THERE'S NO
PLACE LIKE HOME

Secrets OF MY
HOLLYWOOD LIFe

THERE'S NO
PLACE LIKE HOME

secrets of my
HOLLYWOOD LIFE

a novel by

Jen Calonita

poppy

LITTLE, BROWN AND COMPANY
New York   Boston

Poppy

Hachette Book Group
237 Park Avenue, New York, NY 10017
For more of your favorite series and novels, visit our website at www.pickapoppy.com

Poppy is an imprint of Little, Brown and Company.
The Poppy name and logo are trademarks of Hachette Book Group, Inc.

The publisher is not responsible for websites (or their content) that are not owned by the publisher.

First Paperback Edition: November 2011
First published in hardcover in March 2011 by Little, Brown and Company

The characters and events portrayed in this book are fictitious. Any similarity to real persons, living or dead, is coincidental and not intended by the author.

Calonita, Jen.
   There's no place like home : a novel / by Jen Calonita. — 1st ed.
      p. cm. — (Secrets of my Hollywood life)
   "Poppy."
   Seventeen-year-old Kaitlin Burke is back in Los Angeles after her brilliant run on Broadway, but her new sitcom is such a success that she finds herself again wishing for a normal life when a bad run-in with aggressive paparazzi puts her boyfriend Austin in danger.
   ISBN 978-0-316-04556-8 (hc) / ISBN 978-0-316-04555-1 (pb)
   [1. Actors and actresses—Fiction. 2. Television—Production and direction—Fiction. 3. Paparazzi—Fiction. 4. Celebrities—Fiction. 5. Dating (Social customs)—Fiction. 6. Los Angeles (Calif.)—Fiction.] I. Title. II. Title: There's no place like home.
   PZ7.C1364The 2011
   [Fic]—dc22

                                                                                  2010018672

10 9 8 7 6 5 4 3 2 1

RRD-C

Book design by Tracy Shaw

Printed in the United States of America

Secrets of My Hollywood Life novels by Jen Calonita:

SECRETS OF MY HOLLYWOOD LIFE

ON LOCATION

FAMILY AFFAIRS

PAPARAZZI PRINCESS

BROADWAY LIGHTS

THERE'S NO PLACE LIKE HOME

Other novels by Jen Calonita:

SLEEPAWAY GIRLS

RealityCheck

For Cindy Eagan, Kate Sullivan, and Laura Dail
(or, as I like to think of them the Tin Man, the Scarecrow,
and the [not so] Cowardly Lion).
I couldn't have followed the yellow-brick road
without the three of you.

one: Goman Nasi *Means "I'm Sorry" In Japanese*

"This is take fourteen, scene six. And action!"

Suddenly I feel wind on my face and my curly, caramel-hued hair starts whipping around like I'm in a tornado. I'm holding on to the railing of what is supposed to be a huge ocean liner, with the sun dipping into the sea behind me. Call it movie magic—I'm actually standing at a fiberglass replica of a ship's bow with a green screen behind me that will be filled in with that glorious sunset later. There is a large group of beautiful, well-dressed "passengers" milling about around me, along with a terrific violinist and the ship's waitstaff, who are handing out drinks and hors d'oeuvres.

The scene is meant to look the picture of bliss, and I know I feel that way. How could I not? I get paid beaucoup bucks for a thirty-second commercial, I'm back home in Los Angeles after my summer on Broadway in New York, and I get to look this nice for work. I'm wearing a green satin floor-length Max Azria dress that is the exact color of my eyes with killer black tribal-beaded Jimmy Choo sandals, and my makeup is all dewy and sparkles. If that's not bliss, I don't know what is. The sound crew re-creates the ship horn, and I smile and put my arm around Sky Mackenzie, my longtime costar and sort of newish good friend. It's a big breakthrough for us. We used to want to strangle each other.

"Beautiful, girls," our director, Preston Hartlet, coos, giving feedback via megaphone. "This is the take! I can feel it. Show me the love."

Sky stiffly hugs me back—hugging is not usually part of her repertoire—and then it happens. The whole scene falls apart. Again.

When we hug on cue, the extras around us stop their anonymous mingling and start clapping madly as if the two of us have found a way to create peace in the Middle East. Of course, I start to giggle, which makes Sky start to giggle. This has happened every take. Preston winds up calling "Cut" and we have to start all over again. I feel terrible, but as soon as the extras start the applause, we lose it! Why would our hugging make everyone clap? We asked Preston this, but he just shrugged and said it's what Takamodo Cruise Lines, the Japanese company we are making this commercial for, wants. I guess since Takamodo is paying, it's their call, but the gesture makes me crack up. I can't help it!

On this take, Sky's brown eyes lock on mine like a bullet, willing me to stop the giggles, and it actually works. We instantly compose ourselves. I silently order my funny bone that there will be no take sixteen. The sound crew pumps in a melodramatic instrumental as the shot pulls away from the ship. After ten seconds, Sky and I say our one line: "Takamodo Cruise Lines. Tranquility is a cruise away."

"EXCELLENT!" Preston yells exuberantly and pulls on his goatee. "Let's set up the final close-up!"

"Yes!" Sky screams and pulls her hand back from where it was resting around my waist. "God, I love commercials!"

"Me too," I agree, slipping my right foot out of my shoe to give it a little breather. (Gorgeous shoes, but they're pinching my toes.) "This is like making a mini movie in half a day."

"True, but that's not why I like making commercials," Sky says and dances around on her gold, crystal-encrusted Gucci stilettos. "A commercial is like getting a year's salary in four hours! And these dresses are killer." She looks at the digital clock hanging above the soundstage exit doors. It's only one PM. "We should be out of here in an hour, and then we've got to go somewhere good. We cannot waste these outfits or makeup." She twirls around in her John Galliano, the beaded salmon skirt fanning out like an umbrella.

I stifle a laugh. "Where exactly could we wear these dresses for lunch without looking ridiculous? They're sort of red carpet material."

"I want to go someplace fun!" Sky pouts. "I just made easy money and got a free dress, and we have nowhere to go?"

"Would you keep your voice down?" I hush her. "I don't want the Takamodo people to hear you. They'll think we're being rude." I look over at the Japanese executives who have been watching the shoot. I give a little wave and Sky grabs my hand, her chunky, gold bangle cold against my wrist.

"K, you're such a kissbutt. All Takamodo cares about are our gorgeous mugs..." She pauses. "*My* gorgeous mug and your decent mug." I swat her arm and see a small smile starting to spread across her lips. "Fine. All Takamodo cares about is that *our* gorgeous mugs are hawking their ship. That's all they want. I can say whatever else I please." She looks away, but I see her side-eye me. Sky knows when she's wrong.

"You could at least try to be friendly," I scold playfully. "You missed the breakfast they had for us this morning, and you haven't said hi yet. Now, they're heading our way. If you want that free press trip to Tokyo this hiatus, then be nice! Just say sorry about breakfast, and make some small talk. Think of your Galliano! Now you have something to wear to the Save the San Marino Sea Lions black-tie dinner this weekend."

Sky twirls her black hair around her finger. "I guess. Okay. I'll apologize for the breakfast snafu." She gives me an appraising look. "You're always thinking of others, K. God, I wish I could pretend to be like that." I hold my tongue as Sky plays with her gold bracelet, sliding it up and down her toned, tan arm. "I don't know if you've noticed, but some people think I have a sensitivity chip missing."

My lip starts to quiver. "You? Never!" I burst out laughing and Sky nudges me again, but she's laughing too. It feels so good to have this sort of relationship with Sky after all those years of backstabbing and jealousy on *Family Affair* (or as we called it, *FA*), the long-running, popular TV show we starred on together from the time we were preschoolers up until a year ago.

"Watch me be like you, K," Sky whispers and starts shaking her raven hair like she's doing an ad for Pantene. No fair, I do *not* hair shimmy! Sky smiles at the incoming executives from across the set and bows her head at them while she talks out of the side of her mouth to me. "Namaste, right?"

"Sky," I groan. "That's Hindi!"

"So?" Sky clucks her tongue at me. "Big dif."

"They're Japanese," I remind her. "This isn't yoga fusion at the gym!" I think fast. "Make nice so we can film our last shot and get you to the SunSmart Smoothie Beach House for freebies. The publicist said the house is only open till seven."

Sky slaps my airbrush-tanned arm excitedly. "I forgot about the SunSmart House! I can't miss those Theory leggings, but we need to eat first. I'm craving steak from Boa. I've eaten at crafty all week, and the sugar is killing me." She pats her tiny stomach. "Fine, I'll say hi quickly and then we can do our last take and be off." Sky bats her dark brown eyes and opens her perfectly plump lips (they aren't real), which have been puckered in a wine-colored gloss. Then she freezes. "How do I say 'I'm sorry' again?"

I sigh. Our agents taught us several Japanese phrases to say to the executives who flew in for the Takamodo Cruise Lines shoot today. Things like *Oaidekite Koei desu.* ("It's a pleasure to meet you!") And *Kohi demo ikaga desuka?* ("Would you like a cup of coffee?") And *Anata no fuku nante suteki!* (I'm not sure I need to know "What a gorgeous dress you're wearing!" in Japanese, but it sure sounds cool. *Anata no fuku nante suteki!* I may start saying that all the time.)

My agent, Seth Meyers (no relation to the *SNL* comedian), says doing a Japanese commercial is like eating a tub of Sprinkles Cupcakes frosting—a pure treat. And he's right. My treat to you is that this is the first of many new HOLLYWOOD SECRETS I'm willing to share.

HOLLYWOOD SECRET NUMBER ONE: Doing Japanese commercials is a no-brainer. Even if your star wattage is too bright to be seen hawking hair gel or cars on American TV (which some ego-crazed celebs really believe is beneath them), you'd be a fool not to do a commercial in Japan. The payoff is huge—and I don't mean just monetary, even though, well, yeah, that's the best part (think upward of a cool million). American stars are a big deal in Japan, so companies there pay through the roof for Hollywood royalty to shoot a thirty-second spot. Everyone from Tom Cruise to Anne Hathaway to Britney Spears has shot Japanese commercials, and it's easy to see why. The shoot is usually short (half a day), and you don't have to leave Los Angeles to do it. You don't even have to learn Japanese! Most of their celebrity-featured commercials use stars' real voices and American music. Japanese writing or a Japanese voice-over explains what the commercial is about if it's not simple enough to make sense on its own. Our Takamodo commercial, touting their newest luxury liner, speaks for itself. Of course, you don't want to do anything *too* crazy, or your ad will become a laughingstock on American YouTube, like Arnold Schwarzenegger's.

"Goman nasi," I say slowly to Sky.

"GO-MAN NAH-SAY," Sky tries to enunciate, and I can't help but giggle. I don't sound great either, but Sky sounds terrible.

"Never mind," I say quickly as the executives approach. "Just say your line. They've been begging you to do it all day."

Sky groans. "K! Nooo! I don't do it anymore. That phrase ended when *Family Affair* went off the air. It's too embarrassing. Do you know how many people stop me on the street and ask me to say it over and OVER?"

"I know, but it will go over huge," I insist, knowing the clock is ticking. The executives are so close they can hear us. I just don't know if they understand English. "Just say it one time in Japanese. Please? I know you learned how to do it for that Japanese *Family Affairs* press tour a few years back." She shrugs and I know I'm losing her. It's time to change tactics. "You're an incredible actress, Sky. I'm sure if you say the line in Japanese, they'll forget all about the fact that you missed eggs Benedict and they'll start thinking: What can we cast Sky Mackenzie in next?"

Sky's eyes widen at the thought of dollar signs. "I never thought of that, K." She takes a deep breath, and then her whole face relaxes into a bright, beautiful grin just as the executives reach us. I have to hand it to Sky. When it needs to be turned on, she can turn it on. "Onnanoko niwa Onnan-

7

oko no jijo ga aruno," she says, which means "A girl's got to do what a girl's got to do." It was the signature catchphrase of Sky's conniving character, Sara, on *FA*. My goody-two-shoes character, Samantha, didn't really have one. She just said, "That's so sweet!" A lot. She was kind of vanilla.

The Japanese executives stop short and look a little confused—Sky's version probably doesn't sound exactly like the translation should—but they must get the idea because they applaud. Sky is so pleased she actually curtsies and then starts to bow. I yank her away before she does anything she regrets. Like talk about her paycheck again.

I'm sure a lot of people are wondering why anyone in Japan cares about Sky and me. Well, it turns out our beloved former TV show—which is where Sky and I met, brawled, became frenemies, and then finally became friends post-show this past summer in New York—is syndicated there, and the ratings are HUGE. Apparently Sky and I are a bigger deal there than Richard Gere. (I know, I know—who? The Japanese love him. He was huge here a while back when he did all these rom-coms like *Pretty Woman*, which is a classic you *so* must watch if you've never seen it.)

"Sky? Kaitlin?" Our director, Preston, is standing by, waiting for us. His silver Ray-Ban aviators are nestled in his heavily gelled brown hair, and his tan arm ripples with muscles as he runs a hand through his stiff locks. You can totally tell Preston was good-looking back in the day. He is in his fifties, and while he used to make major explosion, kidnapping–type action flicks, now he sticks to Japanese

8

commercials. He's apparently in high demand. "Think we can get this close-up done in less than five takes? I pride myself in always coming in under budget for commercial shoots. It's not all about spending money, you know." His brown eyes look at us intently.

Oh God. He heard Sky's crack about money, didn't he?

I glance back at the crowded set. The lighting guys, boom operator, production assistants, and harried hair and makeup people are scurrying around, retouching, relighting, and setting up the shot again. The catering crew is restocking the table with bagels, cold cuts, salads, cereal, and assorted fruit and candy (you can't have a catering table without gummy worms in my book). Beyond them I can see my own crew—my assistant, Nadine, and my dad, who came to watch the action and try to, um, make some connections. (He's a producer who is in between gigs right now. He hasn't worked in over a year, actually. At the moment his full-time job seems to be golfing and talking about cars, or lately, boats.)

Sometimes I forget how many people it takes to make just one little actor look good. Suddenly I feel guilty about my onset of giggles. The last thing I want is for Preston to think I'm some overindulged teen actress who has no clue how the business works. I love acting, and sometimes it's easy to forget how grateful I should be for every opportunity I get, and I get a lot of them.

I give Preston my best smile and the friendliest face I can muster, hoping I look all earnest and hopeful and sweet, like

my old *FA* character. "Preston, we feel terrible about before."
I nudge Sky, who is busy scrutinizing her Galliano again to
see if I've dislodged one of the thousands of beads on her
one-of-a-kind skirt. "I'm sorry it took us so long to do that
shot. This next one will be quick, I promise, and exactly
what you're looking for."

Preston smiles and looks at Sky for further clarification.
It's hard to tell if he's okay or annoyed in this lighting. The set
is so brightly lit that the behind-the-scenes area seems really
dark, just like Preston's wardrobe (worn navy tee and dark
denim jeans, the director's attire of choice). I nudge Sky, hoping she can think of something that will win Preston over.

Sky turns on her charm. "We really are sorry! It won't
happen again. Thank you for being so decent about breakfast too. I'm going to tell my agent how great this experience
with you was." Sky glances in my direction. "He said if we
liked you we could probably suggest you for our future
commercials and then maybe even a guest directing spot on
this little show K and I are working on. Maybe you've heard
of it? *Small Fries?*"

Preston's expression is unmistakable. His whole pale face
seems to shine, and his eyes are like saucers. "Of course I've
heard of *Small Fries!* That's why I took this commercial, you
know. My kids loved the pilot and said I had to work with
you two. Everyone is talking about it." He scratches his
goatee. "Guest directing, huh? You know, we all need time to
warm up." Preston looks at Sky, who pretends to be very innocent. "Don't worry about those chuckles! I want you two

to have fun!" He laughs and slaps Sky's bare shoulder. She gives him a dirty look, then stares down at that darn dress again to check the beading. I raise my eyebrows at her while Preston prattles on. "Wow, *Small Fries*? I, um, yeah, tell the studio to call me. Anytime. Day, night. My phone is always on vibrate." He turns away, his clipboard in hand. "You girls take your time—when you're ready for that last shot, I'm ready!"

"We're ready!" I say in my best cheerleader voice.

"God, he's a tool," Sky mumbles when he is too far away to hear. I hit her.

"Um, the dress?" She points one long, French manicured nail at the beading. "K, I get the nice girl thing, but to everyone? It's not Preston's money that is being spent on overtime, and seriously, we didn't do that many takes." I give her a look. "Okay, maybe we did a few more than we should have, but who cares? We were having fun, weren't we?" She sort of smiles. "We really do work well together."

"Aww . . . Sky." I hug her stiff frame. "I love working with you too."

"I didn't say *love*," Sky clarifies.

I frown. "Do you really think we should be offering guest spots on *Small Fries* already? Yes, the pilot was huge, but . . ."

"K, I keep telling you to stop worrying. Our show is here to stay. Everyone thinks so!" Sky plays with the big, jeweled ring on her finger. "You have to play to your strengths."

"You mean like you?" I tease. "Should I offer the cop an autograph when I'm pulled over for driving forty miles an hour in a twenty zone?"

Nadine and I carpooled with Sky this morning because Rodney, my driver and security, is doing stunt work for a commercial of his own today. Everyone in Hollywood seems to have two careers—acting, and whatever they do when they're not acting so they can pay the rent.

"Maybe you should, but first you need a license." Sky's long face is devilish.

"Nice." I blush. "I'm going for my road test in six weeks."

"You've been saying that for two months!" Sky reminds me. "K, you're totally going to pass. You've been practicing for ages. And even if you slip up and hit a road sign, you're going to get your license. The DMV won't flunk an Emmy nominee!"

"I don't want special treatment," I insist, looking down at the scuffed floor. "I want to get my license the way everyone else does."

"Yeah, yeah, real girl versus actress. I know your deal." Sky winks at me. "Save the sweet talk for your next *Seventeen* interview."

I'll fix her. "Oh, you mean my cover story for *Small Fries?*"

Sky's eyes widen and her face gets red. "I can't believe you'd do a cover for our show without me!"

"Gotcha. You're stuck with me."

"K!" Sky wails. "That was mean! Anyway, I wouldn't really call it stuck." Sky grins. "Now let's get this over with so we can go have steak! And hash browns! I'll pay for it later with my trainer." She eyes my backside skeptically. "Hmm . . . maybe you should join me too. You could use a good workout."

I don't say anything. Pick your battles, Nadine always says. I don't tell Sky that I don't mind doing more takes either. Pretending to be on an ocean liner is fun. Especially when you're with a friend.

Sky yells over her shoulder, "We're ready, Preston!"

"Great, let's go for it," Preston says and heads to his camera.

Sky and I take our marks on the ship's bow, and the extras close in around us. The violinist starts to play again, and a couple clinks wineglasses. When the wind machine hits my face, I know it's time. Big smile, perfect pose, act happy. It's not hard to do.

Preston lifts his megaphone. "And action!"

Sunday, November 1
NOTE TO SELF:

Mon./Tues. *Small Fries* calltimes: 5 AM
Must get caffeine first! And Froot Loops!
A stopping by set: Mon. 4ish
Ellen taping Tues.
The View taping Wednesday. Calltime: 9 AM
On set for *SF* following taping
Ryan Seacrest phoner: Wed.
SMALL FRIES PREMIERE – Thurs. @ 8:30 PM
SF calltime 4 Fri.: 6 AM
Dinner w/Mom/Dad/Seth/Laney: Sunday after *EW* shoot

Homework . . . ??? Check with Nadine!

SMALL FRIES
SF103 "Give It the Old College Try"

SCENE:
HOPE and TAYLOR'S dorm room. It's packed with people—
band members with tubas and drums, cheerleaders, the
geek squad, goth kids, every cliché group there is.
People are squished into the tiny, very girly dorm room
like sardines, and music is playing at full volume.
HOPE opens the dorm room door and screams.

HOPE:
What is going on in here? *(covers ears to avoid the tuba
blaring in her ear)*

TAYLOR:
Hey! Isn't this great? We're having a Freshman
Fifteen Party.

HOPE:
Do you mean the weight gain thing? *(looks around)*
If you're trying to set a Guinness World Record for the
most weight in a room . . .

TAYLOR:
No! No! It's a play on having fifteen people in our tiny
twelve-by-twelve room. Although I think there are thirty
or forty people at this party. Funny, huh?

HOPE:
*(panicked. She reaches in her pocket for a very dingy,
frayed, small pink blanket.)* Party? I don't do parties. I
told you that.

TAYLOR:
You do now! This is our party. I figured we deserved one after a rough first week of classes. Plus, I finished all my reading for the week, so I thought we should blow off steam.

HOPE:
You finished two hundred pages in an afternoon?

TAYLOR:
I'm a fast reader.

HOPE:
(freaks out) Well, I didn't start reading yet, and I need quiet. *(The tuba blares in her ears again.)*

TAYLOR:
Come on, Hope! The closest you've gotten to a large gathering is probably freshman orientation, and that doesn't count. We've got to help you assimilate. You won't survive four years here if you don't try to fit in.

Dorm room door opens again and GUNTHER bounces from HOPE'S bed to the floor, dances with a few cheerleaders, and finally squeezes past two drummers before stopping in front of HOPE and TAYLOR.

GUNTHER:
Whoa, Taylor, you were right! We can up our room occupancy to sixty. We can totally fit fifteen more people in here. (holds up the microphone around his neck) Who's ready for Fat Fifteen Freshman karaoke?

ZOE:

I am! *(squeezes through the crowd)* Karaoke burns calories, and I only got a two-hour workout in at the gym this afternoon. The spin instructor said she wouldn't let me in a third class. Something about me being a liability.

TAYLOR:

(mumbles) In more ways than one. *(to GUNTHER)* So should we invite more people in?

HOPE:

NO! This is a twelve-by-twelve-foot room! I don't even think my backpack can squeeze in here. *(looks at TAYLOR pleadingly and rubs her blanket on her face)*

GUNTHER:

What's with that rag you're carrying?

HOPE:

(scrunches it up and pushes it into the top of her jeans) It's nothing. Nothing worth talking about. Just something I've slept with practically since I was born, but no biggie. I don't have separation issues.

ZOE:

It looks that old. Haven't you ever heard of Shout? My mom sent me here with two bottles of it.

GUNTHER:

I prefer Resolve, actually.

HOPE:

Can we get back to the point here? You've got to get

these people out of here. I know you want to burn off steam, Taylor, but if Edison gets wind of this get-together, you'll get a yellow warning slip for sure.

TAYLOR:
(gasps) A yellow slip? (starts freaking out) I thought they were green.

ZOE:
Aren't they orange? I got one of those last week.

GUNTHER:
I think that was an invite to last night's Freshman Orientation Dinner.

ZOE:
Oh.

HOPE:
Whatever! Green! Blue! Polka dots! (to TAYLOR) You'll get a warning. You. Miss Straight A. It will ruin your dean's list chances for sure.

TAYLOR:
(grabs the microphone that is hanging around GUNTHER'S neck) EVERYBODY OUT! NOW! HELLO? (panicking and looking at HOPE) They're not moving!

HOPE:
I'll do it. OUT! YOU MUST GO NOW! PARTY IS OVER! Gunther, they're not leaving!

GUNTHER:
Um, maybe they would if you turned the mic on.

HOPE:
Gotcha. OUT! NOW!

(*Dorm door opens again and it's EDISON. He sees the crowd and drops all his books. The crowd sees him and storms the door. EDISON comically pulls himself out of the way before he gets run over. He's hanging from TAYLOR's weight-lifting bar, and the others come and stand under it.*)

EDISON:
What was that?

TAYLOR:
What was what? (*looks at the others*)
I didn't see anything, did you guys?

ZOE:
Nope. Just a few dozen people. (*HOPE nudges her.*)
I mean lab rats. They were lab rats. We were working on our science project.

HOPE:
It was a study group.

TAYLOR:
A freshman study group since we freshmen have been worked to the bone our first week here and we're not ...
(*HOPE nudges her*) we love it here.

EDISON:
You four, my office now.

GUNTHER:
Yes! I've always wanted to see the R.A. lounge!

TWO: *Do You Want* Fries *with That?*

I can hear Peter Frimmons, the network top dog, speak to the crowd of journalists visiting the *Small Fries* set through the crack in the soundstage door, and my stomach is doing excited flip-flops. Peter is gushing—*gushing*—about our show. A new show that just aired last night! I don't think I've ever heard a network executive go on record and say: "I'll give up my bonus if this show doesn't make the top ten." And Pete just did!

"Can you believe Fritz flew all these writers out to L.A. to meet us?" Sky asks me as we huddle together outside the soundstage doors. We're eavesdropping and hoping not to be noticed. "He really must think *Small Fries* is his key to owning a small island off the south of France if he's spending this much dough on us."

The network really is pulling out all the stops for *Small Fries*. They've invited major entertainment journalists from around the country to watch us tape a scene and interview us in person. But even before this meet and greet, the early press for the pilot has been real good. Not that I want to get too ahead of myself. We just debuted last night, and we don't have final numbers yet. Seth says I shouldn't worry. He smells a hit.

"Why are you smiling so big?" Sky asks suspiciously. She looks every bit the college freshman in a really cute but simple green scoop-neck top and dark denim jeans. Her black hair is actually pulled back in a Blair Waldorf–style plaid headband. I never thought I'd see the day she'd wear one of those. "And your neck is getting blotchy," she adds. "What's wrong with you?"

"Nothing. I'm just happy." I shrug. "I'm in L.A. again, things with Austin are good, and after all those months of worrying what some lousy publicity would do in my career, here I am, waiting to be introduced to the press as a star on the most talked-about show of the season."

Sky rolls her eyes. "You're so dramatic and mushy." She purses her full lips. "But I think you're right. We're on a hit, baby! I don't think you spend this much green unless you love a show, and I think Fritz really loves us, which is a huge boost. No one wants another *The Jay Leno Show* snafu on their tanned hands." We both wince at the memory.

"And now, I'd like to bring out the *Small Fries* cast!" Pete says, and I hear the applause. "First up, Ian Adams as Gunther!" Ian, my wacky costar, jogs out, his brown, curly mop of hair bouncing as he goes. Ian is just as nutty as his character, and every bit as charismatic. He's slightly gawky too, being so tall and thin, like a pro basketball player, with huge

21

feet. This is his first sitcom, but he did a failed pilot last season and before that had some bit parts in a few Judd Apatow films.

"Brendan Walk as Edison!" Brendan is the next to fly past me, but he walks instead of runs onto the soundstage, taking his time and savoring the applause. Brendan is nothing like the tightly wound R.A. he plays on *Small Fries*. Incredibly good-looking with short, light brown hair, brown eyes, a strong, angular face and body, and a deep voice that makes the extras melt, he's slightly cocky too, having just finished shooting a potential blockbuster with George Clooney and Brendan's so-called best bud, Robert Pattinson.

"Kayla Parker as Zoe!" Pete yells, as if he's introducing the Jonas Brothers. As Kayla saunters past me, I hear whistles.

"Show-off," grumbles Sky. Kayla is gorgeous, and Sky is a tad jealous, even if she won't admit it. Kayla is the classic Barbie doll come to life. Tall, blond, and thin, with measurements that would make even the *Sports Illustrated* swimsuit models envious. Kayla is definitely the show hottie. She's also a model-turned-actress doing her first show and as such, her face is definitely the draw. Her acting, not so much. Sky, of course, likes to harp on that.

"Sky, stop pouting," I tell her lightly and fidget with the drop-waist peach silk tunic by Twenty8Twelve that my microphone is hidden in. I've got on black leggings and tall Gucci black buckle boots too. Our show stylist has the cutest clothes for us to wear. It's all stuff I wear in everyday life too, so sometimes I forget whose clothes are whose!

"Pete said you get announced last, which means you're the most important person in our cast."

This makes Sky smile. She smooths her dark hair, making sure not to get any strands caught in the dangling green gem earrings she's wearing, and stares down at her feet. She's wearing Tory Burch ballet flats. I'm not sure the average college freshman could afford those, but Sky is happy to have them on. "I know you put Pete up to it." Sky's eyes flash at me, and I play innocent.

I did put Pete up to it. He wanted us to walk out together, but I thought Sky could use an ego stroke. She lost out on a *Vanity Fair* cover this week to Scarlett Johansson and she's been a little depressed.

"I don't know what you're talking about," I insist and make sure my ponytail is in tight. Last week during filming it fell out, and we had to stop rolling.

"Please help me welcome Kaitlin Burke as Hope!" Pete's voice rings in my ears.

I wink at Sky and then run out from the back of the soundstage, forcing the reporters to turn around. I stand next to Brendan and Kayla in front of the dorm room set while the media applaud. We have four sets total—Hope and Taylor's dorm room, Brew, a coffee hangout on campus, the R.A. room, and the cafeteria. (We have other sets too, but those are put up and ripped down as needed.) Above my head are hidden lighting fixtures, and in front of me is the camera crew. We also do some scenes outdoors on the back lot so that our show will appear more "real."

Originally *Small Fries* was supposed to be a multicamera comedy taped in front of a live audience. Then suddenly single-camera shows became all the rage (think *Modern Family*), and our producers quickly retooled us. I would have been happy either way, since I'm used to the live audience thing thanks to the Broadway play I did last summer, *Meeting of the Minds*. I used to get worried when producers and studios retooled projects, but now I realize they second-guess themselves just like I do. The biggest mistake the networks ever made (in my opinion) is still fresh in everyone's mind.

I'm talking about Leno-Conan gate.

If you thought it looked messy from your living room, you should have seen what was going on here in town. There was Team Coco (aka Conan) and Team Jay, and it felt like everyone had an opinion and their secrets.

HOLLYWOOD SECRET NUMBER TWO: For all the joking Sky does about collecting a nice paycheck, at the end of the day, good work is not about the money. The Leno-Conan debacle made Hollywood remember that. You had two guys who loved what they did and despite the payouts they would have gotten to probably go away quietly, neither of them did. There was Conan, who obviously loved his new gig very much and was sad to see it go, and then there was Jay, who has so many millions he could have retired years ago and avoided all this negativity. And yet he didn't want to go away either. That's what I want: to love a job so much that it's not about the money, it's about the love of the work. I think *Small Fries* could be that work.

"And finally Sky Mackenzie as Taylor!" Pete says, and all of us—the reporters and the rest of the cast—applaud for Sky. I don't know Brendan, Ian, or Kayla that well yet, but they seem cool. For now we're all pretty stiff and polite with one another. Everyone is constantly saying things like "Great take!" I worked with most of the same people on *FA* for almost a decade, so it felt like a family, but this could be one too if we're on the air long enough.

God, I hope we are.

"Before we start taping," Pete tells the large group, "the *Small Fries'* executive director has an announcement to make that is so important we wanted to share it with the cast and all of you at the same time."

Sky and I look at each other, and I feel my stomach flip-flop again. They wouldn't call the executive director out in front of critics unless the news was HUGE.

The group quiets down—you can practically hear recorders click on—and our show runner, Amy Peterson, walks out in a beautiful khaki pantsuit and matching Anna Sui heels. "Hi, everyone," says Amy, who looks like a tiny gymnast. She's barely five feet—shorter than me!—and has a hip brown haircut that is long in the front and shaved short in the back. "I'm glad you could join us for *Small Fries'* third episode taping. As you know, our show debuted last night."

I inhale and Sky's and my hands touch. We've been on set all day, and everyone who works on *SF* has been asking/talking/whispering/wondering the same thing: Were our ratings good enough to make it another week? Being a critical darling is great, but it's not going to keep you on the air forever. You still need good ratings. We've been worried because we were up against *Megan*, Megan Moynahan's hit sitcom. The early numbers Seth got this morning looked good, but nothing was official till this afternoon. Everywhere I look—from the camera crew to the grip, to the P.A.s, to the cast—everyone is holding their breath. I look at Amy's face, and she breaks into a smile.

"*Small Fries* was the most watched show of the night!" Amy practically screams, unable to hide the enthusiasm in her usually reserved voice. "Not only that, but in the key eighteen to thirty-four demo, it beat *Megan* in the eight thirty PM hour."

Brendan fist pumps the air, and Kayla throws herself at Brendan. "We've survived another week!" I squeal and hug Sky. "Another few weeks like this one, and we'll get a full-season pickup for sure."

"Survived? We're beating *Megan*." Sky sounds giddy. "I knew we would! It's their fourth season, and that show is going down!"

I stop jumping up and down. "We've only beat *Megan* once." I bite my lip. Ratings talk makes me nauseous. I'm not used to worrying about it. *FA* was on forever and was so popular that whether we were number five for the week or thirty-five in the ratings, I knew we weren't in danger of being cancelled. "This was just our first week. What if no one tunes in next week?"

"You *can* get excited, K," Sky tells me, sounding pumped

herself. "Numbers like this out of the gate are a good thing."

"You're right," I say and start jumping around again. It feels too good to stop. "I just want us to do well. I like it here, and I never thought I'd like anything as much as *FA*. It's not home or anything, but it's a lot of fun and doesn't feel like work and . . ."

"Rambling," Sky says, pointing a long, red fingernail at my mouth. "This show rocks, and so do we. I'm sure we're going to get bigger and better." She looks around. "They wouldn't be doing all this otherwise. Amy is going to have us do a zillion more interviews and TV appearances next week to keep the momentum flowing. You'll be too tired by Wednesday to even freak out about this anymore."

Very true. Nadine told me this month we're doing news shows, radio shows, print interviews, and Sky and I were on *The View* on Wednesday because they're shooting in L.A. Normally I'd be exhausted just thinking about all that smiling and saying "I love *Small Fries*!" over and over, but I'll do anything, even go on QVC and sell T-shirts, if it means making this show work.

It's still mind-boggling to me that we're even on the air already when it's only November. When I got back from New York in August and officially signed on, we were slated to be a mid-season replacement show. We quickly shot the pilot, and execs loved it so much they aired it straight away, right after, believe it or not, an episode of *Dancing with the Stars*. (As much as it kills me, that confounded show is popular! I'm *still* never doing it.) Networks have found doing a special VERY early "sneak peek" of an upcoming show can bring in big buzz, which is exactly what happened when they aired our pilot for the first time. Our ratings were through the roof, we got a fast-tracked November premiere date, and suddenly everyone wants in on *SF*, as Sky and I have started to call it (it's our own personal ode to *FA*).

"We're going to set up the scene you're going to see today, and then we'll do interviews," Amy tells the reporters. "We'll break for a half hour first to set up. See you in a few!" I use the time to run back to my new dressing room and dial Laney and Seth. My phone is already ringing when I get there.

"You heard the news, right?" It's Seth, my agent, and he's practically crying. "I told you this was a winner! Didn't I say this was the one? Your mom was happy, of course, but you know her. She couldn't come out and actually thank me for pushing TV again. She was too busy asking whether you will get a raise." Seth laughs. "Let's survive the next few weeks first, shall we?"

"Absolutely." I take a swig of the sparkling water I left on my dresser earlier. I also grab a few Sour Patch Watermelons. It is so nice having a craft services cart in my life again!

"KEVIN! Line two is ringing!" I hear Seth yell to his assistant. "Sorry, shining star. I'll see you Sunday night for dinner. I know you have that cover to shoot for *Entertainment Weekly*, so don't worry about the time. I'm sure I can persuade the kitchen at the Polo Lounge to stay open late if I have to."

Laney is beeping in, but someone is knocking at my door,

so I let her call go to voicemail (she hates when I'm talking to two people at once even though she does it all the time). The knocker must be Nadine. She had some errands to run for me off the lot. Before I can reach the door, it flies open.

"We just got a full-season pickup!" my younger brother, Matty, screeches. He's in costume and covered in fake blood. "They just ordered the back thirteen episodes!"

I jump up and hug him lightly to avoid staining my own costume with red dye number thirteen. "That's awesome! Are you really surprised? You guys have been killing the competition."

"Yeah, well, you know." Matty shrugs slightly and, seeing my Sour Patch Watermelons, takes a bunch. "You never know. Anything could have happened."

See? All actors are superstitious. It's not just me.

"I wanted to watch you this afternoon, but I'm sort of in the middle of a pretty big battle," Matty says and points to his attire. He looks so terrifying that if I didn't know it was him, I would probably scream. His honey blond hair is matted in blood, his face is dripping red goo, and he's got a fat upper lip. His shirt is torn and his jeans are shredded at the knees, like he's been attacked by a werewolf (which he may well have been). But his green eyes are sparkling.

"Looks pretty bloody. I hope you're winning. Aren't you exhausted? You've been on set all day."

"Not really." Matty perches himself on a high stool in front of my mirror. "I had math and science this morning, lunch in the cafeteria with you, and then history and English. I only started taping an hour ago. If I get done around seven and you're still here, I'll stop by."

"You can watch me another time. I want you to go home and get some sleep." I don't care what Matty says, he looks tired.

"Stop worrying about me." Matty reads my thoughts. "I'm fine. I'm having a great time! I know you worked too hard at my age, but I promise I'll learn from your mistakes, and I won't overdo it. Is that what you want to hear?" He grins a smile that will someday soon make girls faint.

"I know I'm overprotective, but I don't want you burned out."

"I'm not," Matty insists. He looks wistfully at the couch, but I know he doesn't want to stain it with fake blood. "Let's talk about something else. I heard you guys pummeled *Megan*. Nice."

"It's a good start." I play with the chunky, gold Michael Kors watch I'm wearing. "We'll see what happens."

"Mom was on the phone with Laney earlier," Matty tells me, swiping some more Sour Patch. Mom has been dividing her time between Matty's set and mine. Thankfully we're on the same lot, but the way she trots back and forth we keep joking she's going to have to give up her stilettos and start wearing sneakers. ("Over my dead body!" Mom declared.) "They've got you booked on everything on the West Coast they could squeeze in next week."

"I can't believe I'm in such high demand all of a sudden. It's kind of nice." I sink back into the couch. This thing could really use some throw pillows. I've been putting off adding a personal touch to my dressing room (superstitions!), but hearing that news makes me feel more at home. Heck, I'm going to buy pillows and an area rug too. If we get cancelled, I'll find a place for them in my bedroom.

There is another knock at my door, and my costar Kayla peeks her head in, her blond hair falling around her face. "Hey, Kaitlin. I was just running down to crafty before we start. Want to join me?"

A new show feels a lot like a new school year. Well, if I went to an actual school. Even though I want to hang with Matty, I feel like I should join Kayla and get to know her better. "Sure." I glance at Matty. "Kayla, this is my brother. I don't know if you two have met."

"Hi there," Matty says in a voice much deeper than his own. He shakes Kayla's hand, and if I didn't know any better, I would think she's blushing. Isn't she sixteen? She's a little older than Matty. "I've seen your work the past few weeks. You're really good."

I almost gag on the last Sour Patch Watermelon I swiped when Matty wasn't looking. Kayla is not good. She's good-*looking* and very sweet, but she's no Meryl Streep.

Kayla plays with her hair thoughtfully. "Thanks. That means a lot coming from a star like you."

"Star? Nah." Matty seems flustered. "Well, maybe. But I'm new too, you know. I've been in your shoes so I get where you're coming from. Listen, if you ever need some advice . . ."

Oh brother . . .

"I'd love some advice!" Kayla says with glee and beams at me. "Your brother is awesome, Kaitlin."

"*Awesome* doesn't begin to describe him," I say wryly and give him a look. He pretends to be looking at my dressing room's dull, white ceiling.

"Oh, I'm sorry," Kayla says to someone we can't see, and I hear a muffled voice. "Yeah, she's right in here." The door opens further, and there is the best delivery I could ever get: My boyfriend, Austin Meyers, is standing in the doorway holding a small bouquet of daisies.

"What are you doing here?" I gasp, jumping up and practically leaping into his arms.

"I got out early, so I thought you'd like some company." He smiles and stares down at me with his incredible blue eyes.

I can't help but grin. Austin has one of those faces that just sticks with you, and it's not just because his eyes suck you in or because he has great hair. (It really is great. His bangs are long and his hair skims the bottom of his ears.) His face is practically hand-carved and tan, and then when your eyes trail down to the rest of him, you can't help feeling all gooey. He gives being fit new meaning, thanks to daily lacrosse practice even during off season, and I love his muscular arms. He's a great dresser too. Today he's in a navy, long-sleeve, Abercrombie tee and dark denim jeans with low, brown Diesel shoes that I got him at a gift suite.

"I know we have a date later, but I figured we'd start early," he says, handing me the flowers.

"Sounds good to me," I agree and kiss him.

We had a rocky summer apart—I was in New York and he was at a lacrosse camp in Texas—but ever since we've both been back in Los Angeles, it's been bliss. Well, bliss on a much tighter schedule. My new show has required some seventeen-hour days, which doesn't give me a lot of time for date nights, but Austin has been incredibly understanding. He's always doing romantic things like popping by the set.

Austin sits down on the couch and grins at Matt. "Nice outfit."

"Thanks, man," Matty says, standing up and puffing out his chest, which you can sort of see through his ripped, blood-soaked shirt. I'm not sure if the effect is for Austin, who Matty is always trying to impress, or for Kayla. "Just keeping it real."

I look at Kayla and realize we've kept her waiting. We probably have to be back on set in five minutes. "Kayla, I'm so sorry! You remember my boyfriend, Austin, right?" The two quickly say hi. "I didn't mean to keep you from crafty," I apologize. "Go without me. Can we go together some other time?"

"Definitely," Kayla says. She looks at Matty. "Do you want to go with me, maybe, before you go back to *Scooby*?"

"Sure," Matty says a little too eagerly. He clears his throat. "It's not like they can start without me, right? I guess I can take ten more minutes." Matty looks at me. "Kates, have a great taping. A, I'll catch you later. I'm heading from the set to the gym." He puffs out his chest again and sneaks a glance at Kayla. "I'm really bulking up for this role."

"I see that," Austin says, and I think I see the corners of his mouth twitch.

I resist the urge to giggle till Matty has led Kayla down the hall. "You may have to help me bring Matty down a peg," I tell Austin as I close the door behind them and snuggle up next to my boyfriend on the uncomfortable couch. "Can you imagine how inflated his ego will be by the time his show finishes taping in March? We won't be able to fit him through the studio gates."

Austin chuckles. "It's not so bad yet. He was trying to impress a girl."

"True, but if he starts giving me or Kayla acting or workout tips, I'm staging an intervention." On the other hand, it is nice to see Matty so confident. He seems really happy.

Austin grins as he plays with my hands. "Deal." He looks around the bare room. I never realized how bad the lighting was in here. "We have to do something about this space of yours."

My new dressing room is nothing much to look at—yet. It's standard; lots of mirrors, a couch, bad art on the wall, a lounge chair, blah beige walls. I did pin up a promo poster they made for *Small Fries*. It's supposed to look like a fast-food ad. The cast is in knockoff McDonald's uniforms and the tagline reads: "Supersize your Thursdays. Get (*Small*) *Fries!*" It's pretty cute. But that's my only personal touch so far. Sky started redoing her dressing room immediately. She painted her walls hot pink and bought a faux zebra rug, but if we're only here a few weeks, I don't want to get too attached. Still . . . I look over at the tiny paint swatches I've taped to the rear wall where no one can really see them. If things go well, I am so painting this room a warm, buttery yellow.

"Maybe we should paint and get you some posters?" Austin suggests. "From what I just heard out in the hall, it sounds like you're going to be here awhile."

"Can you believe it?" I squeak. "We beat *Megan*! *Megan*!" Sky is right. That is amazing!

"My mom said *Small Fries* is on this week's *TV Guide* cover and the article said you were the show to watch," Austin marvels, throwing his arm around me. "You guys have *hit* written all over you, Burke."

I bite my lip. "I can't believe this is happening. It's overwhelming, but in a good way." I play with Austin's hair. "I feel really lucky."

"You are, but you also earned it," he reminds me. "I'm so proud of you, Burke. Everyone at school was talking about the show today. Principal P. even mentioned it during morning announcements."

Austin's principal and I go way back. She was a major *FA* fan.

"I really like it here, Austin," I admit. "The cast seems great, Amy has a cool vision for the show's first season, and it feels right doing TV again. I know I've been logging a lot of hours," I feel the need to add, "but once the show gets off the ground we'll be able to hang out somewhere other than my dressing room. At least you've had college applications to keep you busy." Austin and my best friend, Liz, are in full-on college mode, a thought I try to block out since both seem determined to go to places as far from the Pacific Ocean as possible. I have to be supportive, as much as I wish they'd stay close to home. And to me. "How's that going, by the way?" I ask.

"Good," Austin says easily. "My English lit teacher read over my Boston College essay and she really liked it. Did you look at any of the applications that Nadine pulled for you yet?"

"No," I admit, feeling ashamed. "But I will."

"It's your call, Burke," Austin says and leans his head back against the cinder block wall. "You don't have to do the college thing if you don't want to. You do have a pretty good thing going right here."

"I know, but . . ."

This is the one area of my life that I don't have an answer for yet. Go to college or forget it? I'm so torn. Sometimes I wish I could split myself in two. I'd be Kaitlin the actress and Kaitlin the regular girl. Then I wouldn't have to make a choice.

"Don't worry about this tonight." Austin reads my mind as a P.A. knocks on my door and announces I need to be on set in ten minutes. "For now, let's figure out when we're going to have a dinner that isn't catered by crafty."

I love that Austin is using Hollywood terms now, like *crafty* for craft services. I grab my iPhone and scroll through the calendar. Nadine found this great application that syncs our calendars, so mine is always up to date. I start scrolling through the next seven days. "Saturday we have that Turkey Tasters thing," I remind him.

"What are we doing again? Cooking turkeys?" Austin looks confused.

"We're making turkey care packages for Turkey Tasters," I explain.

"Why do turkeys need care packages?"

I give him a look. "They don't. They're care packages sponsored by Turkey Tasters, with turkey items inside, I guess. Mom says I need to do more charity work, so she signed us all up, including Sky and Liz. Hopefully we can go out after." I look at the next few days' schedule. "I told Mom you and I were way overdue for a proper date night, so she should leave some nights free next week, and she said she would. I know I'm free Tuesday night and Wednesday and . . . HEY."

"What?" Austin sounds surprised at my tone.

"Every night next week is booked up with interviews or meetings!" I say indignantly. "Nadine even has a note next to each event that says 'booked by your mom.'" I guess she knew I'd be mad. I can't believe Mom did that to me. Okay, I *can* believe it, but I can't. Grr . . .

"Breathe," Austin says soothingly and strokes my arm. I take a deep breath and place Austin's hands in mine, tracing a heart on his calloused palm (too much time cradling a lacrosse stick).

"I just want more time with you." I sigh.

"You have time with me," Austin says softly. "Only it feels like we're on house arrest or *Big Brother*." I giggle. "But it's okay, Burke. Like I said before, I just want you to be happy, and I know this show does that for you. You know what makes me happy?"

"What?" I whisper, even though I think I know the answer.

"Being with you." He kisses me again.

I really do have the best boyfriend.

"FIVE MINUTES TILL TAPING." I hear the P.A. loud and clear.

"Maybe I can beg for ten," I murmur between kisses.

"We'll deal with five," Austin says, super supportive as always.

And then we go back to kissing.

Friday, November 6
NOTE TO SELF:

Saturday: Turkey Tasters event/go out with A
Sunday: *EW* shoot followed by dinner w/Seth/Laney/
rents

Talk 2 Mom re: next week sched. Need date w/A!

Driving test: FIVE weeks away!

THree: *This Party Is a Real Turkey*

My *Small Fries* costar Brendan scoots past me on his brand-new (free) skateboard before he veers out of control and nearly careens into the giant tower of canned cranberries that are set up in the Turkey Tasters Feed the Homeless Photo Lounge. Two Turkey Tasters workers, who are dressed in green aprons with pictures of the cartoon Tom Turkey Taster on them, run for cover as a photographer snaps pictures of the impending disaster.

Brendan thankfully stops himself inches from the towering processed Thanksgiving favorite, but the shutterbug continues to snap away. "Who put these cans here?" Brendan demands more for the sake of his wounded ego than the almost ruined display. "I could have dropped one of these babies on my head and wound up with a real shiner. I have a taping tomorrow!"

Three Tasters employees rush over to make sure there isn't a scratch on widdle Brendan's chinny chin chin (hee hee) while two more Turkey Tasters sponsors give Brendan more freebies to soothe the only thing he did bruise—his ego. One hands him the latest iPad while the other offers the newest edition of Rock Band, both of which he practically salivates over. The event photographer snaps a photo of him holding his loot.

"Your costar is a total tool," my best friend, Liz, says under her breath. "This is a charity event, not a gift suite! And yet, here we are, packing food for the needy while someone tries to photograph us wearing the latest 'it' jacket. Why are they giving us iPads and coats? How is that related to giving thanks?" Liz asks, getting fired up. I notice one of the Tasters people staring at us, and I give a little wave. "They should be spending all their time and money on the people that really need it, not pampering the likes of him."

We're at the packaging station putting together boxes of Thanksgiving goods to feed Los Angelenos in need, and I'm afraid Liz may throw a box of Turkey Tasters crushed cranberries at someone's head. I look at Austin and Liz's boyfriend, Josh, hoping they can calm her down, but they look just as worried as I do.

"You're completely right, Lizzie," I agree quietly. She's right about everything, but if someone overhears her, I'll take the heat for it in the press. "I never would have dragged you guys here if I knew it was a freebie haven masquerading as a cause."

The Turkey Tasters Feed the Homeless event, which is being held inside a rented beach house in Malibu, is a good idea in theory. Turkey Tasters, which is best known for its gravy, asked stars to come out and put together over four hundred meals for families in need. All of the food was donated by local supermarkets and celebrities (I was photographed coming in with my Whole Foods bags) and will be delivered by various stars on Thanksgiving eve. Donating your time to a worthy cause is a great idea, but somehow tonight's event turned into an elaborate gift suite/photo op as well. One of the Tasters people slipped and told me the RSVPs were so poor, they got desperate and had to bring in other sponsors to entice celebrities. They're calling the house the Turkey Tasters Beach Retreat, and they've set up a huge gift suite armed with an array of products stars can take in exchange for donating their time to charity. As if getting the chance to help others isn't fulfilling enough.

HOLLYWOOD SECRET NUMBER THREE: I'm sure you're wondering the same thing I was the first time I heard about these celebrity-frequented beach houses: What's the deal and why do I keep reading about them in the tabloids? I have an answer for you. Every summer big brands and corporations lure the Lauren Cobb and Ava Hayden types to a fabulous Malibu beach house with the promise of two types of celebrity catnip: free stuff and guaranteed paparazzi coverage. Free stuff is something celebrities covet everywhere, especially at gift suites, which I know you guys already know all about. But it is the guaranteed paparazzi coverage that makes minor stars and reality show wannabes who are desperate to extend their fifteen minutes of fame flock to the beach house. Usually the more famous stars stay away.

(Do any of us really need another picture in *Hollywood Nation*? I think not. Do any of us need a fourth iPad? Ditto.)

"I thought this was going to be an event of substance," Liz continues, shaking a metal can up and down so hard that I'm afraid cranberry is going to explode into the air. Her cool pink-and-purple Pucci tank dress is barely visible under the harsh green apron. Her curly dark brown hair is pulled off her face and held back with a purple headband, and you can see her funky purple beaded earrings madly swing back and forth. "Your mom said Clooney was going to be here, and he doesn't do anything that isn't worthy."

"I know." I quietly pry the can from her hands. I'm careful not to tear the sleeve of my Anna Sui silk shirt on the edge of the basket I'm loading. At least my new J Brand jeans and cream Prada ballet flats are a little more practical for an event like this.

"*This* is nothing like that," Liz continues, waving her now empty hands around wildly. Behind her I can see one of the *Jersey Shore* dudes posing in a new pair of sunglasses.

"We're still helping others," Austin reminds Liz and places a can of the new Turkey Tasters crushed cranberries in the basket he's putting together. "I've always wanted to give back at Thanksgiving. I think it's pretty cool a company would at least *try* to do something decent. Sure, they haven't done things exactly right," he adds, when he sees Liz's skin start to prickle, "but we're still doing good. You're not going to walk out on giving Thanksgiving to four hundred people who can't afford it themselves, are you?

42

Besides, this could be a great conversation starter at a college interview." He winks at me, and I have the overwhelming urge to kiss him.

Even in that Turkey Tasters apron, Austin looks good. His navy polo and dark denim jeans stand out against the weird green apron he has on, and his blond hair looks too lush to be wasted on a boy.

"Austin Meyers, you are trying to soften me up, aren't you? It's working." Then Liz smiles for the first time since we arrived, when they offered her a Turkey Tasters Snuggie, and she burst out laughing.

"I like the positive thinking, Meyers," Josh says, pointing to his forehead. "Mind if I steal the college angle too?" He clears his throat. "Yes, college interviewer, I do think I can change the world. Just the other night I was overcompensating for a bunch of half-baked celebrities readying baskets to feed the homeless and I thought to myself, 'This isn't enough for me. This is too small scale. Four hundred homeless? Pish posh. What can we do on a more *global* scale to help others in need?' That's what I hope to find out through my studies here at Brown University." Liz chuckles. She adores Josh, and not just because he looks like a young Brad Pitt. He makes her laugh. A lot.

"You guys are terrible," Liz says, wagging a finger in their direction. "But you may be on to something. I might have to work this into my essay for UCLA."

"UCLA?" I ask, trying not to get too excited. "Since when did that get added to the mix? Are you really considering

West Coast schools now? Los Angeles area or northern California? Just California or as far north as Seattle?"

"Slow down," Liz tells me, holding a bag of spaghetti like a shield. "I'm not saying I'm staying in So. Cal. I'm just exploring my options. NYU is still on the table, but I still have my doubts about East Coast living. Unlike Josh, I'm not sure I'd look cute in snow boots. Does Burberry make any?"

"If they do, I'm sure they're not as cute as the Burberry *rain* boots, which you'd get to wear often if you stayed here," I say hopefully, and Liz just shakes her head.

A huge box of supplies lands with a loud thump in the middle of our table, and cans roll out in all directions. The four of us scramble to catch them before they slide off the table.

"Sorry about that, guys," Trevor Wainright apologizes. "That Tasters guy said you were running out of Turkey Tasters soup."

Trevor is Sky's off-again/on-again boyfriend and has been since we were all on *Family Affair* together. At first I thought Sky was just taking advantage of Trevor's wholesome Iowa-raised sweetness. He's a farm boy turned actor, and he has the looks to match—bright blond hair, blue eyes, tall, and muscular all over. But I soon realized that Sky really had a thing for him, even if she does have a funny way of showing it.

"Trevs, go get more whole-grain bread." Sky snaps her fingers at him. "And bring the rest of our stuff over here too. If I have to hear Baron Darter talk about *Dancing with the Stars* for another minute, I might throw a Turkey Tasters Gravy Maker at his head!" Sky nudges Austin with her hip. "Move down and make room, A. I need elbow space."

"You got it, Skylar," Austin quips and winks at me. He can't stand when Sky calls him A, so he's started calling her Skylar. The two of them have developed a friendly-snipey relationship like she and I used to have.

Sky wipes her brow, and I'm about to tell her she's sweating (Sky claims she doesn't perspire), but I think better of it when I see the annoyed look on her face. Her black hair is pulled back in a low ponytail, and she's wearing simple emerald earrings that match her green Stella McCartney top and coordinating cream skirt. I think she's also wearing Prada pumps, which aren't really appropriate for standing on your feet for hours doing charity work, but that's Sky. "This event is lame," she whispers loud enough for all of us to hear. She's looking at me when she says it though. "We should *not* be here, K. Skits on *The Tonight Show*, yes. Cooking with Rachael Ray, fine. But packaging Tofurky with Mario Lopez is out of the question. I could kill your mom for telling my mom about this!"

"I'm with Sky." Liz is neatly organizing our new supplies. The boxes of stuffing look like the Leaning Tower of Pisa. "You two do not belong with all these reality show stars and C-listers. If your mom thought you needed to do more volunteer work, then there are a zillion soup kitchens that would have loved to have you. This lowbrow event is beneath you guys."

"I'll say." Sky gives one of the former *The Hills* stars a dirty look as she pretends to kiss a frozen turkey for a shutterbug.

"I'm sorry, guys." I sigh. "Mom is so obsessed with making *Small Fries* a huge hit that she says yes to everything these days. She probably was so distracted when she took the call that she thought the Tasters people said Clooney instead of cranberries," I try to joke, but no one laughs. "She's overwhelmed," I admit. "I think she's got a touch of the career anxiety I had last summer, and juggling Matty and me seems to be a lot of pressure on her. She's so upset about not having time to do the Darling Daisies out here. I knew this event was off base, but I didn't want to get her all riled up."

I don't add that I did try to get out of tonight. I casually mentioned tonight's RSVP list to mom—think the *Jersey Shore* stars, the Lohans, and Tori Spelling—but she barely heard me. She was prepping for a conference call with Matty's producers and had the network's publicity department on hold about something with me at the same time. "Kate-Kate, I can't talk right now," she said, sounding weary. "Can we discuss this around two over Ice Blendeds? Just you and me and Coffee Bean?" I agreed, excited for the one-on-one time, but there wasn't a later. When I came to get her, Anita told me she left a half hour earlier to take Matty to a photo shoot.

"Kates, if this was a one-time thing, I'd get it, but your mom never listens to you," Liz says gingerly, taking a box of pasta from Sky, who nods in agreement. "It's like your opinion doesn't count at all, whether it's about a movie role, a dress to wear to the SAG Awards, or going out with us instead of turning up at a lame event."

"She doesn't do it on purpose," I say, feeling suddenly unsure of myself. "And Mom doesn't do that all the time, does she?" I ask Austin.

He looks uncomfortable. "She did book up all your free nights, even though you asked to leave them open so we could hang out."

"She didn't!" Liz drops an orange on the floor. "Kates, you've been saying for weeks that you need a few nights off from the publicity machine. You have to put her in her place."

"Liz, she's my momager," I remind her. *Momager* is the word for moms who are also their kids' managers. "The normal rules don't apply. Momagers are sort of like Emperor Palpatine." I glance at Austin for confirmation on my *Star Wars* reference. "Too much power sometimes goes to their heads, and you have no control over how they act. My hands are tied."

"No, they're not," Sky says and tosses a thing of apples in the box that she's carelessly filling. "Do what I did. I fired my mom this week. Her manager duty is over."

I drop a box of instant sweet potatoes and stare at Sky. "You did what?" I stutter. "But how? What did she say? Did she flip out? Didn't she, well, didn't she say no?"

Sky laughs. "K, she can't say no! It's my decision. I am nineteen." She says that last part quietly. Sky's age is a sore subject. This mean costar we had on *FA* outed Sky's true age to a tabloid, when she had been claiming to be a teenager a few years younger. "I'm old enough to make my own decisions about management, and I've decided my mom is better off being just my mom."

"She took it better than I thought she would," Trev adds, as he joins us again. He's got two boxes on his shoulders, and he effortlessly lowers them down to the table. Loaves of bread and apples roll out. "She went out and booked a vacation to Tahiti. She didn't even buy a return ticket."

"She may stay there through Christmas, and then it will just be me and Daddy eating Wagyu beef at Cut on Christmas Eve," Sky says gleefully.

Wow. I mean, really wow. Sky fired her mom! I never . . . I mean, it wouldn't even occur to me to . . . I'll be eighteen next month.

Does that mean . . . can you really do that? No, no, that's crazy. No one could do a job as good as my mom.

Actually, they probably could.

WAIT. WHERE DID *THAT* COME FROM?

My mom would be crushed! She loves managing me.

At least she used to. Now it seems like everything is another battle, another nuisance, and she's listening to my say less than ever. We have no time to talk, ever, and when we do talk, it's about work.

"Kates, are you okay?" Liz is looking at me, the corners of her mouth twitching. She must be thinking the same thing I am. "Did Sky's mom news throw you?"

I look at my hand still resting on the dropped box of

sweet potatoes. "I'm fine," I insist, adding a spray of sunflowers to my basket. There. That looks pretty. Making baskets really is mindless work, which means your mind can concentrate on other things like . . . wow, Sky fired her mom!

"Makes you think about things, doesn't it, Kates?" Liz pushes, looking sort of satisfied. "Maybe you should throw around the words *job termination* in front of your mom."

"My mom is nothing like Sky's mom." I look at Sky. That sounded harsh.

"You're right," Sky agrees. "Your mom is *worse*. At least my mom doesn't cancel my dates with Trev or make me feel like an employee."

Ouch. That was a little harsh too, but . . . Mom shouldn't be canceling my dates with Austin or giving me no free time. I know that. I've always known that. It's been part of my argument for as long as I can remember—I need a say in things. We've talked about this before, and she swore she'd change. Mom keeps saying how she wants us to be closer, but this latest snafu isn't helping.

I add a box of Turkey Tasters stuffing and voilà! My twentieth basket of the night is complete. I stare at the large table. Except for a few miscellaneous cans, and Sky and Trevor's stuff, I think our work here is done. "Why don't we get out of here and get something to eat," I suggest, hoping for a topic changer. "I think we've done our fair share here."

"Between the four of us we've put together fifty baskets," Josh says, wiping his hands on his apron. "That better be enough to spring us."

"It's six thirty," Liz says, looking at her Gucci watch. "We'll never make our seven o'clock reservation at Il Sole. Where should we go?"

"A Slice of Heaven?" I suggest.

"Grease it is." Liz pulls her apron off her head, and instantly a Turkey Tasters rep is there to grab it.

"Where are you guys going?" she asks nervously. "We haven't played Turkey Tasters bingo yet. The money raised goes to charity, you know. And you really must take time to go to our thank-you gifting suite. Brendan is back in there now picking out an unreleased version of Guitar Hero."

"Ooh, I want one of those!" Sky raises her hand wildly, and Liz slaps her.

"Tasters gifting suite?" Liz's voice rises an octave. "At a charity event? You can take your Guitar Hero and your bingo and—"

I grab Liz's arm and smile serenely at the rep. "What she's trying to say is we don't need any gifts. We were happy to help." I look at the others, who nod in agreement. Liz is still pouting. "But we really must be going. Sky and I have another commitment this evening."

The Tasters rep looks disappointed. "Could you take one last picture? We haven't gotten one of you with Tom Turkey Taster yet." She motions to the guy in the oversized turkey costume. I glance at Sky. She looks like she'd rather eat Tom than pose with him.

"Just one," I tell her. The Tasters people rush him over, and I look at the others. "I'll text Rodney to bring the car around. Then we should call Antonio." Liz starts to dial our favorite pizza place's owner's number.

Josh pokes Liz. "Make sure he puts some garlic knots on."

"And mozzarella sticks," Austin adds.

"Salad pizza," Sky calls out, and Trevor groans. "Hold the cheese. I'll bloat."

I'm not that hungry, so I don't add to the order. All I can think about is Sky firing her mom. I feel a vibration and pull my iPhone out of my pants pocket. I look at the message in horror.

> MOM'S CELL: Change of plans. Need 2 move UR Seth dinner mtg 2 2nite. Rodney will pick you up ASAP and bring U to the Polo Lounge. Hope you're dressed for dinner.

"What's wrong?" Austin asks, touching my shoulder.

"Nothing," I insist, typing quickly.

> KAITLIN'S CELL: Mom, I have plans with my friends. Remember? You wanted me 2 come 2 this Tasters thing 2nite and I did. Now we're going out.

> MOM'S CELL: Sorry. I'm double-booked tomorrow. Everyone already on their way. This is more important! See you at the Polo Lounge.

"I hate when she does this!" I complain, yelling in Tom Turkey Taster's beak without realizing it. "Sorry. Pictures. Right."

We snap a handful, and then I break the bad news.

"She can't keep doing this to me," I say, exasperated. "What if I couldn't leave the event right now? Then what would I do? I have to talk to her about her Darth Vader choke hold!"

"You go, Kates!" Liz cheers. "Do it for real this time. You can always meet us afterward. Antonio will keep the place open so we can hang out late. You know that."

"I'm sorry," I feel the need to say again. "I'll be as quick as I can, but remember, this is a dinner meeting so it could take a few hours."

Austin hands me my coat. "We'll be waiting."

I kiss him and rush outside to meet Rodney, practically knocking down one of the guys from *The Bachelor*, who is hauling a huge box of loot to his car.

I fight the urge to laugh. Only in Hollywood. Even if it is weird, I wouldn't want to be anywhere else.

Saturday, November 7
NOTE TO SELF:

Try 2 Keep Dinner 2 2 Hours!!!
Call Slice when I am on my way.

Cover Story
Banking on the Burkes

November 8

After a bumpy spring, Kaitlin, her brother, Matty, and the entire Burke clan are cleaning up their act and (finally) taking Hollywood by storm.

By Adrianna Locket

Last March, the Burkes looked like they were cashing in a one-way ticket out of Hollywood. After a promising career on the beloved *Family Affair*, Kaitlin Burke crashed and burned under mounting pressure to find a new job, succumbing to the same fate so many other promising teen stars had before her: She chose to trade her SAG card in for VIP status at Shelter. Sprinkle in a short-term friendship with notorious party girls Ava Hayden and Lauren Cobb and a trip to Cedars-Sinai for panic attacks, and Kaitlin's star status was in danger of plummeting to earth. Kaitlin's brother, Matty, who had been gifted bit parts on

Family Affair before it went off the air, was left without a paycheck as well—and no one was knocking down his door to give him a new one. Ditto his parents, whose sole source of income is managing and producing the Burke empire. "It was tough," Matty tells us. "I knew the only reason I got the *Family* gig was because of my sister, and then my sister's minor meltdown was keeping me from getting callbacks for even *Celebrity Apprentice*, which, no offense, I wouldn't want anyway."

Summer bloomed and the Burkes (thankfully) all but disappeared from the Hollywood landscape and the gossip rags (except for a lame little feud with fame-loving Hayden and Cobb, which isn't even worth rehashing). That's when the Burkes started making some seriously smart career moves. Kaitlin resurfaced in New York to guest host the season ender of *Saturday Night Live* with Sky Mackenzie, which the media went gaga for, and to take a role in the decidedly unflashy Broadway play *Meeting of the Minds*. Her reviews weren't shabby, and her quiet little summer and *SNL* stint had Hollywood in a tizzy. They wanted her back. "As much as I love Los Angeles, I think we needed a break from each other," Kaitlin admits. "Those three months in New York were wonderful for me. I got to be sort of anonymous, learn about live theater, and work on the stage. It was get in, get out, and find my purpose in life again, which I did." The creator of a pilot called *Big Fish, Small Pond* took notice. "I always thought Kaitlin was a talented young actress," says Amy Peterson. "I thought she lost her way a little, but I knew she'd find her way back. Her guest hosting gig on *Saturday Night Live* slayed me. I had no idea she could do comedy! When I realized that, I didn't just *want* Kaitlin and Sky Mackenzie for

my pilot. I *had* to have them."

Amy needn't have worried. Kaitlin and Sky wanted in, and soon all the other pieces fell into place, including a name change for the pilot to *Small Fries*. (Maybe you've heard of it?) A risky marketing ploy—airing the mid-season show in the early fall after an episode of *Dancing with the Stars*—paid off and was followed by YouTube clips and catchy ads that featured the cast in fast-food chain ensembles with the tagline "Do you want fries with that?" The PR blitz worked and *Small Fries* debuted in the top ten its first week out of the gate. Critics love the show (including *Tome*'s own Sam Sherman), saying it's: "*Friends* for the younger set, told with a fresh, funny voice and lots of style and charm."

Matty also had a good summer, nabbing the part of Velma's sort of goofy but totally kick-butt boyfriend in a new live-action *Scooby-Doo*. Already a bona fide hit on the CW, Matty is reaping the rewards of being patient. "I'm so glad I didn't jump at the first thing I found," he says happily from his decked-out dressing room on set. "*Scooby* is a great show and a wonderful place to work. I couldn't be happier." Neither could Matt's mom, Megan Burke, who has more than enough managerial duties between her two kids to keep her busy. "It's a lot of work," she says when she phones in from Matty's set at 10:00 PM, "but who knows my kids better than me?"

"I didn't just *want* Kaitlin and Sky Mackenzie for my pilot. I *had* to have them."

With two kids on two hit shows, Megan's job is only going to get tougher and more lucrative. Matty says he is already fielding movie roles to film during his summer hiatus, and rumors are flying that Kaitlin is up for the highly anticipated, top secret James Cameron project shooting this spring. "Wow, James Cameron, huh?" Kaitlin says, sounding surprised when we mention it. "I would take a job shining that man's shoes! You can tell him I said that."

We don't think we'll have to, Kaitlin. All you have to do is wait for his call, and we're sure it's coming along with a million other well-deserved offers too.

Welcome back, Burkes. We missed you.

Four: *Another Sticky Situation*

We're driving to dinner after watching Liz, Josh, Sky, Trevor, and Austin drive off toward A Slice of Heaven, and I don't even have to look up from applying my lip gloss to know why Rodney put this song on. It's Celine Dion's "My Heart Will Go On," the theme song from James Cameron's *Titanic*. I look up anyway, and I can't help but smirk. "Rod! It's bad luck to play that right now!"

"Oh, shush," Rod admonishes me. He's sipping a vanilla shake from Carl's Jr. and has his other hand on the wheel of the Lincoln as he cruises down Sunset Boulevard toward the Beverly Hills Hotel where I'm meeting my family, Seth, and Laney for dinner at the Polo Lounge. "That rumor is legit!" he says. "You are going to work with the king of the world!"

"You're about to become a Na'vi expert," Nadine adds giddily, referencing the alien species in Cameron's *Avatar*. Rodney picked Nadine up on the way to get me so that we could go over some work stuff before my dinner. She's sitting next to me, scrolling through her BlackBerry. On the seat between us is her binder, aka the bible, which has my call sheets, measurements, and everything else one might need to know about me on the fly. Nadine can't stop herself from going on. "Everyone is dying to know what his post-*Avatar* series movie is going to be!"

Ever since Laney got an early copy of the new *TV Tome* cover story that mentions the Cameron rumors, everyone I know can't stop thinking about the possibility of me being in his next film. I'm trying not to let those thoughts out too often, though, 'cause I'm worried I'll press my luck. James Cameron is on fire. He's known for creating well-drawn female characters and could get press for reading a phone book. Could I really be lucky enough to get called in to read for something he's doing?

Nadine goes for overkill. "This could lead to an Oscar nomination!"

I cover my ears. "Stop! Stop! Don't get me excited! That rumor might be nothing more than a rumor."

HOLLYWOOD SECRET NUMBER FOUR: Sometimes rumors really are just rumors. I know I usually say that where there is smoke there is fire, and that's true a lot. Sometimes the tabloids get a story right months before it breaks. Even celebrities with ironclad confidentiality agreements find that their nannies or housekeepers or ex-boyfriends can find loopholes allowing them to spill the details of their private lives. But sometimes a rumor is nothing more than an overeager agent, publicist, spin doctor, or studio higher-up talking about what they want to happen rather than what is really happening in Tinseltown. Maybe James Cameron never even called about me. Seth just wants him to and, by putting the rumor out there, he's hoping the phone will ring.

Nadine gives me a look. One I know well from years of working with her. It means "don't pretend to be humble when you know the real deal." Her shoulder-length red hair was just trimmed, and it's layered and trendy. She's wearing something equally hip: a black sweater dress and black knee-high boots. Nadine says she has a hot date tonight, but she's keeping mum on the details so she doesn't jinx it. "You're going to get offered that Cameron gig, and you know it!" Nadine says, and then her face softens. "I hope you take it. Wherever it's shooting. You've waited your whole life for an offer like this, Kates. You deserve it."

"Thanks." I squeeze her hand. "But Seth hasn't called to say there even is an offer."

"I know it's real," Nadine says knowledgeably and turns sideways in her seat to talk to me, making the leather squeak. "And it's not the only offer you're going to get tonight, which is what I wanted to talk to you about."

"How do you know?" I ask. I cross and uncross my legs again, praying I don't crease my black Tahari trousers. Nadine brought me a change of clothes to wear to the Polo Lounge. What I had on for the Turkey Tasters event was not business dinner–ready. I've paired my new pants with an Aryn K plum sateen blouse and gray, snakeskin, peep-toe Prada heels. I spend way too much time changing in the back of this car. "Did Laney tell you? You guys seem so tight lately."

"You give us a lot to talk about," Nadine reminds me. "I've finally learned Laney isn't that tough to talk to if you know how. Sometimes she has great advice."

"On what?" I ask. My diamond chandelier earrings hit the light, and I can see the reflection dancing on Nadine's face, practically blinding her.

Nadine squints. "Nothing worth discussing now when we have bigger things going on." She looks at me intently. "You're going to get offers that are equally big and just as enticing as the Cameron one tonight, but *do not* try to take on more than the one. Don't overdo it this hiatus, Kates. One major movie is enough. Your hiatus may seem long, but it's shorter than you think, and I don't want you getting burned out before your second season. That one will be even tougher than the first. You've heard of the sophomore slump, right?" I nod. "We can't let that happen with *Small Fries*. You need to be on your game, and I think one big film and some downtime is the way to go. Plus, if you choose to take any college classes this fall . . ." She pushes a gold folder I haven't noticed out of the binder and over to my side of the seat. I look down and see the crest is embossed with the lettering UNIVERSITY OF SOUTHERN CALIFORNIA.

"The application isn't due till January eleventh, so you have time to fill it out," Nadine says before I can say anything. "With your SAT scores and your life experiences, you're a shoo-in if you write a good essay. I know you can nail this year's question: 'Have you changed your life, or has your life changed you?'"

"Deep," Rodney chimes in from the driver's seat. "I'm going to have to think about that one."

I finger the raised lettering on the folder. "We've talked about this, Nadine," I say softly. "With a new show, my schedule is haywire. I'll never have time to take *one* class, let alone two. There's no way I can pull it off. College will have to wait a year."

"And then next year it will be another excuse," Nadine argues. "I've always said I was going to go to Harvard Business School after a few years, but my story is the same as yours. I have every excuse in the book. I'm no closer to moving to Boston than I was four years ago when I moved out here. I don't even *want* to move east anymore. I can't do winters." She looks out the window for a second and pats a strand of red hair in place. "Business school is just not in the cards."

"Don't say that," I fret, feeling bad. "Why can't you go here? Does it have to be Boston?"

Nadine shakes her head. "I don't want to go to business school anymore. I have other dreams I want to pursue but the point is if you don't do it now, you might never do it, Kaitlin. Even if it's just one class at a time, you should try to get your college degree. If you don't, you might always regret it." She taps the folder. "Start with the application. If you decide not to go next fall, then fine, but you can't go without getting accepted first." She grins. "You'd love it at

USC, by the way. Rod and I went there the other day to pick up the application, and I could picture you reading at one of the outdoor verandas."

"They happened to be having SnowFest," says Rodney, looking at me in the rearview. "They brought in actual snow! In L.A.! Students were everywhere checking out ski and snowboard stuff. I would never believe it if I didn't see it myself. How cool is that?"

"That is cool." I place the folder carefully in my new handbag. It's November and it seemed only fitting I trade in my snakeskin bag from New York for a new winter bag for not-so-wintery Los Angeles. This one is a warm, buttery yellow leather bag with black stitching. I like it, but I can't say I'm in love with it. I'm still looking for a bag that screams "me." "I'll think about the application."

"That's all I ask," says Nadine as the car rolls to a stop. I look out and see we're in front of the valet stand at the Beverly Hills Hotel. I gather up my things and look at Nadine. She's staring at me as if she's waiting for an answer. "Have a good meeting and remember what we talked about. You're having such a blast with *SF*. Don't ruin it by overextending yourself. You still need time for *you*."

"I know." I've learned that lesson the hard way. I grab the door handle. "Have a great date—I want all the juicy details."

"You've got it," Nadine says. She turns to Rodney. "Cue the music!"

Celine begins to blare loudly through the speakers again, and I laugh. "I'll call you after," I promise as the valet opens the car door. I accept his hand as I step into the warm night air, then I walk along the Beverly Hills Hotel's red carpet under the green-and-white-striped awning toward the entrance where doormen in black suits with striped cuffs are holding the doors open.

I've just walked into the yellow hotel lobby with its huge chandelier hanging over the cozy seating area of low, fluted velvet chairs and 1950s palm-print carpet when I bump into Dad. He's wearing a white polo shirt and khaki chinos, which means he either went golfing today or took a job at a chain restaurant.

"Hi, Kate-Kate!" He hugs me gruffly. "I saw an early cut of your Takamodo Cruise Lines commercial today. You had that engine at full throttle, I could tell." My dad uses car analogies for everything. Before he joined the family business (Hollywood), he was a car salesman. "Mom will be thrilled. She's already talking about your next Japanese commercial."

"Thanks, Dad. Did you, uh, get to talk to Preston at all?" Dad's been looking for his next producing project for a while, and he was hoping *SF* would be it, but the studio had enough people attached. It's not like Dad has a major track record yet. He's worked on a few of my projects that Seth negotiated into my contracts, but Dad's own production business hasn't, um, well, ever really taken off.

Dad coughs. "Well, you know, Preston's a busy man. Very busy." He looks around and reaches for an antique end table to lean casually. "I only saw him for a second when I stopped by his studio. He said he'd give me a call tomorrow or next week." His voice trails off. "He's not sure if he has any producing needs right now."

"Oh." I lower my eyes and stare at my shoes. "I'm sure he'll call, Dad. Or someone else you've pitched ideas to will."

Dad runs his hands through his thick, dark hair. "It is too bad *Small Fries* didn't need me, but business is business. I can't work on all your projects." I nod knowingly.

"And besides, I'm plenty busy between watching you and needing to be on set with Matty," Dad reminds himself. "Then there is the house to consider—your mom wants to remodel, the pool needs updating, and I've been looking at cars for you." He smiles, his teeth blinding me. "Your first ride is the one you'll always remember, Kate-Kate."

"We don't need to decide just yet," I say nervously. Just thinking about getting my license after all this time makes me freak out.

"True," Dad agrees. "It's a good thing, I guess, because I am not liking what I'm seeing at these Beverly Hills dealerships. These salesmen just don't know how to sell a car! It's appalling. I mean, in my day, we cared about the customer first and the sale second. These guys heard the last name Burke and they tried to sell me every car in the place in the first fifteen minutes. Before I even took a test drive!"

"Terrible," I agree, looking around for the others. I guess we haven't been seated in the restaurant yet. "What are you doing out here anyway? Is there a wait for a table?"

Dad shakes his head. "We're all inside already. I came out here to check on your mom. She had to take a phone call." He motions to my right and I see a tall woman with honey blond hair that closely resembles my own sitting on a velvet chair. She's wearing a black Elie Tahari pantsuit, and a large, turquoise, beaded necklace tangles over her low-cut, cream silk tank top. She taps one cream Gucci heel nervously. Mom doesn't seem to see me.

"Was that today?" I hear her say to someone on the phone while she consults one of two very thick notebooks. Papers are sticking out of all ends. "I'm so sorry. I had it down for to-morrow at three." She laughs. "I don't know where my head is. I probably left it someplace between studio A and B."

"We should really get this dinner going." Dad nudges me. "Seth has somewhere to be at nine thirty."

That means dinner won't be super long and I can make it to A Slice of Heaven to see the others. "Why don't you tell everyone I'm here, and I'll get Mom."

"Sounds good," Dad tells me and heads toward the res-taurant. He winks at me. "Try to keep her from talking on the phone too long."

"Tuesday?" I hear Mom say, and then she's rustling through papers. "Well, I can try to move a few things around, I think . . . um, I have a meeting at eleven, a lunch at twelve thirty, Matty's fitting at two . . . wow, this day is packed! Kaitlin's at four, but maybe if I . . . no, no, no! It's not a bother. I *want* to do this. The Daisies are very important to me."

Mom is quiet as she listens to the caller on the other end. She looks stressed. That's how she looks all the time lately. I wait a few minutes more hoping she'll wrap up.

"I can fit it in," Mom insists. "Nancy, you're being ridiculous! I missed one meeting. Okay, two. That doesn't mean . . . if you'd just . . . don't worry *how*. I just will." Long pause. "I can make this work, sweetie. If you'd just . . . but . . . just . . . think about it. Please? Don't make this decision yet." Mom starts flipping through papers again frantically. "Tuesday at eleven forty-five AM Pacific time! Yes. I can talk over my whole proposal then. Yes. Fifteen minutes is all I need, I swear." Mom's face breaks into a small smile. "GOOD! Thank you, darling. Talk to you then." Mom hangs up and I see her rub her temples in a circular motion. It's something I do myself when I'm worked up. Maybe I should book Mom a massage.

When would she have time to go?

"Mom?" I question. I feel like I'm interrupting a very private moment. "Is everything okay?"

"Oh, hi, honey," Mom says and quickly composes herself. Her makeup is flawless, but her green eyes are cloudy. "Everything is fine. That was Nancy Walsh on the phone. She's very close to getting the chapter off the ground, you know, and things are very hectic to say the least."

When we were in New York this past summer, Mom worked with Nancy Walsh on a bunch of charity projects, but her favorite was this group called the Darling Daisies Committee. They beautified the New York landscape by planting—you guessed it—daisies all over the city. Nancy adored Mom and said she was a shoo-in to run their new Los Angeles division. But that was before managing Matty became a job of its own—his under-sixteen status means there are a lot of laws to navigate. Now she's so busy with him I don't see or hear from her as frequently and, secretly, it's been kind of nice. Plus, Matty has gotten so popular with the tween set that he's getting cover offers from *Teen Vogue* and *J-14* and every teen book out there. Mom can barely keep up with his requests.

Not that she'll let on that she's swamped. She snaps constantly, but she's always telling us she has everything under control. The only time she seems relaxed is when she's doing something for the Daisies.

"What's happening with the president position?" I perch myself on a nearby tufted ottoman with gold legs and watch as Mom gathers up her things. First she drops her Black-Berry and the battery pops out, then she drops a pen, then her notebook. It shouldn't be a biggie, but Mom actually yells something loudly that I shouldn't repeat. "Mom?" I ask worriedly.

"She's giving the job to someone else," Mom says flatly and scoops everything up and drops it in her oversized Louis Vuitton bag. "She didn't say that exactly, but I know she is. She doesn't feel I have time to devote to the Daisies."

"Oh, Mom, I'm so sorry." I reach out and touch her wrist. She wasn't this crushed when I lost out on that Steven Spielberg movie.

"She's giving me fifteen minutes on Tuesday to prove myself, but I know I won't change her mind." Mom's voice is strange. "The bottom line is she's right. I don't have time."

66

"Make the time," I stress, trying to get Mom to look at me. "Maybe if you cut back on other things, like"—I take a deep breath and think of Sky— "me, you'll have the time you need for the Daisies."

Mom looks at me like I've suggested she put me up for adoption. "What do you mean, cut back on you? I can't do that!" Her voice starts to rise a little. "You *need* me."

"I know I do," I backpedal, side-eyeing the guy in the business suit sitting across from us that is staring. "I just meant you seem so overworked and stressed all the time, and that makes me worried. My career is doing great now—you could cut back and Nadine could take up the slack. I never get to see you anymore. I miss you."

Mom waves her hand dismissively. "Oh, Kaitlin, now you're being dramatic. I see you all the time!"

"No, Mom," I say quietly. "I mean, *really* see you. Not at work, not about work; as my mom. When's the last time you and I did anything that didn't have to do with filming?"

Mom's face sort of crumbles when I say that. "Honey, I know it feels that way sometimes, but I love you and your brother more than anything in this world," she says, sounding genuine. "I love being part of your careers and it's so important that I am because I feel so fiercely protective of you two. No one looks out for your interests the way I do, and when I see you doing so well with *Small Fries* and getting these incredible offers that we're going to talk about tonight, I feel so proud. You and Matty doing well at something you love, that's the most important thing to me.

I want you two to be bigger than Angelina Jolie and George Clooney!"

I can't help but laugh at that one, and Mom pulls me in tightly, giving me a rare hug. I breathe deeply, taking in her Beckham perfume, and try to remember the moment.

"If Nancy Walsh thinks my job with you two will take away from the Daisies, then let her. My children are more important than some silly flower project." She touches my chin. "I am never cutting back on you, ever." She pulls away from me, and I notice her eyes are sort of stricken. "Unless you don't want me to manage you anymore. Is that it?"

"Of course not!" I blurt out quickly, feeling guilty for even bringing it up. Look at her—Mom would be devastated if I ever sent her packing. I couldn't do that to her. At least this way I get to see her every day. Sure, she makes me crazy and doesn't listen to my opinions, but if she wasn't my manager anymore, maybe we'd have no relationship at all.

"Good," Mom says, breathing out slowly. "I got worried for a minute. I just wish . . . forget it. It is what it is. This is what we wanted, right? To be busy and successful." She puts her arm around me. "And we are. That's what's most important."

"Mom, you love the Daisies—" I start to say again, but she cuts me off.

"Forget the Daisies." She grabs my arm and leads me through the lobby toward the entrance to the Polo Lounge. "Tonight we have more important things to worry about, like your future."

FIVE: *An Offer You Can't Refuse*

Stepping into the Polo Lounge at the Beverly Hills Hotel makes you feel like you've time-warped to another decade. You half expect to see Tinseltown legends like Jimmy Stewart and Marilyn Monroe sitting in a booth having cocktails. The cozy restaurant is known for its famous brunch on the gorgeous patio, but tonight we're having dinner inside at a table that has cushy, fabric-covered, wood-armed chairs and a view of a massive tree in the courtyard. Jazz music is playing, and the dimly lit room and candles soothe me instantly after the conversation I just had with Mom.

I find Seth, Laney, Matty, and my dad sipping drinks and eating bread. (Well, Matty and Dad are at least. I don't think Laney has had bread since 1986.) Dad looks up from his TAG Heuer watch to Mom and I as we sit down.

"Everything okay?" Dad asks Mom. "You were on that call for a while."

"It was Nancy Walsh," Mom says reluctantly as a waiter places a napkin on her lap. "She thinks I have too much on my plate to handle the launch of the Daisies on the West Coast. I'm going to convince her otherwise." Mom starts punching buttons on her BlackBerry, her new diamond Rolex sparkling brighter than my water goblet, which a waiter just filled to the top.

"You know, sweetie, your schedule is very full," Dad says delicately and touches my mom's hand. "This is the first time we've had dinner together in over a week. You haven't called Victoria Beckham back, and she's called three times."

Wow, Mom is ignoring the Beckhams? She really must be swamped.

"I could help with Katie-Kat more," Dad offers and winks at me. "I've been hanging out at her shoots while you're busy with Matty, and I feel like I did when I test-drove the Maserati GranTurismo with the Poltrona Frau leather upholstery! I'm sure I could swing things for a while until your datebook settles down."

"*Swing* things?" Mom stops typing and looks at him sharply. Any trace of the warmth in her voice from our conversation is gone. "When you're a manager you don't *swing*. You shake. You shimmy. You make your client the best darn thing this town has ever seen!"

"You mean our daughter and son, right?" Dad asks, sounding slightly embarrassed and yet annoyed at the same time. "Are our children just clients now?" Mom looks a little shocked at herself. "We talked about blurring the line, Meg. This is what I meant. Look at how you're acting!"

Matty and I look at each other worriedly. Now my parents are fighting? And in public? They never fight. I think. It's not like I'm around that often to see, but they're always so happy when they're off on a double date with Tom (Hanks) and Rita (Wilson). I nudge Laney, praying she can rein them in before they cause a scene. Jack Nicholson is eating at a table nearby, and he's staring at us.

"Meg?" Laney tries. "Did I tell you *Vanity Fair* is booking their Young Hollywood cover?"

The words *Vanity Fair* jolt Mom out of her tirade. "Have they called for us yet?"

Laney sips her iced tea. "I'm sure they will any day. If not, believe me, I'll call them. They owe me big time."

You do not want to get on Laney's bad side. Her twenty-something look—Brazilian-straightened blond hair, petite figure, cute fitted suits (tonight she has on a black Elizabeth and James stretch jacket over a white tee and black trousers)—makes her seem like a teddy bear. She's more like a grizzly bear. Laney protects her clients—and their extended families—like they are her own cubs. Most of Hollywood is deathly afraid of her wrath. Even I still get a little nervous around her, and she's been my publicist for years.

"You're right. They'll call us. I can't handle making another call this week." Mom motions to the waiter. "I'll have a glass of Merlot, please."

"Actually, we'll have a bottle of your best Merlot," Seth tells the waiter. "Tonight is a celebration. Our shooting star is officially a planet!" Seth looks at me, his laser-white teeth dazzling. His short, brown hair is freshly highlighted, and he's wearing a gorgeous brown Tom Ford suit. Seth always looks like he's at the most important meeting of his life, even if we're doing something as routine as going over my call sheets.

When the wine arrives and Matty and I have our sodas, Seth grins at me over his glass. "You've done it, Kaitlin. You've officially arrived." He starts to applaud me. Here. In the middle of the restaurant. I could die. Especially when Dad joins him.

Matty clears his throat. "Not that Kates doesn't deserve her moment to shine, but . . ."

Seth slaps his hand on the table. "Matt, you're right! Sorry, dude." He raises his glass of Merlot. "And to Matt for getting the part that Ty Crawlord was stupid enough to let slip out of his fingers." Everyone clinks glasses.

I look from one person to the next, hoping I will get filled in. Matty smiles like someone who swallowed a canary.

"I'm going to be Dusty Dermont in *Hope, Guts, and Glory 2*," he says proudly before giving the waiter his order. (I just heard Laney give hers. She's starting with a salad and then moving on to Alaskan halibut.) "Ty Crawlord tried to get the studio to pony up a huge pay raise, and they balked. He's being replaced by me!"

Hope, Guts, and Glory raked in over two hundred million at the box office thanks to direction from Quinn Tartaglia and a ragtag band of unknown stars willing to play American soldiers battling zombie mutants in an African rain forest. Released last Halloween, it broke box office records, thanks in large part to the college crowd. Ty Crawlord looked to be the breakout star, and he's already signed on to two other films. I guess *Hope, Guts, and Glory* 2 won't be his third deal.

HOLLYWOOD SECRET NUMBER FIVE: You would think a high-profile project and a well-liked part would be an unbeatable combination, but sometimes if a star threatens to walk off a sequel, they'll let him. It would be awfully hard to imagine anyone playing the young Obi-Wan Kenobi other than Ewan McGregor, but sometimes established actors are recast in film franchises. If a star is being difficult, or they locked in early for a sequel, the studio may look elsewhere to fill that character's shoes. Sure, you'd rather go with the original, but franchises can survive without them. *Harry Potter* isn't going to tank because they've replaced the person who plays Quidditch player number four.

"Matty, that's incredible!" I tell him, my face beaming as brightly as his. "When do you start?"

"Hiatus," he says and takes a sip of his Sprite. "We're shooting in Brazil. Mom is coming with me."

"But don't you worry, sweetie," Mom says after she's placed her order (same as mine—the truffled Jidori chicken breast. Mom is starting with chilled leek soup, and I'm starting with the Santa Monica Farmers Market salad). "I will fly back and forth to your sets, and Daddy can give me updates. We know you're going to have a crazy hiatus as well."

I shrug, trying not to look too excited.

And I certainly try not to think: *James Cameron. James Cameron. James Cameron!*

AAAAH!

"It's not like I've been offered anything yet." I try to inconspicuously sneak a peek at the rest of the table. Seth's face makes my heart start to beat out of control.

"That's what you think," he says and throws a heavy bound book of pages at me (well, he sort of places it in front of me, but you get the idea). The word *CONFIDENTIAL* is stamped all over it. "This is for you. You're going in to read and meet with Jim next week."

I glance at the cover and see a name I've only dreamed about working with: James Cameron. I bite my lip to keep from screaming at the top of my lungs. "Is this what I think it is?" I can barely breathe.

"You bet your future Oscar it is." Laney looks satisfied. "I told you your life was changing! This part, the stellar press—you're moving in the right circles and people have noticed."

Seth explains more. "It's an action flick set in the near distant future, but it's not an apocalyptic film." Seth rolls his eyes. "I'm so sick of those. This is more of a think piece that focuses on a research team exploring a cure for the greenhouse effect on the planet of Abaronza, which is in the middle of an intergalactic war zone. Brad Pitt just signed on to be the head astronaut, and Sandra Bullock is his co-pilot."

Laney nods approvingly. "I've been telling Sandy for years she needed to do sci-fi. That and paranormal are so in."

"I get to be an astronaut?" I squeak. And work with Pitt and Bullock? EEEEEE!

Seth grins. "Jim already likes you, but if he likes you when you meet, the part is yours. You'd be locked in for a trilogy, should the first film do well enough to warrant more."

Ohmygodohmygodohmygodohmygodohmygodohmygod ohmygod!

OH MY GOD!

I feel like I might pass out. Never in my wildest dreams did I think I'd ever be offered a part like this. Me! Working with James Cameron! With two of the most talked-about actors of this generation! I can't believe it. I really can't believe it! I need to excuse myself so I can tell Austin and Liz. They are going to flip.

"You've arrived, shining star," Seth says, his eyes, I think, actually glittering with tears. I look at Laney. She is misty too. As is Dad. The four of us actually clutch hands. I look at Mom for approval.

"There's more," she says, pulling a dog-eared script out of her bag.

"Meg, I thought we decided to table the other offer till we know Jim's timeline," Seth says lightly, but he looks peeved. If his eyes were lasers, the new script piled on top of my Cameron one would explode.

Mom smooths her napkin. "I don't want to table it."

Uh-oh.

"Why does she have two offers and I only have one?" Matty whines.

"I don't even want to hear it," I joke. "Nothing is better than working with James Cameron. I want to take this one!" Seth and Laney laugh.

The waiter brings over our starters, and my yummy salad stares up at me begging to be eaten. I had lunch almost six hours ago, and I'm starved. As I take my first bite, I hear Mom's reply.

"Of course you're going to do the James Cameron movie, but you're going to take this one too." Seth just looks at her. So does Dad. "What? This script is incredible. To pass it up would be insulting."

"Meg, every five minutes someone in Hollywood is insulted," Seth points out. "This Cameron project is massive. There is no time to do both."

"You said yourself that we can make time if she wants to," Mom reminds him.

"*If* she wants to," Seth says and looks at me since he probably knows I'm confused. "Your mom is right that the other script is a winner too. Clint Eastwood wants you to play George Clooney's estranged daughter in his new film, which he also wrote. The part of the mom will be played by Julia Roberts, and rumor has it they've confirmed Robert Pattinson as the boyfriend."

Whoa. That is pretty good too.

"The film is shooting during hiatus, and it's an intense

six-week shooting schedule," Mom tells me knowledgeably. "Clint's people told me they'd be willing to work with Cameron so that you could squeeze in both." Mom pauses, takes a sip of wine, and takes my hand. "Kaitlin, you've never had offers like this before. How can you pick just one? The Eastwood film could mean Oscar."

"So could the Jim project," Seth reminds me.

When Nadine said it, I thought she was joking, but now that Laney has mentioned it, and Mom and Seth have said it in all seriousness, I can scarcely breathe.

"The screenplay is amazing," Seth agrees. "I didn't bring it to you first because I know you've always wanted to work with Jim, and that one is a trilogy offer and—"

"Your job is to bring her all offers," Mom reminds him.

"Meg," Dad warns. Matty and I look at each other.

"Are you saying I'm not doing my job, Meg?" Seth's voice is tight.

"No, but—"

"We shouldn't overwork her." Seth is firm. "I want her fresh when she goes back for season two of *Small Fries*." He winks at me. "We know there will be one. I've put a call in to Eastwood's people to check on start dates. Maybe if the Eastwood project is pushed back then we can—"

"That's a good idea," I agree quickly.

"No," Mom insists. "We're not losing this." She grabs my hand again and shakes it. "Kate-Kate, I know it's a lot of work, but you can handle it. I know what's best for you. You know that. Don't you trust me?"

"I do, but . . ." I falter.

"You can multitask," Mom says. "We can squeeze in both, and you can do sci-fi and work toward Oscar glory. Sweetie, I want you to have it all."

Laney looks at her plate. Seth looks annoyed. Matty seems a tad jealous. Everyone seems to think this is a bad idea except for Mom. I know it's Eastwood and Clooney, but Seth makes the schedule sound like climbing Mount Kilimanjaro. I'm intrigued, but how am I going to do it all? I think of what Nadine said. "I don't want to be worn out before I even begin work," I say gingerly. "The second season of the show, should we get one, is so important. Maybe I should only pick one film."

"Kaitlin." Mom's smile fades and her voice sounds strained. "You don't have to pick one. Didn't I just explain how this would work?"

"Yes, but doing both feels like a lot." Suddenly I feel very small.

"It's not a lot!" Mom's voice is shrill. "You can do it all! I can do it all! I manage you and your brother, and I'll persuade Nancy about the Daisies. If I can do it, you can too."

"But . . ." What if I don't want to do it all? What if I want a life too? That's what I've always wanted—work and a real life and to keep them both separate. But I don't say that part. I'm too afraid of upsetting Mom and making her turn into a female Hulk.

"Sweetie, maybe you should go freshen up," Dad suggests and puts his hand on Mom's shoulder.

"Yes, I could use a spritz of Evian." Mom is trancelike. "I'll be right back." We watch her walk away.

"I'm sorry," Dad apologizes to the table. "She's been under so much pressure lately. With Matty taking off and Kate-Kate doing so well, it's a lot." He wrings his hands hopelessly. "I don't know what to do. She won't let me help, and I've got enough time on my hands." He laughs sort of bitterly. I don't like the mood my parents are in one bit.

"I'm sorry Meg is overwhelmed," Seth says gingerly, "but that shouldn't affect Kaitlin. I'm her agent, and I don't think doing both projects over hiatus is in her best interest. If I can move one . . ."

Dad shakes his head and looks at me with sadness in his eyes. "Your mom always does right by you, Katie-kins. If she thinks you can do both, I'm sure you can. But the decision lies with you."

"Yeah, right. Mom will make her do it even if she says no," Matty mutters and takes another bite of his thirty-nine-dollar Kobe beef burger.

Matty's right. When Mom gets something in her head, there is no changing her mind. She's going to push and push till I say yes to both movies. Why not save myself the headache and just say yes now? Maybe if I psych myself up the next few months, when the hiatus rolls around I won't even notice the extra workload.

I'm lying to myself already. I'm definitely going to be overworked.

I think of Mom again. I've never seen her so close to the

edge. She's my mom. I can't let her down as much as this schedule might kill me. I've done worse, right? I'll survive.

I hope.

"I'll do both," I say reluctantly and Seth looks pained. "Set up meetings with both directors."

Saturday, November 7
NOTE TO SELF:

Book Mom spa day.
Read scripts by Monday.
Find time to read scripts by Monday.
Have Nadine read Eastwood while you read Cameron.
Hopefully have time to switch.

DMV test: Less than five weeks away!!!

SIX: *A Slice of Real Life*

Forty-five minutes after Mom's mini meltdown, I'm sitting snugly in a corner booth at A Slice of Heaven, my favorite pizza place. Well, everyone's favorite pizza place. Austin, Josh, Trevor, and even Sky are pretty hooked on it too. It's nothing much to look at—checkerboard tablecloths, old chairs, a linoleum floor that has seen much better days, and the requisite faded posters of Italy on the walls—but the pies are just as good, if not better, than the ones I had in New York last summer. That might be because Antonio ran a restaurant there before he moved to Los Angeles. Because it's so late, we pretty much have the place to ourselves. Antonio let us change the satellite radio station to my current favorite, Arcade Fire.

"I cannot believe you're going to work with James Cameron!" Liz screams after I've finished telling them about the two projects I'm considering. "James Cameron! Kates! This is HUGE!" As soon as I sat down, I had to spill what happened at dinner. I was so excited and confused, I was going to burst. Everyone has been debating which film I should take since. They don't know I've, um, committed to both if my standard meet and greets with the directors go well next week.

"The other offer with Clooney, Eastwood, Roberts, and that vampire guy sounds like gravy too," Austin says with a grin as he dives into another slice of pizza. Liz just put in an order for her and my specialty—a pie with extra cheese, peppers, and broccoli.

"She's not doing both," Sky interrupts, sounding a twinge annoyed. "She can't! We don't have enough time off. Your mom is nuts to consider it. But"—she smiles slyly—"you could pick one and give me the other offer."

"Ah, the truth comes out," I tell her and pour myself a glass of Sprite from the giant plastic pitcher in the middle of the table.

"I'm just saying." Sky picks at her salad pizza, overflowing with walnuts, cranberries, endive, and blue cheese. "I was probably first on their list, but then they heard I already had a project for hiatus." Trevor nods supportively. "Working with Jason Reitman is nothing to sneeze at."

"Absolutely not," I say with sincerity. "*Up in the Air* is still on my top ten list."

"I turned down Steven Weitzman's new one." Sky blots her mouth delicately with a napkin. "I so don't want to be part of a project with a release date that gets delayed twenty-three months."

"Hey, that was one movie," I point out. "You don't know that it will happen again."

Sky shrugs. "Why chance it?"

HOLLYWOOD SECRET NUMBER SIX: Movie release dates get pushed back all the time. It shouldn't be a huge deal, but it still is. When you hear about a delay, some people in the industry immediately think it's because the movie is a bomb, or it wasn't finished on time and it needs costly reshoots. Those could be the reasons, but there are legitimate excuses for moving a film release date too. Sometimes two big movies are booked for the same opening weekend, and one moves to avoid getting thumped by the other at the box office. When *Harry Potter and the Half-Blood Prince* moved from a November release to a summer release, there were no other major movies coming out for the Thanksgiving holiday. So *Twilight* was bumped up from a December release—where there were plenty of other movies coming out and providing competition—to a Thanksgiving release so that it could snag the box office glory. Smaller films have issues too. They might be waiting for a distribution deal at one of the film festivals, where someone offers up the money to get into theaters. Whatever the case, delays make actors nervous. They don't want to see a movie they made three years ago show up on theater screens *after* another flick they've made more recently. It just looks bad.

"So?" Sky prods, touching one of her emerald earrings. Her green Stella McCartney top looks a bit dressy for a pizza place, but then again, we all look overdressed, having come from the Turkey Tasters event, and me having changed for dinner at the Polo Lounge earlier. "Which movie are you going to take *if* you get them?" Sky emphasizes the *if*.

Everyone looks at me expectantly, and instead of answering straight away, I take a huge gulp of my Sprite then quickly mumble the answer into my napkin. "Both."

"Did you just say both?" Liz drops her current slice back onto the plate. "Kates, are you insane? This totally goes against your work and real life separation thing."

"Separating life and work is impossible for actors," Sky interrupts. "I keep telling you guys that. You can't split yourself into two people. You are who you are and you make it work." Sky wags a fork holding walnuts at me. "But I do agree with Liz—are you insane? You can't do both. There's not enough time, and both of those directors are perfectionists and immersive-type workers. You can't switch between the two. Unless you want to put out two mediocre performances *and* screw up the second season of *Small Fries* when we go back to work in late July."

I look to Austin for support, but he seems as shocked as the others. His face practically goes as dark as the navy polo he's wearing. "Burke, they're both killer offers, but it seems like overload."

"It isn't," I insist, launching into a sales pitch. "Seth and Mom will work out an agreement with the studios, and I will do one day here and one night there and split days and weekends and ..." I trail off and my shoulders slump. "Who am I kidding? It's just not possible! I don't care if Mom has a coronary. I have to say no to one of these, right?"

"That's what I said five minutes ago," Sky says lightly. "Now you've wasted five minutes of my night off. Thanks." I give her a look.

"You know, up until this film-offers fiasco, I've been loving the newfound freedom I've got thanks to Mom being tied up with Matty's blossoming career," I admit. "But now that Mom is back on my case, I'm starting to feel overwhelmed again! She's trying to make sure she gives equal time to both of us, but instead of having Mom-and-Kaitlin quality time, like she promised, she's just overbooking me and piling on the press."

"I'm sorry, Burke. Things were going so well." Austin puts an arm around me and rubs my right shoulder.

"She's not going to stop pushing till I sign on the dotted line for both movies," I say sadly. "There's no fighting her. I'm just going to lose."

"I told you," Sky interrupts. "Do what I did. Fire her."

"I *should* fire her," I blurt out. My eyes widen and I slap a hand over my mouth. "I didn't just say that."

"Whoa," Trevor and Josh say at the same time, actually taking a break from wolfing down garlic knots long enough to join in the conversation.

"Yes, you did." Liz points at me accusingly before fixing her purple headband. Her pink-and-purple Pucci print dress is as fiery as her temper at the moment. "Finally!"

"I don't know, it's just that . . ." I feel so flustered. "I don't want to have no relationship with her, but I'm sick of her bullying me into things that my agent thinks is a bad idea."

"So you *do* want to fire her," Sky says, her eyes lighting up. "Good, because I think I found the perfect manager for us both."

I picture myself giving Mom the heave-ho, and then I see her crushed face. The same one she had at the Polo Lounge when I lightly mentioned her taking a step back. "Forget I said anything. I can't do it."

"Baby steps," Austin says gently. "No one says you have to fire your mom . . ."

"I do!" Liz and Sky say at the same time.

Austin gives them both a look. "We just want you to be happy," Austin says delicately. "If your mom is one of the things making you unhappy, then maybe you have to change your relationship with her. But not tonight." He looks at the others. "Why don't we talk about something else?"

"I decided to add Berkeley and Penn State to my college applications list," Liz offers excitedly, sounding like she's been holding this in all night.

"How many schools does that make now, Lizzie? Fifteen?" Josh tries to keep a straight face.

"There is no cap on the number of schools you're allowed to apply to," Liz tells him and grabs a slice of the hot pie that just arrived—our favorite. She quickly slides one onto my plate too. After what happened with Mom at the

Polo Lounge, I barely touched my dinner. Now I'm starved, but I hope I don't get grease on my plum sateen top. It's Aryn K!

"I know—you're keeping your options open," Josh finishes and winks at her. "So you keep telling me."

"Is that why I got an application from Berkeley today?" I ask, rubbing my fingers on my napkin to get rid of the grease on my hands. "That's the fifth application package I got this week. Mom freaked when she found the ones for UCLA and Boston University." I cringe at the memory. (Mom actually yelled, "BOSTON? THEY DON'T SHOOT MOVIES IN BOSTON! ARE YOU TRYING TO KILL ME?" They do shoot movies there, but I didn't want to argue with her.) "Did you have the school send them to me?" I ask Liz.

Liz shakes her head. "I don't have time to get you applications. I barely have enough time to finish my own."

I look at Austin questioningly. "Same here," he says. "I'm up to ten schools myself."

Sky rolls her eyes. "I don't get the point of college. If you know what you want to do, just go do it."

"If you can find a lawyer who doesn't have a law degree and you still want to use him, let me know," Trevor argues.

Sky glares at him and looks at me instead. "K, you're not getting wrapped up in this nonsense too, are you? I don't need our show taking off and you disappearing on me, between school and the three billion projects your mom is twisting your arm about."

"I'm not going anywhere," I tell her, blowing on the hot cheese. "I don't know why I keep getting these applications. The only one I got on my own is University of Southern California. Nadine wants me to apply."

"Are you going to?" Austin asks.

"Please don't," begs Sky, tugging on my sleeve with her greasy fingers. She should know better! Trevor nudges her. "What? K is a good actress. Well, not as good as me, but . . ." She looks at me with laser-sharp, dark eyes. "You don't need college. You already have a career. You know what you want."

"Sky, zip it," Liz warns her. "If Kates wants to go to college, she should go to college."

"But she has a career already!" Sky sounds exasperated. "You know you want to be an actress, right?"

I stir my Sprite with my straw, staring into the bubbles. "Yes," I say slowly, "but I still think it's smart to study other things. Making a career choice at the age of four is pretty much unheard of."

"I always knew I was doing what I was meant to do," Sky says, her chin held high. "I can't imagine sitting at a cramped little cube, listening to people drone on and on about their problems over the coffeemaker." She shivers. "No offense."

"None taken," says Josh. "I'm itching to have a cube someday. Not."

"K, why do you seem so wishy-washy about this?" Sky looks suspicious. "You wanted this TV show!"

I sigh. "I know. I love TV! It's just . . ." Maybe it's just the shock of Sky firing her mom. Or how tired I am after three events in six hours. Or how drained I feel from dealing with my mom's recent mood swings. Whatever it is, I'm in a reflective mood. "When I walked into A Slice of Heaven tonight, it made me think of the past. Lizzie, we sat in this booth the night I came up with the Clark Hall idea, remember?"

"That was here, wasn't it?" Liz smiles and plays with one of her hoop earrings. "God, that seems so long ago."

"Even though Sky outed me"—I give her a look and she just shrugs—"I loved being at Clark. I think I finally learned a little about having balance. Maybe that's why I still crave it. I like being an actress, but I like having a life too. I've managed to have both up until now." I rub my temples, not caring if I ruin my foundation. "Just thinking about working twenty-four/seven during hiatus makes me tired."

"I know one thing no one is making you do," Josh says with a wink. "Take your driving test—that's all you, Kaitlin. It's about freakin' time." Liz hits him in the arm.

"Kates likes to take her time with things," Liz says in my defense, "and I can't think of a better time to get your license than on your eighteenth birthday."

Eighteen. I can't believe I'm going to be eighteen in just a few weeks! Austin turned eighteen in October, and we went out for sushi to celebrate. I also bought him the latest version of Rock Band even though the company that makes it keeps offering me copies for free. I just feel like it isn't a gift if you don't buy it yourself. Matty took them up on it, though, and got one for his dressing room. I hear his room has become the place to be on the *Scooby* set when people aren't filming.

"If K fails she'll ruin her birthday," Sky says, chewing happily on a cranberry from her salad pizza. The whole table gives her a dirty look. "What? I'm just kidding! K is going to pass! She's out in the studio parking lot with Rod-O practically every afternoon doing those three-point-turn thingies."

A slow song by Taylor Swift comes on, and all this college talk, mommy drama, and DMV stuff is forgotten. Liz and Josh, and even Sky and Trevor, get up and dance in between tables. I'm so deep in my own thoughts I don't realize Austin and I are the only two left in the booth.

"What are you thinking about, Burke?" Austin asks after a while. He slips his warm hand into mine.

"I'm been thinking about that University of Southern California essay question." I look at my friends on the dance floor. "'Do I change my own life or does my life change me?'"

Austin nods. "I've been struggling with that essay too."

"I didn't know you were applying there." I feel a surge of hope at the thought of Austin staying close to home rather than moving three thousand miles away to go to college in Boston like he's always wanted.

Austin shrugs. "I guess I'm like Liz. I'm trying to keep my options open. Plus I spoke to the lacrosse coach there, and they have a killer team." He smiles. "Maybe they'll offer me a scholarship. I could use one. Besides, the school looks awesome, and they have a good education program." Austin is thinking about being a P.E. teacher, which he would be incredible at.

"We can work on the application together," I suggest. Maybe having Austin in the room with me is just the push I need to actually do it. Wouldn't it be cool if we went to USC together? Walking to class, studying in the library, getting matching USC sweatshirts . . .

Okay, I'm getting carried away.

"You know I'm always up for a joint study session," he teases. He takes my hand and pulls me up from the booth. "But for now, let's forget about college applications. You, my friend, need a break, from work, from your mom, possibly from life. We just have to figure out how to get you there, Burke. And we will."

Austin looks at the dance floor. Taylor's over and everyone is suddenly grooving to the Black Eyed Peas with Antonio, A Slice of Heaven's owner. Sky is bumping butts with Antonio, which is a sight I thought I'd never see. I should so video her with my iPhone and put it up on YouTube. (But I won't.) Josh is twirling Liz around, and she's laughing so hard I'm afraid Sprite might shoot out of her nose. Trevor is singing at the top of his lungs and doing some weird version of 'the robot' that would get him kicked out of the *American Idol* auditions room. I start to laugh—hard. It feels good.

"What do you say we dance off some of your frustration?" Austin asks, swinging my hand. He winks. "A dance-off?"

I smile. "You're on."

Saturday, November 7
NOTE TO SELF:

Read both scripts by Monday and make decision.
Pick one script.
Which script????

USC

UNIVERSITY OF SOUTHERN CALIFORNIA

ESSAY QUESTION: Have you changed your life, or has your life changed you?
(Essay must be at least two thousand words but not more than four thousand. Please type and double-space your essay.)

In answer to the question, have you changed your life, or has your life changed you, I would say I'm . . .

I believe I'm the rare person who has both changed my life and my life has changed me.

Life is never easy, even when you're a teenager. My life is a little more complicated than most because I'm a teenager with a full-time career. I'm an actress. I know that I've changed people's lives and yet my life has changed me.

THAT SOUNDS LAME!

ARGH!

I hate essays. The end.

seven: *How Quickly Things Unravel*

I'm having the best dream. It's my birthday and I'm wearing this incredible lilac Marchesa gown. Austin is dressed like Prince Charming and is twirling me around the dance floor like I'm Belle in *Beauty and the Beast*. We're inside Sleeping Beauty's castle at Disneyland, I think (the real one is nowhere near this big), and the room is packed with people watching us adoringly. Mickey and Minnie are here, and Matty, Dad, and look! There are my former hair and makeup artists Paul and Shelly. I really must convince them to leave their new TV show and join me on *Small Fries*. Liz and Sky are here, along with some of my acting friends like my CW buddy, Gina. Aww . . . there's that cute baby I held for a photo last weekend at the farmers market. Can't believe she's here too. This is all so beautiful. . . .

Is someone yelling?

"Meg, you can't do this without talking to her first. She's going to be furious and she has every right to be!"

"She'll be fine once I explain, Nadine! I know what's best for her!"

I stop dancing and bite my lower lip. My mom is standing on the edge of the dance floor dressed like the wicked witch in *The Wizard of Oz*, and she's arguing with Nadine, who is dressed like Glinda. Maybe we're supposed to be at a costume party.

"Why do you keep doing things like this to her?" Nadine is asking. "If you knew your *daughter*—not your *client*—you'd know she doesn't want press today!"

Eek. This conversation doesn't sound dreamlike. I could totally see Nadine saying something like this to Mom.

"She wants balance!" Nadine adds. "You know that, and yet you continue to make her do every little press opportunity that comes her way. She's too big to do a Turkey Tasters bingo night! Matty is the one who should be doing those things."

God. I can't even have a princess dream without the Turkey Tasters invading?

"Oh, so now you're telling me what's right for Matty to do too?" Mom practically spits. "You're Kaitlin Burke's *assistant* and just Kaitlin Burke's *assistant*."

I wince at the way Mom says the word *assistant*. Nadine hates when Mom belittles her role in my career. I look at Austin, but he's disappeared. I try to go over to Mom and Nadine to beg them to stop, but I can't move that far. It's like I'm in a glass bubble, and I can't stop what's happening right in front of me.

"I don't like your growing attitude," Mom continues, sounding shrill. "You better watch yourself or—"

Uh-oh. Oh no. Mom, *don't* say it. Don't say it! Not even in a dream! You cannot take Nadine from me!

"It's my birthday, remember?" I yell. But in my dream my voice is warbled and it barely comes out, like I'm talking through marshmallows. "We should be celebrating!"

"Or what?" Nadine pokes Mom with her wand. "You'll fire me? Well, guess what?"

NOOOOOOOOOOOO!

I jump up and look around the darkened room. I glance at the clock. It's eight AM. I reach for my iPhone on my distressed white bedside table and check the date: December 11. It really is my birthday. Everything else was just a dream. Thank God. I'm in bed, in my Paul Frank pirate monkey flannel PJs and snuggled in my six-hundred-thread-count duvet. I'm supposed to meet everyone for breakfast at nine thirty before my driving test at one PM.

"I can too fire you! I'm in charge around here. ME! I'm the one who makes the decisions!"

Oh God. Why do I still hear yelling? I'm awake, aren't I? I pinch myself. OW! I'm awake.

"Kaitlin can make her own decisions! She's eighteen now, and if you keep being a dictator she is going to resent you. You're too rash, Meg. You're overworking everyone, including yourself. Now if you'd just let me help . . ."

That's Nadine talking. I look around. No one is in my room but me.

"Help? I don't need help! Why does everyone think I can't handle more than one client? I mean, both my children?"

Oh. My. God. That conversation I heard in my dream must really be going on! I look at the door. I think they're downstairs, but they're screaming so loud you'd think they were lying in bed with me. I better get down there. I've never heard Mom and Nadine brawl like this before.

Nadine gets a little quieter, but I can still hear her raised voice. "I'm not saying you can't handle it. I'm just saying it's a lot of work. It's okay to admit that."

"I want you to leave, Nadine! NOW!"

Oh God. I throw back my duvet and run straight for my bedroom door, throwing it open, knocking down a blurry-eyed Matty as he comes out of his room, past Dad, who is in the exercise room with his earphones on, missing the whole thing, and down the stairs to the kitchen. I make it to the landing just in time to hear Mom say: "Don't come back!"

"HI!" I yell cheerfully, even though my heart is pounding. "Happy birthday to me! It's my birthday!"

I know I sound ridiculous, but maybe if I remind them what today is they'll forget what they were fighting about. Except, they don't look like they're going to forget. If anything, they look madder than I've ever seen them. Mom and Nadine are standing at opposite ends of the kitchen island like they're boxers waiting in their corners. Mom is fully dressed at eight AM in a patterned silk blouse and dark denim skinny jeans with high boots. Nadine looks like she's just rolled out of bed. Her frizzy red hair is pulled back in a small ponytail, and she's thrown on the blue-and-white-striped American Eagle scoop-neck sweater she wore yesterday with baggy jeans. Neither takes her eyes off the other to look at me.

"Guys?" I try again, starting to feel weak. "Please? Don't fight. It's my birthday."

"I'm sorry, Kaitlin, but your mom is out of line," Nadine says, turning to look at me. Her eyes are red. "I did seventy getting over here after I read her e-mail this morning. I just don't think it's right. Not everything you do needs to be on a press release. This definitely shouldn't involve paparazzi! We had enough trouble with them the last time!"

I stop Nadine. "Slow down. I haven't checked my e-mail yet. What's going on?"

When Mom glares stonily at my assistant rather than answering me, Nadine sighs. "Media outlets have been invited to your driving test, Kates. I'm so sorry."

"The paparazzi are coming to the DMV with me?" I look at Mom in alarm and her face confirms my worst fears.

"Sweetie, Nadine is overreacting." Mom hurries around the island and makes her way across the expansive kitchen toward me. She barely misses one of the heavy kitchen table wooden chairs as she rushes to look me in the eyes. "I just invited a few people, and certainly not *paparazzi*, only seasoned Hollywood journalists and photographers." She puts her fingers over my lips to keep me from protesting. "*Celebrity Insider, Hollywood Nation,* and *Sure.* They've all been so good to you, honey, how could I say no?" Nadine laughs bitterly and Mom gives her a dirty look. "They've promised you won't even know they're there."

"Mom, I'm nervous enough as it is," I try telling her. "I don't want to have to be 'on' the whole time just to look good on TV."

"Fine! Forget it!" Mom booms, and I jump.

I hear footsteps and see Dad and Matty. Matty is wearing a Playboy bathrobe that he got as a gift when Mom and Dad wouldn't let him go to what would have been his first party at the Playboy Mansion. Dad is in a white Nike tee and slightly too tight gray sweatpants. They both look as confused as I am.

"I thought you appreciated all my hard work, Kaitlin, but I guess I was wrong," Mom rants. "I try to make you and your brother the best you can be!"

"You can book *Celeb Insider* for me, Mom," Matt pipes up. "I'll let them watch me take my driving test."

"You can't take one yet," I remind Matty, feeling my blood begin to boil. How dare Mom make me feel like this is my fault?

"EVERYONE JUST STOP!"

Uh-oh.

Laney struts into our kitchen at full speed, throwing her oversized Gucci bag on the granite countertop and tossing her keys so that they slide across the island and stop in front of Nadine. Laney is wearing—gasp—workout clothes! A pink tank top and fitted black spandex pants. I didn't even know she owned sweats. Her long sandy hair is in a—double gasp—ponytail. Oh man, she must be mad if she showed up looking like this.

I see Seth walk in behind her. If the whole situation wasn't so upsetting, I would actually laugh. Seth is in sweats too, navy ones, and a gray muscle tee. This is the first time I've seen his hair without product in years. His sunglasses are missing too.

"I cannot believe you did this, Meg," Seth growls. "Kaitlin is getting Oscar-worthy offers, and you dumb down her appeal by letting *Celeb Insider* tape her driving test? What were you thinking?"

"I don't have to answer to you, Seth," Mom says coolly. "What are you two doing here anyway? Kaitlin Burke, did you call them?"

"I did," Nadine interjects, folding her arms across her chest. "Meg, this has got to stop. You're going to damage Kaitlin's career, and just when it's doing so well."

"You invited the press to our daughter's driving test?" Dad asks, scratching his head.

"Yes." Mom doesn't sound the least bit contrite. "Turkey Tasters is sponsoring the segment on *Celeb Insider*, and then I was talking to *Hollywood Nation*, and they wanted in too, so I gave them exclusive print rights and—"

"I take back what I said before," Matty butts in again. "This sounds tacky."

"I'm with Matty," I tell Mom, even though I feel guilty that we're all ganging up on her. "I don't want an audience. Call them and tell them we changed our minds."

100

"It's too late for that. They're already at the DMV setting up," Mom tells me.

I've had it. What has this got to do with *her*? It's my driving test! "I won't show up, then," I tell her, my anger rising. Mom looks shocked.

"Enough is enough, Meg," Laney says firmly. "I usually agree with you on the press front, but booking something behind my back is even tackier than the time Tom and Katie bought me horoscope-sign bath towels." She shudders. "It just should not be done. Neither should this. I won't allow Kaitlin to show up at the DMV if the media are there."

"I'm with Laney," Seth agrees. "If Kaitlin doesn't pass her test today and the entire world is watching, it will be humiliating. This isn't the type of press we should be looking for when she's about to shoot a Jim project."

"And Eastwood!" Mom adds.

"Mom." I exhale slowly to avoid screaming my head off. "I told you, I changed my mind. I am not doing both movies if I have to do them over hiatus. It's too much."

"It's not!" Mom insists, sounding wild. Who is this woman? My mom may be rash, but she's not usually this insane.

Seth looks at Nadine and Laney. "Meg, listen, this is the sort of thing we're talking about. You have too much on your plate. Maybe that's why you're not thinking clearly. We've talked and we all think you should temporarily step down as Kaitlin's manager."

"WHAT?" Dad, Matty, Mom, and I say at the same time.

Why does this idea secretly excite me?

"Just temporarily," Laney stresses. "We weren't planning on discussing this now, but you've left us no choice. We will handle Kaitlin and run everything by you. You can concentrate on Matty's career and when things calm down we can reevaluate."

"It's for the best, Meg," Nadine says softly. "We have to protect Kaitlin."

Mom starts pacing, her knee-high black Gucci stiletto boots clacking on the ceramic tiles, but she doesn't say anything. I'm not sure if this is a good or bad sign.

Suddenly my anger wanes and all I feel is sad. I'm yelling at my mom, she's yelling at me . . . this is not what I want. I wish we had a normal mother-daughter relationship. Now, more than ever, I could use my mother's—not my manager's—advice.

I've auditioned for Jim (he said I could call him Jim!) Cameron and I'm *thisclose* to signing on to spend my hiatus at an airport hanger that has been transformed into another planet! Jim seems incredible and I couldn't be more excited to do this. I auditioned for Clint Eastwood too, but his movie doesn't have a start date, so for now we're in a holding pattern on that one. Seth and I really think I should say no if the Eastwood movie shoots during hiatus. I *think* that's what I should do. Just like I think I should fill out that USC application and try to do that essay I keep trying to write. But I'm still so unsure about college. See? This is why I need my mom! And I haven't had time with my mom in a very long time.

"Meg? Sweetie?" Dad's voice interrupts my thoughts. "Did you hear what Laney and Seth said? I think it's a wise idea."

"Sometimes the press you get Kaitlin puts her in danger of violating her morals clause," Laney explains delicately, tapping her long, red fingernails on the countertop. "Yes, it's just a driving test, but if Kaitlin is drinking an unknown beverage while driving and hits the gas instead of the brake and nips a pedestrian, the last thing we want is for *Celebrity Insider* to be there to capture the whole thing on film. Do we really want to have to issue another statement about Kaitlin's beverage choices? Why get people in a tizzy in the first place? Let Kaitlin keep her Sprite and ditch the tabloids, and we're all happy."

HOLLYWOOD SECRET NUMBER SEVEN: I really do have a morals clause in my contract, just like most young stars my age. It sounds old school, I know, but even Hollywood needs a system to keep their stars in line. For some celebs it's written in broad terms, like don't get a felony rap sheet while you're being paid on the network's dime. For others, like my friends who work for tween-friendly companies, it can be more specific, like no underage drinking or nude photos showing up on the Web. I'm not even sure what's in my morals clause for *Small Fries*. All I know is that I never want to do anything bad enough for them to bring it up. The days of partying, shopping in excess, and hanging with the wrong crowd are long behind me.

"I will not be drinking anything while I'm taking my

driving test," I clarify, "but the last thing I want is to get in trouble, morals clause–worthy or otherwise, with *Small Fries*," I say, rubbing my temples. "I think you should listen to everyone, Mom."

Mom stops pacing and her face is eerily calm. "You think I should step down?"

"Just temporarily." Laney nods, her blond ponytail swishing back and forth.

"You *three*, who *I* hired, think *I* should step down?" Mom repeats, her voice rising. "Maybe you are the ones who should step down."

Uh-oh.

Everyone starts talking at once, pointing fingers, and their voices escalate so loud I think the windows are going to blow out. I can only make out snippets of conversation, but suddenly I hear singing. Anita, our housekeeper, squeezes her round frame through the group, and I see she's carrying a homemade cupcake with a burning candle on top. She's singing "Happy Birthday" to me in Spanish. I think I might cry. At least someone remembered. Matty nudges Laney, who nudges Nadine and Dad and Seth, and everyone joins in (in English). When Anita stops in front of me, I blow out the candle. Peace at Casa Burke seems like a good wish.

"Happy birthday, pumpkin," Dad says. "I'm sorry your day had to start like this."

"I am not stepping down!" Instead of wishing me many more, Mom launches into her tirade again. "I'm sick of everyone attacking me. I'm doing the best I can. I have two careers to manage and no time for myself. None for my charity work. No time to even play tennis with Victoria."

Suddenly she breaks down crying, and I think it's for real. I can't remember the last time I saw my mother cry.

I'm too stunned to speak. Matty and I look at each other. I'm so busy being annoyed that Mom's overworking me and ignoring our relationship that I haven't stopped to think about what the toll must be on her. "I'm sorry, Mom." I touch her shoulder.

"You're sorry?" Nadine explodes. "She did this to herself! She controls what you eat, criticizes what you wear, and comes up with crazy ideas like that 'Paparazzi Princess' song. You are not the one who should be sorry!"

Well, when you put things that way . . .

"Meg, I think what Nadine is trying to say—and not too well, I might add—is that you need to back off a bit," Seth says more diplomatically and gives Nadine a stern look, managing to take authority even in his old gym clothes. "Think of this as a vacation. Just concentrate on Matty. He has so much going on, and he could really use your years of, um, expertise."

"I was talking to Drew last night, and she was telling me about this fab spa in Palm Springs," Laney adds. "Why don't you head down there for a few days and get refreshed? When you get back, we can talk. What do you say?"

We all look at Mom hopefully, but my hope fades fast.

"What do I think?" Mom's voice drips with disdain, her

eyes narrowing behind her now streaming mascara. "What do I think? I think you've ruined my daughter's birthday, and you know what that tells me? That you don't care about her the way I thought you did. And if that's the case, then I don't think you should be part of our lives anymore."

"Mom!" I freak out.

"Meg, think before you say anything else," Dad warns.

But Mom doesn't stop. She gains speed. "I am the only one truly looking out for her best interests. I'm the only one who cares enough to tell her the truth—that cupcakes make you fat, two high-profile projects are better than one, and taking time off for college is career suicide." She glares at all of them. "So what I *think* is that you're done here. You're all fired! Now get out!"

Everyone is stunned into silence except for me.

"MOM!" I screech again, my heart pounding. "You can't do that!"

"Yes, I can." Mom raises her eyebrows at me menacingly. She is daring me to disobey. Normally I don't, but this time is different.

"Mom, I'm eighteen today," I say calmly. "Which means that, legally, I have a say here. I want you to take, um, a short break. My team isn't leaving. They know my career better than anyone. You can't fire them."

Wow, that felt good.

Mom looks at me strangely. "Ask Nadine if she has your back, Kaitlin. I'm sure that is the one part of our argument this morning that you didn't hear. If Nadine has your back

106

so much, then why has she been doing so much *behind* your back?"

I look at Nadine and see her ears are turning red.

"Meeting with Laney, dining with Seth, all without you. Why would she need to do that, huh?" Mom demands. "Unless she's planning a coup d'etat!"

"Meg, you're being ridiculous," Laney insists. "Nadine was asking for business advice, and that's all. It had nothing to do with Kaitlin."

I'm still looking at Nadine. She has been a little odd lately, but I thought she was embarrassed to tell me about a guy she's seeing. She's been dressing up more and doesn't go to all my meetings lately. I'm about to ask what Mom means when I notice the time on the huge Restoration Hardware clock hanging in the kitchen. It's nine AM. I have to meet my friends in a half hour.

"I have to go," I tell everyone.

"Where?" Mom is incredulous.

"Today is my birthday, and some people actually want to celebrate instead of cause fights," I tell Mom, feeling hurt.

"Kates, don't be that way," Matty says. "I want to celebrate with you."

"Thanks, Matt," I say, "but I'm still going." I look at the others. "None of you are fired, and I'm not doing press for my driving test, Mom, so get rid of everyone!"

"Kaitlin, get back here," Mom insists, but Dad cuts her off before she can follow me out of the kitchen.

As I head up the main hall steps to my room to get

dressed, I hear Nadine call to me from the bottom of the landing.

"Kaitlin, I want to explain." She looks upset.

"Come to breakfast," I suggest. "I'll be down in five minutes and I'll meet you in the car. Rod is already out front." Then I dash up the stairs before anyone else spots me.

Considering how my birthday just started, you'd think I'd wear all black, but I want to look nice today. Since I have my driving test, I choose sensible Coach ballet flats (no Manolos), a sweet, green, cowl-neck, short-sleeved sweater (after all, green is my lucky color), and dressy Gap jeans. I take the long way around the house, pausing for a moment to accept a hug from Anita, before I sneak past the kitchen. Everyone is still yelling in there. I slip out the door where Rodney has the car idling in the driveway.

"Happy birthday, Kates," Rod says, and hands me a Jamba Juice cup. He's got one of his own in his other hand. Rod is dressed head to toe in black, and his sunglasses are sitting high on his bald brown head. "It's a Strawberry Nirvana Light smoothie. Your favorite."

"Thanks, Rod," I say gratefully and take a sip of the cool drink. "Ready for your half day off?"

He frowns. "Yeah, but I don't feel right leaving you on your birthday. What if you need me? You are going to be out in public."

"Rod, I'll be fine," I insist. "Austin is going to drive me home after my driving test. We have a whole day planned. We can drop Nadine off too."

"Sure," she says absentmindedly. She looks so serious.

Rodney slurps noisily. "Well, if you're really sure."

"I'm positive. I just need this one ride and then you're off. Enjoy it," I insist, even though I'm not too sure of anything at the moment. I turn to Nadine, who is biting her fingernails. "Are you okay? What was going on in there?"

Nadine sighs. "It's complicated."

"Mom shouldn't have freaked out on you." I check my makeup in my Bobbi Brown bronzer compact. "Mom has definitely overdosed on her vitamin K pills if she thinks I'm changing my team. Don't worry. I'll talk to her and straighten this whole thing out. She's just stressed."

Rodney chuckles. "You always make excuses for her, Kates."

"I do not," I protest.

Nadine gives me a smart look. "You do too. Always. You let your mom get away with murder."

"Sometimes, but she's my mom," I say helplessly. "I want to change things. I do. It's just . . . I don't want to hurt her."

"You should—" Nadine stops herself and takes a deep breath. "Never mind. It's your birthday and I'm sorry if I ruined it. You shouldn't have heard that." Nadine's bitten fingernails tap against the binder she's holding, and I notice she's fidgety. "I just got so mad when I read your mom's e-mail! I couldn't believe she would try to have press cover your driving test without telling us. I texted Laney and Seth, and when they wigged out I knew I was right. I had to see your mom and tell her what I really thought." Nadine looks at me. "I'm worried she's going to destroy your career one day, Kaitlin."

A pit forms in my stomach. "She wouldn't do that," I say hastily.

"Not on purpose, but—"

"Don't say it. If you say it, I might have to agree with you and I'm not there yet. I've never seen her cry like that. And you know Mom's always had a choke hold on me that I've never been able to shake. I don't want it to be like this, but I don't want to lose my mother either. I love her . . . but she drives me crazy." I realize, coming to terms with what is really going on here. I'm so frustrated, my voice goes up in volume. After being the calm one in the kitchen, I finally have a chance to flip out and I'm taking it. "I don't know what to do!"

Even I'm surprised by my sudden outburst, but once the words start flying, I can't stop them. It's as if I've had them bottled for so long, they shoot out like a champagne cork on New Year's Eve.

"She ignores everything I say," I complain. "She thinks she's always right! She annoys the studio executives, embarrasses me at parties, and she never acts like a mother. Do you know how much I'd give to have her do something motherly without having to question whether she has an ulterior managerial motive?" My lower lip starts to quiver.

"Kates." Nadine touches my hand, but I recoil as if she's on fire.

"No! You guys act as if I have a choice here. If I do what

Sky did, my mom will never forgive me. NEVER. I don't want that either."

Nadine grabs my hands firmly so I can't get away. "Of course you don't! But if it's for the best, your mom will realize that eventually and forgive you. She's your mom."

I sigh. "I know, but she would miss managing me so much. And besides, what if I get what I want and my mom still doesn't act like a mom?" That thought scares me most of all.

"That's not going to happen," Nadine says. "You'll get through to her. She might change her ways once she sees how nice it is to have time for a real relationship with you. Then you could hire a new manager."

I laugh. "Like who? At least I trust my mom." On second thought . . .

"Hire me," Nadine says without skipping a beat.

I sit up and look at her determined face, astonished. "What did you just say?"

"Yeah, what?" Rodney asks from the front seat.

Nadine leans forward and talks fast, her eyes glinting excitedly. "Hire me. I know your career in and out. I've been following it for years! I've been talking to Laney and Seth, and they think I have what it takes to do talent management. They said they'd help me find clients and expand my base. Kaitlin, we'd be great together. I know you'd be happy."

I can't get past the first part. If Nadine is going to be a manager, that means she's no longer going to be my assistant. "But that means . . ."

"Yes," Nadine says softly. "I'm resigning as your assistant. I was going to tell you after Christmas and give you a month to find someone new, slowly phase myself out, but after what happened this morning..." She shakes her head.

Nadine is leaving me. She is not going to be my assistant anymore.

I can't live without Nadine! She knows everything about me! I trust her completely! I can't run my life without her!

I should take her up on her offer.

But I can't! Mom would *flip*. I might as well say I want Nadine to be my mom instead of her. I wouldn't put it past her to disown me. She's already mad enough about the college applications. Can you imagine what she would do if she found out I was firing her for Nadine? I can't let her continue on this power trip, though. She can't fire Laney and Seth. I won't allow it. Dad won't either. He'll back me up.

"Kates?" Nadine looks at me questioningly. "What do you think?"

"I don't know." I bite my lower lip. "I'm happy for you. You've said forever that being an assistant was just a temporary thing, but I guess I blocked that out of my mind. I think you're going to be an incredible manager." Nadine smiles shyly. "I'm just going to really miss you." Here come the tears.

"Kates! Don't cry," Nadine says and offers me a tissue from the box in the back of the car. "You don't have to miss me! I'll take on a new role. I know I can do a good job."

"I know you would." I sniffle. "I just don't know what to do. How did this all happen?" I wipe away my tears. "I know you've been talking about business school again lately, but I didn't know you were thinking of a new career."

Nadine looks down. "I wasn't, but then someone asked me to be their manager. I thought they were crazy at first, but when I thought about it, I liked the idea of shepherding someone's career." Her eyes are bright with excitement. "I surprised myself by saying yes."

The car slows to a halt in front of Barneys New York, where we're meeting Austin, Liz, and Sky for breakfast. The department store has a great restaurant on the fifth floor called Barney Greengrass, and we love to have breakfast on the outdoor terrace overlooking the hills. I glance upward and see the tables and the white umbrellas on the top floor. I also see a huge thing of balloons, which are probably for me. That makes me smile. A little.

"Wow, someone asked you to be their manager?" I ask, slightly jealous, slightly in awe. "Who?"

The valet opens the car door and Nadine slips out first. I get out after her and get blinded by a flashbulb. And another. And a third.

"Hi, guys," I say, smiling even though I feel dizzy from both their lights and what Nadine just told me.

"Kaitlin! Over here! Can you take a few pictures?"

"Kaitlin? Kaitlin! Kaitlin!"

Their voices sound grating at a moment like this. I can't smile right now. I can't get it together to pose. I feel bad, but

I always pose for these guys. Can't I pull the diva card just this once? Larry the Liar is not there, but I recognize some of the others. They are an aggressive bunch. The kind I can't stand but tolerate so that they don't make me miserable. They yell the nastiest things if you don't cooperate. Today, I don't care. I wave once and follow Nadine quickly into the department store.

"Nice, Kaitlin! Happy holidays to you too! Way to act like a movie star! You so aren't one!"

Ouch.

I try to ignore their taunts and concentrate on Nadine. She's going on about how torn she's been about this decision and what a great opportunity it is, but all I can think about is who her first client is. Is it someone new to Hollywood? Someone already huge? It could be anyone! Everyone loves Nadine when they meet her. Miley is always telling me how lucky I am to have a great assistant. Did Miley poach Nadine? When we reach the restaurant, the gang is waiting at a table on the terrace. The balloons are for me—pearl, pink, and silver ones are bopping around in the light breeze. The table is set with the standard white tablecloth, but I notice someone threw birthday confetti on there as well. A pile of beautifully wrapped presents lies near one of the bamboo chairs. I'm touched, but I still feel so depressed. (Did Mom even say happy birthday to me?)

"Happy birthday!" Liz throws her arms around me, but she pulls back quickly, looking from Nadine's solemn face to mine. "What's wrong?"

"Are you all right, Burke?" Austin asks and gives me a quick kiss. "You look pale."

"You told her, didn't you?" Sky asks Nadine quietly. She's holding a huge bouquet of sunflowers, and she lets them drop to her side. "I thought we were going to do it together."

"I had to," Nadine explains. "It was a bad morning."

"You know Nadine is going to be a manager?" I ask Sky, looking from her to Nadine in confusion. I can't believe Nadine told Sky before me!

"Yes," Sky says awkwardly, "because she's going to be mine."

EIGHT: *Crash Landing*

"You're Nadine's client?" I freak out. Several well-dressed women sipping English breakfast tea at a nearby table give me a
disapproving look, but I'm too shocked by Sky's bombshell to
apologize. "You asked Nadine to be your manager? *You poached
Nadine?*" My head is swiveling from Nadine's embarrassed face
to Sky's sort-of-defiant one at warp speed. "How did you...
when did you... I don't understand why both of you..."

Austin pulls out a chair and I sink into the green cushion.
I may never leave this chair again. At least I'll have food, and
if I need a change of clothes I can walk inside and buy some
comfy James Perse pants. I feel like the floor is dropping out
from under me. First my mommy issues flooded to the surface, then Nadine's bombshell, and now Sky is taking my assistant? No, *stealing* my assistant? "When did this happen?"

Nadine pulls up a chair next to me, leaning in so I can
hear her every word. "I didn't want you to find out this way,
but you cannot be mad at Sky," she says, her voice insistent.
"I adore you and I only want what's best for you. You're like a

sister to me." Nadine's eyes glisten. "I know you well enough to know why you're mad. It's not because I'm leaving, it's because I'm leaving to be Sky's manager."

"You think?" I fan my napkin out angrily and place it on my lap. I reach for the bread bowl, pulling out a warm roll and taking a bite so that I don't say anything I'll regret, like: How could Nadine do this to me? Leaving me is one thing—I have to accept that. She always said this was a short-term position, and she's been with me for years. But now she's staying in Hollywood and taking on Sky as her client? I glare at Sky. "I should have expected this from you," I say coldly and swipe some butter from the tray with my knife. "Everyone warned me, but I said noooo, Sky's changed! She would never stab me in the back again. We're friends now. Ha!"

Sky takes the seat across from me, and I feel like I'm about to be interrogated. "We *are* friends, K. I did this for both of us! You and I both know Nadine was wasting her talents spending her day picking up Marc Jacobs tops from the dry cleaner and going on Pinkberry runs." She looks at Nadine glowingly. "N here deserves to be a manager. I saw it the first time she laid into you about your mom's career advice. She can do this!"

I feel my cheeks flame. "Don't you think I know Nadine is talented?" I look at Nadine, and my lip begins to tremble. "I always knew you were going to do something great. Like work for the Obamas! I knew this day would come. I just didn't think it would be today."

"Guys, it's her birthday," Austin says quietly, and for the first time I notice how good he looks, standing behind my chair, one hand on my shoulder. He's in an untucked navy blue dress shirt and worn dark denim jeans. "And she's got a road test in a few hours. Can't we put this aside and deal with it tomorrow?"

Everyone looks at him. "No," we say in unison.

Boys just don't understand us sometimes. Once you take the cat out of the bag, you can't cram it back in.

"I don't think I'm up for taking my road test today anyway," I tell Austin and look down at my white plate guiltily. "I don't want to do it in front of the media. Mom invited press to my driving test."

"She did what?" Liz's face is as dark as the indigo headband holding back her curly hair. She stands up, giving me a good look at the drop-waist green Marc Jacobs dress she's wearing. "Why?"

I look at the mountains again, staring deeply at a cool house on a cliff to avoid Liz's piercing stare. "She thought it would be good exposure."

"*Celebrity Insider* filming your road test is good exposure?" Liz is stunned. "Kates! Why didn't you try to stop her?"

"I did, but there were bigger things going on at the moment. She was in the middle of firing Laney, Seth, and Nadine this morning when I found out!" I break off.

"KATES!" Liz's head is going to spin off and land on Wilshire Boulevard. "You didn't let her, did you?"

"I told her no! Just like I told her to call off the paparazzi,"

I insist, my chin held high. Liz continues to stare me down, as do the others. I look away. "But I'm not sure she's going to listen to me."

Sky shakes her head and tsks. "This is why you were so easy to pick on all those years. You are a wet noodle."

"I am not a wet noodle!" I pause for a moment to order my breakfast from the waiter who has been patiently waiting for a break in the conversation. (I order the Jarlsberg cheese omelet. Austin does the same. Sky gets egg whites, Liz a bagel with lox, and Nadine, an omelet.) Everyone stares at me expectedly, and I realize I still have an argument to make. "I stand up to my mom sometimes! Remember when I wanted to go to New York? Or do *Small Fries*? I got to go to Clark Hall for a few months, didn't I? And to be fair, I didn't actually let her fire anyone this morning."

"But now you're back to square one," Liz points out. "When we came up with the Clark Hall idea to give you a few months of normalcy, you *swore* you learned how important it was to have time for you. You said you wanted to be the best you could in front of the camera, and happy when the camera was off. You said you were going to keep balance in your life, but look at you! Just a few months of taping and you're already letting your mom bulldoze you again."

"It's easy for you all to judge, but you don't know what it's like. How do you fire your own mother?" I look at Sky. "How does anyone other than Sky have the guts to fire their own mother? Yes, I should, but she's going to be crushed, and I can't stand that. So for now, I let her pile too much on, and then I make myself miserable in the process." My chest is starting to feel tight. I know this feeling and I hate it. I need to take deep breaths, but that's impossible when you're doing everything you can not to start sobbing.

"I told you, if it will help you out, I'll take the Eastwood project," Sky tries to lighten the mood. But instead I turn on her again.

"YOU don't get to joke." I point my trembling finger at her, the wide arm of my green sweater practically falling in my water glass. Austin pulls it away. "I don't even know what to say to you! You are so not keeping the Bob's Big Boy clock!" Sky gasps.

HOLLYWOOD SECRET NUMBER EIGHT: The Bob's Big Boy clock is a prop in our *Small Fries* characters' dorm room. Yes, it's kind of hokey, but the prop is our absolute favorite, and even though we hope our show is around for a decade, we both joke about who will get the Bob's Big Boy clock if we get the ax (that superstition thing again—actors can't admit when something's going well!). Our set decorator, Bobby O'Shea, is a stickler for finding props that really speak to the characters' places in the college hierarchy (not to mention their wallets). Most set decorators I know do the same. When you're watching a TV show, I'm sure you don't spend much time freeze-framing shots to see specific things on a character's nightstand, or what books are on their bookshelf, but believe me, everything on that set has been placed there with a lot of thought. The cereal boxes that sit on top of our *Small Fries* mini fridge are rotated every taping. Taylor's textbooks are ones that freshmen actually use at Brown University. Even our dry-erase board notes, which can barely be seen behind the large potted plant by the dorm room window, are changed all the time. Decorating a freshman dorm room may be relatively easy, but some shows I know—like *Mad Men*, which needs period pieces from the sixties, or *The Big Bang Theory*, which has tons of scientific gadgets—take a lot of planning.

"You can have the Bob's Big Boy clock." Sky is calm. "If that is what it takes to get you to listen to reason, K. We're worried about you."

"We?" I question, squinting menacingly at the group. There are other traitors afoot.

"Yes, we," Liz pipes up. "I hate seeing you like this. You've been so happy since you got this job."

"She *is* happy." Austin sticks up for me. "Especially today. It's her birthday. Hint. Hint."

"But if it wasn't her birthday, she'd be miserable right now," Liz points out, staring at me like I'm a specimen in her AP science class rather than her best friend. "Ever since that Turkey Tasters event, I've noticed how unhappy you've become. I think a lot of it has to do with your mom. All the stress she's been under launching two stars on two TV shows has finally caught up with her, and she's lost her mind."

"And your mom going loco is making *you* lose your mind," Sky clarifies. "Two jobs? One hiatus? Seriously? She's trying to ruin you. This"—Sky waves her hands wildly in a gesture that is supposed to represent my life—"is not normal."

"You're all overreacting," I scoff. "My life is normal."

"Kates, we love you to pieces, but your life is not normal," Liz says delicately and takes a sip of sparkling water. "You're going to lose *you* in all this work you're doing, I just know it, and that scares me. You won't have time for us." She looks away. "I don't know how long we're going to stand on the sidelines waiting for you to stand up to your mom. You made such strides this summer. It's the most relaxed I've ever seen you. Next hiatus you're going to be a zombie! And you might even lose some friends."

"Is that a threat?" I'm not sure if I should be hurt or angry.

"It's a fact," Liz says simply.

"If you overextend yourself and blow both projects, your future offers will be ones that D-listers would turn their noses up at," Sky adds.

"Plus there is college to think about," Nadine throws in. "We know you're the tiniest bit interested in taking classes at USC. Don't deny it! I saw the essay on your desk."

"That was private!" I gulp. Shoot. I was hoping no one would find it. That's why I hid it under a *Sure* magazine. No one reads that anymore. "What do you guys want me to do? Tell Cameron no? Turn down *Ellen*? I can't!"

"Start by changing your mom's role in your life," Nadine says simply. "She's got to go. Just think of the things she's gotten you into! Remember that 'Paparazzi Princess' song? That wouldn't have happened if your mom hadn't made you go to a meeting with that music mogul, TJ. Then there was the time your mom became obsessed with Alexis Holden and didn't see how manipulative she was...."

"And then there was the time your mom wanted the Burkes to be on a reality show, or when she wanted you to come out to the Hamptons for the afternoon even though there was barely enough time to get back into the city to do *Meeting of the Minds*...." Liz ticks off each indiscretion on her short, silver fingernails.

I close my eyes tight, trying to block out the images. "Don't all moms mess up sometimes?"

"No!" they say at the same time.

I throw my napkin down on the table. "I've had enough." The waiter pours me another freshly squeezed orange juice, and I take a huge gulp before continuing my rant. "She's my mother. I've never once insulted any of your families." Liz hangs her head shamefully. "My mom may book me too many press commitments behind Laney's back, she may not listen to me, and she may be overbearing."

Wow, this really does sound bad, but I'm not letting on.

"But that's for me to complain about, not you guys." Even Sky is starting to look a little guilty. "She's my family, and family sticks together." I begin to choke up, and I push my chair out from the table so I can leave. "And since you guys obviously aren't my family or the friends I thought you were, I think I want to celebrate my eighteenth birthday elsewhere."

"We are your friends," Sky insists, her chunky quartz

Pippa Small ring smacking the table. "K, if you would just listen to us, you'd see we have a plan."

Nadine grabs my hand before I can walk away. "I want to be your manager *and* Sky's manager. I've been trying to find a way to tell you that. I know I could do an amazing job, and you'd be so much happier."

"Listen to her, Kates," Liz agrees. "This is just the change you need."

I look at Liz skeptically. "Really? Firing my mom is the change I need? How am I going to live with her after that?" I question the group. "Bet you guys didn't think of that. Or at least, it's really easy to say when you're not the one who has to do it. Even worse, you really haven't thought through the logistics at all. How am I going to afford Seth and Laney and now Nadine when Mom has control over my money till I'm twenty-one?"

"But—" Nadine starts to say. Nadine's neck is blotchy. She and Liz break out in hives when they're either A) lying or B) very nervous.

"Do you want to hire Nadine?" Sky asks bluntly. "That's the big question. This is your career, not your mom's."

"My mom made my career!" I tell the group. "If it wasn't for her, I wouldn't be sitting at Barney Greengrass right now. I'd be at some mall in the valley buying Old Navy cords! You guys want me to just turn around and tell her 'I'm sorry, I decided I'm better off without you'? She'd be crushed. I can't do that to her." I grab my yellow leather bag. "Enjoy the birthday cake."

"Kates, wait!" Liz begs, but I keep walking, smiling politely at the waiter as he stares at me bewilderedly.

"Burke! Hold up!" Austin trails behind me and grabs my arm. "Calm down. Don't let this ruin your day. You're eighteen! We should be celebrating."

"Kates! Wait!" It's Liz and Nadine again, but I'm already on the elevator down. Four more flights to go.

"Come on, K! Buck up and get back here. Let's talk." Sky is right behind them, but the doors shut and Austin and I are thankfully alone.

I'm furious. "They pick today of all days to tell me everything that is wrong with my life?" I mutter more to myself than to him. "I know I have to fix things, but was today the day to bring it up? I just want to get out of here and go to the DMV."

"Even with the paparazzi there?" Austin asks gently.

"I know." I sigh. "I told Mom to call them off. Who knows if she did? I guess I can call Laney and get an update when we're in the car."

I rush out the front door. I don't want to see my friends and my former assistant. I just keep moving, but I get hit with a flashbulb as soon as I exit.

The paparazzi caravan starts in. "Back so soon, Kaitlin?" I forgot they were here. "Come on, take five minutes to take a picture!" one says, getting right in my face. I try to move around him, but there is another photographer right there. "It's the least you can do! Come on, it's your job! Comeon comeoncomeoncomeoncomeon!"

"KAITLINKAITLINKAITLINKAITLINKAITLIN!"

"LEAVE ME ALONE!" I bark, momentarily stunning them and myself.

"You're rude!" one paparazzo yells back.

I spin around as I start to get surrounded by cameras. "I've got to get out of here," I tell Austin. "I gave Rodney the day off. Where is your car?"

Austin makes a face. "The garage, which I now realize is on the other side of the building."

"Kaitlin!" Liz races out the door looking upset. "Can you hold up a minute? We should talk." Nadine and Sky are right behind her.

"I don't want to talk!" I yell as flashbulbs continue to pop.

"Kaitlin," Nadine says, side-eyeing the cameras. "Come back inside so we can talk about this in private."

"Yeah, Kaitlin, go back inside!" one of the paparazzi taunts as he takes pictures of all of us. "We need a bigger star anyway. You're not going to amount to anything if you can't at least turn and pose for a simple picture."

"He's kidding," another tells me. "Stay and pose. COME ON. You owe it to us!"

"Kaitlin! KAITLIN! KAITLIN!" they sing annoyingly.

"Kaitlin, please," Liz tries, joining the chorus.

"Go away!" I tell Liz. "You're not my friend. None of you are!"

"Aww . . . poor pampered celeb has issues. Wah wah," I hear one of them say. My blood is boiling.

"Burke, I think we should get back inside." Austin takes my hand. "These guys aren't going to quit."

I don't want to stay here, and I don't want to go inside and talk to my friends. I'm trapped.

Then a black SUV pulls up outside. It's a studio courtesy car. I'd recognize it anywhere. It's here to pick up another star, I'm sure, but I'm too upset to feel guilty for what I'm about to do. I rush over and bang on the window as the paparazzi start to surround me. "Hey! Hey! Can you give me a lift?"

"Kaitlin! Just come back inside," Nadine begs.

"Seriously, K, get a grip," Sky barks. "Just take a picture with me and get these goons off your back. We can finish brunch. That's what you want, isn't it?"

I whirl around. My heart is beating fast. "STOP TELLING ME WHAT TO DO!" I scream at the top of my lungs.

Sky looks as if I've slapped her.

I've finally snapped, and I know it. "I'm sick of everyone telling me what to do! What not to do! Where to go, where not to go, who to take a picture with. Just leave me alone! GO AWAY!"

"Kates," Nadine stammers, but I cut her off.

"YOU ALL THINK YOU KNOW WHAT'S BEST. EVERYONE KNOWS BETTER THAN ME, RIGHT?" I'm still yelling, and I don't care that the paparazzi are taking pictures and probably using their camera phones to record my tirade. "Well, fine. Go do what you think is best, and I'll do what works best for me." I'm not even sure I'm making sense. "Everyone takes care of number one. That's what you did, right, Nadine? You got yourself a shiny new gig and forgot about me. So go do it. Sky? You signed on even though you knew I would be upset. So take her. You two deserve each other!" I'm starting to cry, and the paparazzi are still shooting.

"Boo hoo! Poor Kaitlin!" one of the guys says as he zooms in for a close-up of my tears.

"Knock it off," Austin tells them.

"Hey, freedom of speech, dude," one says. "You back off!"

"Austin, forget it." I stare them down. "They're scum!" I know I'm egging them on, and I don't care. "They won't get a good picture of me today."

FLASH. "Who said it had to be a good shot?" one says with a laugh.

The driver rolls down the passenger side window. He's a tall, skinny man in his forties. "Kaitlin Burke, right? Get in already. We'll get you away from these thugs."

"Let's go," I say to Austin and drag him to the car.

"Burke, we don't know him," Austin starts to say.

"Kates, don't go," Nadine says. "Austin is right."

"I can take care of myself!" I feel overwhelmed by all the flashes that keep blinding me. "Stop trying to rule my life!"

Do I control my life or does my life control me?

My life controls me.

That's the million-dollar answer to the essay question, isn't it? At least it's my answer and you know what . . . it stinks. It really stinks!

"I have no control over my life. Everyone has something to say about what I do. Everyone! My mother dictates my every breath like I'm a form of Ashtanga yoga. Laney wants me to be the cover line in every magazine, and the first story on every TV gossip show. All for good things, of course. Liz is on my case about, well, everything. Nadine wants me to apply to college even though I don't have time to take a bathroom break, let alone Psychology 101. Dad wants a piece of every project I make. Matty always wants to know what's in it for him, too. Lauren and Ava want to ruin my career. Alexis Holden *almost* ruined my career. Sky gives me too much garbage to even list."

"You go, girl!" one of the paparazzi says with a laugh.

"Kates, stop," Nadine says through gritted teeth.

But I can't. "Austin is the only one who cares about me for me. EVERYONE has something to say about my life, from the color of my manicure to the shampoo I use to wash my hair. Every part of my life is micromanaged and carefully crafted and I get no say in anything! I'm sick of it!"

"Burke?" Austin tries to get my attention again.

"Now that I really think about it, I hate how controlled my life is. I'm only eighteen! What is my life going to be like when I'm twenty-five? Or thirty? Is my mom still going to be deciding my choice for Emmy red carpet shoes at Fred Segal? Will she make me skip dinner with friends to go to a taping of *The Tonight Show*? How did this become my life?" I feel myself start to hyperventilate.

"Kates?" I think I hear Liz say.

"She's having a breakdown!" one of the photographers comments. "LOVE IT!"

FLASH! FLASH! FLASH!

"I hate you guys! Drop dead!" I scream at the paparazzi. I've never even said anything remotely close to that to one of them in my life. I'm usually so accommodating.

One mutters something I can't repeat under his breath, and I completely lose it. I say the same thing back!

"Kates!" Nadine freaks.

"Get in, Austin!" I bark and he jumps in the car. "DRIVE," I tell the guy behind the wheel.

"Wow, those guys are like animals," the driver says, shaking his head. "Scum." He peels away from the curb, and I fall into Austin.

"You okay?" he says as he puts on his seat belt. I do the same.

"No," I say quietly and start to cry. "I can see my future stretched out ahead of me and I don't like it." I look at Austin. "Press commitment after press commitment, project after project pops up that I know will be squeezed in till I don't have room to sleep. There will be no time for me, for you, for my friends. . . . Why did I decide to be an actress again?"

"Kates, you're upset right now, but you love what you do," Austin reminds me. He's holding on to the seat and suddenly I realize how fast we're going.

"Can you slow down?" I ask the driver.

"Can't! Look out the back!" the driver tells me. "The scum are trailing us. Don't worry, I'll lose them."

I don't even care. What I care about is my life, and I feel

like it's falling apart. Austin is right. I like acting, but it all comes back to this: I can't stand the package that comes with it. I want two lives, and I can't seem to find a way to have them both.

"I do like acting, but forget Hollywood!" I tell Austin as we sway back and forth in the backseat. "My life controls me and I hate it! If this is what happens—someone makes all the decisions and the artist loses all control—then I don't want it. Who wants to be followed twenty-four/seven by Larry the Liar or photographed eating French fries when I'm supposed to be a size four to fit in my new costume?"

"Kates, you don't mean that," Austin says while he keeps his eyes on the driver.

"I do," I insist. "If this is what a life in Hollywood is like, then I don't want it."

SCREECH!

I press my arm against the back of the seat to steady myself as the car veers right with a jerk.

"Hey, buddy, slow down!" Austin says gruffly.

"It's them!" the driver yells. "They're alongside of us."

I look over and the paparazzi are pulling up to us and taking pictures from the window. God, they've never done that to me before.

"See? This is why I have to get away from Hollywood. I have to get away from craziness like this!"

"I hear ya!" the driver agrees. "Don't worry, I'll lose them."

He starts driving even faster and we pull away from the paparazzi, almost hitting the car in the left lane. Whoa. He starts going even faster, and yet the paparazzi are still close behind us. Now I'm starting to get scared.

"Just slow down," I beg the driver. "It's okay. I take it back. Let them get a picture."

"No way!" he says. "You're right about this Hollywood machine. They're not getting a single shot if I can help it!"

The driver just blew a red light! I hear tires screech as we come inches from hitting a car going in the other direction. I grab Austin's hand. My heart is pounding again. I want my life to change, but not like this.

"I don't care," I say shakily. "Just slow down. It's not worth getting into an accident." This guy is nuts.

"Did you hear her? Slow down!" Austin yells at him, banging on the back of his seat to get his attention.

The driver ignores us. I look at Austin again and out the window behind his head. We're going so fast that we're passing blocks without even stopping at stop signs. He's veering in and out of traffic. He's going to get us killed. I start yelling and Austin does too. I see him pull out his cell phone to dial 911. We're both yelling and it feels like we're in a tunnel.

And that's when I see it happen, even if I'm not a trained driver myself yet. The driver goes onto the off-ramp of the freeway instead of the on-ramp.

"LOOK OUT!" I scream.

But it's too late.

You know how in movies when something monumental happens, things sort of slow down and the screen goes slow-mo? Usually it's in war films where the shrapnel flies slowly through the air like it's confetti. That's what a car crash feels like. It's as if time slows down and I'm watching the whole thing happen from the safe confines of my living room couch. I turn just in time to see an SUV plow into the front of the car, and Austin's body swings sideways. The car rattles and screeches and starts to spin. My body lurches forward, then to the left, and I hear a very unsettling crunching sound. Glass begins to shatter all around me, almost in slow motion. The shards begin to hit me like tiny pellets. I hear myself scream, but it sounds like it's coming from outside my body. Then the car comes to a deafening stop that is followed by an eerie silence.

I don't really remember much after that. There was the sound of sirens, and an ambulance and *a lot* of voices. Lots of voices giving various reports that I vaguely remember.

"The boy's right leg is messed up real bad.... He won't leave the girl, though. Her left side is pretty bruised. Could be internal bleeding. Both kids need surgery. Taking them to Cedars-Sinai Medical Center ..."

And then some voices I do know (which sort of make me wince all the same).

"Kate-Kate! Kate-Kate! Oh God. Is my daughter going to be okay? What do you mean she needs surgery right away? She has a taping tomorrow night, and they can't film without her!"

"NO press! I'm in charge of press! None until I say so," Laney demands.

"What about a tweet? Should I tweet her condition to her fans?" I hear Mom ask. "HEY! Let go of my BlackBerry! You broke it! You're going to pay for that!"

"No tweeting!" Seth says.

"Will both of you stay focused here?" Laney snaps. "I'm working overtime to control the media situation, and I'm not even sure I'm getting paid since I think—if I'm not mistaken, Meg—you fired Seth and me this morning."

Mom hesitates. "Well, I—"

"Never mind!" Laney huffs, and I vaguely hear an irritating clapping sound. "People! Yoo-hoo! Nurse folk! Everyone on this floor needs to sign a confidentiality agreement. And get me some Purell. Stat!"

And then, whether I'm just too tired or too tired to deal, everything goes dark.

FADE IN:

BUCHANAN MANOR—LIVING ROOM

The walls are torched, ashes cover the floor, and most of the furniture is covered in soot. In the center of the room, there is a huge burn mark going up the fireplace and through the Buchanan family portrait. DENNIS, PAIGE, SARA, and SAMANTHA search for anything they can salvage. SAMANTHA is sobbing.

SAMANTHA

Mom, our family portrait! *(She pulls it off the wall and the others gather around.)*

DENNIS

It's okay. We can commission another one. It will be even better than the first.

SAMANTHA

(weepy) I liked the first one.

SARA

(sobs) Me too.

PAIGE

Me three. But that's okay. I'll track down the artist, and I'm sure he can do another one. This one isn't in such bad shape that he can't recognize who we are. *(her voice grows low)* Or who we were before . . . *(she looks around)* all this.

KRYSTAL

Guys? The police are here to take statements. Are you up to it, or should I tell Daddy to tell them you'll come down to the station later?

DENNIS

Tell them we'll be right there, Krystal. And thank you, for everything.

PAIGE

Dennis, I'm not sure I can do this. *(sobs)* It's too soon. Too much has happened. If I hadn't . . . if Sam and Sara hadn't heard me, we might not have made it out of here. What if? What if . . .

DENNIS

But that didn't happen! *(grabs his wife by the shoulders)* You made it out of that fire, and you got the girls out too! You're a hero, Paige.

PAIGE

(crying) I feel like this is my fault. I wanted to move. I wanted something different, a fresh start, something new, but seeing this, I miss the old one.

SAMANTHA

(sobbing) It's my fault too, Mom! I've been thinking the same thing. This place is too big, too cold, too drafty. I hated this house. I made this happen, not you.

SARA

Oh please! Would you two quit it? I have bad thoughts every day of the week, and no one bursts into flames. You guys didn't cause this.

DENNIS

Sara is right, girls. This fire just happened. We don't know how or why yet, but we will. We will get to the bottom of this. Do you want to know why? The Buchanans never say die! The Buchanans are a family that fights together and stays together despite the difficulties our adversaries thrust our way. I know the road ahead may look dark and bleak, and we're not sure which way is up from down, but when life throws the Buchanans a curveball we face it head on and find the solution together.

SARA

(clapping) Nice pep talk! Dad, you know we've got your back, right? Even me, and that's saying something because I'm supposed to go out with Tommy Davies tonight.

SAMANTHA

What Sara meant to say is, we love who we are and we are
who we are because of you, Dad. And you, Mom. Whatever
it takes, we'll get the Buchanans back to where they're
supposed to be. Home isn't these four walls. Home is
wherever we are together.

(The family embraces around the fireplace.)

FADE OUT.

nine: *Welcome to the Flip Side*

"Mom?"

I'm talking, but my voice doesn't sound like my own. It's froggy and it hurts to say anything. I'm in desperate need of some Smartwater. I feel very dry and ... WHOA. Is the room spinning? My head feels like it weighs a thousand pounds. Things are blurry, but I can see images moving, and every sound is magnified as if I have my iPod turned up at full volume.

"I'm right here, honey," Mom says. I know I'm sort of out of it, but I think she's stroking my wet forehead. I must have really gotten banged up for her to do that.

"Austin. Is Austin okay?" I ask anxiously, fighting to get the words out. "What about the driver?" I need to say everything as quickly as I can because my head feels like Play-Doh and all I want to do is sleep.

"Shh ... shh ... everyone is okay." Mom's voice is so reassuring. "Daddy and Matty are on their way."

"Where are Seth and Laney? Did they go home?" I ask. It's

awfully quiet wherever I am. Just whispers, some machines beeping, and nurses asking questions like "Would you like another package of crackers?"

"Don't worry about anything, honey," Mom tells me, sounding a bit choked up.

Wow, what happened to me? I must look awful. I try to lift my right arm to take a look. I see some small gashes and red marks, but without a mirror I can't find out what I really need to know—is my face okay? That's an actor's most important asset!

"They're going to be wheeling you to recovery in a few hours," Mom adds. "Right now I just want you to drink this juice and eat some saltines." I hear her pour a glass of juice, and she puts the straw to my lips. The juice is cold and I feel a little better when I swallow. I wonder why Nadine isn't doing nurse duty for me. I half expected to wake up and find out Mom had flown to the Hamptons to recover from the stress I put her through. But then again, Mom did try to fire Nadine and my whole team this morning. I should be mad right now, but I'm just glad to have my mom nearby.

"The car—is it totaled? Is Austin's leg all right? I heard someone say it looked bad. When can I go back to work? Will I miss the taping tomorrow night?"

I can't stop asking questions. I need to know what happened. I said such awful things to my friends in front of the paparazzi. There are pictures of me behaving that badly! I jumped into a car with someone I don't know! Am I crazy? Any bumps and bruises I have are secondary to the mountain of guilt I feel about putting Austin in harm's way. There's only one bright spot to this disaster: At least I didn't get injured on set. I wouldn't want the show to get bad press for my poor choices.

HOLLYWOOD SECRET NUMBER NINE: We all know movies aren't real, but making fiction feel like reality takes a lot of work. There can be hundreds of people involved in a single production. They can dot every *i* and cross every *t* before a pyrotechnic shot, a chase scene, or a helicopter rescue, and use stunt people for everything but close-ups, but actors still get hurt sometimes. Shia LaBeouf got a hip injury while making *Indiana Jones*. And Robert Pattinson supposedly tore a muscle while shooting *New Moon*. Those two incidents were thankfully not life-threatening, but an accident on the set of a movie called *The Twilight Zone*, which was made in 1982, killed two child actors and an adult in a stunt scene gone bad. What happened on that set is part of the reason Matty falls under tougher child labor laws that protect him (and drive him nuts) today.

"Kaitlin, what are—just rest, okay? I'll answer all your questions later," Mom says. "I promise. Everything is going to be fine, sweetheart. Just close your eyes."

Mom being maternal, which is even rarer than seeing a starlet eat a Krispy Kreme donut, is enough to make me listen. I fall fast asleep.

When I wake up, my head feels only slightly heavy, compared to the two-ton block that was resting on my forehead earlier. The room has stopped spinning, and I can finally get a look around. I've been moved to a regular hospital room, and the curtain is drawn around me. A TV is on, and I have a roommate. I can't believe Mom didn't stomp her feet till we got a private room befitting a queen! On my bedside table is a small, sort of scary-looking floral arrangement full of carnations. I'm too weak to grab the card and see who they're from. My eyes drift over to Mom. She's asleep in the vinyl chair next to my bed and she's wearing—WAIT.

It can't be. Is that a plum-colored PB&J Couture tracksuit? *It is!* That wouldn't be a fashion faux pas for most people, but in Mom's book, PB&J is so three years ago. And what happened to her hair? Instead of the warm, caramel hue she pays hundreds of dollars for so that it looks just like mine (she likes to claim it is her natural color), her hair is a mousy brown. I puzzle over this info for a while until I hit on a possible solution. Mom must be in disguise. Clever. Maybe the paparazzi are swarming outside. I should really call Laney, but first I have to reach Austin.

I'm sure they took my bag from the car when they brought me here, but I don't see it anywhere. My iPhone is probably still tucked inside. Hmm ... I'm achy, but I sit up slowly. I pull back my covers, and that's when I see the cast. My right ankle is covered in hard, white plastic from my foot to my knee. Oh God. How are the writers going to explain this one? I'm going to have to order a Coffee Bean coffee cart for a month to make up for this. I slowly drop my legs over the side of the bed, being careful not to bang my cast. I step down on the cold tile and try to steady myself on one foot to hobble around. The only bag I see is a Coach knockoff on the shelf across from me. Where is my yellow leather hobo? Where is Mom's Birkin bag?

"Kaitlin! You shouldn't be walking around!" Mom jumps up and grabs me by the shoulders, steering me back to the bed. She helps me up and then lifts my legs so that I'm sitting. Her expression is stony. This expression I know.

"I'm sorry, Mom. I was looking for my phone," I tell her. "Do you have it? I don't see my bag anywhere."

"I have your phone," Mom says, and she crosses the room and stops at the bookshelf. I watch as she reaches into the Coach knockoff and pulls out a flip phone. "It was thrown from your bag, but it seems to work fine." She holds it out to me and I stare at it.

"That's not my phone. I have the iPhone, remember? And why are you using that bag?"

Mom looks very confused. "An iPhone? *This* is your phone, Kaitlin."

"Mom, I know my head is hazy, but that is not my phone. Mine is the . . . forget it. Can I borrow your BlackBerry?"

"Even all bandaged, you're a riot. BlackBerry!" She chuckles to herself and pulls another flip phone out of her bag. "That new school is giving you delusions of grandeur!"

Instead of arguing, I take the phone from her and dial Austin's cell. It goes right to voicemail. What am I thinking? Austin may not even have his phone if he's in the hospital too.

"Mom, do you know what room Austin is in?" I ask. "I have to see him."

She shakes her head. "I don't know where they took the others. I'll have the nurse find out." She ducks into the hall.

Austin must hate me. Okay, I won't think about that. Right now I'll concentrate on doing something else. I'll call Laney.

Laney's newest assistant, Paula, answers on the first ring. "Laney Peters's office."

"Hi, Paula, it's Kaitlin. Can you put Laney on?"

"Kaitlin?"

I cut her off before she can ask. "I'm fine. I'm banged up and my ankle is broken, but I'm okay. Is Laney back at the office or should I try her cell?"

"I'm sorry, you said you were who?"

Geez, how could Paula not know it's me? "Kaitlin," I say pleasantly.

"Kaitlin who?"

"Kaitlin Burke!" I snap. Mom walks back in and looks at me worriedly. "Look, Paula, this isn't funny. The paparazzi are probably swarming outside, and I need to talk to Laney!"

"I'm not trying to be funny," she says slowly. "I just ... I'm sorry ... I don't know who you are."

WHAT?

I'm so flustered I hang up. Wait till Laney hears what Paula pulled on me. She'll be lucky she lasts the day!

"Kaitlin, sweetie, is your head throbbing?" Mom touches my forehead. "Should I call Dr. Lowe?"

I pull Mom's hand away. I see what's going on. I should have known not to fall for Mom's nice-mom act! "You fired Laney, didn't you? That's why Paula acted like she didn't know me."

"Who is Laney?" Mom's expression is bewildered. "Sweetie, you're not making any sense."

Dad and Matty walk in just in time because I'm about to flip out on Mom. But when I see Matty, I'm almost too stunned to speak. Instead of a stylish pair of jeans and some new designer button-down shirt, Matty is in Old Navy sweats. Full sweats. Like, a sweat suit! In red. His hair is a mess, like it hasn't been cut in a month. It must be a wig. There is no other explanation. Dad looks the same—rumpled button-down shirt, khaki pants—but he's wearing a navy zip-up jacket that says *Jeep* in capital letters.

"Why are you guys all in disguise?" I ask. "Is Larry the Liar outside? He's going to find out eventually that I'm here. I've been trying to reach Laney, but Paula is pretending not to know who I am. It's all Mom's fault! Dad, do something."

"How long has she been like this?" Dad asks Mom.

"Since she woke up," Mom says quietly, not looking at me. "I'm going to page Dr. Lowe."

"You're not going anywhere until you rehire Laney." I slap my hand on the bed. Ouch. Forgot about that whiplash. I lower my voice. "And, um, did you find out what room Austin is in?"

Mom shakes her head. "The nurse says he doesn't have a room."

"Is he still in surgery?" I worry.

"I don't know," Mom admits, looking nervous herself. That makes me really freaked out.

"You have to find out," I beg. I have to get out of this room and find him myself. But how? I'll never make it past the three of them. But I have to. I have to know Austin is okay. "And then you have to rehire Laney!"

Dad looks confused. "Who is Laney?"

"Laney Peters?" I gripe, and Dad still looks at me strangely. "The biggest publicist in Hollywood? The one I've had since I was a kid? Dad, stop pretending not to know who she is! Is Mom putting you up to this to try to make me forget Laney?"

Mom is aghast. "Honey, why would I make Daddy pretend to forget this friend of yours?"

"She's not a friend, she's my publicist!" I say, frustrated, and I lay my head on the uncomfortable pillow.

"Are you talking about Alexis Holden's publicity person?" Matty asks and blushes when Dad looks at him funny. "I read a lot of *Hollywood Nation*, okay? She's always quoted in there."

"Laney took on Alexis as a client?" I flip. "Since when? When I was under anesthesia? Mom, do you see what you've done?" I glare at her. "Next you're going to tell me Sky hired her too!"

"Sky Mackenzie?" Matty questions, running a hand through his messy hair. "She is such a train wreck. I love it.

Did you see this week's *Hollywood Nation*? I was reading it in the waiting room. She is in serious need of rehab."

"No, she's not," I huff. "Sky is completely sober, Matty, and you know it! That's not nice to say. And you know what else isn't nice?" I glance at Mom, who is clutching that Coach knockoff for dear life. "Firing my people behind my back. I'm eighteen now, and I get to make my own decisions. I want Seth and Laney back. And Nadine too! Or else I'll ..." I can't stop staring at Mom. "Or else I'll ..."

Forget it. I still can't threaten to fire my own mother.

"Who is Nadine again?" my dad asks and scratches his head. "Do I know a Nadine?" Mom shrugs.

Cough.

I'm staring at my family, but none of them have coughed. Who just coughed? I pull back the curtain and stare at the thirtysomething blond woman in the next bed. Both of her legs are in traction, but her hands are free and she appears to be taking notes on a notepad. She must be preparing to tell *Hollywood Nation* all about my fight with my family! If it wasn't so hard to get up, I'd pull that pad right out of her nail-bitten hands. Instead I say calmly: "If you even *think* of calling the *Hollywood Nation* tip line and telling them what you just heard, I will slap you with a defamation lawsuit faster than a nurse can bring you Jell-O."

"I'm so sorry," Mom apologizes to the woman and tries to close the curtain again. "She's had quite a day."

But that didn't happen! You made it out of that fire, and you got the girls out too! You're a hero, Paige.

I look at the TV mounted on the wall and cheer up instantly. "Hey, they're playing a *Family Affair* rerun!" That's Spencer talking. He played my dad. He's standing in what remains of the family's living room, and he's giving the famous speech he made when part of the Buchanan mansion burned down (we find out later it was arson).

"Ooh, honey, I forgot what night it was," Mom says to Dad as we continue to play Peeping Tom on my roommate. "Did you remember to set the DVR?"

"Do you guys mind?" the woman complains, holding her bedsheet higher on her chest.

"Sorry," Mom apologizes and pulls the curtain out of my hands as I continue to telepathically convey what will happen if she calls the tabloids. "Honey, put on Kaitlin's TV!"

Dad flips to the channel and uses the remote on my bed to turn the volume up.

"God, I loved this scene," I tell my family, feeling nostalgic and a tad weepy. It must be the anesthesia. My years on *FA* were crazy, but no more so than life has been lately. I still miss everyone in the cast so much. "Remember? Tom filmed Spencer's big speech and it was so passionate, he wound up using the first take."

"And you know this how?" Matty asks.

"I was in that scene." I shrug and look up at the TV screen again. "Don't you remember? It was eleven o'clock at night when we finished filming. It took all day to shoot this five-minute clip because there are so many of us in this one part. I love Sky's and my lines. Especially Sky's. 'Oh please. Would you two quit it? I have bad thoughts every day of the week and no one bursts into flames.'" I laugh.

Oh please! Would you two quit it? I have bad thoughts every day of the week and no one bursts into flames.

Matty is in awe. "How did you know that line?"

We both look at the screen and see Sky, her raven hair ironed straight, her makeup dark and moody. She's wearing a red Gucci sweater. I know because I wanted to wear it and she wouldn't let me. I wore Galliano instead, which isn't too shabby.

"I usually remember the lines in a big scene, don't you?" I ask Matt.

Mom and Dad look at each other again and then at Matt. His jaw is sort of locked in a big O expression.

"Go get Dr. Lowe," Mom whispers to Dad. "Quick."

"Shh!" I tell them. "This is my favorite line in the whole episode. Well, my favorite line that I say: 'What Sara meant to say is, we love who we are and we are who we are because of you, Dad. And you, Mom. Whatever it takes, we'll get the Buchanans back to where they're supposed to be. Home isn't these four walls. Home is wherever we are together.'"

I smile proudly at Matty, impressed I actually remembered the whole speech. He's still looking at me with the same dumb expression. I'm so busy looking at him that I miss the beginning of my dialogue.

. . . And you, Mom. Whatever it takes, we'll get the Buchanans back to where they're supposed to be.

Hey, that's not my voice. I'm not deep and raspy like that. Is something wrong with the TV? I look up and . . . NO.

NOOOOOOOOOOOOOOOOOOOOOOOO!!!!!!!!!!!!!!!!!!!!!!

"WHY IS ALEXIS HOLDEN SAYING MY LINE?" I scream so loudly that my roommate drops her pitcher of ice water all over the floor.

Alexis is playing *my* character, Samantha Buchanan. Alexis Holden, the fiery redhead who I thought was so nice until I learned she was out to swipe my job, is wearing *my* Galliano dress. She's standing next to *my* costars. She's on *my* show, doing lines that were several seasons ago! She wasn't on *FA* till the last season! What is going on?

I look at Mom and Matty. "Did you guys mess with the TV? Why would you do that to me after the day I've had?"

"We didn't," Matty says slowly, staring at me as if I'm dense. "Are *you* playing a joke on us?"

"No!" I find myself getting hot and flustered and entirely uncomfortable. The room is starting to spin again, and I have a headache. Dad rushes back in with a tall, thin, dark-haired guy in a white lab coat. I assume this is Dr. Lowe.

"Kaitlin, are you okay?" Mom asks, sounding out of breath. "Tell Dr. Lowe, honey. Tell him what's wrong. She's been saying the most irrational things," she tells the doctor, who is busy writing on a clipboard.

"I am not saying irrational things!" I freak out. My heart is pounding so hard I'm sure it's going to pop out of my chest. "Samantha Buchanan is my character and yet some-how Alexis Holden is playing my part on this television! I know I was in a car accident today, but I know who I am," I tell him urgently. "I know what happened today. My mom fired my publicist, Laney Peters. My boyfriend, Austin Meyers, is lying somewhere in this hospital, and all I want right now is to go and find him and make sure he's okay. I have to explain myself. Please," I beg, sounding hoarse. I stare into Dr. Lowe's blue eyes. "You've got to help me."

"Oh my God." Mom says softly. She leans on my dad for support.

The rest of the room is quiet except for Matty, who actually chuckles.

My eyes lock on his. "What is so funny?'"

"Um, your fantasy world?" Matty quips.

"Matthew," Dad warns and nudges him. He, Dr. Lowe, and Mom are staring at me as if I'm a rabid animal prepared to attack. "Your sister has hit her head. This is not something to laugh about."

"She must have hit it really hard if she thinks she's a movie star." Matty rolls his eyes. "She's dramatic, yes, but famous, no way. And Austin Meyers wouldn't look sideways at her. Especially not after today."

My heart practically stops. "Did he dump me?" I whisper, and my eyes begin to well with tears.

Matty's eyes almost pop out of his head and he sputters, "Dump you? Kates, he's been going out with Lori Peters since freshman year."

"No," I say and shake my head forcefully. "They broke up a long time ago."

"Matty, don't do this to her now," Dad says, smiling at me tightly.

"Let him continue," I hear Dr. Lowe say. I think. It's hard to tell because a loud swishing sound has started in my ears, and it's coming on like a freight train. "Let's see what she does."

"And you are not on *Family Affair*," Matty says sharply and looks up at the screen, where Alexis and Sky are on to the next scene, laughing merrily in Aunt Krystal's kitchen.

"I was!" I cry. Why are they all being so mean to me? Did someone put my meltdown from this morning on YouTube? Maybe they heard me say I wanted to fire Mom.

"Alexis Holden has played Samantha Buchanan for the past four years. She took over for the original actress, Lilly Amber," Matty says slowly. "You're not a star, Kates. You're Kaitlin Burke, a recent transfer to posh Clark Hall, who hasn't had a boyfriend in like, forever."

I cover my ears to try to block out what he's saying, but it's no use. I can hear him, and like a train wreck, as much as I want to forget it, I want to hear more.

"Your only connection to Austin Meyers is that you swiped him and some of his lacrosse buddies when you hit the accelerator instead of the brake during driver's ed this morning. The car jumped the curb and crashed into them as they were walking to class. I heard you broke his leg and probably cost him his lacrosse career." Matty shakes his head. "People are not too happy with you at Clark Hall."

I look between Dad's, Mom's, and Matty's stricken faces,

and I know Matty is not lying. Dr. Lowe looks at me sadly. Matty is telling some weird, crazy, bizarro version of the truth, but it's still the truth. Right here. Right now at least.

That's when I do the only thing I can think of. I start to scream. The scream is so loud and terrifying that I almost think someone else is doing it. But they're not. It's me. And if any of what Matty just said is really reality, they may have to put me in a straitjacket and throw away the key.

IN THE KNOW

Sky Mackenzie and Alexis Holden Keep Hollywood Haunt Up Late

by **Andrew Harris**

What happens at Teddy's doesn't always stay at Teddy's. When will Hollywood's most talked-about starlets remember that about the hot nighttime club? Someone should remind *Family Affair* costars Sky Mackenzie and Alexis Holden (who play popular fraternal twins Sara and Samantha Buchanan) because their off-the-clock hours are causing more of a stir these days than their on-screen dialogue (snooze…).

Linked arm in arm, the pair arrived at Teddy's for some late-night snacks and drinks, along with twenty or so members of their entourage. When they were told there was not enough room to accommodate them all and that the place would soon be closing, Alexis threw a fit. "She started yelling, 'Do you know who I am?' Manage-

ment went into a tailspin," says an eyewitness. "No one wants to tick off the star of the most popular show on television."

Sky, who is sporting new bleached blond locks against her orange-hued face, was just as difficult. Told the bar didn't serve anyone under twenty-one, Sky still insisted on ordering a seltzer and then refused to leave till she was done nursing it. "That was an hour later!" complained one waitress. "She looked terrible too. Under-eye circles, greasy hair, and her Gucci belt was on backward. Alexis kept yelling at Sky, and she took it. I almost felt sorry for her. Until she didn't leave a tip."

While *Family Affair* is still number one in the ratings, sources behind the scenes worry that the girls' off-screen antics could affect the popularity of the series. It's no secret that Melli Ralton (who plays the girls' mother, Paige) and creator/producer

> ## "[She] makes the network a ton of money. As long as she continues to do that, they don't care who she makes miserable."

Tom Pullman want out. They tried to jump ship last season when they felt plotlines were growing thin (isn't that the truth!) but were strong-armed into staying by the network, which became worried when their cash cows, Alexis and Sky, threatened to walk if the others were let out of their contracts. The show's core audience is still there, but many TV critics have complained that *Family Affair*

jumped the shark a while ago.

Not to worry, fans. As long as they've got Alexis, *FA* isn't going anywhere. "Alexis is a goddess around that studio," complains one source. "As awful as she is, she does all the press she's supposed to do, pretends to be a doll in interviews, and makes the network a ton of money. As long as she continues to do that, they don't care who she makes miserable." ●

ten: *A New Reality*

"Have you gone in to check on her?" I hear Mom's muffled voice through the bedroom door.

"No, I thought you were going to," Dad whispers back.

"I'm afraid to." Mom sounds more hesitant than I've ever heard her. "She's going to start yelling again. All she does is watch that DVD box set she swiped from the living room. Episode after episode of *Family Affair*! She hasn't left her bedroom in days . . . she's not eating. She didn't even eat her favorite dinner, lemon chicken!"

"Maybe we're asking too much of her too soon," Dad says. "Dr. Lowe said we need to give her time. She's got to come out of her room eventually. She knows she has to go back to Clark Hall on Wednesday. Two more days and her engine will be revved to full throttle. I know it."

Dad is still making car analogies. At least some things haven't changed. I hear footsteps and I shimmy further under my covers. I don't remember liking all this pink. The comforter, the curtains, the worn carpet, the rose wallpaper—it's like someone took a bottle of Pepto-Bismol and let it explode in here. My furniture is white, just like my real furniture, but this set has been around the block a few times. There's even some green marker on my bedpost that says my name in a child's script. I don't see any *Star Wars* stuff, though. My Princess Leia clock and blanket are missing.

Even though I miss Han, Leia, and Luke, I have to admit this room is cozy. So is the house. We live in Toluca Lake, which I've always adored, and we're in a side-hall colonial with a modest living room, dining room, kitchen, and den on the first floor and three bedrooms on the second. The house has yellow siding and a beautifully landscaped backyard with a swimming pool (no rock garden or waterfall cascading in it like our real one, but it's still nice). You can't lose anyone in this house. At home I'm constantly running up and down the stairs trying to find everyone, and then when I do, I sort of regret looking for them in the first place. In this house, I don't leave my room—well, except for some late-night kitchen raids when everyone else is asleep. I know I should make more of an effort. If I don't start coming around soon, Dr. Lowe is making me go for therapy! As much as that scenario freaks me out, leaving this bed and facing the crazy reality that is waiting for me scares me more.

"Matt, where do you think you're going?" I hear Mom demand, sounding more like the mom I know.

"Kaitlin asked for some more magazines," Matty tells them. "I was going to buy some on my way home from school, but Rob Murray was hanging outside CVS and I thought he might beat me up because of my last name. I get banged around enough at that school without having to take the heat for Kate's lead foot too."

"No more tabloids," Mom insists. "Kaitlin's becoming obsessed with that Alexis Holden girl! All she does is read about her and watch *Celebrity Insider*. When she isn't watching *Family Affair*, that is."

"She gets this Hollywood obsession from you, you know. Matty probably took that stack of magazines from your pile," Dad quips.

"Are you saying this is my fault?" Mom asks tearfully.

"No. We live next door to Hollywood. It's not unhealthy to want to learn more about the people living in our own backyard," Dad tries tactfully. "Kaitlin comes in contact with celebrities much more now that she and Matty have transferred to Clark Hall. That girl Liz Mendes has gotten the girls into all those premieres lately. I'm sure Kaitlin is just confusing those two worlds in her head."

"Do you think we were wrong to send the kids to Clark Hall High School this year?" Mom asks worriedly. "The education is top-notch, but even before the accident she didn't seem like herself. I like Liz, but I think the two of them are getting too caught up in the Hollywood scene. Kaitlin is changing because of it," Mom continues sadly, "and now she thinks she *is* a celebrity. She's lost her mind!" She starts to cry.

I bury my head under my pillow, hoping to muffle their conversation, but it doesn't work.

"Forget celebrities, Mom. Kates has bigger problems. Someone told me that Lori Peters wants Kaitlin to be expelled," Matty says. "I heard she has a meeting with Principal P. tomorrow to talk about Kaitlin's unhealthy obsession with her boyfriend. Caden Mitchell overheard Lori say that Kaitlin hit Austin on purpose because she's mad that she can't have him."

I can't take it anymore. "I do have him!" I yell from under my blanket. "I'm dating Austin! We've been going out for over a year! Why doesn't anyone remember?" I start to cry too.

"Honey?" Mom jiggles the door lock. "Open up so we can talk. We want to help you, sweetie." She turns the handle, but I just stare at it. I'm not opening that door. "I know you're frustrated, but we're your parents and our job is to help you. Let us do that, Kaitlin. Talk to us or talk to a therapist. It won't be bad, sweetie, I promise. We have to get to the bottom of this other, um, life you keep talking about."

"I don't want to talk," I gulp through my tears. "I just want to be left alone."

I hate talking, because when they talk to me they say this is reality and that other Kaitlin and company that I keep talking about don't exist. I know they're wrong, and I can't stand hearing them say otherwise. I can't accept—I *won't* accept—that my real life isn't real after all.

Eighteen years couldn't be a dream. I've lived too much, experienced too many things. It's just not possible for me to have dreamed it up!

God, I miss Nadine. If anyone could fix this mess, it would be her. I keep dialing her cell and the message says, "The number you have reached is no longer in service. Please check the number and try again."

I hear Mom sigh. "Okay, Kaitlin. Maybe later? I'm making penne à la vodka. You love that dish. When I bring it up, maybe I can eat with you and chat."

I hear shuffling, then more footsteps, and a few magazines are shoved under my door. When the hall is quiet again, I slide out of bed, mindful of my cast, and pick them up. The top one is *Hollywood Nation*, and my eyes are drawn to the cover story: "SKY MACKENZIE AND ALEXIS HOLDEN KEEP HOLLYWOOD HAUNT UP LATE." I flip to the page and read the story quickly, then look at the pictures of Alexis and Sky staggering out of Teddy's. Sky looks like she hasn't slept in a month. Sky may like to be part of the Hollywood nightlife scene, but her reputation comes first these days and she'd never behave the way this article says she did. And Alexis . . . I don't even want to go there.

I fling the magazine across the room, and it lands on top of the white wicker chest in the corner. I'm not even sure what's in that thing because this is *not* my room. This is *not* my life. I want to go home.

What's happening to me?

When my family reacted the way they did in the hospital, at first I thought I was having a horrible nightmare. So I did what I always do when I'm having a bad dream—like the one I have about showing up to cohost *The View* in my underwear—I pinched myself all over (my right arm is still red), closed my eyes, and willed myself to wake up.

Nothing changed. I'm still here. Wherever or whatever here is.

Every "day," if it is a day, is the same. I wake up, sob that I'm here, and then lie in bed watching TV and reading the magazines Matty brings me. I can't stop thinking about where I am.

Could I be in some sort of coma and this is my dreamlike state? It could happen. Maybe things went wildly wrong in surgery, Meredith dropped my spleen, they had to get the crash cart, and McDreamy saved me by the skin of his teeth. Okay, maybe I am watching too much *Grey's Anatomy*. There was a marathon on all day yesterday. But still, if this isn't a dream, maybe I am in a coma or ... GASP. I can't be dead, can I? Maybe this is some sort of Hollywood purgatory where stars go before they cross over to repent for the backstabbing, bad movies, and beyotch-ness they put the world through. Oh God. That's the answer, isn't it?

NOOOO! I don't want to die! I just turned eighteen! I haven't won an Oscar yet or gone to college or visited Australia! How am I going to marry Austin someday if I'm not here to do it?

Oh my God. I want to go to college. I want to marry Austin. I want to!

Those breakthroughs will have to wait because right now my top priority is figuring out if I'm alive, dead, in an alternate reality, or in purgatory. God, this is just as confusing as that show *Lost* was!

Ooh . . . that's it! Maybe I'm on a TV show! This might be like that movie Jim Carrey did where he lived in this giant bubble and his whole life was filmed for TV. They staged every plot point, and Jim didn't have a clue. Could that be what's happening to me too?

Maybe that's my punishment for getting in a car with a complete stranger and for behaving badly in front of the paparazzi. I wouldn't put it past Mom to combine being grounded with media coverage. I stare at the ceiling looking for hidden cameras, then glance around the room. Aha! I knew that teddy bear looked odd. I would never have a cheesy green stuffed bear like that! I pull the bear off a crowded bookshelf and try to rip out his stuffing. Hmph. There can't be a camera in here. I throw the bear on the floor.

Okay, forget the cameras. I don't need them. If I really am on TV right now and Mom put me up to it, all I have to do is apologize and things will go back to normal. Right? I'll apologize on the air and Mom will have to forgive me. It's a brilliant plan.

I step up onto my bed (that way I'm closer to the hidden mics) and make sure my tank top isn't exposing anything it shouldn't be. I smooth down my unwashed hair, steady myself so that I don't break my other ankle, and clear my throat. "MOM? DAD? TV NETWORK? If you can hear me right now, I have something to say. I know I'm on a TV show and this is my punishment for being a star who behaves badly. I want to apologize. I know I was wrong to fight with the paparazzi and to behave irrationally and get into that car. I wish I could take back what I did." I pause. Let me think this through a second. "Well, everything except being mad that you fired Seth, Laney, and Nadine. I want them back. Everything else I'll agree to, okay? I'll do whatever press, print and otherwise, you want me to. Just let me out of this bubble, okay? I want to go home!"

Silence. Maybe they didn't hear me. Or Mom didn't like the terms. My hands start to sweat. I have to get through to her and get out of here! What's it going to take to . . . I KNOW!

"Mom, you can have a raise. You can take twenty percent of my salary instead of fifteen!" I tell the ceiling.

The ceiling doesn't answer. If Mom heard me she would have busted down my door. At least my other mom would have.

"GUYS?" I shriek desperately.

"Kates? Who are you talking to? Do you need Mom to get your meds?" It's Matty. Alter-Matty, as I've dubbed him, and he's right outside my door. *This* door. Not *my* door. This isn't my house!

"Go away!" I crash down onto my bed, sending a deep ache into my broken ankle with the impact. Then I start to cry again.

This can't be happening to me. I'm Kaitlin Burke, TV star, Hollywood actress, high school senior. I'm on a new TV show and I have an amazing boyfriend. Right?

RIGHT?

I feel like Dorothy when she dropped into Oz. Everything is different. Mom is a dental hygienist who is warm and gooey and cooks my favorite foods. Dad is thrilled to be working at the same car dealership he worked at when I was a baby. Matty is a social leper who has gone from cool to drool. It's as if everyone but me is content living the life we would have lived if . . . no, that can't be right, can it? Is that what's different?

Is this what my life would have been like if Mom had never taken me to audition for *Family Affair*?

Knock. Knock. Knock.

"I said leave me alone," I grumble.

"Kaitlin? It's me. Liz."

Liz? My Lizzie? She'll know what to do. "Lizzie?"

"*Liz*," she corrects. "Can I come in?"

I run to the bedroom door and fling it open. It's Liz in the flesh and she looks exactly the same. She's wearing a gorgeous Marchesa dress that I just saw in *Hollywood Nation* and thigh-high black boots. She hugs me and then plops down on my bed.

"You look okay except for the cast, but your brother says you've gone loco," Liz says in between bubble gum pops. "What's going on? You haven't returned any of my calls."

"What calls?" I ask, confused.

"On your cell." Liz looks at me strangely as she pulls her curly dark brown hair off her neck and into a tiny ponytail using an elastic with a silk butterfly attached to it.

I haven't even checked that phone Mom claimed is mine. I don't know the password. It's not the same as my regular one, which is Austin's birthday.

"I've been worried about you," Liz says and pops a bubble to drive home her point. "School is a nightmare. Everyone is talking about your car crash. I keep trying to defend you, but I don't even know exactly what happened because you aren't talking to me. Your mom keeps calling and telling me this bizarre stuff you've said. That you think you're the one who plays Samantha Buchanan on *Family Affair* and Alexis Holden stole your job?" She makes a loud *POP!* with her gum. "You're kidding, right? I know we've been hitting the scene a lot lately, but you don't really think you're a celebrity, do you?"

I lie back on my bed next to her. So this Liz thinks I'm nuts too. If I tried telling her the truth, she'd probably run from the room and never come back. I can't have that. I need someone to talk to. I stare at the carpet and dig my toes into my comforter. "No. I think it's a side effect from all the medication they have me on," I lie, and Liz nods knowingly. "I guess I've been saying some pretty messed-up things."

Liz laughs. "I'll say! You look like hell. What happened to your hair?"

I pull a strand of my honey-colored locks. "It doesn't normally look like this, does it? I've always loved the caramel highlights Ken Paves gives me. He would die if he saw my hair like this."

Liz chuckles. "You crack me up. I meant your hair looks like you haven't combed it in a week. As if you would ever have the money to get Ken Paves highlights—no offense." Liz examines a strand of my hair. "I wish you'd let me pay for it. Or should I say Daddy." She raises her eyebrows mischievously. "Ever since he got Alexis Holden as a client, it's like he's been printing his own money!" Liz flings herself backward on my bed, her head touching mine. "I am just loving this windfall he's on, Kaitlin. It's only been two months, but it's going to change our lives, I just know it. Daddy lets me buy whatever I want and is getting me all these cool clothes, like this dress."

"Marchesa." I nod knowingly and finger the fabric. "Gorgeous."

"Thanks," Liz says happily. "I'm thinking of wearing it to the premiere Friday night. Think you'll be up for going?" She props herself up on her elbows. "We can bling out your cast so that you'll get tons of sympathy. I can even buy you a new dress!" She starts to get excited. "You can't make me go alone. Cara Simeone's going to be there, and I can't stand her." I'm about to ask why, when Liz adds: "I know—we have to kiss her butt if we want to get in her inner circle, but you kiss up better than I do." She frowns and I notice her lips.

Liz's lips! Her lips have never been that plump. She definitely altered them. Something else is different too. OH MY GOD! "When did you get a boob job?"

Liz sticks her chest out proudly. "Happy seventeenth birthday to me! Don't they look great now that the swelling has gone down? I wish we could have scored you a freebie so you could have gotten a new pair too."

EWW.

I'm not sure what to comment on first—the fact that I wanted a boob job or how I can't afford Ken Paves now. A stray tear escapes my right eye before I can stop myself. "I'm sorry." I wipe it away quickly with my flannel PJ sleeve.

"Get up," Liz insists. "Take a shower. Get some clothes on and for goodness' sake, run a comb through your hair. We're getting you out of here. You need air."

Twenty minutes later, I'm wearing what I found in the bedroom closet: a decent Gap boatneck navy-and-white-striped shirt and Gap jeans with one ballet flat. At least alter-Kaitlin has a decent wardrobe. She does well without name designers. And Liz was right. Getting some air did make me feel slightly better. When she pulled out of my driveway and sped through the neighborhood in her brand-new Beamer (this week's big gift from her dad) and jumped on the highway, I felt a small sense of relief. Maybe she can drive me out of this world and into mine. I was even more hopeful when she pulled up to A Slice of Heaven.

Antonio is still here, and the place looks the same. We're sitting at a booth with a spaghetti splat on the red-and-white-checkered vinyl tablecloth, and yet ... everything is different. I'm eating Liz's and my favorite pie—broccoli, extra cheese, and peppers—and sipping a Sprite but I don't feel better. Maybe it's because Liz is talking about our social life, which sounds sort of pathetic.

"Have you listened to a word I just said?" Liz stops chewing and talking and looks at me sternly. "You better get your attention span back or you'll have to kiss that internship good-bye. There are three girls in line behind you just dying for that job. Dad totally stuck his neck out for you."

I stop sipping my Sprite and look up. "What job?"

Liz looks at me like I've just suggested she give back her new black American Express. "Your internship! At *Family Affair*! You know . . ."

I don't know, but suddenly I feel hopeful.

Liz is still looking at me strangely. "The one my dad got you last month because you always wanted a job in Hollywood." She giggles. "At least we told him that so that we could get you close to Trevor Wainright."

I HAVE a job in Hollywood!

"This internship you've got going on is going to be the best score for us," Liz is saying as she pours more Sprite into our glasses. "Forget cozying up to Trevor at the moment. We are *thisclose* to getting our own reality show or something. I can feel it! Then everyone in town is going to want to be friends with us."

I stare down at my pizza. "Celebrities are usually nothing like they are on TV," I say quietly. "Sometimes being friends with people outside the business is much more rewarding." I look at her. "At least, you and I have always felt that way."

"I guess." Liz blots the excess oil on her pizza with a napkin. "We did, but that was before my dad hit the big-time. Now we don't have to pretend we don't want to be part of that world, Kates! We're in it." She smiles brightly. "I hate that you've been out of commission this last week, because so much is going on." She leans in close and I can smell her honeysuckle perfume. "People have been calling *me!*" she says gleefully. "On their own! Kates, we're so in. I mean, yeah, some of them seem a little shallow and self-centered and are not our type, but who cares? Once we're in, we don't need to act like we care about every little thing they say." She laughs so loud we barely hear her phone ring. "HEY, babe!" Liz mouths someone's name to me excitedly when she answers. "What's up? Aww . . . yes, I understand. That so is important!" Liz nods at me knowingly. "How much?" Liz bites her nails. "Um, sure. Of course Kaitlin and I will come to your charity event. My dad can spring for the thousand-dollar tickets. It's totally worth the . . . sure, okay. See you then!" She grins at me. "That was Cora. She had to go, but she wants us at her Save the Dolphins Dinner."

"For a price," I correct. I've seen this sort of thing way too many times to count on my nail-bitten fingers. (I bite my nails now! Like Nadine! EWW!)

"It's a good cause," Liz insists.

Not only am I not an actress, I'm a celebrity hanger-on. From what I've pieced together from our conversations, Liz's dad's business has just taken off, when in the real world, it took off years ago when he took me on as a client. Here, Liz's exposure to Tinseltown has just started, and she doesn't seem to be handling it so well. It doesn't sound like alter-Kaitlin is adjusting to the Hollywood lifestyle that well either.

"Did you have to bring that bag?" Liz groans. "It's so tacky."

I look at the glittery red bag I found in the back of alter-Kaitlin's closet. It's roomy enough to carry books from school, but still small enough that I can wear it on my shoulder to go out to eat. You'd think the glitter would make it look too fancy, but somehow it doesn't. The bag just looks fun, and I could use some fun right about now. It reminds me of Dorothy's ruby red slippers. *The Wizard of Oz* was part of my TV marathon the other night, and I forgot how much I love it. I actually like this bag better than the expensive butter yellow leather one I've been toting around, even if this one isn't made very well. I've never heard of the designer, Riley Pierce. Probably Target. "I like it."

"For dress-up maybe, or for Goodwill, but you cannot bring that bag in public." Liz grimaces. "Imagine getting photographed on the red carpet with that bag. Ugh!"

I hold the bag up and stare at it from all angles. It sparkles back at me happily. This is a happy bag, and my goal is to be happy. It's a keeper. "I think it's cool."

Liz shakes her head and her curls bounce around, falling out of the ponytail that was barely containing them. "I'll buy you a better bag." Her phone rings again and she snaps the phone open. "Hey, you. Yes." Liz mouths another name, but I can't tell what it is between all her chewing. "We'd love to come to your club opening! Sure. What time? I think I have a dinner, but we can come by after. Yes, I get that you have a head count. We won't let you down." She switches calls.

"Mia, sweetums! Hey. Yeah, of course I got the invite.

I'm so sorry I forgot to RSVP. Yep, I'll be there. Plus one, I'm sure. Yes, Kaitlin is on the mend!" She looks at me excitedly. "Okay, doll. We'll see you then." Liz hangs up and sighs. "Three events on one night. How are we going to pull that off?"

"We can't," I say lightly and take another bite of my pizza. "We have to turn one down."

Liz starts texting. "No way! They'll be mad at us. At least Mia remembers you too. Seriously, Kates, you have to be more careful. We can't disappear from the nightlife for more than a night or two. If we do, we'll just be replaced, and I am not leaving when we just got here." Liz seems sort of scared of the thought. Then her phone buzzes in her hand and she reads the text. "You were the one who said to say yes to every event we get invited to and then just not show up at the lame ones." She giggles. "You're so evil."

I am? No I'm not!

She looks up and I guess I must be making a face, because then she says, "Why do you look so worried?"

"It's just," I say slowly, "I didn't know you liked to go out so much."

Liz shrugs. "We both do! But I go out every night. Daddy gets mad, but it's not like I can turn down tickets to a huge movie premiere, you know? What if our new friends stop inviting us?" Liz's phone starts to buzz again. "Ooh! It's Jade."

I shudder. Jade, one name only, is on this totally bizarre reality show on E! She's as C-list as they come. Liz is getting excited about her call?

"This will just take a sec," Liz apologizes, putting her hand over the phone. "Hey, hon! Yeah. That was awesome. Friday? Um . . . yes!"

I stare glumly at the other tables. A few people around my age are staring at me and whispering. They must go to Clark Hall too. This supposed driver's ed crash I caused in alter-Kaitlin-verse was apparently a doozy. No one looked too happy to see me when I walked in here.

"You're hilarious! You so deserve that new pilot. You're going to get it. I just know it."

What's happened to my best friend? Sure, Lizzie's always enjoyed having money, but she's never gotten wrapped up in fame the way she seems to be now. She's sort of morphed into a version of . . .

Liz's phone rings again. "LC! Hey, babe. Yes, I know it's Cobb, not Conrad." She rolls her eyes at me. "How's Ava? Tell her that tantrum she threw at the door at Shelter the other night was hilarious. Friday?" Now Liz looks nervous. "I just made plans, but I'm sure I can stop by. Uh-huh. Yeah . . ."

Liz is friends with LAVA? (That's the nickname the press gave Lauren and Ava Hayden when Sky and I were fighting with them. We're SKAT.) Liz is so above them! At least *my* Liz was.

"Yeah, Kates is with me." She holds out the phone excitedly. "Ava wants to talk to you. She says you haven't taken her calls."

Wait. WHAT? I'm friends with Ava again? And Lauren too?

EWW.

WHY?

I shake my head fiercely. "I think I overexerted myself. Tell her I'll call her later."

"She's using the exhausted-from-the-car-crash excuse again," Liz jokes and winks at me. "I'll tell her. Bye!" Liz snaps off her phone. "She's my least favorite, but what can you do? We need her." She gives the phone a nasty look when it starts to vibrate almost immediately after she puts it down. This time she actually ignores it. "Let's talk about you. Ready for school on Wednesday?"

"No," I say without skipping a beat. I pull at a frayed edge of our tablecloth. It looks like it was singed.

"You need a makeover," Liz suggests. "Something so that no one knows what you look like when you get there. It will keep Lori and Austin's crew from laying into you about driver's ed. Austin just got out of the hospital today, you know." I open my mouth to say something, but Liz beats me to it. "Did you send your favorite crush a card?" She winks. "Probably not, considering you put him there." She laughs. "But seriously. Makeover is in order. We should call Ken and have him squeeze you in. My treat." She starts to dial.

HOLLYWOOD SECRET NUMBER TEN: In my real world, stars make physical transformations all the time and pay for it themselves. When a star makes a physical transformation for a movie role, it's on the studio's dime. Need to drop twenty pounds to play a model? Learn a Russian accent to play a spy? Dye your hair for a superhero character? A movie studio or a producer pays every penny of it. There is only one condition to this rule: the change you're making must be for a specific project or part that you're playing. If you want lipo so you can get the part of your dreams, the check is coming out of your own checkbook.

"I don't want to go to Ken." I push Liz off. "I just want to fly below the radar for a while till I can get out of here."

"What do you mean, 'get out of here'?" Liz gives me an odd look. "LC just told me about a party down on Laurel Canyon. We have to get back out there. I need my wingman. Besides, I heard Lennon might be there." She sighs. "Imagine if he remembers my name? I will just die." As if on cue, her phone starts to vibrate again.

She looks at the screen, but doesn't answer yet. "It's Violet! Holly! NYC." She holds the phone up to me as if for proof. Her face drops. "I want to talk to you, but . . ." She hesitates. "No, I'll let the call go to voicemail. I can do that, right? What if they don't call again?" She looks so crushed I almost feel bad for Liz.

"Take it," I insist and take another slice of pizza. This Kaitlin doesn't have to fit into a size four for her *Small Fries* wardrobe. I take a bite and the gooey cheese burns the back of my throat. I mumble through the pain. "Don't keep Violet and Holly waiting."

Liz grins. "Okay. I won't." And then she goes back to booking our week and weekend plans in the celebrity-hanger-on universe.

Note to Self (handwritten now that I no longer have an iPhone)

Real Me:
Figure out why I'm here.
Figure out how to get home!!!!

Alter-me:
Find outfit in closet for school on Wednesday
Grease Matty and Liz for scoop on my life at Clark Hall

FADE IN:

MALIBU—PICTURESQUE SPANISH-STYLE MANSION

SAMANTHA, PAIGE, and SARA are touring a hacienda with an expansive pool, a giant living room, a state-of-the-art kitchen, marble floors, and high ceilings. The home is fully furnished with upscale furniture and antiques. The atmosphere is warm and inviting, in sharp contrast to SAMANTHA'S mood.

REALTOR #1

As you can see, this home boasts three electric fireplaces. One in the living room, one in the den, and one in the master suite, which also has a Jacuzzi tub and a private balcony overlooking the pool.

SAMANTHA

Three fireplaces? I'm sure you use those a lot in southern California.

PAIGE

(her voice tight) Samantha . . .

SARA

What I want to know is where my bedroom would be. Is it on the second floor? If so, by any chance is there a palm tree outside that one could conceivably climb if I, um, had to escape from a fire?

PAIGE
You'll have to excuse us. My girls have been through a
lot the past few weeks, and sometimes I think none of us
are ready for a move. Other times I think we need this
more than anything in this world.

SAMANTHA
Keep telling yourself that, Mom. Maybe that will
make you feel better about uprooting all our lives. I
understand the need to find someplace new to live after
the fire, but why can't we stay closer to home?

REALTOR #1
Well, as I was saying, this home is four thousand square
feet and has five bedrooms and a separate carriage house
with an additional bedroom, small kitchen, and full bath,
which could easily be converted into office space.

SARA
No gym? Geez, Mom. This place won't work.

PAIGE
Girls . . . *(sighs to the Realtor)* Could we
have a moment alone, please?

REALTOR #1
Absolutely. I'll make some calls in the kitchen.
We have three other homes to tour after this one, so have

a cookie and keep your strength up! *(laughs annoyingly)*

SARA

Oh goodie! Dried-out Entenmann's cookies.
Mom, this blows.

SAMANTHA

I'll say.

PAIGE

Girls, whatever happened to having a big adventure?
When you two were little, all you ever wanted to do
was play what you called "real life." You dressed up in
costumes and pretended you were princesses in foreign
lands or heroines saving their princes from dragons.

SARA

We always were ahead of the curve, even back then.

SAMANTHA

But that was all pretend, Mom. This is real life, and in the
real world, moving stinks. I want our old house back. I don't
want to start over in Malibu and live on the beach! I want
to keep my life the same.

PAIGE

Do you really, Sam? You want your life to be exactly the
way it is now? No changes at all?

SAMANTHA
Yes.

SARA
(snickers) Liar.

SAMANTHA
What? If you guys have something to say, say it.

PAIGE
What I'm trying to say is that for someone who loves
her life so much, you certainly don't seem that happy.
You seem stressed a lot, and tired. Sometimes I think
the four walls around you are going to crash in on you,
that's how overwhelmed you look. Yes, your boyfriend
makes you happy, and your charity work, but what makes
YOU happy, Sam? What needs to change in your life to
bring that smile back twenty-four/seven? *(Sam doesn't
answer.)* Just what I thought. You don't know. But that's
okay, Sam, because whether you figure it out in our old
home or a new one, I know you will find what's missing.

eleven: *Déjà Vu*

"Sweetie?" Mom is tentative. "Aren't you going to get out?"

Mom has pulled into the drop-off zone at Clark Hall High School, and I'm glued to the leather seats in terror. Matty slid out of the backseat as soon as we got here and walked ahead of me to class. I guess even the socially awkward alter-Matty doesn't want to be seen with the girl who supposedly ended Austin Meyers's lacrosse career. A car honks angrily behind us, and soon a whole symphony of honks is begging Mom to move. She can't. I still haven't gotten out yet.

"Go around again," I tell Mom pleadingly. I clutch the sparkly red bag to my chest. It's not a school bag, but there is something I like about this thing that I can't put my finger on. I've taken it everywhere. It's sort of calming.

"This is the last time, Kaitlin. I've already circled three times." Mom gives me a withering look as another driver lays on the horn. Then she adjusts her blue scrubs top. (When she first came downstairs this morning in scrubs and rainbow-colored Crocs, I almost spit my Froot Loops across the breakfast table and started laughing. "What's so funny?" she'd said defensively. "I know they're not the most glamorous threads in the world, but I do my best to jazz them up." I'm assuming the jazzing part is the rainbow ponytail holder she has in her hair, but seriously—Mom in a ponytail?)

I watch out the window of "our" car—a 2005 Town & Country minivan, how horrifying. As picturesque Clark Hall moves out of view again and Mom joins the long line of cars and limos waiting to do drop-off duty, I find myself exhaling a little.

There was a day when I used to dream about coming to Liz's private school full-time. It reminds me of the colleges she and Austin are applying to as we speak in some other realm. (That's my new theory: I'm stuck on a different plane. Hey, it happened on the *Charmed* rerun I saw last night!) Clark Hall sits on ten acres of rolling hills, sports fields, and super green manicured lawns. The school itself is made up of five brick, vine-covered mansions (this was once a private residence). Most of the buildings are connected by brick open-air walkways that are covered with beautiful arches and blooming flower beds. Gleaming silver lockers line separate covered walkways. Thankfully, since I've actually been a student here before—or should I say I was one in disguise for a brief period—I know my way around.

"Kaitlin, I know facing your peers is going to be hard," Mom says, "but what's happened has happened. You can't change the past. All you can do is work on making a brighter future."

I just stare at Mom, my eyes blinking rapidly. "Wow, Mom, that was sort of inspirational." My real mom is inspired, yes, but inspirational . . . uh, not really, unless it involves explaining how I'm going to appear on two live late-night talk shows in the same hour.

Mom smiles and steers the car around the bend. We're four cars away from drop-off again. "It's the truth. Make your apologies, be contrite, and I promise this will all blow over by the weekend. Your father and I spoke with Principal Pearson and no one is pressing charges. They know that you hitting the gas instead of the brake was an accident. The fact that you hurt a few students is a very, very unfortunate mistake, but it was still a mistake. Right?"

I nod unsurely. Who's to say what this Kaitlin might have been thinking? Whenever someone drops a new detail about how I supposedly behave here, I cringe.

Mom touches my cheek. "I'm just glad to see you out of your room."

When I was watching my fourth hour of the *Charmed* marathon last night in three-day-old sweats with an empty box of Oreos in my hands that I couldn't recall eating, a revelation dawned on me: I'm not going to figure out what's happened to me by staying in this room for the rest of my life. If I want to get out of this dream/realm/coma/purgatory, I have to leave the house. And maybe, while I'm here, I can do some good. Like show Matty how to use hair gel and get Liz to see that hanging out with the *Jersey Shore* cast is not something to aspire to.

So here I am.

Mom pulls the car slowly to the drop-off point again and puts the car in park. She stares at me expectantly.

"Kaitlin, it's time," she says kindly, but firmly all the same. "If you need me, just call. The school nurse has your pain-killers if you need them, okay?"

There is no avoiding it any longer. I grab my crutches (my ankle will be in a cast for four weeks) and open the car door. If I had two good legs, maybe I could get up and run away.

"Oh, and honey?" Mom rolls down the car window and calls to me. "Principal Pearson would like a word with you before your first class, okay?"

I nod. It's absolutely okay. Principal P. is always a welcome face, and I adore her. I take a deep breath and step out into the cool December air. I pull my Gap peacoat tightly across my chest, sling my book bag over my shoulder, and use my crutches to hobble down the path. I'm wearing a long green tunic I found in alter-Kaitlin's dresser, black leggings, and a multicolored scarf around my neck. I can't squeeze most of my jeans over my cast till it comes off, so I'm wearing skirts and loose pants or leggings. I also can't wear two shoes. My one foot has on a ballet flat. The other has my toes wiggling through the cast. Still, at least I look decent for my death march. I catch people staring, and I immediately lower my eyes and move swiftly. It's a technique I do well after all my paparazzi run-ins.

"It's *her*."

"Oh my God! Kaitlin Burke is back."

"Look who had the nerve to show up."

Ugh. This is not going to be fun. But what choice do I have? I have to figure out what I'm doing here if I want things to change. And *change* is the operative word. The first thing I want to do after I leave Principal Pearson's office is find alter-Austin and apologize.

Austin.

Just saying his name makes my stomach ache and flip-flop at the same time. I've called him every night, but no one picks up. Maybe if I can apologize for being selfish and putting both Austins in harm's way, all will be forgiven, and I'll wake up in the real world again.

I find my way to the main office without a problem, but I can't figure out a way to open it while I balance my crutches.

"It's Kaitlin! Did anyone tell Lori she's back?"

Move crutch to the left, try to balance on my right foot without the crutch. Grab door handle. Nope. Doesn't work.

"I so would have transferred, wouldn't you?"

Use both hands to grab door handle. Okay, now what? How do I get through without my crutches?

"Go home, Burke!" someone yells.

Great, I'm a leper. How am I supposed to get to the bottom of alter-Kaitlin if I can't get through a door?

"Need some help?" a custodian asks me and holds open the door.

I smile gratefully and head into the office, but as soon as I do, I wish I could use my crutches to pole vault out of there. The secretaries stop talking, the teachers who were chatting by the coffee machine stare me down, and I swear even the phone lines stop ringing. Then I see my history teacher/driver's ed instructor, Mr. Michaels, and oohh...his face looks like it really hurts. His left eye is black and blue, he has cuts on his arms, and his right hand is bandaged. Matty said he hit his face on the dash when I stopped violently short. He uses his injured hand to pull on his salt-and-pepper goatee.

"Ms. Burke," he says stiffly and gathers his papers quickly, as if I might try to ram him with my crutches. "I trust I'll see you in third period."

I have history third period! Okay, at least I know where to go for one class. "Mr. Michaels, I just wanted to apologize," I start to say.

Mr. Michaels pushes his wire-rim glasses up on his long nose. "I don't want to discuss this in a public forum, Ms. Burke. If you have something to say to me, make an appointment after class." He pushes through the office door, practically hitting the speechless custodian, and disappears into the crowded walkway. Needless to say, I have a feeling I won't be getting an A this semester.

"Kaitlin Burke? Principal Pearson will see you now," says one of the secretaries.

I don't think I've ever moved so fast on crutches. As I hobble through the door, I notice Principal P.'s office looks the same as it did when I was a student. Plaques hang on the wall behind her cluttered mahogany desk, and a flat-screen TV is anchored to the opposite wall. Principal P. is leaning back in her chair, so engrossed in whatever is on TV that she barely sees me walk in. She looks the same as she does in the real world—short and plump with graying black hair and off-the-wall style. Today she has on a lime green polka-dot dress, which makes me sort of dizzy.

"I, uh, will be right with you, Kaitlin," says Principal P. in hushed tones. She waves like an air traffic controller to a leather seat opposite her desk. I place my bag on the chair next to me and freeze when I hear Sky's voice.

Oh goodie! Dried-out Entenmann's cookies. Mom, this blows. I'll say.

The second line should be mine, but instead, I cringe when I hear Alexis. My nails dig into the book bag next to me to keep from screaming. *Family Affair* cuts to a commercial break, and Principal P. picks up her TiVo remote and starts to fast-forward. She does a double take when she turns and remembers I'm waiting.

"I'm sorry!" she chuckles. "I get so wrapped up in this show sometimes. Silly to love a soap so much, I know."

"Not at all," I disagree, feeling the need to defend my legacy, even if, at the moment, it isn't mine. Here's what I've pieced together about the alter-*Family Affair*: it's still running, but the storylines are ones I did back in the past. It's as if every season is jumbled up. "I love *Family Affair*. It's never been just a nighttime soap, even though people try to dismiss it as such."

"That's what I always say," Principal P. agrees in solidarity. "I get so mad when people call it fluff! *FA* was the first show to feature a gay couple in prime time."

"And they did some groundbreaking storylines about transgender couples and climate change," I remind her.

Principal P. breaks into a huge smile. "I had no idea you were a *Family* fanatic too!"

That's what *FA* fans call themselves. They were a very loyal bunch. Principal P. could have been their fan club president. She was the only person other than Liz who knew my true identity when I was at Clark, and she used to pump me for *FA* information.

"I loved this episode, by the way," I gush, pointing to the screen.

Principal P. beams. "It's excellent, isn't it?"

"I feel like Samantha finally got to break out of her comfort zone a bit this season, you know?" It's a relief to talk about *FA* without someone offering me a straitjacket. "It was one of my favorite storylines when they had her go off the deep end and refuse to move to Miami." I smile, waiting for her to respond.

Instead Principal P. just stares at me, her mouth slightly agape. "I, it's just ... they moved to Miami two seasons ago and then moved back last season. Now the mansion has burned down again and they're thinking of moving to Malibu."

Huh? "Oh. I guess I got this episode confused with an older one."

Principal P. blushes. "It is kind of similar to the episode

they did when they toured their new home in Miami, isn't it?" She wrings her hands together. "God, my friend Shelly is right. *FA* is jumping the shark!"

I keep forgetting I'm the only one that knows these storylines already. I laugh heartily. "No, it's not," I insist when I see how upset she's become. "I just got confused. I've been reading all these episode recaps in *FA Fans* magazine."

She looks hopeful. "Are they not moving to Malibu, then? I feel like the show is at its best when they live in the mansion, but Shelly said she read online that Alexis is dying for the show to do beach locations again. She gets a better tan from natural sunlight."

Now it's my turn to blink rapidly. "I don't know."

She grimaces. "The storylines just aren't that good this year. Still ..." She looks at the TV again as the show comes back on. "The episode only has five minutes left. Do you mind if we finish it?"

"Of course not," I say, even though it kills me to watch Alexis playing, well, me.

Principal P. presses play and the two of us watch in silence. Paige is standing there, looking like the perfect mom, as usual. God, I miss Melli.

Girls, whatever happened to having a big adventure?

I'm engrossed in the dialogue. Some of it is similar to lines we had in the episode when we toured houses in Miami. God, the writers couldn't come up with anything new? How do they get away with copying themselves? Other lines are brand-new. *I don't want to start over*, I hear

Alexis say. She is not a good actress, but I freeze listening to the words coming out of her mouth. *I want to keep my life the same.*

As Paige gives what is supposed to be a heartwarming speech, I find myself roped in, listening to her every word as if she's giving the advice to me personally.

Yes, your boyfriend makes you happy, and your charity work, but what makes YOU happy, Sam? What needs to change in your life to bring that smile back twenty-four/seven? Just what I thought. You don't know. But that's okay, Sam, because whether you figure it out in our old home or a new home, I know you will find what's missing.

"Kaitlin, are you okay?" Principal P. asks me from somewhere far away, but I can't answer. My mind is racing.

Do I need change in my world? I've been so insecure since *FA* ended because I thought it meant the end of life as I know it. But from where I'm sitting now, I can see it really was for the best. I've tried so many wonderful things since *FA*—I got to do Broadway, I am on *Small Fries*, I'm going to do a James Cameron movie. I've become so anxious about what isn't working in my life, I guess I've been blind to how lucky I've actually been.

"I'm fine. Just getting wrapped up in the dialogue." I choke back tears. "I'm still a little out of sorts. My head is so foggy I can't even remember my schedule."

"You poor thing!" She quickly types something on her computer, and the printer next to it springs to life. "I can take care of that. I'll print you a copy of it right now."

190

"Thank you," I say gratefully.

"Do you need a tissue?" Principal P. passes me one and looks at me sadly with big, gray eyes. "I thought you might be a bit weepy today. I may be principal, but I'm in tune with the student body and I know what everyone is saying." She smiles sadly, and I notice her red lipstick is on a little crooked. "I've already made an announcement to the student body about last week's accident. I want the gossip to stop. It was an accident and nothing more. Mr. Michaels is okay, and the other boys weren't injured. Austin Meyers will be fine, thank God, even if he can't play lacrosse this spring. I'm hoping he'll run our spring carnival instead and that it will take his mind off sports. We'll make a lot of money with the celebrity dunk booth Liz Mendes's father is helping us put together."

"That is a big draw," I agree. Liz made me do it last year, and I spent more time in that disgusting water than I did in the dunk chair. "Thank you for making me feel better, Principal Pearson."

"You're welcome." She blushes. "Let's talk about something more pleasant. Have you heard anything intriguing on the set? I know you're interning at the show. That must be incredible."

"Incredible," I repeat, my mouth twitching at the irony.

The two of us are so busy talking that I don't notice the first two periods fly by. Principal Pearson is fascinated by my stories about the cast ("My *Family* fanatics group would flip if they heard this!"), and she "refreshes" my memory about new storylines this season. The whole show seems to have been turned upside down, and I have to bite my lip really hard to keep from screaming when she tells me what's gone on. Aunt Krystal having an affair with my character's dad? Paige leaving Dennis for a CEO at a rival empire? Sara dating a teacher? BLECH. The Tom Pullman I know never would have approved these storylines. I can't believe people are actually watching this garbage! After we've talked *FA*, we move on to celebrities and Principal P. asks me—a studio intern—what I've heard about different stars' plastic surgery rumors, affairs, and money woes.

"That Melli Ralton is stunning. Just stunning!" she marvels about my TV mom. "I've heard it isn't all good genes, though." She points to her nose and her chest. "But Melli says in every article that she's never had plastic surgery, so I guess we'll never really know for sure."

I know for sure.

HOLLYWOOD SECRET NUMBER ELEVEN: Plastic surgery is still a taboo subject in Hollywood, especially for women. There are two camps on plastic surgery: There are the Heidis of the world who use their time under the knife to get magazine covers and generate watercooler topics. Then there is the rest of Hollywood, the ones that swear their skin is as perfect as a baby's bottom, even at the age of fifty-five. Aging is a worry for any star, but women tend to take the brunt of the burden. That's why so many get a little lift, a little tuck, disappear for a month, and voilà! They look as good as new! Well, *they* think so. Personally, I would never do plastic surgery. I hate that surprised look so many stars have after they've gotten a face-lift. In Melli's case, she has had work done, but she lies to protect her career. If Melli cops to a boob job or an eye lift, some casting couches may not offer her a seat. Melli knows to keep her mouth shut if she wants plum parts.

Principal P.'s jaw drops as I finish explaining my theory. "How do you know all this?"

Hmm ... maybe that was a bit too much info for an intern to know. "I'm doing a paper on celebrity culture for my psychology class," I lie.

The intercom buzzes and the two of us jump. "Principal Pearson? Ms. Jasons says Kaitlin hasn't shown up for her appointment. She wants to know if she came to school today and whether she is in your office? You were supposed to take Kaitlin to her appointment during first period."

My principal looks at her Timex watch. "Oh my! Look at the time." She wags her finger at me. "I made you miss almost two periods, and I still haven't gone over what I needed to discuss with you. No matter. We'll tell your teachers we had a lot to talk about." She winks. "Just don't tell Ms. Jasons." She clicks on the intercom button and asks her assistant to send Ms. Jasons to us.

Who is Ms. Jasons? I take a shot in the dark, hoping Principal P. will give me a clue. "Is Ms. Jasons here to talk about the accident?"

Principal P. fidgets slightly as she takes a seat behind her desk again and shuts off the TV. "No. We scheduled this appointment with you before the accident even happened. To be honest, Kaitlin, she's worried. You haven't had one meeting with her about college applications, and they're due in a few weeks."

I sigh and slouch in my seat a little. The college talk keeps coming up no matter where I am. "Oh."

"We'll sort it out," she says and folds her hands across her large chest. I notice her red nail polish is the same color as my sparkly bag.

There is a knock on the door, and Principal P. waves in a short, thin, strawberry blonde with wispy bangs and long hair. She smiles at us both. This must be Ms. Jasons.

"Kaitlin, I hope you're feeling better after your accident," says Ms. Jasons kindly.

"Yes, thank you." I shift awkwardly in my chair, and it squeaks.

"I apologize for doing this to you your first day back, but this is pretty urgent." She drops a stack of folders on top of Principal P.'s desk. "To date, you have not handed in one college application. They're nearly due, so I thought we could discuss ones you've mentioned a passing interest in." She fans a few out in front of me. "I'm happy to go over essay questions if you want. If I give you a deadline of two weeks, we'll have time to do revisions, if necessary."

I wonder if Ms. Jasons is this reality's version of Nadine. I stare at the large stack and my eyes glaze over. I guess the me in this reality isn't sure what to do about college either. "I'll take care of them," I lie and pick up the folder on top. Boston University. Huh. Looks pretty. Austin likes Boston...no. No. I have to concentrate! What's important is getting home, not college applications. Besides, at home the problem is the same: I'm too busy to worry about this. When would I have time to do any application other than the USC one I promised I'd do for Nadine anyway?

Ms. Jasons clucks her tongue. "Yes, well, you've said that before, and you still haven't turned anything in." She looks at me sharply, and I'm slightly terrified. "I don't want your applications to be late, Kaitlin. You're the only student I have who has failed to complete this assignment. As you know, Clark Hall has an unprecedented record for graduating seniors. One hundred percent of the graduating class goes on to college. I would hate to break that record. I think we've been more than patient"—she looks at Principal Pearson—"but I will be forced to call your parents if you don't get your applications in."

I feel my skin start to prickle. This is the same issue I have in the real world! I cross my arms defiantly. "I don't mean to be rude, Ms. Jasons, but going to college is *my* decision, no one else's."

"That's true," Principal Pearson says softly, "but don't you want to go to college, Kaitlin?"

I look away. "I'm not sure."

She sighs. "Not to get too personal, but I've spoken to your parents at length. They want you to have the best education money can buy, which is why they saved so hard to send you and your brother to Clark Hall this year. They don't want you to sell yourself short."

"I'm not!" I find myself insisting. "But I don't have to go to college to keep that from happening. People can find great jobs without going to college too, you know. If I find a craft I'm good at that doesn't require a degree, say, like acting, why should I take time away from that to go to school?"

"Going to college isn't just about finding a career, Kaitlin," Ms. Jasons explains. She plays with the silver pen in her hand, clicking it open and closed. "It's about finding yourself." She leans in closely, and I watch her whole face light up as she talks. "College is your chance to study subjects that you might not otherwise. Philosophy, fashion, literature from the 1800s, Greek myths. There are courses you can't even fathom! Then, of course, there's the social aspect. In college, you'll meet people from all walks of life and backgrounds. You'll learn perspectives you might never have if you hadn't stepped outside your own world." She smiles. "You might learn a few things about yourself too. Maybe you'll find that being a history teacher isn't what you want to do, after all. After a few semesters of psychology, you might learn that being a school psychologist is actually more up your alley." I see a blush creep into her cheeks as she nervously brushes her light bangs away from her eyes. "At least I did."

Wow. I have to admit I just got a bit swoony at that passionate speech. If she's lying just to get me to fill out some applications, then I should get her a job on *FA* right away.

But why would she lie?

Maybe there is more to college than just finding a career. I have always wanted to learn more about Greek myths and philosophy ... and when I think about it, my favorite part about being at Clark Hall eons ago was actually sitting at a desk surrounded by people in the heat of discussion. When you're one-on-one with a tutor your whole life, the only debate you have is whether or not you can postpone a pop quiz to do a phone interview with *People*.

"A degree opens doors that would never open otherwise," Ms. Jasons continues. "I think it's great that you're interested in being an actress, but it's a very hard profession to break into. Don't you want to have a backup plan if it doesn't work out? That's what a dual degree—in theater and another major— could give you." She pats the large stack again. "I'll tell you what. Pick one application. Just one. Do that and I won't call your parents. If you get through that first application, maybe I can convince you to do more." She grins. "I can at least try."

I stare at the folders. "Okay," I agree. I blindly pull an application from the middle of the stack. When I look down at the folder, my eyes widen.

University of Southern California.

That's the school Nadine wants me to go to! And the folder looks exactly the same as the one Nadine gave me! How weird is that?

"That's a good school, Kaitlin." Ms. Jasons nods approvingly. "They'd be lucky to have you. You'll have no problem with this application or the essay."

"Is it 'Does your life change you or do you change your life?'" I ask, holding my breath.

Ms. Jasons looks surprised. "Why, yes, how did you know?"

Here come the goose bumps again. "Someone told me."

The bell rings and Principal Pearson looks at me. "We should really let you get to class, Kaitlin. I'll tell your teachers in the first three periods that I held you up." I take the USC folder and look at Ms. Jasons.

"We'll be in touch," she says. "Come see me if you need any help, but I'm sure you won't. Let's aim to go over everything next week, okay?" I nod.

When I leave their offices and head into the crowded walkway, I feel a little lighter somehow. The University of Southern California application is tucked into my bag, and I rest my hand on it through the crutches.

I wasn't lying about doing that application for Ms. Jasons. In the real world, I don't have a single application done, but suddenly I *want* to do them. I may not know how I'd pull off filming a show that tapes sixteen-hour days and going to college, but I want to give it a shot. Nadine would be so ecstatic to hear me say this.

For the first time since I've gotten here, I feel . . . excited. I don't know if it was hearing that *FA* speech about the future or Ms. Jasons's rousing pep talk, but I feel positive somehow that there is a reason I'm here for the moment. Even the dirty looks I'm getting from the people around me can't get me down. That USC application has to be a sign that I'm going to get out of here. It has to be. I never get signs. If anything, I'm the one that . . .

"OUCH!"

I was so busy talking inside my head that I forgot to look where I was going. Now I've accidentally planted my crutch on someone's foot.

"I'm so sorry. Are you . . ." I look up to apologize and inhale sharply. "AUSTIN."

Austin. My Austin is standing right in front of me.

TWELVE: *Everything Is Not What It Seems*

Austin is standing right in front of me, and my good foot is glued to the sidewalk in a mixture of panic, terror, and pure adrenaline-fueled excitement.

I don't know what to do. My initial instinct is to burst into tears, throw my arms around him, and sob "Thank God you're okay!" over and over along with "I'm so, SO sorry." I want this Austin and the other one out there in the universe to know that even more than I want to get out of here. But freaking out like that would be a little dramatic, even for an actress.

"Uh, could you take your crutch off my good foot?" Austin asks bluntly.

"Oh, yeah! Sorry." I can't stop staring. There are so many thoughts running through my head, like the one saying I should kiss Austin as hard as I can and not let go. But that would be inappropriate.

Darn.

"That's better," he says when I lift my crutch, and then he

smiles. Smiles! "I was wondering when I'd see you," he adds, as if we're friends. Are we friends here? "I wanted to talk to you before this whole thing spiraled out of control, you know?"

I'm not paying too much attention to what he's saying because all I can think about is that after almost a week of imagining this moment, Austin is *right here*! Standing in front of me! I take in every inch of him from the top of his blond head to his toes—okay, his cast. Ouch. His whole left leg is in a cast, and he's on crutches, just like me. I did that to him. I put Austin in a cast, both here and probably in the real world too, and the guilt of that will never go away no matter how many times I apologize. The rest of Austin appears fine, thankfully. His hair looks exactly the same—long bangs, sort of wavy locks—and his face has that sun-kissed glow you get from spending hours on a muddy field. I don't re- cognize the outfit he's wearing, but I like it. He has on a red Abercrombie pullover and navy wind pants that are rolled up on his left leg.

"I . . . I . . . are you okay?" I ask nervously.

"If you call being in a cast okay," he says, acknowledging his leg with a small shrug. But the way he says it, it doesn't sound mean. Just matter-of-fact. This conversation is going better than I expected.

"I'm so sorry," I blurt out. "I don't know what happened!" Literally. "One minute we were driving, and the next the world was upside down. The last thing I'd ever want is to hurt you." He looks at me curiously. "For anyone to get hurt," I clarify.

"I know." He exhales sharply. "You kept saying that when we were being put in the ambulance. Why would you want to run me down? We're sort of friends."

We're friends! This is a good sign, and yet, we're *just* friends. Hmph.

Austin sighs. "At least we *were* friends."

Ah. There it is. He's friend-dumping me for running him over.

He runs his fingers through that blond mop of his and looks away for a second. "I want us to be friends, but it's tough. I've told you that. It's hard." I nod, even though I don't know what he's talking about, and he looks at me guiltily. "Don't look at me like that."

"Like what?" I ask, surprised.

"Like you're disappointed," he says. "I know I have issues, but you do too, you know."

Oh, I know.

"You've become as obsessed with being popular as I am," Austin reminds me.

"I have?" Maybe he's not dumping me. Maybe . . . this is a conversation that he and I started before I ran him over?

"Yeah," Austin says. "You're not in the in-crowd here, which makes it hard for us to hang out, but you're still on the popularity kick. All you and Liz talk about is getting into Hollywood parties and hanging with stars like Lauren Cobb and Ava Hayden. You tell me not to get suckered into doing what's popular, not to let the people at Clark Hall rule my life, but you're doing the same thing yourself. I don't get you, Kaitlin Burke."

Uhh . . . let me get this straight: Austin and I definitely aren't dating, but there might be something between us that neither of us can act on because he's hugely popular and I'm not (not to mention, he has a girlfriend). And I turn him off with my fascination with being a Hollywood wannabe.

Wow. My relationship with Austin in this world is much different than it was back home. "I don't get myself sometimes either," I tell him, which is the truth. "Forget about all that other stuff for a minute. The important thing is that I'm sorry. About everything."

"I know that." There is that smile I love! Sigh.

"Does that mean you're not mad at me?" I ask hopefully.

Austin leans on one crutch. "I was. I mean, I wanted to be, but I can't stay mad at you."

Now what does *that* mean? What was our history before the accident? Were we secretly talking about wanting to be together, but he was afraid of what his friends would say? I wish I knew the truth, but my heart thumps so loud I think Austin can hear it.

"*But*, if it wasn't for you, I'd be on my way to a game against Southside in an hour," Austin adds.

I look down at my feet—one is in a cast, and one is wearing a ballet flat. "I can't believe you can't play. Did they say how long?"

"At best, two months, at worst, not till next fall, *if*

someone even wants me to play for their college team when they can't see me this spring." He grimaces. "And you? How long are you going to be in—"

"Haven't you caused enough damage, Tread Marks?" A guy appears out of nowhere at Austin's side and pokes me hard in the shoulder.

I look at him and realize it's Austin's best buddy and lacrosse teammate, Rob Murray. "Murray!" I exclaim excitedly before I can stop myself, which I should have because the look Murray gives me makes the Terminators running around in *T3* seem friendly.

"Who you calling Murray?" he asks, leaning into my face rather menacingly. I've never heard him so angry before, and I sort of stumble backward. Austin reaches out to help me, but then stops. "Only my friends call me Murray, and you are not my friend, Tread Marks. You could have killed us the other day! You better watch yourself. After what you did to my boy here"—he nods to Austin—"you're at the top of our Tipster List."

"What's the Tipster List?" I ask, even though I don't think I want to know. The Tipster List sounds very bad, and the way Murray's normally wonderful smile is curled up into a snarl, I'm sure I'm right.

"Why are you even talking to her, man?" Murray asks Austin gruffly.

"I'm not," Austin says to my surprise. "I was just telling her where she can stick her crutch." He laughs awkwardly and puts his hand up for a high five.

Wow. Austin's so afraid of being unpopular that he'll do anything to avoid being kicked out of the in-crowd himself.

"Nice." Murray nods appreciatively, then scowls at me again. "A, I can't even look at her, man. I'm outtie. See you in history. Or not."

"Not." Austin laughs as Murray walks away. He looks around before talking to me again, and his face is pained. "I'm sorry. You've got to understand, especially now, we can't be seen together. I should go." He sticks his right crutch in front of my left one, but I'm too quick. Using one of my crutches, I block his path.

"Wait," I insist. "Do you mean to tell me we're covert friends?"

Austin sort of sighs and hangs his head, which is yet another thing I've never seen him do before. But then again, I've never cost him a lacrosse season before. "Kaitlin, you know how things work around here. I have a rep to maintain."

The real Austin has told me that before we met at Clark Hall he wasn't always such a great guy. He struggled with doing the right thing versus maintaining his popularity. If alter-Austin has been with Lori the whole time we would have been together in the real world, then the pull of being popular is that much stronger. Still, he must want to change, a little, if he's friends with a "loser" like me. I may not be here long (I hope), but while I am, I've got to help him.

"What are you more worried about?" I ask. "Your rep or where you're going to be a year from now? You won't even see these people then! You'll be back on that field before you know it and you can still wow the scouts at Boston College. In the meantime, can't we both stop worrying about what's popular? I don't think the real you cares about rep that much." Blech. I sound like his mom. I stare at the sidewalk because it's less scary. Concrete is nice even if it is covered in gum. Haven't these people ever heard of garbage cans?

"How do you know about Boston College?" Austin asks. "I haven't told anyone that BC is one of my top picks."

"You told me," I lie. "Remember? The morning of the accident." Austin seems to think this through.

Shoot. I have to be careful about spoiling secrets real people have told me. This makes me think of HOLLYWOOD SECRET NUMBER TWELVE: TV show spoilers are sometimes leaked on purpose. George dying on *Grey's Anatomy*. Charlie coming back for *Lost*'s final season. These types of secrets are too big to be kept under wraps till the episode airs, so the network is savvy enough to take care of matters themselves and beat the gossip rags at their own game. Creators and producers may not come out and tell you exactly what will happen, but they will tease that "something monumental will change the lives of all the characters." An actual spoiler, of course, is a specific plot point, which no TV person in his or her right mind would give away on purpose. But a teaser is okay. Sometimes they're a thank-you to fans who are so obsessed with their favorite show that they can't wait another millisecond to know what will happen next.

What I just did to Austin wasn't a tease. It was a spoiler that the real me knows, but obviously alter-Kaitlin and the rest of this universe is not supposed to.

"I don't remember saying something, but if you know, I guess I did," Austin says and then smiles again, just a little. "I really have to go now."

"Please don't go," I say before I can stop myself. I know this is not my Austin, but he's still Austin, and I feel better just being around him.

"Kaitlin—" He says my name like it hurts. But that's the last thing he says before I get knocked sideways by his girlfriend, Lori Peters. In the real world, he broke up with her a long time ago, right after he met me.

"God! Haven't you done enough to my man already, Tread Marks?" Lori says. "Austin, why are you talking to her?"

"I'm not." Austin shrugs. "I was just on my way to find you." Lori smiles at me smugly.

Blech.

The alter-universe has been just as kind to Lori as the real one. She's as beautiful as ever, unfortunately. Perfect platinum blond pin-straight hair, Barbie's proportions, height, and killer clothes. She's wearing a Dolce & Gabbana black dress with knee-high Jimmy Choo boots.

God, I really miss my clothes.

"Leave. Him. Alone. You cost him the upcoming spring lacrosse season and our school's chances at being five-time champs!" Lori points a long, pale pink nail in my face.

"I know that," I counter. "I came over here to apologize."

As soon as Lori opens her mouth, people start to gather round, like they're watching a taping of *Ellen*. I bet they've been waiting all day for someone to tear into me like this. Austin looks as uncomfortable as I am, but he lets her yell at me anyway.

"He doesn't care about your apology," Lori continues and crosses her arms defiantly. "It doesn't change things. He still can't play lacrosse, and you're still a loser." She smiles at me wickedly. "Austin, from now on, Tread Marks is number one on our Tipster List."

"Tell me something I don't know," I snap. I can't stand either version of this girl.

"Lori, let's go," Austin interrupts, not looking at me. "She's not worth it."

Even though I know Austin doesn't believe that, hearing him say it still hurts.

"You're right. She's not," Lori sniffs and hikes a Gucci backpack over her bony right shoulder. "She's nobody." Lori starts to lead Austin away.

Someone snickers and I snap. No one talks to me—real me or alter-me—like that. Austin may not have the guts to say what he feels, but I do. "I am not a nobody," I tell Lori loudly. "I have a life, and a pretty good one, that doesn't include the likes of you. *You* are the nobody, Miss Head Cheerleader. You can't even get a cheerleading scholarship from UCLA." Ha! Pays to know stuff. Liz told me about this last week.

Lori's jaw drops. "How do you know that? No one knows,

I mean, I haven't even, she's lying," she sputters, but Austin is staring at me curiously. I focus on him.

"You're somebody, Austin," I stress. "And you're better than these people. Don't stoop to Lori's level."

Lori looks at him angrily. "What is she talking about?"

"I don't know what she's yammering about." He looks away. "Let's get out of here."

"Yes, let's," Lori agrees and gives me a dirty look. She puts her arm around Austin's back, staring menacingly at me as she goes, and grabs his grubby navy messenger bag. "We are out of here," she tells the growing crowd. "She's Tipster List, number one! Don't forget it, people!"

Where is my guide? In the movies, whenever someone gets stuck in a coma or an alternate reality, there is supposed to be a guide to help smooth things over. Where is my Glinda the Good Witch?

"God, you made things worse," I hear someone say. It's Liz, looking great in a Burberry headband, fitted red shirt, and a tan Gucci skirt with Tory Burch flats. "I know we can't stand Lori's crew, but do you have to make things intolerable during school hours?"

"Thanks for your support," I grumble and take a huge step with my crutches to get ahead of her.

"I can't believe you tried to talk to Austin," Liz says as she catches up and walks along next to me. "We went over this—he's never going to own up to liking you, Kaitlin. You should move on."

I stop short. "Austin really does like me?" Why does

this make me so happy? It's not like this is the *real* Austin.

Liz gives me a look. "*You* think so. And yes, it sounds like it, but come on! That guy is too weak to stand up to his friends, especially now." She throws an arm around me. "Besides, why would you want to waste your time on a high school guy when you could be with someone like Drew Thomas?"

"Eww, Drew Thomas?" I freak. Liz is talking about my self-absorbed ex-boyfriend and costar in *Pretty Young Assassins*. He practically cost me my relationship with Austin a while back. "I would never date Drew!"

Liz laughs. "What are you talking about? You were majorly flirting with him two weeks ago at the Motorola party! You better get going on that. You said yourself you need him to take you to a premiere before he moves on to the next hot thing."

Oh gross! "I think I'm going to throw up."

"Oh, stop!" Liz looks at her Movado watch and then at the fork in the cobblestone path ahead of us. Each walkway leads to a different brick mansion. "Fourth is basically over, so why don't we just skip and head over to the caf? We need to read this week's gossips so we can figure out who to hang with next." I must not look that enthused because then Liz adds, "Added benefit to an early lunch: You can probably avoid being target numero uno on the Tipster List if we eat now."

"I'm in." The thought of sitting in class doesn't seem that appealing at the moment anyway.

Liz starts texting while we walk. Well, she walks and I

hobble with my heavy red bag—do I really need to carry this many books for class? "I've got so much to do before Thursday night. I could really use a new dress for the party—I mean *parties*—and some cute shoes and maybe an airbrush tan. You should go through my closet and pick something out that has a label." Her phone pings and Liz squeals. "It's Lauren!" She holds the text up proudly. "She's inviting us to the after-party. You in?"

"Doesn't that start at three AM?" I ask, knowing how these kind of parties work. "My mom will never let me go to a party that late." Here's one time it pays to have alter-Mom. She's much more concerned about my beauty rest.

"Just say you're staying over at my place. Please?" Liz begs. "Don't make me go alone. We've got to wow these girls or they won't invite us out again. I know it's late and you've got a long day on Friday with the internship, but you can take a nap or something. Please?"

Friday! So that's when I have the studio internship. "I forgot I had work on Friday. What time do I have to be there again?"

Liz looks at me. "Two PM, like always. You get to skip ninth period since it's study hall. Did you forget to take your meds today?"

I nod solemnly. "I do feel a bit foggy."

"You're coming with me to that party," Liz insists. "You need to get out. I'm telling the girls you're in before you can say no." She types too quickly for me to stop her. "There! I hit send. Now you have to come or Lauren and Ava will dis

211

us. You don't want to be on their Tipster List too, do you?"

I bite my lower lip. "Liz, what exactly is the Tipster List anyway?"

Liz groans as she holds open the door to the mansion that has been converted to Clark Hall's cafeteria and culinary school. The noise level is definitely high, and I can see the large eating area is packed with tables of teens.

"If you don't remember, I'm certainly not telling you," Liz says. "It's too depressing to explain. You'll never leave your room again." Liz walks into the room and heads straight to the lunch line.

The place is packed, and I look longingly at the wall of French doors leading to the outdoor tables we used to sit at. I hope we're going out there. This room is loud, and I can already hear people whispering about me. Liz already has her tray and is moving down the line, grabbing a mesclun salad and ordering a panini.

"Liz! Wait! I could use some help." She doesn't hear me. Fine. I can do this. I stare down at the pile of faded orange trays in front of me and try to figure out how to pick one up and manage my crutches. I bend forward and grab a tray, but I can't really walk like this. I look at Liz, hoping to send her a telepathic message to turn around, but instead all she does is answer her cell phone.

"Need help?" a girl behind me asks. It's Beth, and next to her, Allison. Saved! Beth and Allison were great friends to me here when I was at Clark Hall, and Liz adores them. I look at the girls nervously, half expecting them to be as changed as everyone else in this alternative universe, but thankfully they look the same. Beth is still petite, dark-skinned with curly black hair, and Allison still has brown hair and is super tall, which works for an aspiring ballerina. Neither has had a boob job, lip plumping, or gone overly tan! They both smile shyly.

"Beth! Ali!" I exclaim, and they sort of take a step back. "I mean, thanks. That would be great. Liz didn't hear me call her." I hobble ahead of them.

"What do you want, Kaitlin?" Beth asks, adjusting her black wire-rim glasses before picking up my tray.

"A roast beef sandwich and a Diet Coke would be great. Thanks so much. How are you guys doing?"

"Are you feeling okay?" Ali sounds concerned, and she looks at Beth curiously.

"Much better, thanks," I say. "What about you two? What have you been up to?"

After Beth gets my food, we chat a bit as we move down the line. We're so engrossed in a conversation about *Glee* (just another show I've discovered now that I have nowhere to be at night—I guess that's one good thing about this reality, all the TV I can handle) that I don't hear Liz.

"Kates, what are you doing?" Liz says slowly, talking to me as if I'm about to wear a pink shirt with orange pants. She looks so shocked I'm afraid she's going to drop her over-packed tray.

"What do you mean?" I shrug, looking from Beth to Allison, who are starting to fidget. "I'm getting lunch."

Liz smiles thinly. "I'll take that, thanks," she says in this super-chipper voice, but as she yanks me and my tray away from the girls without giving me a chance to say thanks, her tone changes. "Are you trying to make things worse?" she hisses. "What are you doing talking to *them*?"

"What's wrong with them?" I look at the girls again and see them sit at an empty table near the back of the cafeteria.

"They"—Liz begins slowly, smiling even though she's mad. She nods slightly in Beth and Allison's direction—"are social suicide girls. Talking to Beth and Alexandra will make you less popular than you already are at the moment."

"Allison, not Alexandra!" I say incredulously.

"Whatever." Liz shrugs. "No one talks to them, and if you're seen talking to them then your stock will go down even more."

"You're not friends with Beth and Allison?" I ask quietly, looking back to see what could be so social suicide-ish about those two compared to Lauren Cobb and Ava Hayden. They're both nice-looking and dressed normally. Allison has on this pretty green sweater and khaki cords, and Beth is in this cute gray cardigan and dark denim jeans.

"Not since third grade, and neither are you," Liz says and heads to the double doors that lead to the eating area outside.

"That's so sad. They're really nice." I follow Liz to an outdoor table that I remember Lori sitting at, the one in the perfect shade. Liz starts to laugh as she sits down. "Seriously,

Kates, I think you may be delirious. You're acting totally unlike yourself. Why are you so concerned with this place anyway? It's high school. We have a better life outside these walls. We have to concentrate on that rather than swoon over Austin Meyers, who will never give you the time of day." She takes a forkful of the salad on her tray.

Now I'm really depressed. "I think I'm going to skip lunch today," I say, hoping to find a quiet place to process all that has happened this morning. I grab my tray through the crutch, and my sandwich and soda starts to slide. I am never going to be able to walk like this.

I've barely righted my tray when I hear Liz yell, "Look out!" My tray flies into my chest, and my sandwich and open soda ooze down the front of my shirt along with the roast beef, mayo, and lettuce. I cringe.

"And that's how you work the Tipster List!" shouts Murray as he high-fives a guy in a lacrosse jacket. Lori and her best friend, Jessie, are at a table behind him, and they stand up and cheer. Austin looks sort of bothered, but there he is, clapping too, and I give him a dirty look before looking away.

Tipster List. Now I get it.

Clever.

"Hope you liked your first taste, Tread Marks," Murray adds with a chuckle. "I'm sure there's more where that came from."

With the dignity I have left (which isn't much), I let the tray drop to the floor, sidestep the remains of my sandwich, and hobble back inside, ignoring the stares of everyone around me. All I want to do now is find the nearest bathroom, lock myself in, and cry.

Note to Self:

1. Give Matty an image makeover. Make him more assertive!
2. Get Liz to see how Hollywood really works before she becomes a mini Lauren and Ava.
3. Get through to Austin's thick skull that he's better than the goons at Clark Hall that he hangs with.
4. Find something plastic (a raincoat?) to wear to school. Might be easier to clean if I stay a Tipster List target.

UNIVERSITY OF SOUTHERN CALIFORNIA

ESSAY QUESTION: Have you changed your life, or has your life changed you?

(Essay must be at least two thousand words but not more than four thousand. Please type and double-space your essay.)

Who cares what the answer is? Either way my answer is the same: I HATE IT HERE!!!!!!!!!!!!!!!!!!!!!!

Why did I ever think I'd be happy at Clark Hall? The place is filled with poseurs and celebrity wannabes—even the teachers want to be stars (I'm talking about YOU, Ms. Lyden!). My parents have wasted their money on this McMansion hellhole. I can totally tell I've learned NADA at this place (if you discount the Tipster List, which I am now way too aware of). Clark doesn't give you a life, it takes your life from you! Look at Liz—she's a caricature of her former self. Austin is one step away from becoming Lori's lackey (or maybe he already is), and my brother is a walking Lifetime movie waiting to happen. Would it kill him to turn off his computer?

And then there is me—I'm just the kind of person I used to hate—a celebrity hanger-on. In less than a year, I've turned into a Lauren Cobb. I'm one step away from my own reality show.

I don't want to be a bottom feeder. I want my old life back! I should be the one on the red carpets, working charity events, signing autographs. That's where I belong. Instead I'm just so . . . weak. Maybe if Mom wasn't so full of sunshine and penne à la vodka recipes I would actually toughen up a bit!

I don't care if I changed my life or it changed me. All I care about is the fact that I hate everything about this place! I hate my scratchy bedspread, Mr. Michaels's little comments, my crutches, the Tipster List, and being part of this bizarre family!

December 18

Can TV's most popular nighttime soap be saved?

By Gabby Bremston

Backstabbing, bickering, catfights. It sounds like a regular episode of TV's hottest show, *Family Affair*, but this time the action is happening off-camera. Unnamed sources confirm to *TV Tome* that America's favorite soap is in turmoil. "Alexis Holden and Sky Mackenzie have ruined that series," says a source close to the production. "They're constantly questioning their lines, complaining if their scenes are too short, and trying to get Melli Ralton and Tom Pullman fired." Melli plays the girls' mom, Paige Buchanan, and Tom is the creator of *FA*. Seems impossible that either would be let go, but sources say that Alexis and Sky have such a tight rein on executives that the network would rather lose the series creator and show matriarch than Alexis and Sky. "It's awful watching Melli and Tom bow down to two teens," scoffs another source. "They don't want to be part of this show anymore, but they're locked in to a long-term contract. Now Sky and Alexis want to see them gone? It's ridiculous. Those girls should not have this much power."

If the fighting doesn't stop, some fear the show will be shut down and retooled, which means we'll be without episodes for quite a while. If we even get them back at all. "*Family Affair* was such a great program for so long," says one source sadly, "but it is not the same anymore. If this is what working at *FA* is like, most of us don't want to be here."

THIrTeen: *Be Careful What You Wish For*

Aaah! I missed the bus! I hobbled as fast as I could to the bus stop outside the Clark Hall campus after eighth period to catch the bus to the studio for my internship, and I missed it by two minutes. Another one doesn't come for an hour.

I can't wait an hour because then I'll be late to work, and I can't be late on my first day. Well, it's technically "my" first day. Alter-Kaitlin has been going for a month, and the real me started on *FA* when I was four, but the me stuck in this alternate universe has never been an intern before. God, I'm giving myself a headache just trying to work out the logistics of this scenario!

I really want to make a good impression. Part of me is secretly hoping when I walk on that set that everyone will see me and realize I'm the one who should be playing Samantha. Then they'll kick Alexis to the curb.

As if that would ever happen. But at least I'm thinking positively for a change. Last night I tried writing my USC essay again, and even though I came up with zilch, I did have a mini breakthrough. After I ranted and raved about how much I hate it here for the umpteenth time, I came to the awful realization that I might NEVER get out of here.

What if I'm stuck here forever? Then what?

I can't mope around and complain about how this life can't hold a Jimmy Choo to my real one forever. As long as I'm in this place, I'm going to get my life together. I'm going to change my life, and I will try to make this world as close to my other one as possible. First step: reclaiming Hollywood, which I've slowly begun to realize I miss more than I ever thought possible. I need to get on set at *Family Affair* and take a look around.

If only I had a ride to the studio! I can't jog there on crutches, Mom and Dad are both working, and Liz ditched school at noon to go to the Lavender Hills Lotion gift suite and spa with Lauren and Ava. I loved Rodney before, but his stock just went way up in my book. When I get home, he's getting a raise.

I need a car. Fast. I start racking my brain for people I can call, but it's hard when this world is so different from my old one.

And like a gift from fate, a horn honks.

"Do you need a lift?" Austin's pulled up to the curb in his mom's car, and the engine is idling loudly. He's got the passenger's side window down, and he stares at me expectantly, like I should run to the car and just jump in, thanking my lucky stars that the most popular guy at Clark Hall would offer me a lift.

Why would Austin offer *me* a ride after the way he treated me this week? That's A. And B is majorly important too: "How are you driving with a cast?"

Austin grins. "Left leg. Don't need it to drive, remember?"

Ah. Gotcha. Back to A then. "So I guess it's okay to offer me a ride now that your friends aren't around, huh?" I question, feeling touchy. "Shouldn't you be alerting the Tipster List brigade so they can chase after me with today's lemon chicken surprise?"

Austin shifts the gear into drive. "Never mind."

Sigh. Being catty is no way to win Austin over. I have to swallow my pride. "Wait. Forget what I said. I do need a ride."

Austin presses the unlock button, and I see his mouth twitch slightly. "Say please."

My eyes narrow. "Are you kidding me?"

"Fine. Get in." He leans across the cabin and throws open the passenger door.

I slide into the seat next to Austin, throwing my crutches in the back next to his. I hold my red bag close, and I avoid eye contact. I'm trying not to get freaked out.

That smell.

Just putting my seat belt on and breathing in that warm vanilla cookie air freshener makes me feel dizzy. This car smells like home. I've spent so many hours in here: going to Disneyland, on dates, to the beach in Malibu to watch the sunset. I touch the dash without thinking and trace my fingers along it.

"Where to?" Austin asks.

"It's pretty far away," I admit and pull the bus schedule Mom gave me out of my red bag. She looked at me like I was crazy when I asked how to read it this morning. "You can drop me at the Santa Rosita Boulevard stop. There should be a bus coming by in fifteen minutes." I glance at the clock on the dash. "Don't you have to get to ninth period?"

He gives me a serious look, which is sort of cute. Of course he's cute. He's Austin. "Like they're going to flunk me. All they care about is me getting off crutches and back on the field. I said I had a doctor's appointment."

Sigh. Changing Austin is going to be harder than I thought. "Don't you have, um, English ninth period?" He nods. "I thought you liked English."

"I do, but . . ." He hesitates. "Look, I'm here and I'm not going back to school, so do you want me to drive you or not?" His voice is sort of gruff. "I have nowhere to be since I can't practice, so I'm in no hurry."

"Burbank," I say reluctantly, because I really do need to get there. "I have an internship on Fridays at *Family Affair*."

Austin puts on his black aviator shades. They're not the Ray-Bans I got him, but they still look good. "The chick show. Got it. Let's drop the English pep talk and get you to Burbank." He slowly pulls away from the curb.

I should protest about that chick show comment, but he is giving me a lift, and it feels so nice sitting in this car.

Austin turns on the radio. Some Coldplay-sounding knock-off song fills the silence, and he begins cruising the short distance to the highway.

"You know, I don't skip class that often," he says, like this has been on his mind the whole time. He doesn't look at me.

"I know," I say, because my Austin wouldn't. "You're better than that."

"Why do you always say that?" he asks wearily. "I deserve better, I should know better, I need to do better, I'm better than those guys." He gives me another hard look. "You're one to talk. It's not like you've done so well at Clark yourself."

Touché. "That is why I'm overhauling myself." I smile. "Kaitlin 2.0 is in full effect. You won't recognize me in a week."

"Don't change too much," he says, avoiding the subject of himself. "I liked the girl I met on the first day of school." He smiles and I find myself blushing. We stop at a light, and Austin starts rummaging around the center console, then looks in the dash, leaning over me to get to it. I catch a whiff of his signature smell—good clean soap and after-shave—and begin to feel woozy.

"What are you looking for?" I ask to distract myself.

"The GPS. I thought my mom kept it in here." He checks under his seat, then behind his seat, then checks the center console again and frowns. "I thought we could punch in the address so that we can go right there, but I can't find it. Are you good at directions? Lori can't find her way off the football field. We'd never get there if she was sitting where you are."

"It's a good thing she's not sitting here, then," I say stiffly at the mention of his girlfriend. But come to think of it, I'm not sure I know exactly how to get there either. It's been a while and Rodney always drove. We need that GPS. I'm pretty sure I remember Austin commenting once that his mother keeps the GPS in the most non-sensical place possible—the trunk—because she's afraid it'll get stolen, but what's the point in having one if you can never get to it when you need it? But I can't tell him that. He'll think I'm Crazy Stalker Girl. I keep quiet and hope he'll remember.

"I'm just going to pull over and call my mom." He dials and I hear his phone go to voicemail. "No answer. I may have to take you to the bus stop after all. Sorry."

I am not going back to the bus stop now. I'll be three buses behind! Men! I'll take care of this myself. I lean back and shimmy myself with one stiff leg halfway into the bench backseat.

"What are you doing?"

I slide my butt back then reach my hand out to grab the strap in the middle of the backrest, the one that conceals the mini console. With it down, I can see the small door to the trunk. I turn the knob, reach my hand inside, and pull out the GPS. "Here."

Austin stares at me wordlessly. "How did you know where it was?"

How do I explain this one? I look away—I hate lying. "My mom keeps hers there."

225

"Right." Austin nods as he hooks up the GPS. He doesn't look convinced, but he doesn't say anything either. "Guess we're going to Burbank, then."

He's got his eyes on the road—real Austin is a serious driver too—but his face has relaxed finally. It's as if we're far enough away from Clark Hall that maybe shades of the real Austin come out. "Tell me the truth about the GPS. You're stalking me, aren't you?"

I'm a little insulted. I don't stalk! Larry the Liar does that. "I am not!"

He starts to laugh. "It's kind of cute, in a creepy sort of way," he says. "You can admit you like me."

"I do not," I insist. But I do. Sort of.

"You do," Austin says, sounding slightly arrogant, which just makes me mad. So much for the real Austin shining through. "You wouldn't be so concerned about me going to class if you didn't."

Only two highway exits to go and for the first time ever, the exit ramp doesn't seem backed up. I look at Austin's smug face, and my annoyance level creeps up.

"Well, maybe you like me too," I blurt out, "but you're too afraid to say it." The smile wipes off Austin's face. "You like being around me, but you're worried about your reputation so you only talk to me when no one is watching. You're nice to me—again, when no one is listening in. Any guy who got hit by a driver's ed car would not talk to the girl who ruined his lacrosse season unless he liked her. Not to mention know what bus stop I was waiting at, Mr. Stalker." I'm on a roll. "I just wish you'd realize that you don't need to be a jerk to be popular."

Austin's face twists slightly, and the car grinds to a halt. "This is your stop." The large, decorative wrought iron gates to the studio are right in front of us. Austin stares straight ahead.

"I guess I'll get out here," I say, my voice much softer than it was a moment ago. "Thanks for the ride." I go to shut the door when I hear Austin.

"Maybe I am the one who is the stalker," Austin says uncertainly, and my heart feels like it will need a defibrillator. "But knowing that won't make it any easier. You make it sound so simple, but I'm trying."

He looks at me expectantly and all I want to do is hug him, but I know that won't help things. Instead I pull my glittery bag onto my shoulder and grab my crutches. "Try harder," I say quietly and shut the door. I don't bother looking back.

My confidence deflates quickly after that. That's because the *Family Affair* soundstage is nothing like my *Family Affair* soundstage, starting with the large pictures of Alexis Holden that greet visitors in the lobby. Alexis winning an Emmy! Scenes with Alexis! Alexis swimming with dolphins!

Gag. Gag. Gag.

I may be sort of getting through to Austin, but how am I going to change anything at a major television show?

"Kaitlin?"

A woman I don't recognize is sitting behind the receptionist desk wearing a large headset, and she's staring at me. Where's Pam, our regular receptionist? "They're waiting for you in hair and makeup. Can you manage to get down there on your crutches?"

"Absolutely." As long as the hair and makeup room is where it was when I was on *FA*, I should be fine.

"Word of warning: She is in RARE form today, even for her," the woman says, giving me a look. "Try to stay clear. I heard even Tom is hiding in his office."

Is she talking about Alexis? That doesn't sound too promising.

I head down the hall toward hair and makeup, and my walking slows down to a complete crawl. I can't help feeling sort of misty and nostalgic as I move through the soundstage. I want to take in every picture on the walls, every face that passes me. I want to remember the stage's fresh paint smell (they were always painting some set), the sounds, the wires...all of it. Being here makes me miss *Family Affair* in a way I haven't in a while, but it's more than that.

I miss working.

It's been weeks (*I think*—it's hard to tell when you're in an alternate dimension) since I've been on a soundstage, and I can feel the pang in my heart as I see familiar things, like tiny stars on dressing room doors and the craft services cart being wheeled by. I miss *Small Fries*. I miss reading scripts, doing wardrobe fittings, eating lunch with Matty and Sky in the cafeteria, getting gummy bears from crafty. I . . .

I miss my very complicated, very overbooked Hollywood life.

If my ankle wasn't broken, I would kick myself for being such a fool and wishing it away. I want it back. All of it, warts and all, just for the chance to slip on a costume again and emote about a problem that isn't my own.

I take a deep breath and move out of a P.A.'s way as he runs by me with a box full of strange electrical items. I have two choices at this moment: I could burst into tears and cry about the cruel twist of fate that is my new life, or I could do the job I came here to do.

After all, I am still on a soundstage. The *FA* soundstage. Yes, I want to go home, but if I have to be anywhere other than home, this is a great place to be. In my world, the *FA* set is no more, but here it is up and running and everyone is still here looking happy and . . .

Well, actually, come to think of it, no one I've passed actually looks happy. If I study the harried faces of P.A.s, lighting folks, union workers, and assistants running past me, no one looks even remotely cheery. They look stressed and sort of freaked out and . . . is someone yelling? It's coming from the hair and makeup room. I freeze outside the door when I see who is causing the commotion.

"GOD, PAUL! You call this a half pony? This is not a half pony! I could do a half pony better in my sleep!"

My old *FA* hairdresser, Paul, is the one taking the tongue

lashing. He's still impeccably dressed and has great dark, curly hair, but his tall frame is slumped forward and his face is blank while she tears into him.

"I told you what I would do if this happened one more time, just one more time, didn't I?"

It's Alexis, just as I remember her, and she's pointing a finger at his chest. Her long, fiery red hair is pulled in what looks like a decent half ponytail to me, and her green eyes narrow. She's so tall, she towers over him in knee-high black Gucci stiletto boots. Her model-ready figure looks great in a black strapless dress.

"I don't care what Tom says, you can't do hair. I've been saying it for a year! You need to be replaced. Max Simon runs circles around you."

Shelly, my old makeup artist, snorts. "Max runs circles *for* you, Alexis."

"Shel," Paul says witheringly.

"No, Paul. Let her fire me too!" Shelly booms. "It would be a blessing! I can't stand coming here anymore. I won't answer to an eighteen-year-old." Shelly glares at Alexis. "You want Max because he's in your posse. As far as hair goes, no one does as good a job as Paul."

Alexis looks like she might breathe fire. "You're lucky I'm obsessed with the way you do my eyeliner and airbrush tanning, or you'd be out on your fat butt yourself."

My jaw drops. I can't believe Alexis called Shelly fat! Yes, she's plump, but that's not Alexis's concern. Alter-Alexis is ten times more obnoxious than the real Alexis was, and I think I know why. Here, she rules, just like it said in that *Hollywood Nation* article I read. If Sky and I hadn't beaten Alexis at her own game and gotten her fired from *FA* way back when, she could have ruined everything for all of us. If Alexis stayed as beloved as she was by the media—who didn't have a clue how vindictive and awful she was—she could have become the tyrant she is here and now.

I shudder so violently that I drop my right crutch. It lands with a smacking sound on the hardwood floor, and Alexis whirls around, ready to bark. Then she sees me.

"Oooh, the Make-A-Wish Foundation girl, right?" Alexis says, gliding toward me and picking up my crutch before I can answer. "Let me get that for you, honey, and let me sign your crutch. Would you like that? I have a ton of other stuff for you in my dressing room. I can get someone to carry you down there to get it." Alexis signs my cast before I can stop her. I'm so flabbergasted I can't speak. She looks around. "Where's your reporter for the story? And the photographer?" Her shoulders slump. "Do you mean we just missed this moment? Now we're going to have to do it again!"

Paul and Shelly burst out laughing. "That's Kaitlin Burke, Alexis. Remember? She's one of the studio interns."

Alexis rolls her eyes. "I wasted all that on you? UGH. Give me back that crutch."

No way. "I don't think so. I need it to, you know, walk."

"Fine." Alexis runs a hand through her thick hair. "But if you screw up like that again, you're off the lot. I don't need to be humiliated by a . . . by a . . . what was she again?"

"Intern," I finish for her, smiling sweetly.

"Just get out of my way." Alexis shoves me aside and click clacks down the hall. "Paul?" she yells back. "You can stay—for now."

"Lucky me," Paul mumbles under his breath, then smiles at me. "Sorry about that, Kates." He knows me! And I'm just a lowly intern. "You know how the red dragon gets." He raises his eyebrow. "Too bad she doesn't hate us enough to fire us." He sighs. "But you almost had an out there. You should have gone for it."

I want to be fired? How bad has *FA* become?

"You better get down to the set and bring this." Shelly hands me a fancy water spritzer. "You know how Alexis gets if she doesn't have her mineral water spritz on the sidelines. It's your job today. I have to hang back here and do makeup for the Make-A-Wish girl. Alexis is worried she'll look too pale and sickly without bronzer." Shelly gives me a look. "How that girl wields so much power around here, I have no idea."

Speechless, I head back down the hall and head straight toward the soundstage. At this point, people are running back and forth and yelling things.

"Alexis needs Smartwater! She only has three bottles."

"Alexis wants Melli on set pronto so she can switch some lines!"

"Where is Tom? Alexis has questions about her dialogue!"

"Did the Make-A-Wish kid get here yet? Alexis doesn't want her screwing up her lunch hour."

Alexis, Alexis, Alexis! My god, where is Sky in all of this? I've never heard of her being so outdone.

Maybe my fantasy of working on *FA* again is not such a good one, after all. Why would anyone want to work here?

The light isn't on above the door to the soundstage—you can't enter if they're in the middle of taping—but I have to wait for a grip to open the door for me and then I limp inside. My breath catches in my throat.

There in the middle of this oversized hanger is my old TV show living room! To an outsider it would look strange to see three sheet-rocked walls of a room being held up by two-by-fours on the outside, but to me, this is my Buchanan family living room. Directly next to it is the set for the kitchen, the girls' bedroom (which doubles as our parents' bedroom), and the screened-in porch. Behind all the sets you can see pieces of rooms lying against walls, waiting for their turn to come to life. If you walked around the exterior walls of the set, you'd have no idea where you were. You'd see a ton of wires taped to the floors, and black-painted walls leading to nowhere, but if you turned the corner and got onto one of the sets, you'd feel like you were in a real house. The Buchanan house after the fire. The fireplace, the leather couches and ottoman, the family photo . . . AAH! My family photo! But of course, where I would be standing, next to Sky as Samantha, is Alexis.

My heart sinks. Do not cry. Do not cry. This is *not* real. It can't be!

"Where is my mineral water?" Alexis barks.

I move as quickly as I can around the wires on the floor, but it's hard with crutches. People are so frenzied that no one notices I'm having trouble. I feel a hand on my arm.

"Let me help you there, Kaitlin."

"Rodney!" I throw my arms around his large frame. "God, I've missed you. How are you?"

Rodney just looks at me. "Okay, I guess, for someone who is stuck being Alexis's bodyguard."

ALEXIS'S BODYGUARD?

NOOOOO!

"You feeling all right, Kaitlin?" he asks, adjusting the black sunglasses that are pushed back on his bald head.

"Fine," I say hastily. "I, uh, just missed you last week and wanted to say hi."

"Can I help you get to Alexis? You know how she is about being kept waiting." As Rodney talks, I see his gold tooth. It's still there. But there's something different. His smile is missing. And he's much quieter when he speaks.

"Yes, that would be great." Rodney links arms with me through one of my crutches, and slowly we make our way over to Alexis, sidestepping cables. Alexis is busy filing her nails, so she doesn't see me.

"Rod. Where is my pink nail polish?" she demands. "Did you get it from my dressing room?"

"Not yet, Alexis."

"Well, what are you waiting for? You have to do that, get my dry cleaning, pick up those Jimmy Choos I have on hold at Fred Segal, and I need you to fill my Zantac prescription. God, you're useless!" she tells him, and he winces. "I should get rid of you too. All of you!" She points to the people milling around the stage.

"Don't you have an assistant to do those things?" The words escape my lips before I can stop them. No one talks to my Rodney like that. NO ONE.

"You again." She snaps and blows on her nails to dry them. "Where is my mineral water, *intern*? I need to be spritzed, like now."

I want to hurl the bottle at her, but I remain calm and spritz her face.

"Don't move more than two feet from me at all times," Alexis reminds me, waving her hands. "I will yell 'SPRITZ!' when I need you. Got it?"

"Got it," I mumble. I wish I could spritz her right out of here.

"It's three thirty, Alexis," a P.A. says quietly.

"SKY! SKY!" Alexis barks. "MELLI! WHERE ARE YOU? WHERE IS TOM! TOOOOMMM! GET DOWN HERE! I AM LEAVING AT FIVE THIRTY WHETHER THIS SCENE IS SHOT OR NOT!"

I almost drop my crutches when I see Melli and Tom come running from opposite directions. Tom is still portly, with thick black glasses and a chrome dome. He looks more haggard than I've ever seen him, and I've seen him really spent, like when we shot a live episode. Melli is still beautiful, with long black hair and the smallest waist you've ever seen, but she has black rings under her eyes that even the best concealer can't erase.

"Where were you?" Alexis questions them. "Didn't I say three fifteen?"

"I was trying to do homework with my son in the dressing room," Melli says stiffly. "I'd rather do it at home, but apparently I have no choice in the matter."

Alexis sighs. "I told you. I'm not having you killed off. My agent did the numbers, and the polls say they prefer Samantha to have a mom. Deal with it."

Melli looks like she is ready to reenact the scene where she tried to strangle our aunt Krystal before they both fell into a pool, fully dressed in evening gowns. Instead, Melli looks over at Tom, and he is scratching his head over and over, like he has a nervous tic. I can't believe what I'm seeing. What has Alexis done to this place? No wonder everyone hates being here. I hate being here, and I never thought I'd see the day when I felt like that.

"Where is Sky?" Alexis snarls, and no one answers.

"I think she's sleeping it off," someone says.

"That girl is a train wreck." Alexis rolls her eyes. "Wake her up and get her down here now."

It only takes a few minutes before someone practically carries Sky onto the soundstage. I say *carry* because it looks like she can barely walk on her own and ... holy hot mess!

Alexis is right: Sky is a train wreck! A complete train wreck! Her black hair is knotty, her tan skin is all sallow, and she has huge bags under her eyes. She's thinner than ever, and not in a good way. She looks like she could be snapped in two, and her fitted red minidress with a drawstring waist is sort of hanging off of her frame.

"Sky?" I put a hand on her. "Sky? Are you okay? What's wrong with her?" I ask the others frantically, but Sky waves me off, mumbling the word *fine* over and over again.

Alexis shrugs. "She's been out all night again. Big whoop. Give her a Red Bull. Make it two, and she'll be up and running. SKY!" she yells in her ear. "TIME TO WORK OR NO PREMIERE PARTY TONIGHT!"

Sky's eyes flutter wider. "I can't miss the premiere. I'm here!" She looks around. "Wherever here is." She frowns, and then it looks like a lightbulb goes on in her head. "Duh! This is work, right? What's my line?"

"Someone give Sky her line," Alexis tells the others as she checks her hair in the mirror a P.A. is holding. "I need her up and running for the *Mind over Matter* screening tonight. It's with Angie, Brad, and Jen, and it's only running for two weeks so I am not missing it. We need to film so Sky and I can jet."

Two-week screening. Yeah right. Especially if the world's most well-known love triangle is in it. HOLLYWOOD SECRET NUMBER THIRTEEN: Tinseltown is full of gimmicks because gimmicks bring in big money. One of their favorites: limited engagements. We're talking TV shows that only air for eight episodes before a long hiatus, or films that hit theaters for only two weeks. What's the point, you ask? To drive people to their TVs and to theaters so that they

237

don't miss out on this exclusive, once-in-a-lifetime chance to view history in the making! Of course, once a show or a movie does pull in the big bucks, the studio is likely to renege on their limited engagement deal. Look at Michael Jackson's *This Is It* or Miley Cyrus's *Hannah Montana* concert film. When ticket sales went through the roof—surprise, surprise—those films' theater runs were extended. In Hollywood, money is still the most coveted prize.

"SKY!" Alexis snaps her fingers, bangles tinkling viciously, when she sees Sky sink into the couch pillows and close her eyes. "Drink your Red Bull and let's go."

"Don't talk to her like that," Melli scolds, her dark eyes blazing. "It's your fault she looks like this. Dragging her out every night, insisting she go to every party on the planet to keep her job. If you had actual friends, Alexis, you wouldn't need to make Sky go everywhere."

Alexis wags her finger. "Watch your tone, Melli. I'd hate for the studio to hear you yelled at me."

"I'm tired of this." Melli freaks out. "One second you're threatening to keep me on, the next you're threatening to fire me. Look what's become of Sky. She can't even hold her head up!" Sky barely seems aware people are talking about her.

Alexis shrugs. "Some of us can't party as well as others. What can I tell you? I need her to go and stay at these things to make sure I'm well represented when I go home early and get my beauty rest. Right, Sky?"

"Right," Sky says, looking exhausted.

"Let's just shoot, shall we?" Tom's voice is strained.

Everyone walks onto the set and takes their positions. When Sky stands up and walks unsteadily to her mark, I think I'm going to burst into tears. Alexis is ruining everything I ever loved about being at *FA*! Alexis may be getting *FA* good ratings, but I see why the tabloids think the show is in trouble. No one wants to work with her. People look like Alexis is holding them hostage. It's enough to make me lose my lunch.

When I was on *FA*, everyone loved being there. *I* loved being there. And when it was over, I was sad for a long time. Probably too long. Instead of appreciating all the time I had on set, I've continued to long for more. I've compared everything I've ever done to *FA*. Doing that has kept me from moving on the way I should. Seeing what's happened here, I realize how keeping the show alive could have ruined *Family Affair*. We left on a high note. I never would have wanted to work at *FA* if it was like the one Alexis created. I want to throw down my mineral water spritzer and start screaming at this spoiled brat. I don't care about me anymore—I care about my *FA* family. Someone needs to put Alexis in her place and show her how a true Hollywood star behaves.

"I said, let's go!" Alexis insists, clapping her hands together loudly. "Snap snap! Taping time diminishing. HELLO, TOM? Can we start?"

I'm stewing, but I'm not going to open my mouth. I don't want to get thrown off the set. They need me here more than I realized. I look at the crew. No one will look at Alexis. They're glancing at the lights or the wires on the floor, or they're rolling their eyes at each other. Alexis has ruined all of them. I've never met an actress this selfish, and I've come across some doozies.

"AND ACTION!" Tom yells as he takes his seat behind a monitor and puts on his headset.

"It's not every day you make the honor society," Melli (aka Paige) says to Sky (aka Sara). Melli looks so calm and relaxed, in sharp contrast to her mood only seconds earlier. She has always had great composure, even in times of stress. "How you had time to study in between all your dates, I'll never know."

Sky laughs. "Some of those dates were with straight-A students, Mom. They were great study partners in more ways than one."

Wow, even dead tired, Sky is still good. I remember this scene well. When we shot it, it was for the girls' sophomore year, and the whole episode revolved around a cheating scandal at school.

"Great job, sis," Alexis says, sounding stilted. "Who knew you had it in, um, uh, you were, um . . . ARGH! LINE!"

I hear a few people groan.

How could Alexis have forgotten her line?

Tom reads from the script. "Alexis, it's: 'We knew you had it in you to prove you were more than just a cheerleader.'"

"I knew that," Alexis tells the crew, giving them the evil eye. "Roll again."

Alexis gets it that time, then gets stuck again two lines later.

"She's dreadful," I hear a P.A. next to me whisper to the person standing next to her. "Why does the public like her again?"

In between blowing lines, Alexis yells. She makes Sky feel smaller than she already is, insists Melli miss a call from her kid, and threatens firing Tom and half the crew. My nails dig into the mineral water spritzer. Alexis doesn't appreciate the success she's been given. A million girls would kill for her job, and here she is treating everyone like they're the gum on the bottom of her spiked heel. Alexis shouldn't have this role, this paycheck, or this fame. Whether this is the real world or not, someday karma will catch up with her. She won't have the career she has forever if she doesn't start appreciating it now.

The same goes for me.

I swear, if I can have my old Hollywood life back, I won't gripe about it anymore. No one wants to hear a celebrity complain about how hard her incredible life is. I'm going to be grateful for the good and the bad that comes along with having a career at the age of eighteen. My life is pretty darn fabulous, and the parts that need fixing? Well, I can fix them if I finally get up the guts to do it.

"Sam, what do you mean you saw Miss Carmichael changing answers on Lexie's test?" Melli asks.

It's my line—Alexis's line—and she's stuttering again.

"I was . . . I was standing . . . I, um, uh . . ."

Oh, enough of this!

I march onto the set, stick my crutch in front of Alexis to hold her back, and say the line the way it was meant to be said. Melli and Sky stare at me with wide eyes.

"I was standing in the doorway watching her, Mom," I tell them, fully feeling my former character's heartbreak. "She kept changing all of the answers from the wrong ones to the right ones. She gave her an A, when she should have gotten a D. I saw it with my own eyes, and yet I didn't do anything about it. I stood there and watched her, and I knew it was wrong. What do I do now, Mom? I can't live with myself if I let her get away with it."

There. Nailed it!

The whole set is quiet. *Stunned* would be a better word. I hear someone say, "She's good. A million times better than Alexis."

I can't help but grin, and I see Melli smirk. Then someone pushes me. Rodney reaches out to grab me, but Alexis knocks his arm out of the way.

"YOU." Alexis points a shaky finger at me. "How dare you? Grandstanding like that, trying to make me look like a fool . . . it's . . . it's . . ."

"You are a fool," Sky mumbles under her breath.

Alexis looks around the room crazily, and am I dreaming or do people seem to be enjoying this? "YOU ARE FIRED!" she yells at me, looking satisfied.

I spritz her face with the mineral spray, shooting the mist

hard so that it drenches her face and her makeup smears. Then I drop the bottle at her feet. "No, Alexis," I say calmly. "*You're* fired."

Alexis laughs and crosses her bony arms. "Never."

"Yes, as if." I grab my crutches. I start making my way through the crowd, and Rodney winks at me. "That's where you're wrong, Alexis." I smile with satisfaction. "You just don't know it yet."

Note to Self:
Appreciate what you have and stop griping about what you don't.
Meet Liz at 7 PM for premiere party at Boa.

fourteen: *Party Poopers*

I hear a knock on my bedroom door, and I remove my iPod earbuds. "Come in!"

Mom is standing in my doorway looking very grave. Even so, I have to resist the urge to burst out laughing. She's wearing a cook's apron. An apron! On the front it says "Irish Women Make the World's Best Cooks!"

Mom's one of the world's best cooks? God, if my real mom could see this, she would need an oxygen facial at Medi Spa for sure. Mom's holding two things: a wooden spoon in one hand and a piece of paper in the other. I can't see what's written on it, but it's typed and most of the lettering is in caps.

"Kaitlin, I was on the Food Network Web site to double-check the recipe for Rachael Ray's goulash, when I hit a button and this popped up on the screen." Her voice is sort of strained. "You know I'm not very tech savvy, but I believe this is yours."

"Thanks! You can leave it right there." I slide off my bed

and hobble to the closet on one foot. I can't stand using my crutches to walk just a few feet. I still need to find something in this closet that is right to wear to Boa Steakhouse tonight. They're hosting a movie premiere party for Tom Cruise's latest, and I'm going with Liz, who is going with Lauren and Ava.

Gag.

Just the thought of making small talk—not to mention butt-kissy small talk—with the gruesome twosome is enough to make me want to hurl my dinner from crafty. Even though Alexis banished me, the crew was so proud of me for standing up to her that they snuck me over to the craft services cart (Alexis never visits since she doesn't eat). It felt so good to have crafty on set today. It felt normal. Free-range chicken on a bed of greens with a side of gummy bears just can't be beat.

Liz says going out tonight will be even better. I doubt that, but I still have to go. Liz needs me there to help her realize Lauren and Ava aren't the perfect party wingmen. Liz can do it fine on her own without getting caught up in the fame and excess that have taken down so many before her. At least I hope so. Matty's already showing improvement. Yesterday I got him to wear jeans and a polo instead of a sweat suit to class, and I'm *thisclose* to getting him to join the winter formal committee. I told him it is much cooler than that lame online virtual prom he's been talking about.

Mom is still standing in the doorway, holding the paper and staring at me. "Are you okay?" I ask.

"Not really." She sits down on the edge of my bed and smooths the lumps in my comforter. This Mom is a mini Martha Stewart. She's always mopping the floors, dusting the furniture, and saying how a housekeeper is "so unnecessary." Anita, our real world housekeeper, would get a good laugh out of that one, but I actually think the change in Mom is nice. This Mom will actually stop what she's doing to help me with homework, watch a TV show with me, or be Matty's number two on a computer game she doesn't know how to play. She loves to go shopping, but she doesn't care what designer is on the label. She eats pizza without blotting the oil off the top. She doesn't mention celebrities in every other sentence. She insists on the family sitting down for dinner together every night (which I admit is pretty nice), and Dad is just as involved. The other day he asked me to meet him for dessert at work just so we could catch up. (He had to work late all week at the dealership.) I like spending time with all of them, even if I feel a little guilty. The truth is if my actual family life could be half as nice as this alternate one, I would really have it all.

Mom holds the paper out for me to take and looks at me sadly. "When did you write this?"

Uh-oh. Alter-Mom printed out my lame attempt at the stupid college admission essay, which starts off with the all-caps sentence "I HATE IT HERE!" From there I go on to say what a nightmare my life is. Oops. "I was upset about something at school when I wrote this."

Mom nods. "So I see." She looks down at the comforter

and traces her fingers along one of the flower designs. "I didn't realize we were making you so unhappy by sending you to Clark Hall, Kaitlin. I thought you could tell me anything, but you've kept your feelings about school and your family a secret." Her lower lip begins to quiver. "I know Dad and I don't do as well as Liz's dad and you wish you had her life, but I didn't know our non-celebrity lifestyle made you so miserable."

"It doesn't!" I don't know if I should hug her or stay where I am, pulling at the threads on a black sweater dress I just found buried in the back of alter-Kaitlin's closet. It has a cowl-neck collar and a cross knit at the waist, which is really flattering. If I pair this with my heeled boots, this could be a killer outfit.

"Apparently it does," Mom says softly. "You've been unhappy ever since you went to Clark Hall. I guess transferring you was a mistake. Clark Hall has made you feel like you deserve a different life. You've gone to all these parties with Liz and stayed out to all hours with people like Jay-Z and Rihanna. I should have realized that our little world wouldn't compare to what Hollywood has to offer."

I hang my head a bit, feeling guilty. Alter-Kaitlin sounds like she's been a troublemaker.

"But you know something, Kaitlin? I like our life," Mom tells me, her face brightening. "I have enough time for my work and for my family. I feel like I have some balance. So does your father. He loves working at that dealership, and someday he'll own one, I just know it. That's always been his dream."

My ears perk up. "I didn't know that."

Mom nods. "When I met him, that's the first thing he said to me." She chuckles. "He was so nervous he talked about cars the whole time! Can't get enough of them, which is why he's always saying all those weird mechanical expressions. I'm sure you find them dorky, but I've always loved that about him."

I have too, actually. My real dad seems so lost these days. He's got no job to speak of and Mom won't let him help run my career or Matty's. I bet he'd love to work at a dealership again, even if he was just the guy who greeted you at the door. Mom would never let it happen, though.

"But you, Kaitlin, I can't figure out." Mom rests a hand on her face. "We've always known you would do something great, but we wanted you to figure out what that was on your own, without any interference from us. You know I'm not the type of mom to pry or dictate."

Don't laugh. Don't laugh. Don't laugh.

"I want you to find yourself, but to be honest," she chokes up, "I don't know if I like who you've become."

"Mom." Ouch. That hurts. Even if this isn't me, I don't want to see her so disappointed. "That letter isn't real. I was just angry and blowing off steam. It's been a rough two weeks. And look," I point out, "at least I was starting a draft for a college admission essay."

Mom's eyes are teary. "So you do want to go to college?"

I think of my conversation with Ms. Jasons again and smile. "I think so."

Mom leans in, her green eyes full of newfound excitement. "That's good to hear. I think you'd love it." She sits on the edge of the bed. "Have you thought at all about where you might want to go?"

"Not really," I admit and walk toward her, still holding the black dress in my hands. I sit down next to her, hesitant to open up about something my real mom would frown on. "I looked at the USC application, and they have a lot of good programs. The campus looks pretty, in pictures at least."

"Maybe we should make an appointment to take a tour," Mom suggests, getting excited. "We could meet with an advisor too, and you could talk about majors. Or maybe we could find someone who goes to USC to sit down and talk to you about it?"

She's rattling off suggestions so quickly, I find my head growing heavy and my heart sort of anxious. It's too much at once. I've barely decided I want to squeeze college in. I don't need a weekend tour just yet. Still, I say out of habit, "Sure."

Mom gives me a look, and then her right eyebrow raises ever so slightly. Wow! Just like my mom's! "You're not ready for a whirlwind tour yet, are you?" I shake my head. "Then tell me that," she stresses, shaking my arms slightly as she reaches over to grab me and pull me closer. "I want you to be open with me, you know that." She hugs me tight, and I let her stroke my hair. It's very relaxing. "I'm sorry if I push too hard, Kaitlin. I just want what's best for you and Matty. I guess sometimes I forget that you guys have opinions and dreams of your own too." She laughs. "That's a mom for you. We never stop mothering."

Maybe that's the mistake my real mom has been making—smothering instead of mothering. She basically admitted that to me the night we were at the meeting with Seth and Laney. She wants what's best for me, but her idea of what's best and mine seem to be two different things.

What I want, I realize so strongly that I wish I could say it right now even though it wouldn't make sense, is my mom back. Someone else can run my career, but I want a mom who I can have this kind of conversation with.

"I like that you mother me." I mean that. I really do.

Mom and I sit just like that for a while, neither of us saying anything, until my phone rings, and I see it's Liz. She's waiting for me outside.

The whole car ride to the premiere I think about my conversation with Mom, and when I'm not thinking about that, I think about the fact that I'm minutes away from hanging out with Lauren and Ava. As much as I'd like to see this Tom Cruise movie I've never heard of (maybe it's an alter-Kaitlin-verse exclusive?), I could do without seeing LAVA. I wish I could just watch the Cruise flick at home in my comfy bed. Sometimes it pays to be as big and powerful as Tom Cruise or the president because then you can do just that.

HOLLYWOOD SECRET NUMBER FOURTEEN: There are only a few who can call up a studio head and tell them to send over a movie print that is currently in theaters or isn't even out yet. Think Cruise, Spielberg, Prince William, or the first lady. If you're going to all that trouble, you're probably not watching the movie on a flat-screen TV in your den. No, these folks have actual screening rooms in their houses with movie seats and large projectors. (Dad has always wanted one of those.) But like Cinderella at the stroke of midnight, a Hollywood screener must return to its rightful place (aka the studio). For repeat viewings, you'll have to get out a wig and dark sunglasses and go to the theater like everyone else.

"Isn't this exciting?" Liz asks as she grabs my arm and we whisk through the velvet rope into Boa Steakhouse in West Hollywood. "I hope Lauren and Ava saved us seats at their reserved table." She adjusts her funky purple headscarf. I convinced her to wear it with her new black Prada dress to add a splash of color. The real Liz would never settle for an all-black ensemble. "Do you think they remembered we were coming?" Liz frets. "I texted them three times today to say we were, but I never heard back."

"We don't need them to have a good time," I insist, taking a look around. I've only been to Boa Steakhouse once, for dinner with Seth, but the fare is what you'd expect from a big meat and potatoes place (with more unusual stuff like a Kobe beef corn dog thrown on the menu too). Boa is very feng shui—modern and sleek—with walls of marble and glass bricks, cylinder light fixtures, a steel floor-to-ceiling wine case, and bare tree branches dotting the landscape between the tables.

The crowd is just as cool as the digs. Everyone I know under twenty-five is here, including some of my real-life celeb friends like Gina. I can't help but say hi as she walks by, but she just smiles at me politely and keeps going.

"She had a huge fight with Ava a few weeks ago," Liz confides when Gina is out of earshot. "Remember when she got mad at Ava for hitting on Pierce? Ava said it's not like they're married or anything."

"How mad would you be if Ava hit on your boyfriend?" I ask.

She shrugs. "I guess I'd have to have one first."

"What about Josh, that cute guy at your kickboxing studio?" I hint hopefully. Liz's face instantly shuts me down.

"Josh? He's not going to help me get in anywhere!" She shakes her head, her gold hoop earrings shining in the light. "I need someone who can up my profile, not sink it. That's what Ava says."

I can't help but groan. "I told you! *We* don't need her. We can hang out at these things without getting obsessed with all the freebies and the wannabes."

I can tell she's only half listening to me as she scans the room. "Look! They've got a table over there."

"Let's get our own table," I beg, and Liz looks at me like I've hit my head again. "We can draw our own crowd! People will love us."

Liz drops her eyes and stares at her new snakeskin Gucci heels. "I heard about the studio thing today."

"You did?" My eyes widen. Oops.

"Daddy got a call," Liz says. "He's going to try to smooth things over. What were you thinking? We were this close to getting on Alexis's radar. Now we're going to be banned for life."

"So?" I huff. "We don't need people like Alexis or Lori Peters who think they're better than everyone else. If we get sucked into this world and do what everyone tells us to, we could wind up like . . . Sky Mackenzie." I wince at her name. "All this partying has pretty much ruined any chance she has of having a career after *Family Affair*."

Liz rolls her eyes. "Now you sound like my dad! What's so wrong with fitting in? Look at this crowd!" Liz says, scanning the room of beautifully clad people, each more wisp-thin than the next. "They have it all! Is it so wrong to want what they have? You seemed to agree with me a few weeks ago, but ever since that accident, you've become holier-than-thou, preaching about morals and what losers our Hollywood friends are." She puts her hands over her ears. "I can't stand it!"

I'm so shocked by her outburst, I don't know what to say. Thankfully a waitress walks over with a tray of drinks and offers us some pink nonalcoholic smoothie they've named the Smooth Cruise Control, which has mango and papaya juice. I take one and play with the funky purple straw, swirling the ice crystals around and around. The two of us just stare at each other, and I blink rapidly to avoid crying.

"I'm sorry," Liz says flatly, not looking at me. "I shouldn't have freaked out on you. It's just . . . you've been acting so weird."

"I know," I say, my voice hoarse.

"I want the old Kaitlin back," Liz adds.

"Me too," I say. I think we're both thinking of different Kaitlins, but no matter.

Okay, I'm going to cry now.

"Maybe we should take five," Liz suggests before storming off. "Since you want your own reserved table, take this one. I'm going to go say hi to the girls—and I don't want a lecture because I'm doing it." She's got my Liz's fire, all right, but she's using it in all the wrong places.

I stand there, thinking away the tears that I know are seconds from dropping. I can't live in a world where my best friend thinks I'm a nightmare, or where Sky looks the way Sky does. I can't be someplace where a person as awful as Alexis Holden controls a whole studio of good, decent people that I love. I can't live with this Austin. I know I'm trying to make things right, but the more time I spend here, the less sure I feel about anything.

"Kaitlin?" I look up. Austin is right in front of me wearing a rumpled blue dress shirt untucked with brown cords. "You okay?"

"What are you doing here?" I whisper, wiping my eyes. God, I hope he didn't see me crying.

Austin gives me a strange look. "Uh . . . you invited us? Me and Lori." I must look confused because he rambles on. "Lori said you wanted to apologize for the accident and for giving her the impression you liked me when you don't." He says the last part in a weird voice and then takes a seat across from me. "Is that the truth? What was all that stuff you said in the car the other day, then? Were you just laying it on thick to get a ride to Burbank?"

"No," I fumble, getting more upset. "I do care." I hesitate. "It's just . . . it's complicated."

Austin runs his hand through his hair. "You're so hot and cold. One minute I think you want to be with me, the next you're telling Lori you can't stand me."

"I never said that," I insist. "And so what if I do want to be with you? You're with Lori. You're not ready to make that stand. You've made that clear."

Austin leans in close and ignores the question. "One second I think we can be friends, the next you're calling my girlfriend behind my back. Why would you want to smooth things over with someone you can't stand?" Austin's blue eyes widen. "Unless you're just playing me to rise up the popularity ladder yourself."

"Liz must have set this up!" I tell him, and the tears start flowing. "I didn't even know you and Lori were coming! This has nothing to do with me."

"Sure." He shakes his head. "Maybe I was wrong about you. You are just like the others. See you around, Kaitlin." When he gets up and turns around, he bumps right into Lori. She takes one look at my tear-stricken face and then at Austin's angry one, and she erupts.

"What's this?" Lori asks, folding her arms. Her glossy

blond hair is big and curly, and she's wearing a lilac dress from the new Marc Jacobs collection. She looks perfect. Sigh.

"It's nothing," Austin mumbles. "Let's get out of here. I don't want an apology from her. I wouldn't believe it."

"Well, I want one." Lori's eyes narrow. "And a promise that you'll stay out of my boyfriend's way. If you see him in the hall, walk the other way. If you get assigned as his partner in science lab, come up with a fabulous excuse to get out of it. I don't want you breathing the same air as him, got it?"

"Lori," Austin starts to say, looking taken aback.

"What, Austin?" I ask, holding my chin up high. "Do you actually have your own opinion you want to contribute to the conversation? I'm all ears!"

"What is she yapping about?" Lori asks.

"Nothing." Austin grabs her arm, pulling her away from me. "Come on, Lori, let's get something to eat."

Suddenly I have the urge to scream so loud that the DJ would stop spinning. Liz, Austin . . . this isn't going as well as I thought it would. Everyone around me is laughing and eating finger food and having a good time. Everyone but me.

"HOW DARE YOU TALK TO MY CLIENT WITHOUT CONSULTING ME FIRST!"

Hey, I know that voice!

"NEXT TIME YOU PULL A STUNT LIKE THAT, I'LL CALL PAGE SIX AND HAVE YOU CANNED SO FAST YOU WON'T EVEN HAVE TIME TO TAKE A NUMBER-TWO PENCIL WITH YOU!"

It's Laney! She's sitting alone at a booth two feet away from me. Her plate is empty, and she has a tall clear drink in front of her, but as usual, her pleasure comes from berating someone via cell phone. She looks exactly the same—pin-straight blond hair, lithe body, great clothes, and two Bluetooths glued to her ears. I'm so excited, I could race over and hug her. But I don't. I bet this Laney doesn't like hugs either. Instead, I listen to her continue to yell at someone. It's like music to my ears. Laney is exactly the same in alter-Kaitlin-verse. So far she's the only one.

I must be staring at her for a while because she looks up and gives me an appraising look. "Reese's party, right? You won the Guitar Hero contest?"

Eee! Laney is talking to me! "I don't think so."

"I must know you from someplace." She pulls the Bluetooths off her ears like diamonds and drops them in the oversized bag sitting next to her. She's wearing a white wrap sweater and wide-leg black trousers with very high heels. She pats the seat next to her. "Are you an actress?"

"No." Ouch. That hurt. I sit down next to her. "My name is Kaitlin Burke. I'm here with a few friends, but I've, um, never acted before. Although I think I could do better than Shayla Stevens." God, I hope Laney doesn't represent her.

She groans at the mention of Tom Cruise's costar in the movie tonight. "Wasn't she the worst? I know they like to pair Tommy with beautiful unknowns, but they couldn't have found someone who could at least enunciate clearly?"

"It's not like the lines were that complicated. How hard is it? 'Quick! They're on to us!'" I use a thick Russian accent, better than the one Shayla used, and look around frantically, bobbing and weaving my head as if bad guys are behind every table. "We need to find a safe haven until this smoke clears. If we don't, I don't think we'll be around to do the second circus performance tomorrow."

I miss acting. A lot.

"Impressive." Laney appraises me. "That was very good. You're also much prettier than Shayla. You have great bone structure, wonderful skin, and your tone is wonderful. Great name too."

"Thanks," I say, happy to bask in Laney's glow. "Are you a casting agent?" This is fun!

Laney perks up. "God, no! I'm a publicist, and I have a lot of clients here tonight. Tommy is my boy. Did you like the film?"

I hesitate. "Yes." It was okay, I guess, but Cruise playing a circus clown? I don't see it.

"But?" Laney presses. She can read a person like a book.

What the heck. It's not like I'll ever see her again. "I liked the premise, but I thought Tom was too big a star to play a circus freak. The whole story would have worked if he did something different, like own a Disney-esque amusement park instead of a circus company. And Hulk Hogan as the bearded lady?" I shake my head. "Gerard Butler wasn't available? He would have been perfect."

"That's what I thought!" Laney is flabbergasted. She takes

a sip from her drink. "I pushed for Angelina in this thing too."

I nod. "She would have been better in Shayla's role. Someone Shayla's age would have made an awesome sidekick, but I didn't think the star tightrope walker was her thing."

"I agree," Laney whispers. "You sure you aren't in the business? I could swear I've seen you in a Tide commercial."

I've been in several, but I can't say that. "I pay attention to the trades and casting news. *Variety* is bedtime reading."

"Smart girl." Laney raps her long, dark red fingernails on the glass table. "You and I should take a meeting. You don't have representation, do you?" She looks at me smartly. Laney hates liars.

Alter-Kaitlin taking a meeting? God, if I could act while I was here, it would be better than finding my way to a nearby Sprinkles for a dozen cupcakes. "No," I say, trying to hide my excitement. "Do you have a card?"

Laney pulls one out of a sleek black holder. In the real world, she has a Louis Vuitton one that I got her for her birthday. "Give me your info too," she says as her Bluetooths start beeping again. I scribble it down on a piece of paper she hands me. "I'll call you tomorrow. Have you ever eaten at STK? I'll take you there this week. I want to introduce you to a few agents that would go gaga for you. Trust me."

I love STK! Laney and I go there on the down-low without Mom. Mom never lets me order anything fried, but

Laney does. She says I have a good metabolism. "Okay," I agree.

Alter-Kaitlin has a meeting! Alter-Kaitlin could have a publicist! Alter-Kaitlin could even get an agent!

I'm in such a good mood, I say good-bye to Laney and decide to look for Liz to smooth things over.

I find her on the other side of the restaurant, holding court with Austin, Lori, Ava, and Lauren. Ava is wearing pink satin and petting Calou, her puffball of a tiny dog, who is wearing a matching pink satin top. Ava's blond hair is pulled back, and curls bounce around as she laughs. Lauren's brown hair is done the same way. She's wearing a Versace jumper that, if Alter-LAVA is anything like the one back in the real world, I'm sure was stolen. Both of them have a shoplifting habit, even though they can easily afford their threads. The girls are hanging on Liz's every word, and she's too engrossed in storytelling to realize I'm a few feet away. I guess it is crowded and dark enough not to notice one more person loitering nearby.

"Call the psych ward, stat, because Kaitlin needs to be committed," I hear Liz say, and I stop short. "She must have really hit her head in that accident because ever since then she thinks she's Mother Teresa." Liz pretends to pray. "I have to right my friend's wrongs."

"Hysterical!" Ava laughs, and Calou barks in agreement. She feeds him a tiny filet mignon on a piece of toasted bread. "Seriously, Lizzie, why do you even chill with her? I knew she was no fun."

"No, I mean, Kaitlin is fun, or at least she was." Liz fiddles with her hoop earrings almost as if she's in a trance. "Whenever we used to go to these things, she always chatted up the hottest star in the room. She's so charismatic. Maybe that's why I've overlooked this ridiculous makeover campaign she seems to be on."

"You could so do better," Lauren adds.

"I've never liked her," pipes up Lori, who looks thrilled to be surrounded by D-listers. "She's always stalking my boyfriend. It is so creepy."

"She's not creepy. You just don't know her," Austin surprises me by saying. They all look at him, and he glances down at the table and plays with a chicken kebob he hasn't eaten. "Go easy on Kaitlin. She's had a rough few weeks."

"Go easy on her? Look what she's done to you!" Lori hisses and her head whips around so fast, her curled hair looks like Medusa's snakes. "Listen, Liz, I know it was you who invited us, not Kaitlin. Still, no can do with the apology thing. Your girl is cuckoo. I think I want to look into getting a restraining order for A."

Ava snorts and grabs another pink drink from a passing waitress, who stops short to avoid toppling her tray. "Sweetie, so easy to get. I have several myself."

"You mean you have several *against* you," Lauren clarifies. She sucks in her already tight stomach when a hot guy walks by but deflates quickly when he doesn't give her a second look. "Not the same thing."

"Maybe I need a restraining order," says Liz as she

munches on a small crab cake. "We've been friends all year, so I feel like I should help her, but now I don't know."

"You're such a generous soul," empathizes Ava, and she feeds Calou a cucumber roll from her plate.

"The last thing I need is to wind up on crutches like you, Austin," Liz adds, as she looks from Ava to Lauren for approval. "Who knows who Kaitlin will run down next?"

They're all so busy laughing, I don't think they see me stomp over to the edge of their table and toss the remains of my smoothie at them full speed. It sprays out, hitting Liz, Lauren, and Ava the most. I can't help but be the one to laugh now. I'm not the only one; Austin's mouth looks like it's twitching when Lori starts to sob into his shoulder about the pink goop in her hair.

Ava is the first to shriek, and Liz's eyes widen in horror when she realizes who's responsible for the attack. "You little freak!" Ava wipes the thick, pink goop from her eyes. "Laur, get her tossed from the party. Get security!"

"Don't bother!" I snap. "I'm leaving."

Liz is pale. She grabs my hand. "Kaitlin, I . . ."

"Liz," Ava says sternly as a waiter hands her and Lauren white cloth napkins to dab their clothes with.

"Forget it," I tell Liz and drop her hand. She looks away in embarrassment. "To think I thought you were my friend. And these two D-listers you so desperately want to impress?" I point to Lauren and Ava. "You don't realize you're heads above them. They know it, or they wouldn't be hanging out with you."

"That's ridiculous," Ava says quickly, side-eyeing security as they approach.

"Kaitlin, I'm sorry," Liz starts.

"Don't be. You think I've changed?" I question. "*You've* changed. The Liz I know is smart, sassy, and cares more about her friends than she does an invite list." I start to choke up. "She doesn't make herself fit into this perfect little box to impress others. She stands up for herself, and that's exactly what I'm going to do now. I'm out of here."

Austin calls my name, but I don't look back. Security is standing guard with a smoothie-spattered Lauren, whose Versace jumper looks almost tie-died with the smoothie clinging to the Lycra material. I feel so satisfied with myself that I storm right past them and head for the exit.

If there is anything I could leave in this alternate universe I'm trapped in, it would be Lauren and Ava. But I won't let them hurt me—not here, not in the real world—and I won't let them hurt my friends either. It's time I take control of my real life. It's not going to be easy, but I'm ready to fight for the things I love, like the right acting projects. And to refuse the things I don't (losing my mom just to have a manager). I need to be the one in the driver's seat. Nadine was right, just like she always is.

Nadine.

NADINE!

OF COURSE!

If anyone could get me out of here, it would be alter-Nadine.

I hike my sparkly red bag onto my shoulder and push through the crowd of onlookers. Liz tries to pull me back.

"Can't we talk? Please? Where are you going?"

"Harvard." I squeeze toward the doors and head to valet, hoping they can call me a cab. As angry as I was a few minutes ago, I'm smiling now. I know what I want, and I know how to get it back. Nadine can fix this. She can fix anything. I just have to track her down, and I think I know exactly where to look.

Note to Self:
Find out cost of ticket to Boston.
Get spending money.
Leave town. Immediately.

FIFTeen: *Boston or Bust*

I find a pink duffel bag in the back of alter-Kaitlin's closet, and I stuff it with a bunch of clothes, some one-hundred-calorie snacks, and the eighty dollars I found in the badly painted piggy bank on my dresser. I lug it down to Matty's room and knock on the door.

I hear two locks turn—who needs double locks on their bedroom door?—before Matty appears in the doorway looking rumpled. His blond hair stands up on end, he's wearing a baggy LEGO *Star Wars* tee and wind pants, and he has on wire-rim glasses. "What do you want?" he huffs. "I'm in the middle of a crucial battle scene in *Hero War Battle of the Titans*, and if I step away from the computer for more than fifteen seconds, Daryl from Cleveland might win."

"I'm sorry to bother you, Matty. I need your help."

"I told you—it's *Matthew*," he corrects me. "Since when does anyone call me Matty? I'm not two."

He has a point. The real Matty thinks the nickname sounds "hip." "I'm sorry, *Matthew*. I'll be quick." My eyes dart around the dark, messy room. The shades are drawn, his bed is unmade, and there are constellation maps on the walls and a picture of Albert Einstein. This kid should have "desperately seeking friends" stamped on his forehead. "Can I borrow some money?"

He views me skeptically. "So you and Liz can hit some party and not invite me? No way." He starts to shut his door.

I put my hand up to keep the door from closing. "I'm not going out with Liz. This is something for me."

"What are you buying?" he asks suspiciously.

"I can't say." If I tell Matty where I'm going, he'll probably crack under pressure when Mom and Dad come looking, and then he'll be in trouble right along with me. I can't have that.

He scratches his head. His blond hair is in serious need of some styling. It's way too long on the sides and too short on top. "I'll bite. How much do you need?"

Umm . . . how do I say this without sounding suspicious? "Eight hundred dollars."

I checked the flights going out of LAX to Boston, and a last-minute ticket to Boston is around six hundred dollars. Then I need cab and T (subway) fare, and some money to crash at a bad hotel. Even eight hundred is going to be stretching it, but how much can I ask for?

Matty laughs at me. Even his laugh is different. He sounds like a hyena. "Sure, let me just get that money out of my vault." He gives me a withering look with our similar green eyes. "What do you need all that money for anyway?"

266

"I told you. I can't say."

"Then I can't help you." He starts to close the door again, but I stick my hand up to stop him. The door bounces against my flat palm, flies backward, and almost hits him in the face.

"It's an emergency!" I sound desperate, I know. "This money could be life-changing for all of us."

"Are you going to Vegas?" Matty asks, horrified. "You're underage!"

"I'm not going to Vegas." I cross my arms and try to keep my good foot from tapping nervously. "It's nothing illegal."

He mulls the proposition over. "Changing my life sounds good to me, but I don't have that much cash. I can give you something, though. Close your eyes." I start to protest. "Just do it. No peeking!"

I hear him poke around the room, a key turn, something slam shut, and then I feel money in my hand. I look down and see he's handed me a hundred-dollar bill. It's a start.

I grab his thin frame (no muscles on this Matty) and hug him. "Thanks, *Matthew*. You have no idea how important this trip is. Wish me luck, okay?" I pause. "And stall Mom and Dad, for at least the next several hours. Just say I'm out with Liz or at a study group." He starts to laugh. "Okay, say I'm at a pep rally."

Matty grins. "That will work." Then his face clouds over with worry. "Are you coming back?"

Er . . . sort of? "Yes. I just might be gone overnight. Or two." Matty's eyes widen. "You have to trust me."

"I do trust you. This you, not the one before the accident," he clarifies and fiddles with the key still in his hand.

I put the money in my red bag and look at him. "What do you mean?"

"You're nicer, that's all. And a little wacky." He shrugs and scuffs his foot on the brown carpeting. "That's okay, though. It's fun to watch. I'll cover for you today, if you cover for me sometimes." His computer screen IM pings madly. He stares back at the laptop. "If I ever have someplace decent to go in the real world."

Aww ... I grab his chin and stare into his eyes. "You'll have plenty of places to go in the real world, I promise. You just don't realize it yet, but you're going to be fine, Matthew Burke. And more popular than you can ever imagine. I love you for it, even if you do drive me crazy sometimes." Matt blushes. "Can you do me one more favor?"

"Another one?" he asks incredulously.

"This one is easy. Tell Mom and Dad I love them."

Because I do. I really do. This Mom and Dad are so ... what's the word I'm looking for?

Happy.

They're happy to be with us and be part of our lives, and they worship each other rather than the scene around them. Maybe it's living in Toluca Lake, or the fact that neither work in the industry, but they're not consumed by Hollywood, and that's a good thing. Dad needs to go back to working with cars. And Mom, well, I want a *mom* back. And when I get home, I have to figure out a way to make that happen.

Matt's quiet. "You're not coming back, are you?"

I mess up his hair some more. "You'll see me again. I promise."

"Do you want to see the flowers that just came for you before you go?" Matty asks and skirts past me into the hall-way. Sitting on our black hall table is the most beautiful arrangement overflowing with peonies and sunflowers.

"They're gorgeous!" I thumb one of the sunflowers care-fully. "Who are they from?"

"Who do you think?" Matty says wryly. "Mom's bestie, Victoria Beckham."

I turn around so fast that I pull a sunflower out of the vase. "What did you just say?"

Matty looks at me strangely. "I said look at the card."

"No you didn't, you said *Victoria Beckham*," I insist and start fingering through the arrangement, looking for the card.

"You're getting weird again," Matty warns just as I find what I'm looking for. The card is from Liz, not Victoria.

I'm more sorry than you can ever imagine.
   —Liz

"I must be hearing things."

"Doesn't seem that unusual these days," Matty tells me.

I hug him one more time, pick up my bag, and walk downstairs, taking a last look around before I go. Then I walk outside to a waiting cab and get in. I look back at the pretty yellow colonial with the maroon shutters, and I pray

I'm seeing it for the last time, no matter how homey the house and the family inside really is.

* * *

An hour later, I'm at LAX and I have one hundred and ten dollars in my pocket. It cost me seventy dollars to get here! Geez, cabs in Los Angeles are expensive. Now what do I do? There is no emergency credit card in my wallet—Allison and Beth seem to have those, but I do not—and I need money. Fast. Even if I got hired at the local airport hamburger joint (and I can't stand the smell of microwaved meat), it would take me weeks to make that cash.

"Kaitlin?" I turn around. "IT IS HER!"

Liz comes flying toward me, and she's got . . . no. It can't be. Is that Austin?

Liz throws herself at me. "Thank God we found you!" she gushes, and I catch a whiff of her lilac body mist. I see some people on the check-in line smile, thinking we're having some long-overdue reunion. "I knew you'd be here. I said you'd never wait around. You get something in your head, and you have to do it right away." She looks at me with her dark eyes, hopeful. "At least the old you did."

I push her off. I'm still mad. New Liz, old Liz, whoever she is, it doesn't matter. She's not my friend. "What are you guys doing here?" I hold the duffel tightly and push the red sparkled purse deeper inside. I don't want them seeing my notebook. I have tons of notes about where Nadine could

270

be, things she's said to me over the years about Boston and where she'd go if she lived there. I'm going to cover every lead I can. If I actually get there.

"We're here to help you," Austin says and smiles that smile that always makes me melt. God, he looks good today. He's wearing a zip-up navy-and-green sweater over a white tee, and he has on distressed jeans. Even his cast matches his outfit. Oooh, must concentrate. Alter-crush and friend are bad. Real boyfriend and girlfriend are good!

"I don't need help." I walk toward the nearest ticket counter, pushing my duffel with one of my crutches. I don't actually have the money to buy a ticket. I guess I'll just pretend and eventually they'll walk away.

"Yes, you do!" Liz insists, folding her arms across her chest and sending several gold bracelets on her arm into a landslide toward her wrists. She stares at me, determined, her face as dark as her purple Rebecca Taylor top. She has a funky plaid scarf wrapped around her neck, and she's wearing skinny J Brand jeans with . . . are those the Jimmy Choo boots we bought a few weeks ago? Liz and I have been eyeing them for ages, and Mom finally gave me permission to buy a pair. We had them on hold at Fred Segal forever (not that they hold merchandise usually, but I asked very nicely).

"Where did you get those?" I point to her shiny black feet.

"At Fred Segal, with you, a few weeks ago. We both got a pair." Liz taps her toes happily. "Don't you remember? We had them on hold forever and the guy was like, 'Are you taking them or not?' but you didn't have permission from your mom to get a pair because you still owe her money, and then finally she said yes."

But that doesn't make any sense! Alter-Kaitlin wouldn't have money to buy those. "I don't have those boots in my closet."

"Yes, you do."

I shake my head impatiently. "I don't." If I did, I'd be wearing them right now. "How would I have the money for those?"

Liz and Austin look at each other. "Forget it," Liz says. "It doesn't matter. What matters is we're here to help you get to Boston. That is where you're going, right? When you said Harvard I figured you were heading to Massachusetts. Either that or there was a hot new club in L.A. called Harvard that I didn't know about . . . and I know about all the new hangouts in town." She raises an eyebrow. "I won't ask why you're going to Massachusetts. I just want to help."

The line inches forward. "I don't need your help," I say stubbornly. "Why are you here anyway? You're not my friends. I heard what you said at the party, Liz. Don't even try to deny it. And you." I point to Austin. "I'm sure Lori doesn't know you're here. That would put you on the Tipster List right alongside me."

Austin's blue eyes lock on mine. "Actually, she does know," he says, and I try to resist the urge to gape at him. "I told her that you and I were friends—or maybe more than that, I don't know." My face starts to flush. "I told her where I was going, and I said I wanted to be there for you, for once, the way you've tried to be there for me." He grins. "Not counting the time you tried to run me over with a car."

Does he have to keep bringing that up? "You really told her that?"

Austin nods. "I did." The two of us stare at each other.

"I told Lauren and Ava I wasn't going out tonight or the next night or all weekend," Liz adds. "They weren't happy, but I don't need to be their plus one. I have my own invites." She sighs. "Besides, you were right—they're not so great. After you left I started listening to them talk, and I never noticed what airheads they are! Or how obnoxious! I don't want to be like that, even if I have been lately." She grabs my hand. "Can you forgive me?"

I squeeze her hand and feel the multitude of rings on her fingers. Just like real Liz. How can I say no? "Yes."

So that's it, then. Liz and Austin are changing, I have a meeting with Laney Peters, I told off Alexis Holden, I had a heart-to-heart with my mom for the first time in forever, and Matty is finally coming out of his room. I've started to fix this universe and make it feel more like my own.

But I don't want to make it my own. Even if I have ten meetings with Laney and I get Austin to ask me out, this still isn't my life. I miss acting, and my friends, and even my zany schedule. I wish I could take pieces of this life back with me—my family time, my downtime—and make it work in my world. But even if I can't, I'm ready to go home.

Liz looks relieved. "Good. So that's it, then. We can go home. You don't need to go to Boston now, do you?"

Uh ... "I'm glad we made up, but I still have to go to Boston."

"But why?" Liz whines.

"I feel it in my gut." I pat my belly, hidden beneath the two sweaters I have on—one a sage green turtleneck, the other a thick, chocolate button-up. I'm wearing skinny jeans and the cutest navy wellies I found in my shoe rack. Hey, it's cold and snowy in Boston! Even if people are looking at me oddly in the airport, it will work where I'm headed.

"That's not an answer," Liz says, sounding more like the Liz I know. "What's the real reason you're going there?"

"I ..." I look at their curious faces. I can't tell them the truth. They'd never believe me. Sometimes I don't believe it myself. And if Nadine can't get me home, I don't want to come back to Los Angeles and have everyone here think I belong in a box of my favorite cereal, Froot Loops. "I'm visiting a friend, and I need to get there right away," I explain. "I think she can help me figure some things out."

"Next! Counter five!" A Delta attendant standing at the front of the line makes crazy arm motions, pointing to the next available attendant. Austin grabs my duffel bag from the floor, and Liz walks alongside me as I make my way to the attendant. It really is helpful having someone with you when you're traveling on crutches.

"Can I help you?" the tall, dark-haired woman behind the counter asks me.

"Yes, I need a ticket to Boston for today," I say clearly, and try not to side-eye Liz and Austin.

"I have a flight leaving in an hour. The ticket costs six hundred and eighty-four dollars."

Um . . . do you think she'd settle for one hundred and ten instead?

"Kate, what are you doing?" Liz shakes my arm, which is sweaty, thanks to the double sweaters. "You don't have that kind of money!"

"You just said I had the money to buy Jimmy Choos," I counter.

"You don't own Jimmy Choos." She sounds puzzled. "Are you talking about liking mine?" She looks down and poses. "They are pretty snazzy, aren't they?"

But she just said . . . I am so confused!

"Miss? Do you want the ticket?" The attendant is starting to get impatient.

Liz slaps down her American Express card. "She wants the ticket. She wants three tickets."

The attendant goes to take the card, and I swipe it from her.

"No," I say and hold the Amex above my head. "You are not buying my ticket! And you guys aren't coming with me. I have to do this alone."

Liz's shoulders drop. "But why? Why can't we come?"

"Because you don't really want to, you just think it's the right thing to do."

"I do want to." Liz stares at me earnestly, and for a moment I feel like all the sounds of the airport have been sucked out. "I want to make things right between us, Kaitlin. We're best friends, or at least we were before all this Hollywood stuff came between us. I can be a good friend if you let me."

"Let her pay," Austin urges. "Aren't you the one who is always saying how important it is for friends to help each other?"

"You know you need help," Liz says confidently. "You're just stubborn! I know you don't have the money to buy that ticket. Or the money to get around town. Let's face it." She grins mischievously. "Like it or not, you need my plastic."

I just realized who this Liz reminds me of: Sky. My Sky. And my Sky, as grating as she can be, is usually right.

"What do you say, Kaitlin?" Austin encourages me.

The four of us (the fourth being the attendant) are momentarily distracted by yelling and an annoying clicking sound that has taken over the departures area. Alexis and her entourage are heading toward the security area. The paparazzi are hot on her trail, which seems to annoy her to no end. That's probably because she has bed head and is wearing a velour tracksuit. Hee hee. It's tough to hide from the paparazzi, even if you do have a disguise. Most stars don't even bother with one. The paparazzi will figure out it's you anyway.

HOLLYWOOD SECRET NUMBER FIFTEEN: It's not easy to evade the paparazzi when you're white-hot. And white-hot is what the paparazzi want. If your name is Robert or Kristen and you've been in a little film called *Eclipse*, then good luck. I can't help you. My best advice would be to act annoying and hire a P.U.H. (personal umbrella holder). A P.U.H. can keep the paparazzi from getting a clear shot. The other choices you have are tougher: You need to act boring. Be in a long-term marriage, move to Texas, stay away from scandal. Or drop out of the public eye completely. If not, you're fair game, and quite frankly, what are you whining about? You've got money, fame, and the world at your feet. Get over yourself.

Hmm. Where did that come from? That sounds like something Nadine would say to me when I border on bratty celebrity territory. And she's right. Right now, I'd kill to have the paparazzi trailing me.

"I do need you," I admit to Liz. I try not to let my mouth twitch into a smile. Two heads are better than one, and if I'm being honest with myself, I don't want to do this alone. I'm scared. If I make it to Boston and I don't find Nadine, or I do find Nadine and she won't help me, then what do I do?

I don't even want to think about that.

I look at Austin. "Are you coming too?" Part of me wants him to. I always want him there. Even though he's not who I want him to be. Just being near an Austin of any kind is intoxicating. It could also be distracting.

Austin shakes his head. "I can't miss class. I want to get those grades up. Try to get into a better school. Maybe even one in Boston?" He winks at me. "I think you two have this covered. I just wanted to make sure you were okay. I'll see you when you get back." He touches my shoulder. "Good luck, Kaitlin." He disappears into the busy airport crowd while Liz pays for our tickets.

I hear the attendant asking for my photo ID and whether we have any bags to check, but I'm not paying attention. I drop my red bag and zip through the crowd on one crutch, calling Austin's name. When he turns around, I plow right into him. I wrap my arms around his neck, lean up on my good toes, and kiss him before he can even react, sending all our crutches clattering to the floor.

"For good luck," I say.

And to kiss him one last time, in case the next time never comes.

"Good luck," he says softly. "I hope you find what you're looking for."

"Me too." I unwind myself, feeling sort of sheepish as I lean over to pick up his crutches for him, and then back away slowly, afraid to turn around and for him to be gone. Who knows who I'll be seeing next time—my Austin, or this one, or no Austin.

I'm starting to get a headache.

"Kaitlin!" Liz is yelling and jumping up and down at the counter. The attendant looks peeved. "We need your ID. NOW!"

I hobble over and don't look back.

Even if I want to.

sixteen: *The Magic Maker*

I was too tired to look at my watch to see what time we landed at Logan International Airport in Boston. All I know is it was late. Too late to check into a nice hotel like a Westin. We stayed at the airport motel, paid cash, and shut our phones off because they were ringing nonstop. Liz said she was extremely achy from flying coach, but she thought if she bought two first-class tickets her dad might have flown to Boston and escorted her home personally. I hit the pillow so hard I could have gotten a concussion, and before I knew it, the sun was up, Liz was pulling on a North Face jacket and me a Gap parka, and we were walking to the T to take the ride to Cambridge. Harvard is smack in the middle of beautiful, brick-lined streets and historic buildings, and Nadine is hopefully there too.

We just needed to find someone who would tell us for sure.

We spent two hours at the Harvard registrar's office trying to convince them to tell us whether Nadine was registered there, but even with my best acting skills, I couldn't get the girl behind the counter to open up. (Apparently it's against the rules to give nonstudents information about actual students.) Liz tried to pay a student to find out for us, but he said it was unethical. Do all these Harvard types have to be future politicians?

Finally Liz was able to bribe a cute guy in a navy peacoat and a striped beanie cap to check Nadine's registration. "There's no one by the name of Nadine Holbrook registered at Harvard—past or present," he told us, covering his mouth with his coat to fight the cold.

"Did you check undergrad?" I questioned, wiggling to get warm. It had to be twenty degrees here, and I could see my breath as I talked. The sky was gray and sort of gloomy, which was just how I was starting to feel. "What about part-time? Future registrants? She has to be here! I know she is!"

"Thank you," Liz said and dragged me away before I could cause a scene. The last thing we needed was the cops wondering why two eighteen-year-old high school girls were this far from home alone the week before Christmas.

"How do you know your friend Nadine goes to Harvard?" Liz asks me a short time later as we sip mocha lattes in Peet's Coffee & Tea in Harvard Square. I remembered Nadine telling me about liking this place when she came to Boston to check out the campus.

At least the real Nadine came here. But what if I'm wrong about this Nadine? What if she's not in Boston? What if she's still in Chicago, or her family moved? What if she doesn't exist at all? My mind is spinning, my hands are cold from being outside for so long, and my heart is beating out of my chest.

If Nadine doesn't exist, what does that say about my other life? Does that mean it doesn't exist either? How could I have made all that stuff up?

Celebs lie all the time, I know, but no one makes up a lie this big. This is a Madonna-level lie. You've heard of a Madonna-level lie, right? HOLLYWOOD SECRET NUMBER SIXTEEN: Stars lie. It's a plain and simple fact. We do. Just like you. And there are many reasons for it, especially if you're Madonna. She told the press she was not getting married to Guy Ritchie. Then she hopped on a plane to go marry him (not that the marriage lasted, but still). A secret wedding you can kind of understand. Getting drunk—or worse—and appearing on a talk show, and then totally denying it like so many stars I know have done? Not really understandable. Own up to your mistakes, I say. But stars won't. Many think they're the victims in this tabloid-loving world. They feel like they give their all to their careers and that some part of their life should still be private. I'm all for it, I just don't know if it's possible.

"Kates?" Liz butts into my thoughts. "Did you hear what I said? When was the last time you talked to Nadine? Are you sure she's still in Cambridge?"

"I heard you." I'm feeling too blue to actually make conversation or give her an answer. I couldn't have made my whole fabulous Hollywood life up.

Could I?

"What if she went home for Christmas break?" Liz blows a chunk of whipped cream off the top of her confection. "It is just a week away."

Bah! Humbug!

"Yes," I snap, and Liz looks taken back. "Sorry. I'm just frustrated. Nadine has to be here!" How do I explain how I know this? "Back when she, um, lived in L.A. she always talked about going here and how she was going to enroll right away."

"Are you sure she had the money for tuition?" Liz frowns. "Harvard looks pretty expensive, even to me."

I stare out the window and watch the people walk by with bags and wrapped packages that are probably meant for the holidays. I haven't even thought of Christmas till today. Is it almost Christmas at home too? What if I miss it? What if no one misses me?

What if . . . what if I never get back?

"KATES." Liz's voice is louder now. "Stop feeling sorry for yourself," she scolds. "You're going to find Nadine. I don't know why she's so important, but I know you're going to find her. You can't give up now."

I feel sort of teary, and Liz is making me more so. "Thanks. That sounded very best friend–ish."

Liz smiles triumphantly. "I knew it did. Just like it was best friend–ish when I lent you my favorite Marc Jacobs dress a few weeks ago for the *Family Affair* DVD party without even wearing it first, remember? What friend would let you do that, huh?"

Family Affair DVD party? How does she know about that? That final season party happened in my world, not here. And come to think of it, I did wear Liz's dress.

"How do you know about the *FA* DVD party?"

Liz looks up from her drink. "What's *FA*?"

"You just said—" I stop when Liz looks confused.

"I said you have to keep thinking of places Nadine could be," Liz reiterates. "We came all the way here, and we're going to find her." This is just like my Liz to be this stubborn. "Now think of the other things she told you about Harvard."

"Well..." I take a long sip of my drink. "She's wanted to go since she was twelve. She said that Boston was one of the epicenters of politics, so she'd be in the right place for her future work." I smile. "She wore the Harvard sweatshirt she got for her fifteenth birthday so much it fell apart. Her parents didn't have the money to pay for all her tuition, which is why she got a job to help cover the costs." I don't say that job was working for me. "Nadine wanted to make the money on her own and stop their fighting. She said her mom would rather be poor than let Nadine pay for college, but her dad argued they *would* be poor if they took out a second mortgage to do it."

"Sounds like something my mom would say." Liz taps her long, purple nails on the table. "She said she'd rather be poor than live in an empty mansion that Dad was never home to enjoy anyway." Liz says it bravely, but I know the divorce is a sore subject. Her mom lives in Maine now, and Liz hardly ever sees her. Liz's expression changes. "Hey. Do you think Nadine's parents got divorced?"

I shake my head. "They're happily married."

"When was the last time you talked to Nadine? Maybe they got divorced right before she came to Harvard." Liz is jumping out of her seat now.

"I guess they could have." I stir the drink around and around, watching the whipped cream melt and fade away. "But that doesn't change things. She'd still be here, and she's not. There is no Nadine Holbrook at Harvard."

"That's right." Liz is practically gloating now and I don't get why. "There wouldn't be a Nadine Holbrook here because she's not Nadine Holbrook anymore."

I stop stirring. "I don't get it."

"When my parents got divorced, my mom hated my dad so much that she changed her name legally back to Rosenfeld," Liz says animatedly. "I kept Mendes because I'm closer with my dad, but who would Nadine have sided with if her parents' split got nasty?"

I give her a look. "This is a stretch, Liz."

"*Think*, Kates," Liz pushes. "If they went through a messy divorce, whose name would Nadine have kept? What was her mom's maiden name? Do you know?"

I actually do know. Nadine uses it to check me in to hotels because the name is so funny, no one would ever suspect it was me staying there. "It's Funkhouse." I giggle at the thought of it. "She would have been Nadine Funkhouse."

"You're looking for Nadine Funkhouse?" the guy behind

the counter interrupts. He's cleaning the countertops with a scary-looking rag. "She comes in at three."

Liz and I look at each other in shock. I feel shivers go up my spine.

"I should be on *CSI.*" Liz is beaming. "I have good instincts."

I look at the clock on the wall. It's a quarter to three.

Oh. My. God.

I'm going to throw up. Could it really be her? Now she's Nadine Funkhouse? But why? How? Okay, concentrate.

"Are you friends of hers?" the guy asks as he continues to scrub down the countertop with that grimy cloth.

"Cousins," I say, and I give Liz a look to keep quiet. "Long-lost cousins. My mom said she worked here." I grab my crutches and walk toward the counter with Liz right behind me. "I just want to make sure we have the right Nadine Funkhouse. Longish red hair, petite, fiery temper, loves to preach to people?"

He laughs. "That's Funky Funkhouse. But her hair isn't long. It's super short. I keep teasing her that she looks like a guy. She says she can't afford to grow it long and use all those styling products. She has to save her coffee money for rent."

Ohmygodohmygodohmygodohmygodohmygodohmygod! It's Nadine!

"Okay, now you really have to tell me why we're here." Liz has her hands on her hips, and from her expression I know she's not going to take "I can't" for an answer.

My Liz is in there. Somewhere.

"I'll explain everything," I say, even though I'm not sure I mean it. "Later."

"She should be here any second if you two want to wait for her," the guy adds.

I think I might pass out now. What am I going to say? How am I going to convince her to help me if she doesn't recognize me? Liz reaches for my elbow to steady me and leads me to a nearby table. "Are you all right? Why are you so nervous?"

But I don't hear anything else. I hear the tiny bell above the Peet's Coffee door ping and the door open. Almost in slow motion, for me at least, in walks Nadine.

"Gary, get the latte machine whirring because I need a double shot of espresso in my no-fat, no-foam latte," she tells the guy behind the counter. "I've got a splitting headache."

It's my Nadine, all right. Aside from the hair, it looks just like her. She's wearing a black long-sleeve tee and worn-in jeans, and she is carrying a Peet's Coffee apron that she ties with one hand while she removes a dingy green puffer coat with the other. She sees me and grins. For a split second I think she's going to walk over and hug me. Instead she makes her way to Gary.

Nadine has no clue who I am.

She was my last hope, and she looked at me like I was a stranger. Nadine is never going to help a total stranger find her way back to another plane/dimension, or wake up from a coma. I know Nadine—she'd never believe any of those things.

Would she?

Gary nods to us as he refills a coffee grinder. "Your cousins have been waiting for you, Funky Funkhouse."

"My what?" Nadine looks us up and down skeptically. "I don't have cousins."

"How could you not have cousins?" Liz asks, without skipping a beat. Liz whispers to me, "Why did we say we were cousins again? Why didn't you just say who you were?"

This is getting dicey.

"My parents are only children," Nadine tells Liz and puts her apron on over her head. "No cousins. So who are you? Are you selling Girl Scout Cookies? Candy bars to raise money for your school? Either way, I can't help you. The only fund I give to is the Nadine Funkhouse fund for Harvard tuition." Gary chuckles, and they turn their attention to two customers who just walked in.

"Why doesn't she recognize you?" Liz asks me.

"It's been a long time." I stall for time. "She was always, um, bad with faces."

I wonder if I can get Liz out of here and talk to Nadine alone. I look at Liz again. She's so curious she'll never leave.

"We don't want money." I hobble back to Nadine's side of the counter. "We just want to talk to you for a few minutes. We're doing a high school paper on coffee shops and working through grad school, and someone recommended interviewing you. Right, Liz?"

"Sure, whatever she said," Liz agrees and sits down at our table again to take another swig of her drink.

Nadine looks at me. What was I thinking? Nadine is not going to believe that. Nadine is skeptical about everything. She questions authority, is type A, and says what's on her mind. She'll never listen to us.

"I go on break at four," Nadine says as she works a latte into a frothy foam.

"Fine, we'll wait," I say cheerily, and take a seat next to Liz, who is staring at me expectantly. "Please don't ask me to explain all this right now."

For some reason, Liz doesn't. Instead she fills the time chatting about benign stuff like Christmas gifts, holiday movies, and her latest celeb crush (Taylor Lautner—which means she's got the same crush as the rest of the world). I tune her out and think of Nadine. What can I say to make her believe me? If she's here, then I must have a chance to make this happen. Right?

At four on the dot—Nadine is always punctual—Nadine slides into the chair across from me. She tosses a bag on the table. "Cookies. I thought you guys might be hungry. Gary says you've been sitting here for hours." She takes a sip of coffee. "I only have fifteen minutes, so fire away."

"Kates? Want to start?" Liz prods and rests her chin on her elbows as if to say, "This is going to be good."

I don't know how to do this any other way. "Obviously we're not your cousins," I say. "But we do know each other.

My mom and your mom go way back. You used to babysit for me when you lived in Chicago."

Nadine looks ready to bolt already. "Where did I live?"

I know the answer to this one. "In Northampton, 1918 Park Drive West."

"What's your name?" Nadine asks, still looking unsure.

"Kaitlin Burke. We lived around the block from you, remember?" I'm sweating I'm so nervous.

"You're lying," Nadine says and takes a bite of a cookie. "There was a library around the block from me." She starts getting up, and I know I'm losing her. I don't have a choice. I have to tell the truth, the whole crazy truth and nothing but the truth.

"I need your help," I say and Nadine turns around. "I traveled three thousand miles to find you, and my friend Liz paid for the tickets. Can you please just give me ten minutes?"

"She really doesn't know you?" Liz asks incredulously. "Then how do you know her?"

"Yeah, how do you know who I am?" Nadine crosses her arms.

"I know everything about you," I explain. "I know you make judgments about people in the first five minutes, so you already don't trust me, but sometimes your judgments are wrong. Remember Carol Barker? You thought she was going to give you an F on your tenth-grade science project because she looked at you funny, but then you found out she had a corn dog for lunch and her stomach was acting up."

Nadine's jaw drops. "How do you know that?"

"Yeah, how *do* you know that?" Liz wants to know.

"Because I know you," I say softly. "Not here, not now, but I know *you*. We work together, actually."

After I give Liz strict instructions not to interrupt even if she thinks I need a one-way ticket to crazy town, Nadine lets me talk. And talk. I talk for her full break, telling her everything about the accident, my family, my friends, Austin, Sky, *Family Affair*, what's changed for the better, and what's worse. I pepper the conversation with anecdotes about Nadine herself—advice she's given me over the years, what she's told me about her life, why she became my personal assistant, and finally, why she left.

"I quit?" Nadine looks astonished. I'm not sure whether she believes me or just thinks this is a good story, but I keep answering her questions. Liz thinks I'm nuts, I can tell, but I keep talking.

"You realized that you wanted more," I explain and hold one of my crutches in my hand for support, in more ways than one. "You were beyond picking up dry cleaning, going to Crumbs bakery for my cupcake fix, and doing my schedule. Even I knew that. I just loved you too much to let you go. You're opening your own celebrity management company, and your first client is Sky Mackenzie."

Liz and Nadine chuckle to each other.

"That train wreck?" Liz says.

"I can't stand that girl," Nadine agrees and takes another sip of her coffee.

"She's not like that there," I insist. "Sky's got it together. We're friends, actually. Good friends," I add. "And she's your first client."

"Why would I want to work with celebrities?" Nadine sounds flip, which she is SO not. "You couldn't pay me to live in Los Angeles. It's so plastic, and I hate tabloids and those TMZ people."

"You do hate those things!" *Though you have gotten over it somewhat*, but I don't add that. "You were making money to go to Harvard," I explain. "You knew you could make the money fast if you came to L.A. You had a friend who did the same thing. Caroline," I remember, and Nadine's eyebrows rise ever so slightly. "She did well as an assistant, so you decided to go out for a few years, make money, and then go back to business school."

Nadine stands up and picks up her coffee. "I can't listen to any more of this. Your story is compelling, I give you that. And you sound like you know what you're talking about, but this is crazy! People don't time travel or dream travel or whatever you think you've done." She waves her hands, and her coffee begins to slosh over the sides of the paper cup. "I would never move to Los Angeles. *Ever*. And fetch someone's dry cleaning? I don't think so. You have the wrong girl, and I don't think you're going to find the right one." She looks at Liz. "You need to take her to a doctor. She needs help."

Nadine starts to walk away, and Liz grabs my hand. "I think she's right, Kaitlin. I'm going to call your parents, and we'll get you home," she says soothingly. She looks a little frightened, actually. "Your story was incredible—so detailed—but it's not real. Maybe that accident caused more trauma than anyone realized."

Liz calling my parents, Nadine walking away from me? No, no, no. This is all wrong. I need Nadine! She can help me, I know it.

"Mark Howards!" I yell.

Nadine stops but doesn't turn around.

"You moved because of Mark Howards." I lower my voice. "He was your first love. He was going to go to Harvard with you. He had the money to go and you didn't. He said he'd wait a year and then reapply again with you, but he lied. He went without you, and you didn't forgive him. You broke up. He came out to Los Angeles to apologize once, but you wouldn't see him and you haven't dated anyone seriously since. You always said he was your one big regret."

Nadine stares at me. "Mark and I broke up last year."

"He didn't go to Harvard with you?" Liz asks, intrigued.

Nadine's smile is sort of sad. "He did go. We both did, and then we broke up anyway. He transferred and I'm still here." She looks around and sighs. "Making life plans with a guy instead of making life plans for yourself is a big mistake. So was coming here," she adds and walks back over.

"But it's all you ever talk about!" I tell her. "'When I go to Harvard,' 'this would never happen at Harvard,' 'I'm too smart to hear you say something that dumb, Kaitlin.'"

Nadine laughs. "I would say those things." She looks at

me wistfully. "But if I could talk to your Nadine—*if* one actually exists—I would tell her that business school isn't what I thought it would be. Neither is politics." She scrunches her nose like she just sniffed expired milk. "I worked on a local campaign last year and hated it." She shrugs and runs a hand through her short red hair. "But I can't not see school through to the end. It has cost my family too much. Even if I'm not happy. Not that I know what would make me happy, except…" She looks at me. "Your Nadine sounds content in a way I've never been living here. Maybe not getting what she wanted gave her everything she wanted after all."

"Give me a second. I'm trying to follow that sentence." Liz looks like she's concentrating hard, and Nadine and I laugh.

Nadine takes my hand. "Kaitlin Burke, I think you're crazy, but maybe it's time for me to do something crazy for once." She gives me a look. "You may not be an actress, but you definitely have charisma. At the very least, you'll keep me entertained while we're at this."

"You'll help me?" I can't believe it. I really can't believe it!

Nadine smiles. "Yes. Let's get you back to your Hollywood life."

seventeen: *Wishful Thinking*

I soon find out saying you want to go home and doing it are two very different things. It's not as easy as when Dorothy dropped back in to Kansas (aka woke up). I can't click my heels three times and get there. I did try zipping and unzipping my ruby red bag three times and saying "There's no place like home," just to be on the safe side, but of course, nothing happened.

It takes the three of us hours before we come up with a scenario that could work. And it has to work, because we're running out of time. Liz's dad traced her credit card yesterday, left her an irate voicemail, and told her that he and my parents are on the next flight to Boston to get us.

I have six hours to figure this out, or I'm never getting home.

Liz thinks I'm certifiable, but she also thinks my story would make a fabulous screenplay. ("I think I could be a director!" she says. How ironic.) So she's sticking around. She also says that friends help friends even if they think they've escaped from the mother ship. Nice.

We've already tried a few things. Nadine dragged me to a palm reader, but she didn't say boo about my other life. All she said was, "If you keep to the map of the life you want to lead, rather than the path others want you to, you'll have a long and prosperous life." Good advice, but I need to get my life back first.

We also tried a psychic and a medium. "Why would we need a medium?" Liz asked. "She's not dead!" Nadine made a face that freaked me out—making me think she did think I was dead—but the medium, thank God, reached only my grandmother, who said hi and to tell my mom to "take a chill pill and stop being obsessed with the Beckhams." At least the medium had a sense of my alternate reality! The psychic got nowhere. Like I care how many kids I'm going to have. I'm only eighteen! I think both Liz and Nadine are having less and less faith in me as the hours go on.

Now we're on our way to Gail Harding, a renowned hypnotist, who Nadine says spoke at one of her psychology classes at Harvard. She agreed to meet with me after-hours tonight, but that could be because Nadine didn't tell her the whole story. If Gail knew I thought I was from another dimension, she probably would have slammed the phone down and changed her mailing address.

"If anyone can figure out what's going on with you, it is Gail," Nadine explains, pulling her plaid scarf tighter to fight the wind. It's blustery here today—the forecast on TV this morning said a nor'easter blew in out of nowhere—and Boston is expecting high winds and rain/snow. "I watched her cure my psych professor's smoking addiction in just one session, in front of our entire seminar! She put him to sleep, made him say a few words, and poof! He woke up cured. He's never wanted to smoke another pack again. The smell of smoke makes him sick."

"But we're not trying to cure Kaitlin of anything, except maybe being crazy." Liz keeps in stride with Nadine. She has on her North Face parka, skinny jeans, her Burberry rain boots, and a heavy red sweater. I have on the green baby-doll sweater I wore yesterday with my unwashed skinny jeans and my wellies. Liz wanted to go shopping yesterday, but she joked she wouldn't be able to lug all the new clothes back on the plane herself when I vanished into thin air after tonight's session.

Wouldn't that be nice?

"How will falling asleep help Kaitlin get home?" Liz asks.

"I don't know," Nadine says thoughtfully. "I still don't know if I believe any of this! I don't know the first thing about dimensional travel, but I do know about hypnosis and it can help in a lot of areas—getting over irrational fears, smoking addictions, weight loss. Maybe she can restart Kaitlin's brain in the right reality, whatever that is."

"She'll put me to sleep and then what?" I ask nervously. "I fall asleep every night, and I wake up the next morning and I'm still here. How will this time be different?"

"I don't know." Nadine sounds exasperated and stops walking. "I'm sorry. I'm just frustrated. I can't stand not fixing things on the first try."

I know.

"I don't know how to help you," she continues and starts biting one of her nails. "All I know is the more time I spend with you and the more I hear about this other life you claim to have, the more fabulous it sounds and the more miserable I feel." Nadine looks at her boots. "What if we actually succeed in this crazy scheme of yours, get you back there, and Liz and I are stuck here, with the lesser versions of the lives you say we lead?"

"I didn't think of that." Liz looks gloomy too.

I take both of their hands and use them to steady myself as another huge gust of wind threatens to blow my crutches out from under me. "If I get back, then you get back too. I don't know what happens to here. All I know is that there, in Hollywood, we're all pretty happy."

That seems to appease Nadine because she starts walking and talking again, about things like her favorite restaurants in town (On The Border, this excellent Mexican place) and the Harvard bookstore. Before we know it, we're knocking on Gail's office door, she's inviting us in, and she's asking us to explain everything. When I'm finished, I get the same reaction I did from Nadine the first time. Silence. At least Gail was scribbling in a notebook the whole time. The sound of her pencil tapping across the binder is the only sound in the room. It's sort of grating, and it keeps getting louder. Come to think of it, that binder looks awfully familiar. . . .

Hey, isn't that Nadine's bible? That's where she keeps all of the info about my life. I'd recognize it anywhere—there are stickers on the back of Nadine's favorite bands, and a picture of Tahiti, where Nadine wants to go.

"Where did you get that binder?" I break the silence. "That's Nadine's. Well, my Nadine's." Alter-Nadine is looking at me strangely. "The picture of Tahiti, the band bumper stickers. That's the binder my Nadine keeps all my stuff in."

"Kaitlin, what are you talking about?" Liz talks to me like I'm two. "This binder has nothing on it. It's a dull navy blue. No offense."

Gail holds it up for me to see and Liz is right. It's blank. But it wasn't a minute ago. I'm sure of it. And there's that tapping again! It's so irritating. But Gail isn't tapping her pen. Liz and Nadine aren't doing anything either. What is going on?

"I know her story sounds crazy," Nadine says hastily, "but I figured if anyone would know how to help her, it would be you. I've read your papers on hypnosis, and the power of the mind is huge."

"That is true," Gail says with a soft smile. She's older than my mom by at least a decade, and she looks more like a grandma than a doctor. She's got short, salt-and-pepper hair and kind blue eyes, and she's wearing a tweed suit. "The mind has a funny way of revealing itself sometimes. In Kaitlin's case, it appears to have been teaching her a valuable lesson about love and loss." She looks at me kindly. "I wish I could help you—and maybe I can, but not now. I don't think you're ready."

Liz's phone starts to vibrate. "Geez, did their plane land

already?" She looks at me. "It's my dad. I'll let it go to voice-mail."

"I am ready," I insist to Gail. "I want to go home."

She shakes her head. "I'm not sure that's the answer. You have to figure out what you really want first."

"I know what I want." I'm growing aggravated. "I want to go home. I want my life back."

"You keep saying that, but I'm not sure you mean it." Gail looks at her notes. "In my opinion, if wishing you were back home and wanting it were the only things you needed to do, you would already be home. Something is holding you here. Even if I put you under, I fear it wouldn't work."

"So you believe her?" Liz sounds surprised.

"It's not a question of what I believe. It's a question of what Kaitlin believes." Gail looks at me. "If Kaitlin believes she's meant to be somewhere else and she's stuck here, then I want to address that first."

HOLLYWOOD SECRET NUMBER SEVENTEEN: It's amazing it's taken me this long to see a therapist. In Holly-wood, everyone I know goes to therapy; belongs to a church, synagogue, or Scientology center; or sees a life coach, does yoga therapy, or visits an ashram before he or she reaches puberty. Remember those Kabbalah bracelets everyone in southern Cali was sporting a few years back? I do. Every costar I knew wore one. In Hollywood, we're always looking for the next big thing that will help us feel fulfilled. As actors, we're always trying to be someone else. Things like therapy help us learn how to be ourselves. Sometimes.

Gail looks at me kindly. "What's holding you back, Kaitlin?"

"I don't know." I feel impatient now. Gail obviously thinks she can help me, but she won't. "If I knew I wouldn't be here, would I?"

"Maybe you would, and maybe you wouldn't." Gail begins tapping her pen again. The sound is beeping in my ear. Or maybe that's my cell phone. I don't remember putting it on.

"My phone is ringing too," Liz says and looks at the screen. "It's Austin. Do you want to talk to him?"

Yes, no. I don't know! I'm so confused. I cover my ears to block out the noise. It's getting louder.

"Hey, A. Yeah, I'm right next to her," I hear Liz say. "She's not talking yet. We've tried everything."

What does that mean?

"Kaitlin," Gail tries again, and I can hear the wind outside howl like a wolf. "As much as you want to go home, I think a part of you wants to stay here. Why?"

"I don't know!" I yell.

"They don't know why she's like this. She should be up by now," Liz says into the phone.

"I am up!" I tell Liz and she jumps. "What are you talking about?"

"What are *you* talking about?" Liz asks. "My dad is beeping in again. Kates, knowing him, he's got some newfangled satellite tracking on me and he'll be here any minute. You better figure out how to get home fast."

"I'm trying!" I freak out. I want to cry. My head is spinning. Things are spiraling out of control. I hate when this happens! I hate when life gets this overwhelming and I feel like I'm drowning and I'll never be in control again.

"Kaitlin, think about your life." I hear Nadine's voice. "You say you adore it. You love being an actress, you love your new TV show, you love your friends, your boyfriend, even Sky Mackenzie. But you also said you wish you could split yourself in two, right?"

I thumb the leather on the chair I'm sitting on. "Sort of."

Nadine leans forward excitedly, happy to be on to something. "I think if you could, you'd want two lives—one that involves acting and one that lets you live away from the cameras like you do here. Am I right?"

I don't say anything. I just stare at Gail's diploma on the wall. Huh, she went to Cedars-Sinai? I didn't know that was a medical school and a hospital. "I don't know about wanting two lives. I just want balance," I say unconvincingly.

"Talk to her." I hear Liz again. "Tell her it's okay. Tell her you're okay." But Liz is not on the phone. What is going on here?

"Now we're getting somewhere. What parts of this life would you take with you, if you could?" Gail asks me.

I blink back tears. "I like my parents," I croak. "I like our peaceful house. There aren't BlackBerries going off at all hours of the night, or powwows with agents and publicists at eleven PM when I want to go to bed. My mom is sane and in my world . . ." I trail off. "She's not. She thinks if she's not managing me then my whole career will fall apart, but . . ."

"But?" Gail leans forward, still scribbling.

"But I'm not sure." I look at Nadine again. "Sometimes when it's just you and me, I feel like I can do anything. I feel like I'm old enough to make the right decisions. I'm not saying I won't run them by her, but there is so much I would or wouldn't do if she let me have a say. Mom gets me so nuts sometimes that I just want to run away! That's how I wound up at Clark Hall the first time. I was so overwhelmed by the paparazzi, the tabloids, and my mom that I wanted to disappear."

"Disappear," Nadine repeats. "Kind of like what you're doing right now."

"But this is different," I disagree. "I don't want to be here."

"Maybe you *do* want to be here," Gail interrupts. "Maybe you don't want to face the future. Maybe what's really holding you back is *you*."

I never thought of it that way before. "So what do I do?"

Gail touches my hand. "You learn to relax. Wanting more than a career comes naturally to you, but maybe it doesn't for your parents. Sometimes you have to teach people new tricks, Kaitlin. Show them there are more ways to do things than the way they've always done them. It's not easy, but it can be done."

"I've always thought the solution to my problems was keeping a clear line between my work and my home life, but maybe I've been looking at it all wrong." I look to Nadine for reinforcement. "Maybe what I should have done was figure out a way to make my two worlds coexist peacefully."

I think about that for what feels like hours, even though it's probably minutes. What would it take to live in my world happily? It's like the essay question: "Have you changed your life, or has your life changed you?" Maybe Gail's right: I'm here because my life has changed me up until now. Maybe it's time I change it instead. "I think I know how to make things work," I say finally.

"Talk to her. Tell her you love her!" Liz says again.

"She doesn't hear me, does she?"

Is that Austin? It can't be Austin.

"Kaitlin, I won't leave you, okay?"

"Nadine, did you just say something?" She shakes her head, and I hear that annoying beeping again.

"Kaitlin, if you really have an answer, this will work." Gail reclines the leather armchair I'm sitting on. It's next to the windows, and I can hear the wind rattling the frames. I try to relax, but I feel like things are poking me. "Close your eyes and listen to my voice." I scratch at my forearms, trying to get rid of whatever's pulling at me there, but I don't find anything.

"I am listening," I murmur.

"No talking, just listen. I want you to think about your life ... the one that is far away from here ... think about everything that's happened to you the past few years and all the things you learned. What changed, what didn't? Think about what you want your life to be there, and think about the home you want. Can you do that?"

I nod.

"Good. Keep your eyes closed and say, 'There's no place like home.'"

I really am Dorothy! "There's no place like home," I whisper with my eyes closed tight. "There's no place like home."

My home. My life. Los Angeles. The thoughts flash through my mind like pictures. I see Austin, Liz, *Small Fries*, Sky, and Rodney picking me up at the studio. I see my life on *Family Affair*, Matty, Mom, Dad, and Nadine. And strangely, I see other things too. Things that shouldn't be there. Like my house here in Toluca Lake and Mom setting the kitchen table for dinner. (There are no takeout boxes on it.) I see stacks of applications, and I see the University of Southern California. I picture Austin and myself walking around campus.

And then I see me. The me I want to be. A girl who isn't bogged down in what she doesn't have or what's going wrong. Someone who knows what's going *right* in her life. I see what I love about acting and how much I want to keep doing it and how nobody, no matter how much I adore them, can keep me from taking charge of my destiny.

And then everything goes dark.

eIGHTeen: *Welcome Back*

"Oh my God!" I hear Liz exclaim. "Is she opening her eyes?"

"Look! They're fluttering! Page the doctor." Now it's Mom's voice I hear, and I hear others too.

"Kaitlin? Can you hear us? We're right here." It's Nadine.

Everyone's voices are magnified a thousand times, and I feel like I'm in some sort of wind tunnel. Someone's heels clacking on the floor sound like thunder claps.

My right hand feels warm. "Burke? You're okay, Burke. We were in an accident, but we're fine. Or we will be when you wake up."

I'd know that voice anywhere.

"Austin?" I croak, and I struggle to open my eyes even though they feel very heavy.

"She's awake!" He sounds so relieved as he strokes my hair. "Hey. You gave us quite a scare there, birthday girl."

It is Austin. *My* Austin. That can mean only one thing: I'm back!

I feel so tired, but I look around to make sure I'm not

still in Gail's office. Liz, Mom, Dad, Matty, Nadine, Rodney, Laney, and Seth are all staring at me, and they're smiling. If Laney, Seth, and Rodney are here, then I really am where I belong.

"I'm home." I choke up and feel tears trickle down my cheeks. "I am home, right? Where do we live?" I whisper, clutching Austin's hand.

Liz giggles. "In the best city in the world—Los Angeles."

"And what do I do for a living?" I ask.

"God, she must have really clunked her head," I hear Sky say.

Sky is here too! "K. You're on *Small Fries* with me," Sky says very slowly, as if I can't understand English. "You're not as good an actor as me, but I carry both our weight."

"I'm an actress! YES!" I want to yell, but it hurts my throat.

It was a dream. My life without my Hollywood career was nothing more than a figment of my imagination.

That was some dream. And yet . . . I feel different somehow. More grateful, definitely, but maybe a bit wiser too.

"Do they have her on Vicodin?" Laney asks. "I get wacky when they give me that."

"Nah, Vicodin would make her more hyper," Sky says. "I had that when I got my deviated septum fixed."

"Aka her nose job," Liz translates.

"Sky? Are you okay?" I ask, reaching for her hand. "You haven't been drinking, have you? Or hanging out with Alexis?"

"No and no!" Sky pulls her hand away.

"Promise me, Sky," I insist, even though my voice is barely a whisper. "I love you too much to see you destroy yourself."

"What is she talking about?" Sky asks the room. "I think that concussion gave K memory loss."

"Sweetie, we're going to get the doctor," Mom says soothingly, which is all the more confusing because now she sounds like alter-Mom. Ouch. My head hurts. "It's going to be okay." She chokes up as she sits down next to Austin and strokes my hair too. "We were so worried about you. When we got the call that you'd been hurt right after we'd had that huge fight, I . . . I . . ." She starts to sob.

"Honey, it's okay," Dad says. "She's okay. Kate-Kate, do you remember what happened?"

"Not really," I admit. "The whole thing feels sort of foggy. I remember the paparazzi chasing us, and that driver egging them on, but the whole thing started because I told them off. This is my fault." I lean my head back on my pillow abashedly.

"No it's not, Kates," Rodney tells me, and I see he has a few bandages on his arm. "I should have been there to stop him. I shouldn't have let you give me the morning off. On your birthday, no less. I should have known something would go wrong. That's why I came back. When I saw those piranha shutterhounds, I tailed them."

"Rod was the first one to get to our car after it crashed," Austin tells me. "He pulled you out."

I look at Rod. "You're always there when I need you." Aww . . . he looks misty. I'll leave it there. Rodney hates to tear up in public. He saves his crying sessions for *Brothers and Sisters* (shh!). "I'm fine, thanks to you." I grab for Austin's hand. "I'm just happy I'm here. That we're all here and everyone is okay." I smile at Austin and look down at his hand holding mine.

Austin has a cast on his right wrist.

"It's just a sprain." Austin holds up his right wrist and I get a better look—a cloudy look—and see the bandages. Everything is sort of blurry. "The doctor says I'll have it off in two weeks. Plenty of time to recover for the spring season."

So he didn't break his leg like the alter-Austin in my dream did. I'm still upset he got hurt, but thankfully I didn't ruin his chances at a lacrosse scholarship. I feel so relieved.

"You're the one we've been worried about," Austin adds. "You had to have surgery, and everything went south from there."

"What happened?" I ask nervously.

"You broke your ankle and had to go under anesthesia to get it fixed," Nadine explains. "They had trouble waking you up. They were worried you had a concussion that was undetected, and they said something happened with your oxygen level."

"I think it's called desaturation," Liz explains, fiddling with the ends of a violet scarf wrapped around her dark, curly hair. "The doctor said to talk to you, so we've been telling you stories."

"They've—*we've*—been watching you and waiting for the last few hours," Austin says.

"Did you mention the new Marc Jacobs boots?" I ask breathlessly.

Liz's mouth, lined in purple gloss, drops open. "You heard me, didn't you? I knew shopping was the key to waking you up!"

"You'll have to use crutches for a few weeks," Mom informs me, "but you're going to be fine. We called the studio to let them know what happened, and they're going to shut down production for a week or two till you feel better."

"So hurry up," Sky jokes.

"It's just so nice to be home," I say, closing my eyes again. Must sleep.

"What do you mean home?" Dad chuckles. "I'd hardly call this posh surroundings."

"Wherever you guys are is enough for me," I whisper and then I hear footsteps.

"There are way too many people in this room," a nurse complains. "Some of you are going to have to leave."

"Sorry, Nurse Gail," Seth says.

Gail? That's funny. That was the hypnotist's name in my dream.

"Kates, we're going to go," Seth tells me. "You need to rest, but Laney and I will check on you tomorrow."

They're fired. I remember Mom firing Laney and Seth. I open my eyes, alarmed, looking anxiously between him and my mom. "But . . ."

Seth winks at my mom, who smiles. "Not to worry. We

told your mom she couldn't fire us when she was under duress. We're all still on your roster."

Thank God.

"You just concentrate on getting better," Laney tells me. "I'll handle the media and run anything good by your mom."

"Yes, do that, Laney," Mom says, her voice slightly jumpy. "We'll only give one outlet the exclusive. Should it be *Today* or *GMA*?"

"Meg." Dad's voice is a warning.

"I'm just trying to make her feel better." Mom folds her arms across her chest and thumbs the beaded necklace she's wearing. "Speaking of which," Mom adds, "you'll be able to do a lot more shopping after tomorrow." Her eyes glitter brightly. "I convinced Seth to bring the contracts for your movie deals tomorrow."

"Mom . . ." Suddenly I feel weak again. The Mom in my dream would never bring up work when I was hooked to an IV. "Can we do this later?"

"Later? I have huge news to share that I gathered while booking Matty's *Teen Vogue* cover. Don't you want to know what it is?" Mom raises her eyebrows, but I'm not biting.

"*Teen Vogue?*" Matty sounds excited. "Mom, that is killer."

"I know, and so is this news." Mom can't stop herself. "If you'd be willing to sign on to both movies tomorrow, you'd get a huge bonus, Kaitlin. HUGE."

HOLLYWOOD SECRET NUMBER EIGHTEEN: Usually when you sign on to do a movie, your paycheck is your salary. But on occasion, you can get bonuses or certain perks, if the movie does extraordinary well—even if it hasn't been made yet. Sometimes studios are so eager to get you to sign on the dotted line (usually for a sequel) that they may offer a car or some other eye candy as a perk. My friend Gina got a Range Rover when they wanted her to lock in to *Hell on Wheels 2: Holy Terror*. Other times, the deal involves giving you a percentage of the profits. Don't get too excited about that bonus—it takes a bundle for a film to make back all its production, marketing, and promotion costs before you see your 5 percent (which tends to be the max).

Mom looks satisfied, but I've gone from elated to dejected in ten minutes. I have plenty to say, but now is not the time. "Can we talk tomorrow? It's been a long day."

Much longer than any of you realize.

"But—" Mom presses.

"Meg." Dad's tone is stern, like the time I came home two hours after curfew.

"Okay." Mom touches my leg over the scratchy hospital blanket. "You're right. We've had enough for one day. I just can't stop thinking of ways to help my children." Nadine makes a face behind Mom's back. "Get some rest, sweetie."

Dad winks at me. "Idle all you want, Kate-Kate. I'll keep her in neutral."

When they're gone, I look at Austin, Liz, Sky, and Nadine, who are still with me. If I don't say something, I'm going to burst. "You guys can't leave yet. I have to tell you what happened to me."

Nadine looks at Sky and Liz. "First, we want to apologize."

"We shouldn't have ambushed you on your birthday." Liz takes Mom's seat on the edge of my bed. She smooths her drop-waist green Marc Jacobs tank dress, which she had on this morning at breakfast.

I can't believe that was only this morning. It feels like a lifetime ago.

Sky rolls her eyes. "We should have remembered you take change badly."

"Not anymore," I say thoughtfully. "And if anyone should apologize, it's me. I really am happy about your new career, Nadine." I look at Sky sternly. "You've got the best running your life now. Don't screw it up."

"I know this isn't the time or the place, but consider coming with us, Kates," Nadine says, her eyes glistening. "I don't think I can do this without you. It wouldn't feel right."

"It is right," I insist. "This is what you're meant to do. Not Harvard business school. Believe me."

Nadine smiles. "What made you think of Harvard?"

"I've been thinking about a lot of things, like how the tabloids are going to have a field day with the awful things I said in front of the paparazzi." I stare at the room blinds. They could use a dusting.

"That was so out of character, K." Sky tsks. "The press is going to call you ungrateful."

"Maybe I was," I admit. "But I'm not now. I'm thankful for everything I have—even that accident."

"That is one thing I would never be thankful for." Liz shakes her head.

"I sort of agree with Liz," Austin says slowly. "That accident was way scarier than any trip I've taken down the red carpet. It was—"

"Terrifying," I supply.

"Terrifying," Austin repeats. "But I'm okay, and it sounds like you are too."

"I really am." I start getting choked up again. I'm so happy to be home. I mean awake. I mean here. "If anything had happened to you, Austin, I . . ."

"If, if, if." Sky sighs. "The world is full of ifs, and you can't do anything with them. It's too late. What's done is done, and you're fine. A is fine. Just don't ever do that again, okay? You completely freaked us out."

Behind Sky, Liz is pantomiming. She rubs her eyes and pretends she's crying. Sky was crying? Over me? Wow, our relationship really has changed.

Austin touches my face. "You should rest."

"I don't want to rest." I struggle to sit up again. "There is so much I have to do now that I have the chance." Nadine stares at me strangely. I look to make sure my door is closed and that I'm in a private room, which thankfully I am. No cranky roommate this time.

"Why are you acting so weird?" Sky groans. "Explain!"

"Okay!" I take a deep breath. Where do I start? "While I was out cold, I had the strangest dream. . . ."

I tell them everything, from start to finish, leaving out none of the details. I talk for so long that Nurse Gail comes in and takes my temperature twice. She also reminds me that visiting hours end at eight and it's nearly seven. But I can't stop. The more I tell the story, the more excited I get, even though while it was happening to me I was freaked out a lot of the time. When I'm done, they're all speechless.

"That is the most elaborate dream I have ever heard of," Nadine marvels. "And the way you described Harvard and Peet's, it's like you were really there! Have you ever been to Boston?"

I shake my head. "Never. I guess I just remembered everything you told me."

"Well, I don't like what you told me," Liz sniffs. "I sound pathetic."

"At least you're not a hungover train wreck," Sky grumbles. "Nice to know you think I'd fall apart without you."

"I came through in the end, so I feel okay." Austin winks. "Interesting about University of Southern California, though. So you were really thinking about going?"

"I was and I am definitely filling out an application."

Nadine grins. "I really do serve a purpose here," she jokes, but I know it's true.

"So now what?" Liz wants to know. "Are you going to tell your mom about this dream?"

"She'd never listen. But maybe she doesn't have to. About that at least."

"Your mom in an apron? Tucking you in at night? Driving you to school and working in a dentist's office?" Liz repeats, her mouth twisted into a cat-got-the-canary grin. "I would pay to hear you tell your mom about your dream mother."

"I think it's pretty cool what happened to you," Sky says, playing with a strand of her long, raven hair. "I wish something like that would happen to me."

"No, you don't," I tell her. "It was freaky, and all I wanted was to come home."

"Maybe part of you wanted to be home, but part of you must have enjoyed it." Nadine is thoughtful. "It's sort of like what you've always wanted, isn't it?"

"What do you mean?" I take a sip of the icy cranberry juice Nurse Gail brought me. I'm sipping it down by the quart, I'm so thirsty from all this talking. And, well, from surgery.

"Kates, you've always wondered what your life would be like if you were just like the rest of us, and it sounds like your dream gave you a chance to do just that." Nadine taps a pen on the bible—my real bible, Tahiti stickers and all. "Now you know you're on the right path."

"That's more than the rest of us can say at eighteen," Liz points out.

"So what do you do now, Burke?" Austin asks.

"A lot," I say simply and rest my head on the hospital bed pillow to think about it. I'm suddenly very tired again.

They must realize that, because they say their good-byes and Austin shuts off the overhead light, but I can't sleep. My mind is racing. It may have been a dream, but this is my second chance. I am going to figure out how I want my life to work, once and for all. This time I'm going to straighten everything out, which is something I should have done a long time ago. If that dream has taught me anything, it's this: You can't wait on things. You have to do what you love, take the time to say what's in your heart, and take control of your own destiny.

I'm finally going to take charge of mine.

SCOOP PATROL

December 19

Kaitlin Burke in Car Crash Involving the Paparazzi

By Ellie Reeseman

Her eighteenth birthday should have been so bright, she needed to wear those Gucci aviators she was eyeing at Barney's that morning. But instead of making a birthday purchase for herself, Kaitlin headed up to Barney Greengrass restaurant at Barneys New York to have breakfast with her personal assistant, Nadine Holbrook; her boyfriend, Austin Mcyers; her best friend, Liz Mendes; and *Small Fries* costar Sky Mackenzie. Witnesses say the birthday brunch went downhill fast, with Kaitlin leaving in tears. "Kaitlin's assistant was giving her notice," says a witness. "She was devastated. I looked away to put sugar in my chamomile tea, and when I turned back they were arguing about college and Kaitlin's mom."

Those familiar with Kaitlin's mother, Meg Burke, know she's been a sour note in Kaitlin's skyrocketing career, pushing her daughter to such lengths that she became the subject of a less-than-flattering cover story in *Sure* last year. "She has been riding Kaitlin hard lately, pushing her to sign on to two high-profile movies," says a source close to the Burkes. "The projects are a huge get for Kaitlin, but taking both during one hiatus? Can you spell exhaustion? Kaitlin seems overwhelmed."

It's no wonder then that on the morning of her birthday Kaitlin wasn't concerned about having a fight with friends in front of the paparazzi, who were busy snapping away. When Kaitlin realized what was happening, sources say she told off the shutterbugs. "She said that she was

sick of her Hollywood life and wished it would all just disappear and for the cameras to go along with it," says one photographer, who asked not to be named. "It didn't sound like her at all."

"Kaitlin said nothing of the sort, and I have three photographers who were present that will confirm our side of the story," insists her publicist, Laney Peters. "Kaitlin was involved in an accident with the paparazzi that she had no control over. Instead of worrying about what Kaitlin was saying as she fled for her life, we should be talking about how the government of California should enact harsher laws against paparazzi and create legislation regarding the invasion of privacy for celebrities."

Following the heated discussion, Kaitlin rushed into a waiting SUV—not her usual car—and sped off with the salivating paparazzi in hot pursuit. What happened next is uncertain, but somewhere on Wilshire Boulevard, the SUV jumped a curb and hit a fence. No one on the street was injured, but Kaitlin, Austin, and the driver, Frank Turnblatt, were taken for medical treatment, with Kaitlin suffering a concussion and a broken ankle. She was released two days later after being monitored for head injuries. "I am so thankful that Austin, our driver, and I are okay and that no one else was hurt," said Kaitlin in her only statement. "Driving is serious business and I, for one, don't think anyone should get behind the wheel when they're upset. I know I won't when I get my license. But after what happened, I think that will be a ways away. For now, I just want to concentrate on my family, friends, and the future. To all my fans who sent their well wishes, thank you. Have a wonderful holiday season. We all have so much to be grateful for."

nineteen: *Finishing the Puzzle*

"Are your eyes closed?" I tease.

"Kate-Kate, you blindfolded us both with my new, never-worn Gucci scarves," Mom sniffs. "Yes, our eyes are closed and we're not peeking. Now what is this about? I'm freezing." Mom pulls her faux mink jacket (I freaked when she thought of getting a real one) tightly around her tan neck.

"Meg, it's fifty degrees," Dad says dryly. "It's certainly not freezing."

"I spoke to Nancy Walsh, and she said it was this cold in New York today." Mom's teeth are chattering. "How can it be this cold here too? My fingers are so numb, I can barely type on my BlackBerry."

"Now that's a Christmas present I never thought I'd get," Dad jokes, and I giggle.

"Enough chatting," Matty says sternly and winks at me. "If you don't behave, then you don't get your present. Well, Dad doesn't. This is really for him, Mom. That's why we said you didn't have to come."

"I wanted to be supportive." Mom blows on her hands.

"You're getting one of your presents from me later on, Mom," I remind her. "Well, two presents."

"Well, where are we now, then?" she complains. "I feel like we're on a highway, it's so loud. I don't like the idea of you driving us someplace without telling us."

"Rodney drove," Matty says. "And besides, that's why it's called a surprise."

Matty looks at me nervously. It took a lot of convincing for Matty to sign on to this present—I paid for most of it, but Matty chipped in too—but I think after I explained things in detail, he agreed with me. This present is going to make Dad happier than he's been in a long time. Matty's not sure Mom is going to like my gift to her so much, but he promised to support me. I told him I have a lot more experience in the Mom area since I've been doing this longer. "Which means she can be more mad at you too," Matty reminded me. That's what I'm afraid of.

"Are you ready, Kates?" Matty asks. "You should do the honors."

"Are you sure?" I ask my brother. He looks so grown-up in that black Kenneth Cole peacoat and jeans. I hobble over to him on my crutches. I can't wait till these things are gone for real. At least they're a good reminder of what I've learned. It's hard to maneuver when you're wearing a heavy green Gap wool coat, but Mom is right, it's chilly. That's why I'm also wearing a black-and-white-striped cashmere sweater underneath with skinny jeans and those much-talked-about Marc Jacobs boots. (I really do own a pair!)

"It was your idea." Matty smiles at me, revealing his perfect teeth. "Which means you get the first round of interrogations too."

"Why would there be yelling?" Mom questions, turning blindly toward our voices. "Kaitlin? Matthew?"

I untie Dad's blindfold first, and then Mom's. "Merry Christmas!" I yell. Matty hollers and I clap, but Mom and Dad stand there dumbfounded.

They're staring at huge glass windows where gleaming cars and SUVS are parked inside the store. We've taken them to Dad's old car dealership; the one he worked at years ago before he joined the Hollywood food chain. The place isn't open at nine AM on a Sunday morning, but that's okay, the staff is here to welcome us. I asked them to come in early to meet their new boss.

"But I . . . don't understand," Dad says, looking from Matty to me in confusion. "Why are we in front of my old dealership? I don't need a new car. My Maserati is only a year old."

"True," Matty says. "Why else would we be here, then?"

Mom sighs. "You two are not getting cars before you get your licenses!"

"We're not getting cars now, but when we do need wheels, we're coming here." I side-eye Matt. "We have an in with the owner."

"Eric Peterman?" Dad asks.

"No, *you*," Matt says. "You're the new owner, Dad. Merry Christmas!"

"What?" Dad's jaw almost hits the sidewalk and lands on a piece of gum.

"We bought it for you, Dad," I say, as Mom yells, "WHAT?" I hug him, holding my crutches away from my body. "You've never been as happy as you were working with cars. Everyone should love what they do."

"But my production deals," Dad stammers.

"Dad, let's face it," Matty says without a hint of irony. "You're never going to be a real producer. You've gotten some gigs from us, or more like Kates, but you're not going to make it out there."

"But that's okay, Dad, because you are a rock star when it comes to selling cars, and we know you've always wanted to own a dealership," I add quickly, since Matty is right but also being kind of harsh. "Now you do."

"I don't know what to say." Dad looks misty as he stares at the dealership. "How'd you know I missed this place?"

I grin. "Someone told me. Congrats, Dad! We hope this makes you as happy as you make us."

Dad bear hugs me and Matty, hitting Matty in the face with one of my crutches. "Are you sure? Really sure? I don't know what to say!"

"Ask how they got access to the money to buy this," Mom gripes, typing furiously on her BlackBerry with her short, pink nails, despite her aversion to chapped skin.

"Our financial planner said having Dad own a dealership

was more cost-effective than having his producing credit worked into all our future deals," Matty explains. "He signed off on this. He said he'd show you the numbers to prove it."

"Kids, I don't know what to say." Dad chokes up. "I have always wanted to own this dealership. I've missed being here. I'm terrible at movies."

"Don't say that." Mom pulls the sleeve of his Ralph Lauren trench coat. "You're brilliant!"

"Meg, I'm not, and I'm not happy doing it either." Dad looks serious, not sad. "Hollywood is not for me. All I want is to watch my kids do well and to enjoy their careers. I'm happy to take a backseat and sell some great cars."

"But, but . . ." Mom is speechless.

If this has her, wait till she sees what's next.

"Mom, you look like you could use a drink," says Matty, leading her to the front door. "The staff has bagels and mimosas and coffee inside to celebrate."

"Afterward, Mom, I'm taking you for a massage." I click clack with my crutches behind her. "I made appointments for us at the Four Seasons Hotel spa, and afterward we're going to have lunch at the Gardens."

"That sounds superb, sweetie," Mom gushes. "How thoughtful. You must really be enjoying your time off."

"Yes, it's been great getting stuff done," I say truthfully and wink at Rodney, who is carrying my new bag—it's a sparkly red Chloé bag that looks surprisingly similar to the no-name one in my dream. One of my errands this week was to find my dream bag and buy it. It's a great reminder of what I nearly lost and what I need to focus on now—getting my life in tip-top shape. "I have my Christmas shopping done, and I have a lot of assistant interviews scheduled."

"You're going to find someone ten times better than Nadine," Mom says. "It was time for you to make a change anyway."

"Change is a good thing," I agree, and try not to smirk. That would be mean. "It's good to have a fresh start, even if it's painful sometimes."

"Absolutely." I'm not sure Mom heard me because she's applying a deep red gloss on her lips and looking in a tiny mirror.

I am making headway on the assistant front, not that it's been fun. Nadine has been secretly interviewing assistants for me while she sets up her shingle as a manager. I don't know how she does it all, but she said she wouldn't feel good about leaving me in the lurch during the holidays. I told her it's quiet this time of year anyway, and it turned out the two weeks I have off to recuperate is actually almost four weeks with Christmas and New Year's thrown in the mix. I have plenty of time to find someone new to help me run my life. I guess. I'll still miss Nadine.

Which is why I'm not letting her go.

* * *

LIZ'S CELL: Tick tock. Tick tock. Time's up, Kates! Focus, focus, focus! It's now or never and I have faith U can do this!! LUV U!

AUSTIN'S CELL: UVE waited 4EVR 2 do this. Rock it, Burke! UVE practiced & R ready 2 face the fire. I'm thinking of U.

SKY'S CELL: K? Where R U? Did U do it yet? Don't chicken out! I need Nadine focused, not whining about U. Get going already!

"Katie-kins, that Swe-Thai massage was excellent!" Mom coos. We're being seated at a table at the Gardens restaurant in the Four Seasons for lunch. The restaurant is supposed to be casual, but I still think it's elegant. They have indoor and outdoor seating (it's too cold for that today), butter-colored walls, heavy drapes, big armchairs, and a nice, easy, California chic menu. Mom's face is glowing. "That was ninety minutes of pure heaven. How was yours?"

"The stone therapy was awesome," I tell Mom as we settle in to the corner table tucked into the back of the restaurant (my request). I'm hoping Mom doesn't question why we're not sitting at a two-seater instead of this six-chair round table. I pull my honey blond hair back in a low ponytail. I'm wearing what I had on this morning—my sweater, skinny jeans, and boots. The outfit is comfortable. And between the massage, the pep talks I've been giving myself, and the texts from my friends and Austin, I also feel confident.

"You were careful with your ankle during the treatment, right?" Mom asks worriedly, checking to make sure she buttoned all the buttons on her baby blue Aryn K silk blouse that has silk flowers for a collar. Mom's paired the beautiful top with wide-leg white trousers and white boots. "We can't risk you being off your feet any longer than you already are. The show gave you a very nice break as it is."

"I know, Mom."

"I've given you a nice break too, you know," Mom says lightly, rapping her fingers on the table. "I've listened to you and your father and given you time to grieve Nadine's departure and to come to terms with your hectic spring." She pauses and looks into my eyes. "I only want to do what's best for you, Kaitlin. I know I push you hard sometimes, but it's only because I love you and want to see you succeed."

Here we go . . .

"I wanted to talk to you about that, Mom." I take a sip of ice water. "I know you have my best interests at heart, but I still think juggling Matty and my careers is taking its toll on you. You can't do it all," I tell her kindly.

"Of course I can," Mom says hastily and almost drops the spoon about to go into her iced tea to stir her raw sugar. "I'm not slacking."

"I didn't say you were slacking," I say hastily and place a napkin on my lap. "I said you have too much on your plate. You . . ." I hesitate. "You don't seem happy, and you look tired."

"I'm not tired," Mom insists and instinctively touches her eyes, which are wrinkle-free thanks to her Botox treatments. But she looks uncomfortable with the subject matter, and she immediately changes the conversation to prove her point. "I'm fine. Now about those contracts, Kaitlin. You have to sign them today. We need to go to Seth's right from here. You can't risk losing one of these movies!" Mom's green eyes look wild, like a tiger's, but they look desperate too. She doesn't like anyone giving her feedback on her job, and she really wants me to follow her guidance. I don't have the heart to tell her that I've already made my decision. I actually signed a contract to do the James Cameron film. I called Mr. Eastwood personally to tell him I was turning the role down, and he was disappointed, but he applauded my work ethic and said he understood me not wanting to over-extend myself. He said they may not shoot till late fall now, so if that happens, he'll definitely give me a call.

I take a deep breath before I answer Mom. "I'm not going there today. I have an appointment tomorrow."

Mom grabs her BlackBerry. "I don't see any appointment for tomorrow. Tomorrow is Matty's *Teen Vogue* shoot, and I'm going to be there all day. I guess I could dash out around eleven for half an hour. No, no, I'm wrong. I have a conference call with the *Scooby* folks then. Um . . ."

"It's okay, Mom, you don't have to be there." I take a roll from the bread basket they've just brought. Mom raises her right eyebrow at me, and I'm not sure if it's because of my comment or because of the bread.

"Of course I have to be there! You can't sign without your manager."

"Sorry I'm late, Kates." Nadine throws down her bag and coat without looking up. "That Ananda facial rocks and . . ."

327

She sees Mom. "I'm out of here." I grab the back of her green sweater.

"You're not going anywhere," I tell her, but she won't sit.

"Then I'm going," Mom says, getting up quickly.

"No," I tell them sternly. "I need to talk to both of you."

"I thought today was my Christmas gift," Mom sniffs.

"I thought the massage and lunch were *my* Christmas gift." Nadine is whiny too. "You're not what I want for Christmas either, Meg."

"This is what I'm talking about, Nadine." Mom points a pink nail at her, and I brace for fighting. "Your flippant attitude is uncalled for. I think you—"

"Stop," I tell them. Then I smile sweetly at the waiter bringing over the salads that we didn't order. I ordered everything beforehand so there would be no interruptions. "To be honest, the spa day isn't either of your Christmas gifts. I needed to get you both in the same place at the same time."

"Well, that was dishonest, Kaitlin," says Mom as she drips dressing on her salad, not even asking if it's low-fat. "Why would you torture us around the holidays?"

Nadine takes a seat on the other side of me and grabs a roll, much to Mom's displeasure. "Surprisingly, Kates, I agree with her."

"Today isn't a Christmas gift you can unwrap, but it is a gift of sorts," I explain. I look down at the crispy lettuce leaves, hoping for a script to appear that would tell me exactly what to say to make them listen. "Aren't you tired of being pushed and squeezed, always trying to catch your breath, doing what everyone else wants you to do?" I ask them both. "Don't you want to be happy?"

Mom raises her eyebrows. "Are you saying we've made you unhappy, Kaitlin?" She sounds very hurt. "I've given you everything you could possibly want and more. Even when I don't understand—like when you and Drew Thomas broke up, or when you wanted to enroll at Clark Hall for a semester—I've let you do it. I didn't realize you were so un-happy."

"You're not making me unhappy." I change my approach slightly. "I think I'm making *you* unhappy, Mom. Look at you!" I tell her. "I've never seen you so stressed. You're not enjoying yourself. I know you've done an amazing job getting me where I am in my career, but at what cost to you? To our relationship? I know you want me to be bigger than Reese Witherspoon, Mom, but I'm only eighteen. I have time to get there."

"I don't understand what you want me to say," Mom says exasperatedly, and her BlackBerry buzzes urgently. She ignores it. "My happiness isn't your concern. I'm worried about you, and if sometimes I seem a little stressed doing it, then—"

"I'm worried about us," I blurt out, and my voice cracks. "I know you could keep doing what you're doing forever, driving yourself into the ground, but I need to see you as happy as Dad is with his new dealership. Your life shouldn't all be about me and Matty. You deserve to enjoy yourself too."

Mom stutters, "I do, I mean, I—"

I grab Mom's hand. "I want more for us, Mom. I want a real relationship, and I don't think we've had one in a very long time. I don't want to be your employer anymore. I want to be your daughter, and I want you to act like my mom, not my manager." My voice grows stronger. "I want to talk about normal stuff, like a fight I have with Austin or what you think of an outfit I'm wearing on a date or what I should do about going to college. And I want you to answer as my mom, not as someone who has a stake in the industry." Tears start to plop down my cheeks.

Mom is teary too and looks completely shocked by what I just said. "Oh, honey, of course I want to be your mom." She leans over and hugs me tight, not letting go. "I thought I was being your mother, making sure your career was on track." She looks at Nadine. "I always worried about someone taking advantage of my children. You see how this town can do that." Nadine nods. "But that's not what you really needed, was it?" Mom looks at me and I shake my head no. We're both crying now, in the middle of the restaurant, and I don't think either of us care. "I want us to have a real relationship too. I know you talk to your dad about things you don't with me. I hate that you think you can't tell me anything important." She strokes my hair and sighs heavily. "So what do we do to change this?"

"For starters," I say and wipe away my tears, "I think we have to separate our personal and professional relationships. I know you don't want to do this, Mom, but I think

I need to find a new manager." She starts to protest, but I cut her off. "You've focused on my career forever, and you've made me a big star," I say quickly. "I'm so grateful for all that you've done to get me here. Now it's time for you to do the same for Matty. He needs you, Mom, and the two of you work well together."

Mom sniffs. "He does need me, doesn't he?"

"Yes. And when you're not working, you and I can focus on our relationship, and you can spend time doing the other things you love, like working with the Darling Daisies." I smile. "That's your other Christmas present—I spoke to Nancy Walsh and told her what a mistake it was not to make you the chairperson of the West Coast committee. I told her you'd have more time to devote to your charity work now that we weren't working together anymore, and she agreed to give the position to you. You're gearing up the launch, Mom!"

Mom looks stunned. "You called Nancy Walsh for me? I . . . this is incredible! Wait till I tell Victoria the news!" She goes to grab her BlackBerry, but then she looks at me. "I can't do it. I can't leave you like this."

I look her straight in the eyes. "I need a mom more."

Mom wipes under her eyes and sighs. "Okay, then. If this is what you really want . . ."

"I do," I say honestly. "I think this is the best thing for both of us."

"So where do we go to find you a new manager?" Mom says and grabs her BlackBerry for real, going straight back to work mode. She starts scrolling through numbers. "We need someone who can devote a lot of time to you, especially with the projects you have lined up, and someone who can—"

I gently pull the BlackBerry out of her hands. "I already found someone." I look at my former assistant. "Nadine."

"Kates, are you serious?" Nadine squeals. "You're not just saying that?"

"You have gotten me through so much," I tell Nadine seriously. "I can't think of anyone who knows me and what I need better than you."

Mom's gentle expression hardens. "No. No, no, no. She's an assistant! She doesn't have what it takes. You're always giving bad advice," Mom scolds Nadine. "Who gives back the pot on five-dollar Friday?"

"The star!" Nadine retorts. "It's meant for the crew."

"Then why put in five dollars?" Mom asks.

I sigh. They're getting off the point, but I guess I should still explain.

HOLLYWOOD SECRET NUMBER NINETEEN: Five-dollar Friday is another one of those morale boosters on movie sets. Or you could call it a lottery, kind of like the one we did with the jar on my last movie set. On five-dollar Friday, everyone in the cast and crew gives five dollars (get it?), and the winner's name is drawn at the end of the day and that person gets to keep the money raised. Even stars participate because it's considered rude not to, but the unwritten rule is that stars don't collect the prize. Mom freaked out when I won one time and Nadine commended me on giving the money to the next person I picked from the hat.

"Kaitlin, you see what's happened on *Entourage*," Mom adds and squeezes my hand. "E can't do anything right for Vince."

I giggle. "Mom, that's a TV show. Nadine knows what she's doing, and she has a lot of people who believe in her." I give the waitress the sign, and on cue, Seth and Laney appear. "I knew you'd have some doubts, so I asked some people here to back me up. Seth and Laney are two of the biggest agents and publicists in the business, and they think Nadine is the right manager for me too."

Seth and Laney take seats, and the waitress brings over the iced teas I ordered them. They're both in work mode. Seth is in one of his pitch-perfect John Varvatos tailored navy suits, and Laney is in a tan slim-fit pantsuit that looks like Chloé. Her long blond hair is pulled back loosely.

"Meg, I know we don't always see eye to eye, but I think Kaitlin is right," Seth says, removing his trademark sunglasses and getting to the point. "Nadine has what it takes. We're going to work closely and make decisions together. I have full confidence in her." Seth smiles at Nadine, who looks like she might burst into tears. "You know I wouldn't hand Kaitlin over to just anyone."

"That's true," Mom says and plays with her fork.

"I think she has the chops too, Meg," Laney adds and actually smiles at Nadine. I notice she's not wearing her

Bluetooths. "This one has never mucked up Kaitlin's career the way so many idiot assistants do. Nadine's smart and savvy and having worked with her for years, I know she's got the guts and the mouth to keep Kaitlin on the fast track to the A-list. Heck, Kaitlin is already there."

"I have already made her a household name," Mom tells herself more than the rest of us. "How badly could Nadine mess it up?" Nadine looks like she wants to snap, but I give her a look. Thankfully, she restrains herself. Mom looks around the table, taking it all in. Then she looks at me. "If this is what you really want . . ."

I squeeze her tight, not caring if I'm wrinkling Mom's blouse. "What I really want is for you to be my mom. You'll know everything going on, and I will always want your opinion, but the work rests with me and my team. You're off duty."

"Matty could use some good torturing, Meg." Seth winks and runs a hand through his stylized do. "You're going to have your hands full."

"I've already had to fend off a dozen rumors of who he's dating." Laney groans and stares at one of her phones angrily. "That boy is going to put my tabloid statements into overdrive."

Mom laughs. "That's for sure! It sounds like I will have my hands full and when I don't"—she looks at me again—"I'm going to be spending time with my daughter. That's the best gift a mom could ask for around the holidays."

I may cry again. Mom is never this mushy. "Merry Christmas, Mom."

"Merry Christmas to you too, Kate-Kate." Mom kisses my forehead. "And an early happy New Year. I have a feeling next year is going to be your best one yet."

For once, Mom and I see eye to eye.

Next year is going to rock.

SCENE:
HOPE and TAYLOR'S dorm room. HOPE'S best friend from
home, KARA, is visiting, and all she can talk about is
how HOPE made a bad choice coming here instead of to
Georgetown with her. HOPE is ready to strangle her, but
TAYLOR and the gang calm her down.

HOPE:
(lets out an ear-piercing scream and throws her pillow
across the room, almost hitting Gunther) If she says the
G word one more time, I'm going to ... I'm going to ... make
her eat every last Philly cheesesteak in the cafeteria.
And she has a dairy allergy!

GUNTHER:
Way harsh, Hopester.

HOPE:
Harsh? Harsh? I'll tell you what's harsh! Kara's hair!
I don't care if everyone at the G word is washing their
hair once a week to save water. It looks terrible! And I'm
not going to tell her that! Let her walk around looking
like a satellite station!

ZOE:
We could help her too, you know. All she needs is a good

deep-conditioning treatment and that frizz
would disappear.

HOPE:
(mocking Kara's voice) The *G* word has huge dorm rooms.
The *G* word has a coffee bar right on campus. The *G*
word has a larger student body, more international
programs, blah, blah, blah! I'll give her an
international program! I'll hit her so hard she lands
in London. That will save her a plane ticket.

TAYLOR:
Hope, you've got to calm down. Don't listen to her!

HOPE:
(plops down on her bed) I can't help it. The more she
talks about the *G* word and what a mistake I made the
more I worry that ... *(She stops.)*

EDISON:
That what?

HOPE:
That I *did* make a mistake. What if I should have gone
to Georgetown instead of here? What if Kara's right?
What if I would have been happier or had better
professors or taken a class called the Politics of
North African Masculinities? What if I'm, as she says,

wasting my noggin?

ZOE:
You are certainly not wasting that. I might be,
but you? Never.

EDISON:
Listen to her, Hope. She's got this one right.

TAYLOR:
Hope, what makes you think George—

HOPE:
(freaks out) Don't say the word!

TAYLOR:
Fine. What makes you think the *G* word is any better
than here? I'm sure we have that class you mentioned.
Plus we have nine million incredible other ones that
you're always yakking about to the point I put in my
earbuds, turn up my iPod, and tune you out.

HOPE:
You do that? I always wondered why you never
answered me. I thought you were trying to be
philosophical.

TAYLOR:

I was bored! But you're not! You love it here, and you
want to know why? Because you picked this place from a
batch of acceptance letters. I'm sure if you think hard
enough, you can think of a dozen reasons why you chose
here over the *G* word.

GUNTHER:

I better be on that list.

ZOE:

Ooh! Me too, please? The only lists I'm ever on are ones
that involve girls who look great in bikinis.

TAYLOR:

(dryly) Poor you. Edison! Stop smiling!

EDISON:

Sorry.

TAYLOR:

Hope? Are you thinking?

HOPE:

I don't have to think. I already know. The climate is
way better. Heck, I could surf and then take yoga all
before my ten AM classes if I want. Kara can't do that
at the *G* place.

GUNTHER:

The only surfing she can do is snowboarding.

HOPE:

I can study outside, I have professors that have worked with Nobel Prize winners, past presidents, and sat in on world conferences.

EDISON:

Keep going. Regrets are for wusses, you know.

GUNTHER:

I have lots of regrets.

TAYLOR:

Well, I have none. You can't look back. Nothing you can do to change it. Only forward. I have a feeling Kara is riding you about the *G* word because she sees how fabulous it is here.

EDISON:

Maybe she's the one doing the regretting. About *G* town!

GUNTHER:

G town. I like that. Could be the name of a rap group.

ZOE:

I think it is the name of a rap group.

HOPE:

What would I do without you guys?

TAYLOR:

You'd be stuck in the lounge area by yourself, that's what.

HOPE:

Okay, when Kara gets back here from the showers...

EDISON:

She's in the showers? I think I need to get something down
the hall.

EVERYONE:

Edison!

HOPE:

When Kara gets back here, I'm not going to let her get to me.
I love it here! I love my new life, and I'm not afraid to say
it. If Kara is unhappy with hers, that's too bad.

TAYLOR:

Atta girl. Oh, and while you're looking forward, could you
look down too? If you don't put your shoes in the closet when
you come in the room, I'm going to start throwing them out.

I can't keep tripping over them.

HOPE:
There is no room in the closet! Your extra textbooks take up all the floor space.

TAYLOR:
Hey, they were a good buy! They're next year's books at this year's prices.

HOPE:
How do you know . . . *(voice becomes muffled. Taylor and Hope continue to bicker, but we can't hear what they're saying.)*

GUNTHER:
Girls.

EDISON:
Wusses.

COMMERCIAL BREAK

TWENTY: *Back on Track*

I walk to my mark across the set, right in front of Taylor's (aka Sky's) bed, which is covered with a fluffy, purple-striped comforter and lots of throw pillows. The wall behind her bed is painted purple, which was part of the plot for last week's episode. Taylor got in huge trouble with Edison for doing it. She tried to use legalese to get out of paying a fine at the end of the year for defacing dorm property.

"When Kara gets back here," I say evenly, staring at Sky seriously, "I'm not going to let her get to me. I love it here! I love my new life, and I'm not afraid to say it. If Kara is unhappy with hers, that's too bad."

Sky nods approvingly. She looks so cute in that fitted sweater vest, collared shirt, and khaki skirt. Her very long dark hair is pulled back in a low ponytail. Very private-school girl. "Atta girl. Oh, and while you're looking forward, could you look down too? If you don't put your shoes in the closet when you come in the room, I'm going to start throwing them out. I can't keep tripping over them."

"There is no room in the closet!" I say, pointing to the closet behind me. I start pulling on my sage green BCBG wrap sweater, which is lodged under one of the piles of books. I hope my tan pleated miniskirt doesn't hitch up while I'm bending over like this and flash the crew. "Your extra textbooks take up all the floor space!"

"Hey, they were a good buy!" Taylor/Sky protests and whips out a large history book, almost knocking Gunther in the head. I do my best not to giggle. I'm not sure she meant for that to happen, but I don't want to screw up and make them redo the take. "They're next year's books at this year's prices."

"How do you know they're going to use that book next year? Huh?" I improvise, since we're supposed to keep talking even as we drop our voices.

Gunther steps forward. "Girls."

Edison shakes his head. "Wusses."

"CUT TO COMMERCIAL BREAK!" yells our episode director.

My family and friends, who are hanging out by the episode director off camera, start to applaud. This is our first episode since our four-week break, and in a show of support, everyone I love came to watch me film. Mom and Dad are here with Laney, Seth, Nadine, Rodney, Austin, and Liz.

"Great job, guys," our guest director, Taye Markenson, says, walking over to where we're still standing. "We're going to take a short break to set up the next shot. Kaitlin? Sky? This is the scene where you're driving Kara back to the airport." Sky and I nod. "We're using the poor man's process, so try not to overdo it, okay?"

HOLLYWOOD SECRET NUMBER TWENTY: The poor man's process is a movie term that is used when you're shooting a scene inside a car or an airplane or another moving object, but you're not actually going to be in a moving object. They sometimes blow out the windows in the car—make them look milky white like you would for a green screen effect—to keep the audience from seeing outside the car. It's a cheap way to get a shot done, but if it's done right, the at-home audience won't know the difference. It's usually the actor who messes things up when they're acting out their driving. I don't have my license yet, so I could be horrible at this. Hmm . . . maybe Sky should be the one who pretends to drive.

"I'm going to go see my family," I tell Sky and grab a bottle of Smartwater to take with me.

"I'll come too," Sky says. "I need to find out if Nadine ever heard back from Judd Apatow's people."

You'd think Sky and I would be bickering worse than the Kardashians now that we both have the same manager, but surprisingly, that's not happening—yet. Nadine tries to keep our affairs separate and usually has something to say when one of us starts questioning what the other is auditioning for. "You worry about your own career and let me worry about hers, okay?" I've heard her say those words to both of us on more than one occasion. Other than that, the transition is going well. Even Mom has relinquished her role without a lot of drama. She still calls Nadine daily to check in, but Nadine has been patient. "She really does have some helpful ideas," Nadine said diplomatically.

My family went ahead to my dressing room, so Sky and I join them there. It's so loud in my little room you'd think we were having a party, which I guess we kind of are. I can't remember the last time all these people were in the same room and they weren't fighting or throwing *Hollywood Nations* at each other. Matty rushes through the door, knocking into me and Nadine. Mom shrieks when she sees him. His face is covered in fake blood, and he has a black eye. His black tee and jeans are shredded, but he's smiling so I know he's okay.

"Did I miss anything?" he asks, sounding out of breath. "I have to be back in ten to do a phoner with *EW*. They're thinking of putting the cast on the cover!"

"Awesome, Matty," I say and give him a squeeze. "But you know you'll have to get in line." I look at Sky.

"K and I are on their next cover," she says and flicks his nose. "'The headline is: 'The Hottest New Show of the Season.'"

Matty's jaw drops. "Hey! That's supposed to be our headline!"

"Yours is the hottest *haunted* show," I tell him. "I checked."

"Okay," he says, thinking a bit. "But we're still going to beat you in the ratings."

"Bring it on, werewolf lover!" Sky teases, and Matty laughs.

"Kaitlin?" Mom says tentatively. "Your last take was

excellent. Your emotion was perfect!" Mom is really trying to work on her mothering. Last week we went for mani/pedis together, and she didn't bring up the Beckhams or the *H* word (*Hollywood*) once.

"Thanks, Mom," I tell her. "That means a lot to me."

"I don't think I've ever heard Meg give a straight-out compliment before," Seth says and winks at her. Everyone chuckles.

"My daughter is a star and I'm proud," Mom tells the group. I hear Matty clear his throat. "Both of my children are stars." She looks at my dad. "That's why I want to share this surprise we have for them with all of you." Mom looks directly at me. "We wanted to wait till we knew for sure before we told you. We're moving."

At first my heart stops. "Where?"

"You're going to be thrilled, Kate-Kate," Dad says enthusiastically. "We bought a house in Toluca Lake!"

"WHAT?" Matty, Liz, and I say at the same time.

Toluca Lake? That's where the alter-Burkes lived! If we wind up living in the same house, I'm going to have to see a psychologist for sure. But other than that, I'm excited. I love Toluca Lake! I've always wanted to live near many of the other studio kids. It's so pretty and residential and doesn't feel so isolated like our home does now. It's also much closer to Austin's and Liz's. "But why? How? What...?"

Dad looks at Mom and plays with his shirt collar. He's in golf mode again, looking like a caddy in his Dockers and button-down shirt. "We've been thinking of moving for a while. At first your mom wanted Malibu, but in the last few weeks, we started looking in other areas, and your mom mentioned how much you like Toluca Lake. We went looking with a realtor and found this darling Tudor."

"I wouldn't call it darling, honey," Mom tuts. "*Darling* sounds small. This is forty-five hundred square feet, but it feels homey. We put an offer in right away, and it was accepted. We'll move as soon as our house sells."

"When can we see it?" Matty wants to know. "Stefan and Jo live in Toluca Lake too. Wait till I tell everyone on set. This rocks, guys!"

I hug my parents, lingering with my mom, who smells like freesia, which is also the color of the cashmere sweater she's wearing with skinny jeans and tall, tan boots. "Are you okay with this? It's a lot to give up," I tell her. "You won't live anywhere near as close to the Beckhams as we do now."

"Toluca Lake is the place to be," Mom says wryly. "I told Victoria she should look herself." Mom touches my chin. "And if she doesn't, then too bad for her. I think we're going to love it there, and that's all I'm concerned about."

"The mileage to the dealership is pretty great too," Dad tells me happily. "I really like the drive. You're going to love it when you get your license, Kate-Kate."

"Speaking of which, when are you taking that test?" Laney asks. "I'm getting sick of answering phone calls about your driving exam. Are you ever getting your license?"

"Hey! I was on crutches for a few weeks, if you recall," I

remind them as they laugh. "I've had a lot going on. Work, meetings, assistant interviews, college applications. Now that they're all in and I'm just waiting to hear, I'll reschedule the test." I look at Nadine out of habit, but she's not my assistant anymore. I'm pretty close to finding one, thanks to her, but I haven't committed yet. Nadine is hard to replace. Mom knows I've sent in college applications. She still doesn't think I need to go, but she said she understands my need to try new things. Like I said—she's growing.

"We are going to throw a party when you take that test and pass." Rodney flashes his gold tooth. "And you're going to pass because I am the one giving you driving lessons."

"Learn from the best, that's what I always say," I joke.

There is a knock at the door, and the Mexican food we ordered for dinner tonight arrives. The scent of enchiladas and melted cheese makes me salivate, but I don't want to get anything on my wardrobe. Instead of digging in with the others, I walk over to Liz, Sky, and Austin. Austin puts his arm around me. His half-zip green sweater feels soft against my skin.

"I think a party for getting your license is a great idea," Austin says. "Liz and I are already on the decorations."

Liz grins. "We're going to have a big banner made that says 'It only took me two paparazzi mishaps, a shady driving instructor, and two years to get my license.'"

"I like it. Will you get plastic plates that look like steering wheels?" I ask.

"We can get a cake that has little cars on it being chased

by the paparazzi," Sky suggests and we all groan. "What? Too much?"

"Too much," I agree. "I don't want to relive that."

Not the accident part, not even the dream part, because my life now is just the way I want it to be. I start preproduction on the James Cameron project in late April and am done by July, a few weeks before I go back to *Small Fries*. Even with *SF* work, I'll still have plenty of time to see Liz and Austin before they head off to college. The one thing I know about furthering my education is that wherever I go, it will be close to home. I'm not giving up *SF*, and I'm not giving up my chance to do college either. Liz applied all over, including NYU ("I'm not heading east, though," she said hastily. "I'm a Los Angeles girl. Right?"). I think she still adores NYU more than she'll admit. Austin has several schools on his radar, and his top picks are all in New England, which is pretty far from here. But after all that's happened the past few years, I'm not about to worry about the long-distance thing just yet.

"What are you thinking about, Burke?" Austin asks, giving me a kiss on the cheek.

"You, me, fall, friends, college, life," I rattle off the list and smile. "Nothing big."

"Yeah, you're not one to worry about anything major," Austin teases. "You take things as they come."

"I do now," I say confidently. "It's a new year, and I'm just grateful to be here, on this set, with all of you."

"You're not going to get weepy on us again like on New

350

Year's, are you?" Sky asks. "I thought I was going to have to take you and Liz outside and throw you in the pool to calm you down."

Okay, so on New Year's I was still a little weepy about what the next year could bring, but I'm allowed to be sad that everyone might be leaving Los Angeles eventually, even if I know we all have to grow up and lead our own lives. "No tears," I promise Sky. "I'm happy."

"It's about time," she says and smiles a little.

"It's taken you a long time to get here, so you should enjoy it," adds Liz and raises her glass of Sprite to me.

"I am," I say and I really mean it. I lean into Austin, with his arm firmly around me, and he kisses my cheek.

I have all I've ever wanted and then some. I'm sure worrying will always be part of my nature—hey, I'm an actress and we tend to be dramatic!—but being happy, having the freedom to do what I want, and looking toward the future with an open mind is the name of the game now. It may have taken me a while, but I think I've finally figured out how to have a Hollywood life I can truly enjoy.

UNIVERSITY OF SOUTHERN CALIFORNIA

ESSAY QUESTION: Have you changed your life, or has your life changed you?
(Essay must be at least two thousand words but not more than four thousand. Please type and double-space your essay.)

I was supposed to write this essay over a month ago, and if I had, I would have written something completely different. My answer would have been how my life had changed me.

That's not true anymore.

Today I can honestly say that I'm in the driver's seat, and I couldn't be happier. I've always been the kind of person that let other people take control. You might think I did it because I was weak, or afraid to disappoint others, but I think the real reason I let others make my decisions was because I was too overwhelmed to do it for myself. My profession (acting) has a lot of pressure, and I've relied heavily on other people's expertise and advice to help me make my choices. I thought they knew more than I did. Now I'm not so sure. I've been acting since I was a child, which means I've been doing this as long as, if not longer than, my so-called life experts. I've learned what it's like to grow up on a soundstage, to have my picture taken while I'm throwing out the trash, and how to deal with backstabbing costars, all the while smiling and acting as if I don't have a care in the world.

I didn't realize that the more I let others be the puppet masters, the more unhappy I became with myself. I've always enjoyed what I did, but the more pressured I felt, the more I wished I could escape. I forgot to love what I did and instead started to loathe it. I was ungrateful, but I wasn't without reason for being so. I let people, work, enemies, even shoplifters (another story entirely) pick away at the things I loved, and slowly all I had left were the things I didn't like.

It took fate to help me realize what I would have lost if I let people take away the things I love most. I thought there could be Kaitlin the actress and Kaitlin the regular girl, but I know now they're the same person. I need to be in charge of both of them if I want a life I can be proud of.

Since I've taken over taking care of, well, me, my life has only improved for the better. I won't lie—being the one in charge can be scary. I'm still worried that I'll make a bad decision, or say the wrong thing and embarrass myself on the *Late Show*, but I know with every mistake I make, I'm learning something too. When I screw up, it's because I'm the one who made the mess in the first place. Is my life still crazy and complicated sometimes? Yes. But it's my life, and I wouldn't have it any other way.

—Kaitlin Burke

EPILOGUE: *Eight Months Later*

"Yes to *Ellen*, no to *The View*. I have an Introduction to Art History class test that afternoon," I say, walking briskly across the grassy knoll, sidestepping two guys throwing a Frisbee and a group of people reading books on an over-sized picnic blanket.

"Apologize and send flowers, though, and tell the ladies I'd love to cohost the next time they're in town," I add, hiking my heavy Kate Spade messenger bag over my shoulder. "Uh-huh. Yep. Eight PM. Tell Rodney I'll be at the southwest corner this time chatting with Larry the Liar." I laugh. "Kidding! But I will be there." BEEP. I look at the iPhone screen and practically scream out loud I'm so excited. But I don't want to draw attention to myself. I've done such a good job of not doing that so far. I put the phone back to my ear and say to my assistant, "Shannon? It's Liz on the other line! I have to take this. Thanks again, Shannon. I'll see you tomorrow." I click over. "Lizzie? How's the Big Apple treating you?"

"Kates!" Her voice comes through loud and clear like

she's standing next to me, not three thousand miles away at New York University. Liz may have thought she was a true-blue California girl, but she realized she had room to love New York too. I'm glad. She belongs there, even if I miss her. "Sorry I missed your call last night," she says. "I tried calling you back, but Shannon said you guys were in the middle of a taping. How'd it go?"

"Great. Season two, episode four is in the can, and we premiere this week." I shade my eyes from the warm California sun. Everyone on campus is in shorts, tees, and flip-flops, and my green Alice + Olivia tank dress sticks out like a sore thumb. I just came from an eight AM table read for the next episode. The rest of the day I'm here, at University of Southern California, taking college classes. The studio has been so accommodating; sometimes I still can't believe it. We worked it out so that I get to take day classes in the afternoon on Tuesdays and Thursdays, after putting in five early-morning hours on set.

"They'd rather make it work with you than lose the hottest star on the planet," Seth explained when he and Nadine put the deal through back in May. "They know how lucky they are to have the George Clooney of current TV on their network." Seth winked. "I'm not exaggerating! Everyone who knows anything is talking about your work with James Cameron, and you being on the network makes them look good. Your film is the most groundbreaking project Cam's had in years. Dare we say Oscar territory?"

"We dare not," I said with a laugh, even though the thought makes my skin tingle. "It's too early to speculate."

"Maybe for you, but *EW* is already saying it, and the film won't screen for months," Nadine pointed out. "Sky forwarded me the article and—don't tell her I said this—she actually said she wants to be on your career path now."

"Wow," I marveled. "After spending months telling me what a mistake I'm making, she's doing a one-eighty." Sky's got me helping her with *her* admissions application to USC now. She's hoping to take a few classes in the spring now that we have this *Small Fries* schedule that works with coursework. "She told me the two of you are meeting with Peter Jackson about his next project."

"You've really inspired her, Kates," Nadine told me. "Even if she won't tell you that herself."

"She does in her own way," I said with a smile.

Nadine continues to inspire me too. She's kicked butt as my manager, not only passing along the best scripts for me to read but filtering through everything Shannon gets offered to make sure I do what's necessary to make it in Hollywood and yet still have time to be a college coed. Nadine's business is doing great. She has four clients, including me and Sky, and has hired her own personal assistant.

A text interrupts my conversation with Liz and pulls me back to the present.

SKY'S CELL: Bored! Thx to U and UR new sched! Meet

356

later for coffee? SOS w/my admission essay. U up to help college girl?"

"Guess what my roommate asked me to see tomorrow night since she got student rate tickets?" Liz is saying. "*Meeting of the Minds*! I feel like I should check it out and see how they're faring without you."

"Last I heard they had a proper trained stage actress doing my part, so they should be fine," I say. "I wish I were going with you, though. Promise we'll get tickets to something when I'm in town in a few weeks to do the morning show rounds for *Small Fries?*"

"Already on it," Liz informs me. "Sky wants tickets to—don't laugh—*Rock of Ages.*"

"Isn't that a little commercial for her?" I ask. "Not that I mind seeing it."

"I think Josh is going to drive down from Rhode Island and meet us," Liz says. "I wish Austin could be there. Then we'd have a real party."

"I know," I say sadly. "I talked to him about it, and he can't miss lacrosse practice. They've got a few big games coming up."

"I miss that boy," Liz says wistfully. "And you. Bet you don't have time to miss any of us."

I laugh. "I'm not *that* busy! Not anymore."

"True," Liz agrees. "Matty's the one on overload."

"And loving it," I add. "Mom booked him two movies for his hiatus and he's doing the Thanksgiving Day Parade and has a guest judging spot on *American Idol* this winter. Mom

357

is elated. She told him he has to mention Dad's dealership and the Darling Daisies at least once during the broadcast." I giggle.

"You mean she's not going to be there with cue cards off-stage telling Matty what to say?" Liz asks dryly.

"Actually, she and I are going to be at the Canyon Ranch Spa that week," I tell Liz, checking my bag for one of my assignments that is due today. I thought I printed it out, but if not, I can just plug my MacBook Air in at the computer lab and make another copy. "We're having a girls' weekend. It was her idea."

"She's really come around," Liz marvels. "If I didn't know any better, I would say she's a clone."

"Lizzie!" I admonish. Although I can't say the thought hasn't crossed my mind. I just thought it was because I watch too many *Clone Wars* reruns.

"Okay, sorry, sorry." I hear her apologize to someone talking in the background. "Kates? My roommate's here, and we're going to grab some coffee before philosophy. I'll talk to you tonight, though, I'm sure."

"I talk to you more now than while you were here!" I tell her. "Of course we'll talk tonight. Love you!"

"Love you too," Liz yells back.

I hang up and quickly text Sky.

KAITLIN'S CELL: U win. Coffee at 8:30. Coffee Bean on Melrose. TTYL.

SKY'S CELL: Took you long enough. :)

KAITLIN'S CELL: Did U just make a :)?

SKY'S CELL: UR fault! If U tell anyone, I will deny it!
TTYL.

I laugh and put my phone in my bag, setting it to vibrate. If anything urgent comes up, Shannon can always text me. She knows not to while I'm in class unless it's an absolute emergency, and she's never had to yet. Only Mom has—to ask me what Matty should wear on *The Tonight Show*. Mom still wins most improved, though.

I check my watch and see it's almost two. I still have a ways to walk, so I pick up my pace and hike my bag on my shoulder. I feel guilty not using the ruby red one I love so much, but it doesn't really go with my green dress. Besides, I hate throwing it on the floor when I'm in a lecture hall. That red bag is still my favorite, and it deserves to be used for special occasions, like the Golden Globe Awards.

Before I know it, I'm walking toward my usual table at the outdoor coffee bar. My date is already waiting.

"We need to get you Rollerblades, Burke," Austin says with a huge grin. I throw my messenger bag onto the waiting chair and lean over to give him a kiss. "You take way too long to get across campus."

Austin was *thisclose* to taking a partial scholarship at Boston College when he got a full scholarship offer for

359

University of Southern California. He couldn't pass it up. "I've been thinking of taking up surfing," he told me, explaining his decision to stay on the West Coast. "I can't do that in Boston in January. And besides, I like the warm weather. I think I'd miss it too much if I went east." He didn't add, "And I'd miss you," but he didn't have to. I knew. I always know when it comes to Austin.

Can I just say how relieved I am that he's still here? Forget just being my boyfriend, Austin has been the best campus tour guide any girl could ask for. A few months at Clark Hall was not enough training for me to fit in on a college campus. Austin showed me around, helped me buy textbooks, and stayed by my side at freshman orientation. I was worried that people would treat me differently because I'm a celebrity, but so far, it doesn't seem like a big deal. Well, other than the fact that everyone on campus has seen my admissions essay. It was leaked and ran in *Hollywood Nation*. (Laney made USC donate a huge chunk of money to the Darling Daisies committee for that slip-up, which made Mom happy.) That sort of mishap is part of the price of being me, and I'm okay with that. Finally.

"Since when should walking around campus be a sprint?" I place my hands on my hips in mock indignation. "Some of us don't get to spend all afternoon outdoors, so we walk slowly and take in everything around us from the birds to the noise of the students, to the architecture of the buildings."

Austin gives me a look, his classic bangs falling across his big, blue eyes with a small gust of wind. "English was definitely the right major for you, Miss Drama. I smell a screenplay in your future."

"Maybe," I say with a smile and let Austin pull me toward him and onto his lap instead of my own seat. "I have time to decide. I'm only eighteen."

"Yeah, but you've already lived a lifetime," Austin semi-jokes. "You could probably write an autobiography at this point. It would be juicy too." I laugh.

"Nah. Some of my secrets should stay secrets." I kiss him lightly on the lips. "I think I've shared enough of mine already, don't you?"

"That's for sure," Austin says with a grin and kisses me right back.

I've got my whole life ahead of me to tell more secrets. For now, I'm going to enjoy keeping some to myself.

Acknowledgments

Cindy Eagan, I will forever be grateful to you for taking a chance on someone who had a big idea, but no clue how to put it down on paper. Thank you for helping me create Kaitlin's world and for letting me follow it through six amazing adventures. Who knew coffee at the Rock Center Café would completely change my life? I couldn't have done any of the heavy lifting without my incredible editors, Cindy, Kate Sullivan, and Phoebe Spanier. Phoebe gave Kaitlin her voice all those years ago, and Kate kept it going and has made it stronger. Whether it was cupcake debates or questions over alternate realities, Kate, you cared as much about getting it right as I did. And here we are at the end of the finish line (on this one at least). I think it's time we had a good cry now. . . .

My wonderful agent, Laura Dail, also gets kudos for taking chances on a complete unknown. Thank you for walking me through every detail and offering feedback where it's needed most. Tamar Rydzinski, you rock too!

To the entire Poppy and Little, Brown Books for Young Readers team, you're the most incredible cheering squad an author could ask for. Thank you to: Andrew Smith, Elizabeth Eulberg, Ames O' Neill, Melanie Chang, Lisa Ickowicz, Andy Ball, our incredible Secrets cover girl, Tracy Shaw, and her sidekick, Neil Swaab.

My family and friends have been the Secrets pep squad since the very beginning. You guys have always showed up at my events (in the beginning, you were the only ones!) and you've practically hand sold hundreds of books with your kudos and praise. Special attention must be given to my mom for helping me out with the boys; my grandfather, Nick Calonita, who loves to tell people he has an author in the family; and to my official go-to girl, Mara Reinstein, who is always just a phone call away when I need her expertise on retail therapy and dining hot spots.

Finally to my boys, Mike, Tyler, and Dylan (and Jack, of course), you make this whole thing possible. Thank you for being such an incredible support system and inspiration, especially Tyler, who was the reason this whole journey started in the first place.

Jen Calonita

on the SECRETS OF MY HOLLYWOOD LIFE series finale,

There's No Place Like Home

How did you come up with the title *There's No Place Like Home* for the last Secrets of My Hollywood Life novel?

I always knew that when it came time for Kaitlin's journey to come to a close, she needed to make a decision about what she wanted from life and stick with it. Kaitlin tends to be very wishy-washy! It's hard for her to stand up for herself because she has people advising her from every possible angle. She has this incredible career, but she's always secretly longed to be a normal teen too, and in Hollywood she's found it's sometimes hard to do both. This book gave me a chance to explore the fantasy life Kaitlin has always dreamed about—and to show how she reacts to the change. It was hard keeping track of all the details, but I loved squeezing in people and places that have been with her from the very first book. I always knew exactly how I wanted the story to end, but I still get a little choked up when I read the epilogue. It was the most fun book to write in the whole series, and I hope readers will enjoy reading it as much as I did working on it.

What was your favorite part of writing Secrets of My Hollywood Life?

I love entertainment! Give me a bowl of popcorn and my TV remote or an hour's worth of movie previews and I'm a happy girl. I started my career as an entertainment editor at a magazine, so I've always had a huge appreciation for movies, TV, and celebrity culture. Secrets has been a great way to keep a toe in that world. Whenever I buy a new magazine or see a movie, I say it's part of my research for the books!

What will you miss most about the series?

Um . . . everything? Kaitlin's world is so much fun to explore. Sometimes I'd read about some catfight in a magazine and think, "That has to happen to Kaitlin!" Or I'd see Selena Gomez wear some gorgeous gown to an event, and I would say to myself, "Kaitlin should wear something like that!" Most of all, I'll miss the characters, who have become like family to me in many ways. (Sky is one of my absolute favorite characters to write.) It's going to be hard putting these characters to bed, but I know it's time for Kaitlin to try something new, and it's time for me to do the same.

What are you working on now?

I'm really excited about a new teen novel I'm writing called *Belles*. It's about two girls named Isabelle Scott and Mirabelle Monroe who come from completely opposite cultures and backgrounds, but find themselves suddenly living under the same roof. Mira's dad is a state senator hoping to run for the US Senate, so her life is all about glitz, glamour, and little responsibility. Izzy's life up until now hasn't been as charmed. She's grown up with much less than Mira has, but she is proud of where she's come from, she's a fighter, and she has a lot of heart. I love fish-out-of-water stories, and *Belles* is definitely that, with, of course, a lot of romance, drama, and splashy parties thrown in too. I love a good party! The book will be out in spring 2012.

As a girl from Long Island, New York, what inspired you to set this new book in the South?

I think I've always secretly wanted to live in the South! I'm fascinated by the culture and the beauty of it all. I would love to hear friends of mine who went to college below the Virginia state line tell me stories about cotillions, elaborate private schools, and how football was practically a religion. I knew I wanted to write about a privileged world set in the Carolinas that gets rocked by an outsider who has very big ideas that don't always jive with the culture.

How are your new leading ladies similar to and different from Kaitlin?

Isabelle and Mirabelle, despite their very different lives, have the same issues that Kaitlin has always had— *Who am I?* and *What do I want for my life? Where do I fit in?* And *Why are boys so hard to understand?* Whether you're the biggest star on the planet or a girl who counts every penny, I think you have the same problems. It's how you handle those issues that makes it different.

What are your new characters' favorite movies? TV shows? Things to do when they're not in the spotlight of Mr. Monroe's political career?

Mira would be into whatever is hot at the time, but I could definitely see her being hooked on the CW and everything on it! She and her friends spend a lot of time planning and going to Emerald Cove events, which require incredible clothes and lots of shopping! Izzie, on the other hand, rarely shops and doesn't go to parties. She's busy, but in ways that don't allow for a lot of TV time. Izzie is a lifeguard and spends a lot of time at her community center, but if she did have a night off, I'd expect her to veg out and watch MTV.

Would Kaitlin Burke have any advice for these characters?

I think Kaitlin would tell both girls to do what makes them happy and not to get hung up on the small things. By the end of *There's No Place Like Home*, Kaitlin has finally learned to do just that.

Read all six novels in the SECRETS OF MY HOLLYWOOD LIFE series

Two Southern girls. One life-changing secret.

Isabelle Scott loves her less-than-charmed life by the boardwalk on the wrong side of the tracks in North Carolina. But when tragedy strikes, a social worker sends her to live with a long-lost uncle and his preppy, privileged family. Unfortunately, Isabelle's entry into the glamorous lifestyle of Emerald Cove doesn't go so well. Rumors and backstabbing lurk beneath her classmates' Southern charm, and her cousin Mirabelle Monroe isn't thrilled to suddenly share her life with an outsider. But it turns out that these two teenage Southern belles may share more than just the roof over their heads....

Turn the page for an exclusive first look at BELLES, a new Southern family drama series from Jen Calonita.

Coming April 2012

One

Isabelle Scott kicked her legs, propelling herself to the ocean surface with a final burst of adrenaline even as her lungs screamed for air. Breaking through the waves, she looked around, focusing on the tiny stretch of North Carolina coastline that she had called home for the last fifteen and a half years. Harborside Beach was still packed at 5 PM. She could see couples lounging on beach blankets while their kids dug in the sand or attempted to bodyboard, but beyond the roped-off swim area, Isabelle was flying solo. She had always preferred it that way. But that was before she'd met Brayden Townsend. As if on cue, he paddled his surfboard toward her.

"Go ahead and gloat, Iz," Brayden said, not sounding the least bit out of breath, even though he had just paddled over the breaking waves. He pushed a beat-up surfboard toward her. His favorite black wet suit, the one with the pirate skull on his chest, looked barely wet even though they'd both been in the water for almost half an hour.

Izzie, or Iz, as Brayden called her (only her grandmother called her Isabelle, when she called her anything at all), rested her arms on the bobbing board. She couldn't help but smirk at Brayden. "I didn't say anything."

"You didn't have to," Brayden grumbled even though his blue-green eyes were playful. Salt water dripped from his short, light brown hair and he wiped it off his face. "You win, Iz. I'm man enough to admit you can swim faster than I can paddle out here, *but,*" he added before she could gloat, "let's not forget that I was carting *two* boards, and pelicans were nose-diving at my head."

Izzie tapped her chipped purple nails lightly on the board, the bathlike water lapping at her upper back, which was the only part of her torso not covered by the unflattering blue Speedo she wore for her job as a lifeguard. After four, she was off-duty, but unlike some of the other guards she worked with, she didn't change into her own suit before going for a dip. Why waste time? When she wasn't working, there was no place she'd rather be than in the ocean. Brayden was the first guy she'd met who seemed to feel the same way. They'd only been friends since mid-July, but they had been meeting up practically every day since, and this was the best time of day to do it. By 5 PM, the soupy North Carolina heat had started to subside and there was even a light breeze. The sun was still bright, but low enough that they didn't need sunscreen, and the water wasn't overly crowded with kids goofing around or adults twice her size who could barely swim. Five PM was "me" time, and when me time included Brayden, it was that much better.

"It only took you half of July and all of August to realize I pretty much know everything there is to know about being in the water," Izzie teased, staring at his woven rope necklace that had a pirate coin dangling from it. "*You* surfers are all alike. Cocky."

"Hey," Brayden argued even as he smiled an extra-adorable grin. "It's not cocky; it's called confident. There is a difference. *You* lifeguards seem to forget that."

Izzie coyly pushed her wavy, shoulder-skimming brown bob out of her hazel eyes. "It's kind of hard not to when we're pulling you guys out of a rip current at least once a day."

Brayden gave her a sharp look. "I told you a million times, I was fine."

"You didn't look fine," Izzie reminded him, wrinkling her freckled nose at the memory. "You were going—"

"Against the current instead of with it," Brayden interrupted, and shook his head. The dimple in his left cheek began to form. "I'm never going to live that down, am I?"

"Nope," Izzie said, feeling at ease, like she always did

around him. They were just friends—friends in a teasing, sort of flirty way—but for some reason it didn't matter. Well, it mattered a little, but they had such a good time together that she almost forgot he wasn't her boyfriend. She knew practically everything there was to know about him, from how much he loved to surf to his favorite iPod playlist. They liked the same bands, preferred water over dry land, and would take a slice of pizza over a hot dog any day. Maybe that was why she was beginning to dread the thought of school starting in two weeks. When would she see Brayden then? They hung out only at the beach. She wasn't even sure where he lived. Whenever she asked, his cryptic answer was always "Nearby."

Brayden looked at the shore as he bobbed up and down on his board, and Izzie tried not to ogle his toned arms. "So, ready to try surfing again? Maybe you can actually stay on the board today."

Izzie pulled herself up on her board and floated next to him, their tan knees touching. Brayden's, she noticed, were beaten up and bruised from some crash landings. "Do we have to keep doing this?" she groaned. "Why do I need to know how to surf?"

"I told you—so you can do it with me. Let's try this again, okay?" Brayden instructed, his square jawline set. "I'll make you a deal. If you can manage to get up this time, I'll buy at Scoops."

Izzie grinned. "You're on, surfer boy."

She reached down and attached her board's leg strap to her ankle. She'd learned her lesson about being untethered last week when she had to swim after a runaway board. Then she paddled after Brayden, trying to remember his instructions — when to stand up, how to lean left or right into the wave for balance, how to hold her legs. Brayden had given her this board after he bought one that had a pirate ship on it. The gift had come with one condition — that Izzie keep both boards in the lifeguard hut for him. Brayden said his board didn't fit in the back of his Jeep. He had just turned sixteen and his parents had bought him the truck for his birthday, which led Izzie to assume that Brayden didn't live *that* close to Harborside because she lived there and no kid she knew owned a car, let alone a new one.

Izzie looked for the balance point Brayden had marked with wax and tried not to "cork" the board, as he'd called it. Something about too much weight in the back. She watched Brayden almost fifteen feet ahead of her — the proper safety distance — and saw him effortlessly stand up on the board as a wave began to crest. She tried to remember what he'd said as she got closer to the waves and pushed up on the board, keeping her legs on the stringer and gripping the board with her feet. She was supposed to look like a sumo wrestler, and it was working. She was up! Was Brayden seeing this? Even her feet were in the right positions! Then two seconds later, she fell and cursed herself for looking down, which is what Brayden had told her *not* to do. The surf was swirling around her, and as she swam to the surface, her board whacked her in the head. She dragged the board behind her as she hit the beach a few minutes later with a scowl on her face.

Brayden watched her as he stood next to two kids playing in the sand with plastic army men. His board was staked next to him, giving him the appearance of a guy who had just won a Teen Choice Award surfboard. Brayden probably could win, for looks alone, if he lived twenty-five hundred miles away in California and was discovered by a film agent. Robert Pattinson's mug had nothing on Brayden Townsend's.

"I can't believe you looked down, Iz! It was going so well!" Brayden said, as if she needed reminding.

Izzie rubbed her head. "I know, I know, and I'm going to pay for it with a big, fat headache."

Brayden put his arm around her, smelling like a mix of coconut and salt water. His black wet suit hugged his taut stomach and Izzie felt her breath get stuck in her throat. "You'll get it eventually, lifeguard. Or maybe not." He rubbed her head like she were a kid brother. "Tell you what: I'll buy even though you screwed up." She started to protest. "You save that paltry salary of yours."

Fifteen minutes later, after they had both toweled off and Izzie had pulled on frayed jean shorts and a tank top over her suit, they flip-flopped across the crowded boardwalk toward Scoops, where her friend Kylie Brooks worked. Izzie knew it sounded silly to have such deep affection for a place, but almost everything she loved about Harborside was on these planks. She'd learned how to play *Dance Dance Revolution* at the arcade, scored her first hole in one with her mom at the Mermaid Putt-Putt, made pizza with Grams at Harbor's Finest, held her first job at Scoops, and had her first kiss on the amusement park roller coaster. But what she still loved best about Harborside Pier was the community center. Sandwiched between the boardwalk and the main drag, the community center had been her family ever since her mom died. And Izzie had very little family to speak of.

"Look who's here! The beach bum and the lifeguard!" Kylie yelled as a tiny bell on the door announced Brayden's and Izzie's arrival at the homemade-ice-cream parlor. Kylie's loud voice startled some of the customers eating at the tiny tables. Izzie and Brayden walked up to the long counter, where Kylie was making an ice-cream sundae. "So what are you guys having?" Kylie asked. She slid the sundae over to the startled customer and leaned toward Izzie, her long blond hair falling in front of her face.

"Um, hello?" said a cool voice. "I believe we were next."

Izzie noticed a well-dressed couple in their twenties at the other end of the counter. The guy nudged the girl, who gave him a sour face. "What? You wanted homemade ice cream, right?" she whispered. "And I want to leave this boardwalk before some pickpocket dips into my Tory Burch bag."

The guy rolled his eyes. "Hannah, you're overreacting."

"You heard what the taxi driver said," she said in hushed tones. "I know you like to 'keep it real,' but I'm not hanging out all night on some dodgy boardwalk when our hotel has a private beach."

Harborside Pier may have been as popular as it ever was, but it was dogged that summer with stories about teen gangs and how shady the area had become. One of the pier shops had been broken into and robbed, and a knife fight earlier this summer between locals and gang members had turned ugly. No one Izzie knew had been involved. Her friends hung out under the boardwalk at night, but they weren't thieves or hoodlums. There just weren't a lot of places for them to hang. Izzie knew she didn't live in Beverly Hills, but she also knew Harborside wasn't unsafe if you knew how to navigate it. She wished she had the nerve to tell the customer that.

"Kylie, you should help them first," Izzie said instead. "They were waiting."

Kylie rolled her eyes and pulled at her stained white Scoops tee. "Whatever." Like most of Izzie's friends, Kylie didn't mask her feelings, even if they stung. "What do you want?"

Brayden glanced at his diver's watch. "I've got to check in

at home. Order for me?" he asked Izzie, then winked. "She'll give you extra toppings." He pulled his phone out of his orange backpack and walked outside as Izzie scanned the day's ice-cream flavor chart.

When Kylie was done serving Miss Uptight her kid-size fat-free vanilla cone, she planted herself in front of Izzie and grinned slyly. "So?" she said meaningfully.

"So what?" Izzie repeated slowly.

"So have you told Mr. Hot Surfer Dude that you want to be the topping on his soft-serve cone yet?" Kylie asked.

Izzie felt her face flush. What if Brayden had heard Kylie say that? She turned around slowly and to her relief saw Brayden's butt leaning against the glass window as he talked on the phone outside. "Kylie, geez!" Izzie said, her color returning to normal. "I told you a million times. We're just friends."

Kylie gave her a knowing look. "You don't act like just friends."

Izzie looked down at the ice cream under the glass counter and stared at the Cookies-and-Cream tub. If she looked at Kylie, her face might give something away. "Well, we are, so would you lay off? Besides, I don't have time for a boyfriend."

"That's true," Kylie said, walking away to wash the ice-cream scoopers in the small sink. "I don't even know how you have time to sleep between work, swim practice, taking care of Grams, food shopping…"

Izzie shrugged and pushed her still-damp hair behind her ears. "It's no big deal."

"It's a huge deal," Kylie disagreed, and then smiled slowly. "Which is why I think you need a little fun." She looked at Brayden's butt and sighed. "And Mr. Hot Surfer Dude definitely looks like fun."

"*Kylie*," Izzie said, starting to feel both annoyed and uncomfortable. "Drop it."

Kylie rolled her eyes again. "Fine. You should snap that boy up, though. If you don't, believe me, someone else will."

The bell hanging from the door jingled, and Brayden walked back in, his flip-flops making a scuffing sound against the sandy floor. "Did you decide what you want yet?"

"Oh, she knows what she wants," Kylie said, staring at Izzie intently. "She just hasn't figured out how to order it."

"A scoop of Oreo, a scoop of Marshmallow Supreme, and one of Butter Toffee," Izzie said quickly, "with gummy bears." Brayden looked amused. "I'm a growing girl."

"No complaints here," he said. "I like a girl who eats."

Izzie tried to think of the appropriate comeback, but before she could, she felt her cell phone vibrate in her pocket. She didn't recognize the number, but she picked up anyway. "Hello?" She instantly regretted her decision. "No. I'm at the beach." Pause. "Nope. I have to stop at the community center first. I forgot my swim meet registration forms." Her smile slowly faded, and the room began to spin around her. "Yeah, I can be there at six thirty. Bye." She snapped the phone shut, her eyes blinking rapidly, and grabbed the counter to steady herself. This couldn't be happening. "I'm going to have to take you up on that free ice cream offer tomorrow," she said quietly, not looking at Brayden.

"Everything okay?" he asked, his brow wrinkling with worry.

"Did Grams lock herself out of the house again?" Kylie asked as she finished Izzie's order and slid it toward her.

Izzie pushed it back. "No, I just have to get home." She avoided their stares.

"Let me drive you," Brayden suggested.

Great. For the first time, Brayden was offering her a ride, and she had to say no. "I've got to go to the center first," Izzie explained, looking up at him. He had to be at least six foot two. "Besides, I'm only a few blocks from there. You stay and hang out. I'll see you tomorrow."

Brayden grinned. "Okay, because you, my friend, seriously need some more surf lessons."

Izzie forced herself to groan playfully. "Don't I know it? See you, Kylie," she managed with a smile even though she felt like the floor was going to fall out from under her.

Leaving Scoops, Izzie unlocked her dirt bike from the rack and raced down the boardwalk bike path, feeling the wind whip her hair around her face as if she were at the top of the Ferris wheel. Then she slowed down her pedaling and reminded herself of the truth: She wasn't on the Ferris wheel. She would soon be on her way home, where her social worker, Barbara Sanchez, was waiting.

The questions ran through Izzie's head almost too fast for her to keep up. Was Barbara there to push foster care again? Barbara and Grams had been discussing the idea ever since Grams's health started going downhill last year, but Izzie was still vehemently against it. When Grams remembered things (which felt like ages ago now), she had said another option was to find a distant relative to take care of Izzie, but Izzie hated that idea, too. She had lived with her grandmother ever since her mom brought her home from the hospital as a baby. Izzie had never met her dad. Her mom hadn't even told anyone who the guy was. So it was Grams who became Izzie's legal guardian when her mom died in a car crash a few years ago. Now that Grams was sick, it was Izzie's turn to return the favor. Grams was the only family she had left, and she wasn't going to let the state of North Carolina take that away from her.

Izzie pressed hard on her dirt bike brakes, the tires squeaking loudly to a halt in front of Chicken, Ribs and More. She let the familiar smell of barbecue sauce and crisp sweet-potato fries wash over her as the reasons behind Barbara's house call began to overwhelm her. Izzie's thoughts were darker than she would have liked, and she shut her eyes to block out the scenarios. Without thinking, her feet went back onto the bike pedals, and within minutes she was in front of the Harborside Community Center.

HCC wasn't much to look at. Weeds poked up around the cracked, aging stucco, and the windows had a permanent film from years of neglect. As rundown and forgotten as it looked from the outside, though, once Izzie walked through the glass doors, the building had a different story to tell. The community center was bustling, loud, and as cheerful as the cinder-block walls that had been painted in vibrant yellow-and-blue beach scenes. Hanging from corkboard strips were bright flyers and banners screaming things in large print like upcoming samba lessons, teen bake sales, Xbox Kinect tournaments, and directions to the next swim meet. Summer camp was winding down for the day just as some of the adult evening classes were starting, and the halls were a mix of young and old voices. Izzie knew most of them and said hello or waved as she walked down the hallway toward the pool.

Mimi Grayson wrapped her tiny wet arms around Izzie's waist as Izzie passed her. "Are you done saving lives, Izzie?" Mimi wanted to know.

Izzie patted the top of her curly hair. "For today." She gave her a mock stern look. "What about you? Have you been practicing your lifeguard training today, too?"

Mimi nodded. "Just like you showed me at swim class this

morning." She mimicked a frog, showing Izzie her breast-stroke. It seemed to be the easiest stroke for Mimi to master, so they'd concentrated on that one first.

"Perfect," Izzie said with a smile, and then began swinging her arms in a circular motion forward. "Tomorrow we'll work on this one, okay?"

"I can't do that one." Mimi's face scrunched up in frustration. "My arms don't go fast enough."

"What do I always tell you?" Izzie asked, and then the two of them said it together: "No guts, no glory." She nudged Mimi with her elbow, and the girl smiled. "I'll see you at nine AM."

Where stories bloom.

poppy

Visit us online at
www.pickapoppy.com